HOT
ALPHAS

W9-AUN-945

OTHER ANTHOLOGIES FEATURING LORA LEIGH

Real Men Do It Better

Honk If You Love Real Men

Real Men Last All Night

Men of Danger

Legally Hot

Taken

HOT ALPHAS

Lora Leigh

Laurelin McGee

Shiloh Walker

Kate Douglas

ST. MARTIN'S GRIFFIN
NEW YORK

These novellas are works of fiction. All of the characters, organizations, and events portrayed in these novellas are either products of the authors' imaginations or are used fictitiously.

HOT ALPHAS. Copyright © 2015 by St. Martin's Press. "Erin's Kiss," by Lora Leigh. Copyright © 2015 by St. Martin's Press. "misTaken," by Laurelin McGee. Copyright © 2015 by St. Martin's Press. "Burn for Me," by Shiloh Walker. Copyright © 2014 by St. Martin's Press. "Tangled," by Kate Douglas. Copyright © 2015 by St. Martin's Press.

All rights reserved. Printed in the United States of America. For information, address St. Martin's Press, 175 Fifth Avenue, New York, N.Y. 10010.

www.stmartins.com

The Library of Congress Cataloging-in-Publication Data is available upon request.

ISBN 978-1-250-06688-6 (trade paperback)
ISBN 978-1-4668-7198-4 (e-book)

St. Martin's Griffin books may be purchased for educational, business, or promotional use. For information on bulk purchases, please contact the Macmillan Corporate and Premium Sales Department at 1-800-221-7945, extension 5442, or write to specialmarkets@macmillan.com.

First Edition: May 2015

10 9 8 7 6 5 4 3 2

CONTENTS

ERIN'S KISS

by

Lora Leigh

For Mom.
Just because I didn't understand then,
doesn't mean I don't understand now.
I love you.

CHAPTER 1

⌒

The night had finally wound down, the last customer urged out the door and the Broken Bar was closed up for the night.

Standing next to the counter, Erin Masters surveyed the pristine area critically, ensuring everything was ready for the next night.

The head bartender and club manager, Jake Manning, had left her in charge of cleaning and restocking the various bottles of drinks kept on hand. The large crowds known to descend on the nightclub on any given night left no time to replace bottles. And he was damned picky about making certain everything, down to the last speck of dust, was cleaned away and the serving area ready to go the next evening.

Glancing to the mirrored wall behind the wide counter she found the neon BROKEN BAR sign. Her gaze moved to the camera eye in the center of it, then gave it her customary wink. She knew the girl that worked the security recordings. The wink was a nightly salute. Gabby would roll her eyes, Erin knew, and remember the night they'd had one drink too many, and revealed how each of them had become fixated on one of the Broken Bar's security agents.

For Gabby, it was Iron.

For Erin, it was the hard, tough Turk Rogan.

Folding the damp bar towel she'd used to clean the wood bar, Erin pushed it into the small plastic bag of towels used that night and tied the bag closed. Picking it up she pushed through the swinging doors to the kitchen, finally relaxing at the thought of going home for the night.

Leaving the bag at the back door for morning pickup she made her way back to the front to check everything one last time. Jake could become highly critical if anything in the bartending section wasn't just right. She sure as hell didn't want him tearing her ass as he'd torn the last assistant's. That one he'd sent running from the club in tears as she quit on the spot.

Flipping the kitchen light out, she stepped through the swinging doors once again and almost ran face-first into one of the nicest stretches of chests she'd ever beheld.

Powerful, not too wide, but rippling beneath the black T-shirt he wore. Her fingers itched to smooth across the expanse of powerful muscles.

He made other parts just ache.

"Turk." She stepped back, looking up into the rough-hewn, hardened features of the security agent working cleanup with her.

Dark, chocolate-brown eyes were set into a brooding expression that gave him a hard, savage look. A sexy rough-hewn toughness that just took a girl's breath away.

His gaze lowered to her lips. That look made her mouth go dry. It made her sex wet.

"Erin." Deep, whispering of sensual delights and wicked knowledge, that voice sent shivers working down her spine as his gaze lifted to hers once again. "Have you finished up here?"

He stepped back, slowly, allowing her to ease from the doorway to the dimly lit bar area as she looked around one last time.

"Let's hope I am." She grinned back, smoothing her hands down the side of the short, black skirt she wore.

Turk's gaze flickered down her body before coming back to hers, the shadow of something hungry in his eyes caused her heartbeat to pick up, racing in excitement as she swallowed nervously.

"Everything looks great." He nodded, finally glancing around himself, his eyes narrowing. "Jake shouldn't be able to bitch—no matter how much he loves doing it."

Amusement gleamed in his eyes as they met hers once again.

"Good." She glanced over the area again though. "Perhaps I'll survive my first night closing."

"You'll survive," he promised as though he'd already decided that on his own. "If you're ready I'll walk you out to your car. The rest of the waitresses have left and I'm ready to head out myself."

"I just need to stop in the lounge and collect my purse." She was already turning for the exit from the tending area, all too aware of the fact that he was walking behind her.

And he walked silently, too. There wasn't so much as a whisper of his footsteps. Quiet, intense, his scarred face was normally implacable, his voice deep. He was the epitome of the type of agent her stepfather preferred as security personnel for the nightclubs that worked beneath the Covert Information Network.

The Broken Bar was one of those establishments, while five of the ten security personnel were longtime agents of the network. Ex-military, Rangers in this case, most of them wounded in some way that had ended their official military careers. The agents for the network were deep cover, their identities changed years before, most without families or ties to pull them back to the lives they had once lived.

Turk Rogan was just such a man. His military career listed him as troublemaker, dishonorably discharged from the Rangers after an accident that had caused his own injuries. The truth was, he was a man with no family, no one to care that he never returned. A Ranger who had nearly given his own life for his country and the soldiers he fought with. When he was offered the chance to continue protecting his nation in another capacity, he'd jumped on it.

Like the agents that worked for the network, Erin kept her past strictly quiet. Being the stepdaughter of the regional director of the network and stepsister of the security director could become uncomfortable if others were aware of it.

Besides, her stepfather and stepbrother weren't exactly men that made others comfortable. As a matter of fact, they were known to piss others off routinely just for the hell of it. Her stepfather often told her that a man that stayed loyal despite his anger was the man he could trust at his back.

There were many of those agents she truly hoped John Delanore—J.D. as others called him—and her stepbrother, John D., didn't have to trust at their backs. One of those men might end up braining those two with a two-by-four. She knew she was tempted to do so often.

Stepping from the bar ahead of Turk she waited as he locked the doors before moving toward the side of the building. As they began walking, his large, broad palm settled at the small of her back, the warmth of it heating her flesh as her heart rate kicked up in speed once again.

Shadows swirled about the parking lot, and a light fog whispered around the deserted area, its moist warmth settling around them as the night enfolded them.

She'd parked her small sedan in the employees' parking area. As they turned the corner of the bar she noticed he'd parked the wicked black motorcycle he rode next to her. He'd been doing that since the first night she'd arrived at the bar.

"Be careful driving back to your apartment." His dark voice was low, intimate as they neared her car. "The fog is wicked tonight."

They lived in the same small apartment complex, his apartment right across the hall from hers.

"I'll be fine," she promised, a little warmed by the protectiveness he hinted at.

He made her feel secure. Not overshadowed or guarded, but secure. She realized she'd grown used to the fact that he rode behind her whenever they left together, that he was there in the early hours of the morning when she arrived home while everyone else was sleeping.

Stepping to the side of her car she pushed the remote lock, hearing the snick of the door unlocking as she turned back to him, the sexual, sensual awareness that flooded her body weakening her knees as she looked up at him.

It was the look in those dark eyes. A knowledge that he had every intention of acting on the attraction that sparked between them like an invisible flame.

"You kept up tonight after Jake left," he stated as a small grin quirked his lips. "You surprised me."

"It wasn't that bad," she assured him, catching the side of her lower lip between her teeth before quickly running her tongue over her lips again. "Jake's a hard act to follow though."

"So are you." His hand settled on her hip as he moved closer, the night suddenly heating as his body brushed hers. "Erin, if you don't want me to kiss you, then you need to get your ass in that car and haul out now."

The suggestion had her eyes widening before her gaze moved involuntarily to his lips.

Would his kiss be as hot and as filled with pleasure as she imagined?

Lowering his head slowly, Turk gave her plenty of time to run, "to haul out" as he called it. She had no intentions of running. She felt as though she'd been running all her life, until now.

As his head tilted, his arms went around her. When his lips settled on hers the whimpering little cry that left her throat shocked her.

It was like pouring gasoline to a flame. Like pouring pure, shocking emotion into an eruption of pleasure.

His lips took possession of hers, dark experience and sensual knowledge wrapping around her as he pulled her against him. The heavy imprint of his erection pressed into her lower stomach. Heat settled immediately between her thighs, her erogenous zones kicking to life with a force that stole her breath.

Pleasure surrounded her.

Like a heavy veil of intimacy it enfolded her, shrouding logical thought, hiding her from the implications of exactly what she was doing as pleasure flooded every area of her body.

That pleasure was immediately followed by a pulse of arousal so sharp it clenched her womb. The sensitive flesh between her thighs grew more sensitive by the second, her ability to think, to process the sensations overwhelmed by the pleasure itself.

It was like being taken, possessed by a hunger she'd had no idea she harbored inside her with such strength.

As his hand cupped the back of her head, broad fingers spearing into her hair, Erin found herself arching to get closer. Her breasts pressed into the heated width of his chest, her nipples hardening to immediate, painful sensitivity as her breasts began to ache for touch.

For his lips.

For his hands.

She shook in the grip of a hunger she'd never known and one that rose with such strength inside her that the hot flares of pulsing sensitivity and exquisite electric sensation became more than she could bear.

Just as quickly as the kiss had begun tearing through her senses, it was over.

Releasing her, Turk quickly stepped back, his gaze locked on hers as she lifted her lashes and stared back at him in shock.

He'd stopped?

Why would he stop?

Reaching around her rather than pulling her back to him, he opened the door of her car instead.

"It's getting late." The hard, dark rasp of his voice had moisture pulsing from between her thighs once again. "You need to get home."

Did she really?

Blinking up at him, Erin was slow to process the rejection. But it finally processed in her passion-drugged senses.

Her knees stiffened. Pulling back from him quickly, Erin gripped the car door and slid inside. Shoving the key into the ignition, she moved to close the door.

The hard fingers still gripping the frame tightened.

Turning, Erin stared up at him, hoping like hell the anger that tightened her body wasn't apparent in her eyes.

"Erin . . ." A grimace pulled at his features as discomfort shadowed his expression in the dim light.

"I get it," she told him softly. "We can discuss it at another time."

"What do you get?" His expression became shuttered, remote.

"Not something you want to pursue at the moment," she said as though she understood. "It's not a problem. And as you said, it's late. I need to be going."

Tugging on the door she almost breathed out in relief as he released it. Pulling it closed Erin slid the car into reverse and accelerated out of the space. Sliding it into gear and pulling from the parking lot moments later, she had to force back a shaming tear of regret.

Damn, it was hard to imagine never feeling his kiss again. A kiss that had burned through her senses like wildfire and threatened every ounce of control she'd ever believed she had over herself.

It was evident, though, that Turk Rogan hadn't felt those same flames.

Wasn't that too bad? For her at least. Because she would have loved to have seen exactly where they would have ended. She ached to feel, just one more time, the calm that stole over her restless spirit, even as excitement churned through her senses as he held her.

That feeling that finally she'd found a place all her own.

Turk watched the car as it pulled onto the main road, a curse slipping past his lips as he pushed the fingers of one hand roughly through his hair and strode to the cycle.

Son of a bitch, he should have known better.

Hell, he had known better, he reminded himself. He'd managed to control the impulse to kiss her every night since she'd first arrived to work at the nightclub. As he'd gotten to know her, the impulse had only grown. And he hadn't been alone. The wary interest in her eyes had assured him he wasn't aching in vein. And aching he was.

His erection throbbed like a wound, fully engorged and howling in protest at the loss of the pleasure that echoed to the hard flesh. Like sweet little fingers of heat spreading from her kiss to his hardened shaft rising between his thighs, his flesh demanded her touch. The pleasure of her hungry kiss mesmerized him. Pulling back from her had been like cutting his own arm off or some shit.

Blowing out a hard breath he jerked his helmet over his head and secured it. Turk told himself it was better that she thought she was being rejected. The truth was far too weird to even get into. How a full-grown man could be weakened by one pint-sized little woman's kiss he couldn't figure out.

The fact was it had been so damned hard to pull back, almost impossible to put distance between them, was a warning he knew better than to ignore. He would have ended up trying to take her there on the hood of her car if he hadn't heeded it.

That skirt wouldn't have stood in his way. Pushing it over her thighs would have been easy. Of course, it might have taken him awhile to finish if he'd given in to the hunger to taste more than just her kiss.

Before the night was over, the security cameras would have recorded a hell of a lot more than one brief touch of their lips.

And Turk would have revealed a hell of a lot more than just his interest in the new assistant bartender.

He'd have revealed a hunger he was hard-pressed to control.

And control meant everything.

Or it had. . . .

For far too many years his control had been all that had saved him. The knowledge that his battle to rout out the monsters that destroyed the life of his baby sister so many years ago could only be accomplished if every part of himself was focused on it.

And he'd sworn he'd never allow himself to care for anyone else to the point that their deaths destroyed him.

Cara Jane had been too little to protect herself. He'd raised her after their parents' deaths. He'd loved her. Two months before he was due home from the military she'd been killed in a suspected terrorist bombing while on vacation with their aunt and uncle in England.

He'd lost the three last remaining members of his family that day. And he'd lost the little sister he'd promised he'd always protect.

Ten years later and sea-green eyes were making him forget the vow he'd made at his sister's graveside to never risk his soul again. To never let himself love anyone else. Not in any way.

Yet, Erin was sneaking her way inside his emotions, and he couldn't seem to stop the slow, steady headway she was making into his heart.

A heart he'd believed he no longer held.

CHAPTER 2

How interesting.

The watcher watched as the prey stalked to his motorcycle and rode off behind the young woman he'd pulled back from so abruptly. Turk Rogan wasn't the first choice for the betrayer, but Erin Masters was definitely the type of woman the betrayer had once shown such a fondness for.

Innocent.

Sweet.

Pretty red-gold hair and mesmerizing eyes, but with a streak of a rebel gleaming in her gaze.

There had been a certainty that drastic measures would have to be taken after failing to identify the prey several months before. The other men suspected had shown no true fondness for any particular female. Without a lover to protect, the betrayer would never reveal himself. He would never make the call that would reveal him.

This woman meant something to Rogan though.

This one was important.

Satisfaction lit a glow of hope inside a heart black with hatred. Perhaps, finally the game would be drawing to a close. Perhaps it wouldn't be necessary to draw the ultimate bait out to lure the prey to his death.

That was a weakness the watcher had feared being forced to use. One that could possibly backfire . . .

With any luck Rogan was the one hiding from a past filled with blood, broken innocence, and destruction.

The one responsible for such betrayal that even now, so many years later, the effects of it were still being felt.

CHAPTER 3

S he was a fool!

Stowing her purse in her locker the next evening Erin closed the metal door and turned the lock with a hard snap.

What made her think that giving in to her fascination for Turk Rogan was a good idea?

It was insanity.

It was a recipe for a broken heart.

Smoothing her hands down the sides of her black skirt before adjusting the black vest over her white long-sleeved shirt, Erin forced herself to still the hurt. Taking a deep, steadying breath she then forced herself to leave the lounge.

Saturday night at the Broken Bar was always too busy, too loud, and filled with far too much excitement. At least for the customers.

Pushing through the swinging doors she ducked her head, pretended to adjust the rolled-back sleeves of her cotton shirt and slid behind the bar where Jake was already prepping for a busy night.

"Hey, Jake. Everyone," she greeted the head bartender as well as the rest of the Broken Bar family gathered around the bar.

The owner, Ethan Cooper, and his wife, Sarah, head of security, Casey, and his wife, Sheila, and the other security personnel gathered there.

"Lookin' good Miss Erin," Iron Donovan greeted her with his customary flirtatiousness.

"Smack him, Erin." Sarah laughed. "He's watching your backside again."

"Hey, it's a damned pretty backside," Iron complained.

"Dig your hole deeper, Iron." Nick chuckled as his wife whispered something in his ear.

Sliding past Jake, Erin shook her head at the lot of them, though she noticed Turk wasn't joining in that evening as he usually did.

"The lot of you need to attend those sexual harassment classes again," she chided them, unable to hide her smile. "You weren't paying attention at the last one."

"We didn't pay attention to the one before that, either," Iron snickered. "We were too busy staring at that cute little instructor's legs."

"Cut it out, asshole." Turk's tone was dark and lacking any sort of amusement.

Erin lifted her head slowly, the sharp retort hovering on her lips forestalled by Jake's next comment.

"Hey, Erin, you did good last night." Growly, not in the least given as most managers to give a compliment. This compliment had everyone staring at the fierce former Ranger in shock.

Erin blinked back at him, frozen in the act of sitting a shot glass on the prep counter as her eyes widened.

Panic had her heart in her throat, trepidation drying out her mouth as she hurriedly glanced at Cooper. He was suddenly staring at the scarred top of the wood bar rubbing slowly at his jaw.

She turned back to Jake, swallowing nervously.

"What did I do wrong?" she asked, trying desperately to remember what she might have forgotten.

His glare darkened.

"Did I say you did something wrong?" he barked.

She just barely controlled a flinch.

"Well, no, but the last bartender you complimented ran out twenty minutes later sobbing hysterically." She heard that story several times. "I'd feel better if you just told me where I messed up now so I can fix it."

His lips tightened, his fierce expression nearly frightening as his jaw bunched.

"Little girl," he snarled. "Learn how to take a friggin' compliment!"

His attitude sucked on a good day.

This obviously wasn't one of his good days.

Feeling everyone's eyes on her now she managed to dry another shot glass and place it on the counter in front of her.

"Thanks, Jake," she murmured. "I'll try to do better next time."

Jake didn't give compliments.

She'd been warned of that by Jake himself.

"Damned women," he muttered behind her. "This is what I get. Next time, Miss Masters, try remembering where everything belongs before you leave."

She turned back to him. "What was left out of place?"

Nothing had been left out and she knew it.

"Your good senses not to mention your supposed good taste," he informed her with another glare. "Get those damned glasses done."

Turning back to the far-too-attentive audience his eagle-like gaze moved to Turk accusingly before he turned and busied himself with the drink bottles that sat in front of the mirrored wall.

"Well, that was interesting." Iron smirked back at her. "Care to explain it?"

"Frightening is more like it." She casted Jake a wary look as she hurriedly finished the glasses. "You explain it first."

Only Turk seemed unconcerned with what had occurred. Leaning against the end of the bar, his arms crossed over his chest, he seemed to be glaring at Jake through the mirror behind the bar.

"Okay, children, playtime's over," Cooper announced as he rose from the barstool. "Iron, you can let the VIPs in now. Casey, you and Morgan get the bouncers in place. Turk, you have security at the bar tonight, Morgan has lead. Let's see if we can get some work done."

The change in positions was surprising. Even Jake seemed perplexed by them as he sent Cooper a probing glance.

Not that Cooper's expression changed. But whatever Jake saw in it, it had him smirking for a second before his expression turned fierce once again.

Moments later the VIP guests were milling in from the large backroom where drinks and appetizers were provided by the chef in the newly built kitchen.

The VIPs were the politicians, entertainers, and even suspected criminals considered powerful regulars, as well as their guests. They were shown in through a private entrance to the comfortable guest lounge on the other side of the main bar area. Watching their faces unobtrusively, Erin memorized their features, filing each in a mental category she would later list in her report.

"Well, hello again, pretty thing." A Corpus Christi talent scout, Tyler Stanley, took a seat in front of her, his smug expression as off-putting tonight as ever. "Change your mind about dinner yet?"

He'd been inviting her out as long as she'd worked there.

"Not tonight, Tyler," she declined again. "Sorry."

He normally took her refusal good-naturedly.

"Are you ever going to say yes?" he demanded, his dark eyes narrowing as his patience was obviously wearing thin.

"Probably not." She sighed, as though in regret. "I told you, I'm involved with someone." It was her standard excuse. She refused to go out with sleazeballs. Tyler Stanley was a sleazeball. "I'll get you a drink though. Another whiskey sour?" she suggested, nodding to his nearly empty glass.

He accepted the drink, obviously still angry. Thankfully, he moved from the bar to make his way to one of the tables occupied by several less savory individuals.

The VIP guests kept her for the next half hour then the rush through the front entrance began.

Halfway through the night a third bartender moved in behind her as bodies packed around the counter and orders flew in. There was little chance to consider Jake's odd behavior or Turk's.

Later, she promised herself. She would think about it later. Because she had no doubt Turk had something to do with it.

CHAPTER 4

The night ended as dawn was peeking at the horizon.

The bar area sparkled. There wasn't a chance anything was out of place or that a speck of dust or smear of a drink remained.

Looking around she gave each area another thorough look, ensuring there was nothing Jake could possibly find fault with. As her gaze moved to the mirror behind the bar and the subtle lights of the neon BROKEN BAR sign, she gave the camera hidden within it a flirtatious little wink.

Gabby would no doubt find that one amusing.

"Ready?"

Swinging around to face Turk, the smile tugging at her lips flattened.

"Looks ready." She shrugged, adjusting her purse on a shoulder and moving for the exit. "Good night, Turk."

The heavy sigh that sounded behind her was filled with male irritation.

"You going to stay mad at me?" he asked softly as he unlocked the door for her.

"I'm not angry with you." What the hell did he expect her to say?

"Of course you are," he murmured.

"Because you forced Jake into that asinine compliment?" she snorted. "Really Turk? It was so obvious."

He simply stared back at her.

"Forget it," she snapped. "I just want to go home."

"Let me lock up and I'll walk you to your car." He didn't argue with her—that was a good thing. She was not in the mood for a confrontation.

"It's nearly daylight. I'll be fine." She almost managed to slide past him when she felt his fingers curl firmly around her upper arm, dragging her to a stop.

"Erin, tempting my patience is the wrong route to take." The warning in his voice seemed designed to just piss her off.

"Give me a break." Mocking, disbelieving, she laughed at the comment. "You just wish I'd tempt you then you wouldn't have to take responsibility for giving into what you want yourself."

He turned the key in the lock with a hard twist of his wrist before turning to face her.

"And just what do you think I want?" he asked, his voice a hard, dark rasp.

The overhead light cast his harsh features in savage lines as his chocolate brown eyes narrowed on her impatiently.

"You're such a man." She snorted in disdain. She had yet to meet one of her stepfather's agents that wasn't an ass. Turk just hid it better.

"Glad you realize that." Powerful arms crossed imperiously over his chest.

"It wasn't a compliment," she informed him, her gaze raking over him. "Look at you. All defensive and displaying such control. Arms crossed, feet braced firmly beneath you. As though you're facing an enemy when what you're facing is your own fear of whatever that sizzle was between us last night. What do you want, Turk? Do you need me to seduce you?" She gave a short, contemptuous laugh. "Sorry but I have things to do tonight. Catch me next lifetime. Maybe then I'll be desperate enough to let you hide from your own hunger and blame me for it."

Catch her next lifetime?

It was all Turk could do to hold back his anger, and his amazement.

Son of a bitch, if only she wasn't so fucking enchanting.

If only she wasn't so damned right.

It was all he could do to keep his hands off her. At the same time, he was dying to push her into touching him instead.

"You've lost it, sweetheart," he growled.

"Have I?" she drawled. "Have I lost it, Turk? Or do you really wish you could lose all the wondrous control you have?" A slender, red-gold brow arched slowly, mockingly, before she turned and began striding away from him.

As though this were finished?

"Where the hell do you think you're going?" he demanded, following her quickly. "This isn't finished, Erin."

Reaching the driver's side door of her little sedan she pulled the door open with a hard jerk before turning back to him, her expression livid.

Eyes sparkling, her cheeks flushed, the full mounds of her breasts heaving within the neat little frame of the black vest secured beneath them. Damn, she was pretty as hell.

"This is finished, Turk," she snapped back at him, holding the top of the doorframe with one hand, the other braced on her hip as she faced him. "It's very much finished, because I'm simply not in the mood to pander to your damned ego tonight."

He was going to burn in hell and Turk knew it.

Reaching out he hooked his arm around her waist and jerked her to him, one hand tangling in her hair to hold her in place as his lips bore down on hers.

Thunder crashed in his head—that had to be his heartbeat, he thought, almost dazed as her lips parted beneath his.

A muted, broken whimper of feminine longing eased past their kiss as her arms twined around his neck. Slanting his lips over hers Turk was helpless against the hunger burning inside him now. Raging at him.

Damn her.

She made him want. . . . He wanted more than just the sex but he was damned if he could put a name to the hunger rising inside him. All he knew was the only relief for it was the woman in his arms.

"Damn you!" Pulling back, Turk stared down at the dazed, flushed features, the mass of red-gold hair falling around her face and her kiss-swollen lips. "I'll follow you to the apartment."

Pretty gray eyes blinked back at him, at first confused, then with a hint of feminine hesitancy.

"Do you need to be seduced first?" he growled then.

A hint of a smile curved her lips. "Of course I do." Stepping back she slid quickly into her car. "Shall we see if you're capable of the seduction?"

Turk couldn't help but grin. "Oh, baby, have no fear. I'm more than capable."

He turned and strode back to the front door, ensured security had engaged when he'd locked the door, then moved quickly to the motorcycle parked next to her car.

Meeting her gaze through the window he nodded shortly, after securing his helmet. As she pulled out he followed. Riding behind her the short distance to the building that housed both their apartments, all he could think about was the woman ahead and the sweet passion that erupted whenever he touched her.

And he intended to touch her quite a bit in the coming hours.

CHAPTER 5

Turk was pulling in beside her as Erin parked her car. His helmet was off as she opened her door. Slamming the door closed she found herself pushed against it a heartbeat later, Turk's lips covering hers again.

She could grow addicted to his kisses.

Hell, maybe she was already addicted. Her body definitely acted as though it were.

The second he touched her, the second his lips covered hers again, his tongue rubbing against hers, pleasure exploded through her system. A vibrant, white-hot pleasure that whipped through her body and left her senses reeling.

She couldn't catch her breath.

She didn't want to catch her breath.

This was what she had craved from the moment she had met him, from that first look to that first kiss then to here. These striking, incredible sensations she'd only just learned existed.

Sensations she'd only found in this man's arms.

Her breasts plumped, becoming swollen, her nipples too sensitive as they pressed against his chest. A flush of heat washed through her body, as though her internal thermometer had gone haywire. Between her thighs, the gold, curved piercing that circled her clit was doing something it had never done before. Where once there had been plenty of room between the piercing and her clit, it now rubbed against the hood covering the bundle of nerves and sent exquisite sensations racing through her.

Even masturbation hadn't swollen that bundle of nerves to this extent.

"Move," he growled, lifting his head as she forced her lashes to part. "If we don't get to your apartment or mine in the next ten seconds, you'll be fucked wherever we're standing."

There was a problem with that?

"No matter who's watching," he groaned as her lips parted on a slight gasp.

Oh, yeah.

Watching. That was right—anyone could be watching.

"My apartment," she demanded. "My bed."

"You'll be lucky if I get the door closed first, dammit."

Taking her forgotten keys from her hand he hit the remote lock to the car, then he was pulling her behind him. Precious seconds were taken in punching the code into the security system at the door. Then the elevator.

The ride took forever. It was torturous as he pulled her back to his chest, the hard ridge of his erection riding against her lower back as his lips lowered to her neck.

Oh, God.

Chills raced over her flesh as his lips found the sensitive curve of her neck and shoulder, playing there with gentle nips and heated kisses.

Her head fell back against his shoulder, one arm curving around the back of his neck as she leaned into him. Her eyes drifted closed as the elevator signaled its arrival at the third floor.

Stepping around her Turk drew Erin behind him, her keys still in his hand as he reach her apartment door.

"Push your code in," he groaned as he shoved the key in the lock. "And hurry."

Hurriedly punching in the six-digit code as he turned the key and pushed the door open, Erin could feel her heart beating faster. Sensual, erotic need rose through her senses and left her breathless.

Pushing the door open, Turk pulled her in behind him. The second the door slammed shut she was lifted from her feet, her back pressed against the wall. Gripping her thighs Turk placed them at his hips, moving between them with a groan.

The heavy length of his erection, held back by his denim and her silk panties, pressed against the sensitive mound of her sex. Damp heat and erotic flares of sensation erupted from her clit through the snug tissue of her vagina to clench at her womb and steal her breath.

Grinding against her, his lips took hers again. His tongue pushed past her lips to find hers as a moan escaped from the erotic caress.

Erin tangled her fingers in his hair, tightened her thighs at his hips, and rode the impressive length of his shaft as she felt her skirt slide up, over her rear. A second later a cry escaped her as the silk of her panties were torn from her.

"Buy you more later," he groaned, pushing his hand between their bodies, his lips moving to her neck as he pulled her blouse aside with his other hand.

Buttons scattered. The cup of her bra was pulled aside as she felt the wide, blunt tip of his cock pressing against the heated, slick folds of her pussy.

"Fuck! I knew this would happen," he groaned, his breath sawing in and out of his lungs as she forced her eyes to open, to stare at the savage features of the man prepared to penetrate her.

"Condom," he bit out, voice rough as he moved the hand clenching the curve of her rear to search a pocket.

She'd forgotten protection, too. She had never forgotten anything so essential.

Pulling the foil pack free, his jaw clenched, his expression tortured, he tore it open with his teeth, removed the latex and hurriedly rolled it in place.

"Now," she whispered as the hard, throbbing crest was pressed into place once again. "Now, Turk . . ."

The muffled, whimpering cry that left her lips at his first thrust was followed by a second as he pulled back. Pushing inside her again, he went farther. On the third thrust he buried deep, a hard rasp of a groan echoing from his chest.

It was so good.

Pinpoints of heat and pleasure pain attacked her flesh as it struggled to accommodate the width of his erection inside her. Sensation built and gathered, swirling through her senses, drawing a muted cry from her lips and intensifying the need already burning through her.

"So damned tight," he whispered, his lips moving to her neck once again, spreading kisses along the sensitive column as he moved toward the needy, hard-peaked breasts below. "So sweet and hot. Damn, Erin. So fucking sweet and hot."

The penetration stretched her almost painfully, the duality of the pleasure and pinching heat making her gasp from the sensations. The pressure it created on the piercing that circled her clit was disastrous.

There was no holding back her response as each pulse and throb of his cock inside her seemed to tighten the gold semicircle with its emerald-tipped jewel tighter around the swollen nub.

There was no holding back any part of herself. She was his. All his. She'd known it since the moment their eyes met, since that first kiss. . . .

Then, he began to move. Thrusting inside her, slow and easy, his lips moved from her neck, along her collarbone to the tight point of a nipple pleading for touch.

Tightening her thighs on his hips, her head fell to his shoulder; Erin could feel her response to him spiraling out of her control. There was no holding back, no pulling back. As though her body recognized the one touch she would always ache for, her senses became consumed by him.

The piercing circling her clit tightened further, rasping over the engorged bud of her clit as Turk moved against her. Drawing back, the heavy length of his cock stroking slowly over sensitive nerve endings, enflaming them with the stretching pleasure-pain.

Pulling free, the broad crest paused at her entrance, Erin drew in a shaky breath, only to expel it in a harsh cry of extreme sensation as Turk powered inside her once again.

The hard penetrations followed by the slow, exquisitely sensual withdraws were intoxicating. Each one pushed her deeper into the merciless storm gathering inside her. Pleasure raged across nerve endings. Heat flushed her body, swirling around her, through her. Flames licked across her flesh, struck at her clit with each inward stroke, then over the slick, inner flesh of her sex.

It was so good.

Sharp, building ecstasy whipped through her, gathering and intensifying as his thrusts began to quicken, to push her higher, deeper into the swirling heat surrounding her.

His lips drew at her nipple, the pleasure there sending shards of sharp sensation to clench at her womb.

Addictive.

She knew she would crave more once he was done. She would ache for this pleasure. She might even be tempted to beg for it.

"Turk." Crying out his name as his hips moved harder, faster, driving him inside her with destructive results, she felt every muscle inside her begain to tighten.

Her clit was so swollen the piercing sensations drove her to the brink of insanity. Her nearing orgasm tightened, brewing in her womb, in her clit, racing toward ecstasy.

The muscles of her vagina clamped on each shafting stroke, tightening on him, pleasure rupturing through her senses as a low, mewling cry escaped her throat.

It hit her then.

An explosion that vibrated so deep, so powerfully inside her that she swore she saw stars. One hard, violent spasm after another clenched the flesh surrounding him. They rocked through her senses, dragging her into a storm of blinding ecstasy.

"Ah, fuck!" Turk groaned, his head lifting from her nipple, his cock plunging inside her again. Again.

As pleasure destroyed her senses she felt him tighten against her, his erection throbbing with one hard, powerful pulse before the feel of his release echoed through her sensitive inner flesh. The final, ever-deepening explosion of her own orgasm drove through her senses with incredible, destructive rapture.

Collapsing against him, Erin was only barely aware of him moving. Holding her close. His arms strong and warm, he carried her into her bedroom and gently laid her back on her bed.

As she drifted off to an exhausted slumber she felt him stripping her. For a moment, she awakened enough to realize he was slowly moving a damp cloth between her thighs, removing the damp proof of her own pleasure.

Thankfully, she slept, Turk thought, unaware of him staring down at her as the sun rose hot and bright in the Texas sky. Unaware of the way he brushed back a swath of red-gold hair before drawing back and snapping and zipping his jeans before leaving her apartment, locking the door behind him silently.

Moving across the hall he unlocked the door to his own apartment, stepped inside, then blew out a hard, deep breath.

"Fuck," he muttered into the silence of his apartment. "I'm screwed."

Because the pleasure had been simply incredible. Better than anything he'd ever known with any other woman. Better than he'd ever imagined he'd experience.

He wanted nothing more than to slip back into her apartment, into her bed, and experience it again.

An addictive pleasure.

And addictions were flat forbidden in his life.

For a reason.

CHAPTER 6

Erin had never imagined what a damned fool she could possibly be.

What had she imagined would happen? That in the space of time it took Turk Rogan to get off that he'd somehow decide he couldn't do without her?

Wasn't she a fool if she had believed that for even a heartbeat?

But maybe, somewhere inside that place where hope still struggled to burn, she'd wondered if it could happen.

Pulling into a parking space on the opposite side of the bar than from where she normally parked, Erin drew in a deep breath. She told herself she wasn't going to act any differently than she had before. Once she left the car her hands would not shake, her heart would not race.

She'd been trained to rein in such a show of nerves before her stepfather had allowed her to join the Covert Information Network.

Another hard breath and her heartbeat slowed. With her body under control she opened the door and stepped from the car. A second breath and her emotions stilled. They no longer raged through her, no longer tormented her.

By the time she stepped into the employee's entrance and relocked the door behind her, she was her normal calm self. Just as she had been trained to be and she was ready to return to the mission she'd been assigned.

She was there to ascertain the security and efficiency of the agents in charge of gathering the information that came through the club. That was all she was there to do. . . .

She hadn't been sent to fall in love.

Turk watched the cameras, his eyes narrowed as Erin parked on the opposite side of the bar than he'd parked. She sat there for a moment before exiting the vehicle. She was calm, poised, no anger, no sense of betrayal showing on her expression as she entered the employees entrance.

There wasn't so much as a hint of nerves.

Dressed in her customary skirt, vest, and white shirt paired with black, low heels, she was so damned sexy she almost took his breath away.

Her red-gold hair was piled atop her head, fringes framing her face, and if he looked close enough he'd see the little mark he'd left the night before, just below her delicate ear.

"She barely looks old enough to work here," the director of the Covert Information Network, J. D. McConnell. stated rather blandly.

"She's old enough," Cooper assured him. "You approved her application yourself."

J.D. snorted at the reminder. "I didn't say she wasn't old enough . . ."

"She didn't do it!" Turning to the two men Turk could barely restrain the anger building inside him.

Son of a bitch! What was wrong with him?

Lifting a brow curiously, J.D. focused his attention on Turk. And that was never a comforting place to be. Penetrating, cool blue-gray eyes stared back at him as the director's imposing features remained remote, nearly expressionless.

"Who else would have?" Cooper asked then, his voice dark with his own anger.

The Broken Bar was his, the men he worked with were the last of the unit he'd once fought with.

"It's not in her nature. . . ."

"Or are you just too involved with the woman to see the possibility of the deception?" J.D. asked coolly. "You weren't quite out of the cameras' field of view the night before last when you were all but fucking her in the parking lot." There was a hint of emotion in his voice then.

Disgust perhaps?

Turk glared back at him for long, tense moments.

"Are you accusing me of something, director?" he asked then, stilling the urge to say more.

"Of playing with the girl, perhaps?" The other man rose from his chair, like a predator moving into place for the kill.

Tall, leanly muscled. Middle age had done nothing to detract from J.D.'s powerful presence.

The white dress shirt he wore tucked into dark gray slacks presented an appearance of thin civility. It was damned thin though.

"I thought we were here to discuss Ms. Masters's attempt to disengage the club's security?" Cooper growled as Turk and the director stared back at each other in growing tension.

"Mr. Rogan doesn't seem convinced she's capable of the act," J.D. pointed out calmly. "I'd like to know why. Is it because he believes in her innocence or because he wants to protect any chance he'd have to get into her bed?"

The bastard.

The icy mockery in the director's tone was starting to piss him off.

"Have you slept with her, agent?" The question had Turk's back teeth clenching.

"That has nothing to do with why I believe in her innocence," Turk argued.

But was it the truth?

Something had happened to him when he'd realized he'd nearly forgotten a condom before taking her. Something he couldn't explain, even to himself.

"I asked you a question," the director stated, his voice growing colder. "Have you slept with her?"

"None of your business," Turk growled.

J.D. nodded slowly, as though the question had somehow been answered before turning to Cooper. "Call her in please."

Turk grimaced, knowing what was coming.

He should leave. If he stayed, he may end up hurting her further. Because seeing the hurt in her face was only going to piss him off more. And that more just may be the stick that broke the barrier he'd placed around his emotions years before.

And how that had happened, he'd be damned if he knew. One thing was for sure though, nothing good could come of it.

Turning his back on the two men, as Cooper made the call to Jake, he glared out the window of the office, teeth clenched, that anger building in his gut until his stomach clenched and his muscles ached.

"She's on her way," Cooper announced.

Turk waited, feeling that inner wall grow thinner, emotions surging behind it, anger battling at it.

Emotions.

Son of a bitch, he didn't want to know what those emotions were, nor did he want to deal with them.

A brief, light knock at the office door and Cooper's permission to enter ended the brief solitude he'd managed to wrap around him, and the moment of reckoning arrived.

Erin stepped into the office, only barely managing to contain her shock as she recognized the tense, furious set of her stepfather's expression.

She was certain Cooper likely missed the rage brewing in J.D.'s gaze, but she didn't. That lighter blue-gray was a sure giveaway that an explosion was imminent.

Cooper sat back in the chair behind his desk, a frown on his face, his gaze sliding briefly to the third occupant next to the window.

Turk.

She looked away from him quickly, closed the door behind her, then moved with a confidence she certainly didn't feel, until she stood several feet from Cooper's desk.

"You wanted to see me?" she asked, keeping her voice at its normal cadence, the nerves beginning to build in her stomach tightly contained as she stood relaxed, her arms at her sides as she met her boss's gaze.

"Erin, we seem to have a problem." It was J.D. that moved from where he stood to the corner of the desk to face her.

Damn, he was really pissed off.

She lifted a brow slowly, watching from the corner of her eye as Cooper slowly tensed in his chair at the familiarity in J. D. McConnell's tone.

"Really?" she murmured. "What sort of problem?"

She could feel Turk moving closer until he invaded her peripheral vision, then moved with a stealthy silence until he stood several feet from Cooper, a dark, steady watchfulness in his deep-brown gaze.

Oh, hell, it was obvious J.D. had not informed them of exactly who she was and what she was doing there.

J.D.'s smile was all teeth.

Oh, God, what had she done to deserve this? Whatever the hell was coming, it was obvious her stepfather wasn't just angry, and he'd gone past furious.

"You've been accused of placing an electronic device designed to reroute the camera feed over the bar to an as-yet-undisclosed location after the club was closed last night."

Her gaze jerked to Turk. They had worked together last night. He would have known better.

"The programming was done from this office," Cooper interjected, his voice dangerously soft. "You were out of Turk's gaze for approximately thirty minutes while taking the trash and soiled rags to the back door, then the time it would have taken you to collect your purse in the lounge across the hall. All recordings from the time just before you left the bar area until this morning were rerouted and erased from this system."

Erin remained silent for a second before looking slowly to her stepfather. His jaw was clenched, the savagely hewn curve not unlike Turk's as well. Both men were silently holding back their fury, and there was little doubt it seemed directed at each other.

She drew in a slow, deep breath. "Not one time did I enter this office, or any other office while out of the bar area," she informed them. "I took the soiled rags and trash to the back door, collected my purse, then went to the employees' bathroom to brush my teeth and collect a breath mint before returning to the bar and leaving."

"You brushed your teeth?" Cooper asked slowly, disbelievingly.

"I did." She nodded. "When I returned to the bar I then looked up at the camera, winked at it as I do every night before leaving, then preceded Turk from the bar. He locked up, followed me to my car, then we drove to town. I didn't return to the bar, nor did I enter your office or mess with the cameras."

"Why the hell did you stop to brush your teeth before leaving the bar?" Cooper snapped as though she would lie about it.

"Because I wanted to," she answered, barely holding back a confrontational tone begging to escape.

"Something you never do any other time," Cooper growled as Turk slowly glanced to the ceiling as though daring to pray. "I've checked the video of previous weeks, Ms. Masters, to ascertain your schedule. If you brushed your teeth last night . . ."

"She did." The snap in Turk's tone had Erin glancing to her stepfather once again.

He still wasn't happy. If nothing else, he was becoming dangerously furious.

"How the hell do you know?" Cooper jerked around to glare at his security agent. "You were in the bar."

"Come on, Cooper," Turk bit out, his expression tightening as his shoulders tensed further. "She brushed her teeth, dammit, and I know she did. Let it go at that."

"I want to know why. . . ."

"Because he kissed her before following her to her apartment where he stayed approximately forty-eight minutes before sneaking back to his own like some damned thief."

Erin flinched at the pure fury reflected in J.D.'s tone now.

"And this isn't some simple-minded little girl you're accusing of treason, Cooper. She's my damned daughter and here at this fucking club by my order."

"Stepdaughter," she felt the need to interject as shock rippled through the room and filled Cooper's gaze.

J.D. turned that glare on her then. "My daughter."

Erin lifted her hand, covered her eyes, and gave a brief, agitated sigh.

Oh, boy, he'd just screwed this puppy right, hadn't he?

Silence filled the office.

Lowering her hand she shot her stepfather an irritated look before shaking her head wearily.

"Thanks, J.D.," she muttered mockingly before turning to Cooper. "I'll collect my things and leave immediately. . . ."

"He didn't hire you, little girl, I did," J.D. snarled, turning on her with a glower that had caused much more seasoned agents to back down immediately. "He has no power over that decision."

"Really, J.D.?" she questioned him with amazement. "You didn't even let the owner know I was coming because it behooved you to take the time out of your busy schedule, then ordered me not to. Do you really think he wants me here now?"

"I'll be damned if you'll stay," her stepfather growled, "after what that bastard pulled last night. . . ." He stabbed his finger in Turk's direction.

"Were you there?" she snapped back at him, mortified.

God, how had he known?

The heat that filled her face was beginning to set a flame to her temper.

"I didn't have to be there, your handler was." Her handler? Her stepbrother? Oh, God, this was getting worse by the second.

"And that misfit stepbrother of mine can go to hell for all I care." She stepped forward, all but going to her toes to go nose-to-nose with him. "He's always overexaggerating everything. He does it just to piss you off."

"Are you trying to tell me Rogan"—he flicked his hand at Turk— "didn't seduce his way into your bed last night?"

"I can tell you unequivocally he's never been in my bed." For the first time she was damned thankful he hadn't joined her in her bed.

"Is he gay?" J.D. snarled then.

Erin backed down and stared at her stepfather in complete shock.

"I'm calling Mom," she muttered before turning back to Cooper and the complete disbelief that seemed to be frozen on his face.

"What in the hell is going on here?" he asked her with impressive control as his gaze moved from her to J.D.

"My stepfather likes to think he somehow has a right to monitor my morality I guess," she answered shortly. "We disagree on that. Often. But that was none of your business, just as he should have never sent me in here without informing you of my identity and the job he sent me here to do. Which was to monitor you and your agents' efficiency in gathering intel from the various suspects that often spend their evenings here. In my own defense, the CIN does employ me as well though. So I really had no other choice but to keep my mouth shut."

Turk cursed under his breath; the latent anger that filled the single, explicit word did cause a light flinch to ripple through her before she stilled it.

"I didn't give you leave to reveal that information," J.D. stated stiffly.

"You should be committed, J.D.," she informed him caustically. "You're a hazard to yourself, your employees, and the world at large. Now I'm going home before I kill you myself and take that pleasure from someone who actually deserves to go to prison for it."

Turning, she left the office, furious, offended, and certain J.D. had just destroyed every iota of friendship she'd found in Simsburg.

J.D. let the smile he was holding back slip free as the door slammed behind his stepdaughter only to be followed by Rogan's exit as well. Damn, he was crazy about that girl. She had so much of her mother's fire and flash temper that he couldn't help but be wary of her as well though.

"Drink, J.D.?" The cool drawl of Ethan Cooper's voice sounded as if a smile turned into an amused quirk as he turned back to the man he'd been friends with since Cooper was a kid barely out of diapers.

"You're pissed," he stated.

He could always tell when Coop was pissed. It was a look the other man had, the way his eyes seemed to still, a hardening of his jaw. . . . Nope, Coop wasn't very happy at the moment.

"You're messing with my club, my agents, and my staff," Cooper snapped as he moved to the small bar at the corner of the room. "I don't appreciate it."

J.D. lifted a brow, though he wasn't really surprised that Cooper had come to feel protective of Erin. It was the same reaction most men displayed toward her mother, Esme, as well. They had a way of drawing a man's protective nature out, whether the males wanted it drawn out or not.

"Of course you don't, neither would I," J.D. assured him as he accepted the whiskey the other man handed him even as he noticed the glimmer of surprise in his eyes.

"Then why do it?" The deepening of his voice was another sign of his disapproval, if not his anger.

Turning, J.D. resumed his seat, propping his ankle on the opposite and staring back at Cooper for a long, silent moment.

"I always send backup up to watch out for her, and my son John D. usually takes that duty," he stated as Cooper returned to the desk and sat down as well. "It would kill Esme and I if anything happened to her. John D. has been watching Turk and Erin dance around each other for three months now, and that's something she never does. That, added to the anomalies showing up here, and I'm damned concerned. It was better to get the truth out in the open and have it done with rather than hanging over her head where that boy's concerned."

"That boy?" Cooper grunted mockingly. "I don't think I'd call Turk a boy and let him hear it."

J.D. chuckled at the thought of the agent's reaction should that happen.

"Probably not a good idea," he agreed. "But, she loves him. Let her have her chance."

"And you know this how?" Cooper was obviously not of the same mind-set.

"And he loves her." J.D. grinned. "I have the pictures John D. sent of the two of them whenever they were working together. Trust me, it's been like seeing me and Esme all over again. And that's a fine agent, a good man. I couldn't have chosen better for her myself."

To which Cooper gave him a wry, mocking look. "Well hell, J.D., sounds to me like that's exactly what you've done."

J.D. only smiled.

Some things, he thought, people just needed a little help with.

Just sometimes.

CHAPTER 7

E rin was on the verge of crying as she pulled into the parking lot of the small apartment complex where she lived. That was something she never did, especially when it came to a man. Regret was a dark, aching wound in her chest. The bitter, painful feeling refused to be pushed away. Realization hounded her, lashed at her emotions.

She was falling in love with Turk. She'd been aware of it, and though she knew she should have fought it, still, that hunger for him, the need for something far more than physical, had grown inside her.

Because she'd believed she had a chance at his heart.

She'd fooled herself into thinking that if she hungered this deeply, then surely he did as well.

Moving from the elevator and walking slowly to her apartment, she still marveled at how easily that hope had blown apart in her face. How quickly the need had lashed back to strike at a heart she hadn't realized was so vulnerable.

But that was no excuse for losing the wariness that had been ingrained inside her since she was a child and she and her mother had endured her father's rages. In the years before J.D. had come into their lives, there had been very little security in it.

It was no excuse for not being aware of the dangers she knew existed in the world though.

It was no excuse for what came next. The second Erin pushed the key in the door of her apartment to unlock it, she knew she made a mistake.

The door was already unlocked and someone was waiting on the other side.

Dragged into the apartment, the force exerted on her arm was excruciating. She let out a scream worthy of a horror heroine.

"Bitch!" The furious hiss accompanied a hard blow to her head, dazing her for a second. But it didn't hurt her lungs. And it seemed screaming could actually be instinct, because she kept screaming.

Pain exploded through her head. Harsh fingers gripped her hair, jerking her head back forcefully a second before they tried to ram her face into the wall. Fighting, jerking against the hold, another cry left her lips as her shoulder took the impact instead, the sting not nearly as painful as a full-face kiss to the dry wall would have been.

She was beginning to think no one was going to hear her. That her screams were being ignored or everyone was just gone. It wasn't that late, surely someone could hear her screaming.

The grip in her hair tightened as she reached back, her nails digging into skin as her assailant cursed and tried to ram her into the wall again. Turning quickly, the pain to her scalp enraging her, Erin kicked, scratched, her cries more guttural now than loud. She fought each attempt to disable her as she twisted, trying to claw at his face, knee him in the groin. She refused to stay still, refused to give in to the pain or allow the son of a bitch enough of a grip to actually succeed in quietening her.

"Erin!" The sound of her name being called, the voice harsh, power resonating in the voice, was followed by the heavy thump of something crashing into her door.

"Turk!" Screaming out his name, powerless to stop the coming crash as she was thrown to the floor, Erin rolled with it instead.

Coming against the wall as her door was kicked in, Turk's large, powerful silhouette rushed the room. His entrance was followed by the sound of glass shattering.

"Oh, hell no." Scrambling to her knees Erin turned, staring at the hole in her living room wall where a large, picturesque window now lay shattered.

She couldn't believe it. Wasn't this just the perfect ending to this night?

"That was my window," she whispered, shocked as Turk rushed past her, the weapon in his hand held ready as he braced himself against the side of the wall before quickly looking out.

The sound of a motor gunning and racing away could be heard, followed by another. John D. or his partner, possibly both, would be following the bastard. If anyone could catch the assailants it would be them. Scrambling across the floor she jerked her cell phone from where it had fallen to the floor, flipped it open and hit her stepfather's number.

"Get out of there!" J.D. barked into the phone. "John D.'s trailing them with backup en route. Get to Turk's place now, Erin. I'll be there later."

The line disconnected.

Collapsing against the wall behind her, she braced her arms on bent knees before looking up at Turk as he reentered the kitchen from the short hall that led to her bedroom.

Moving to her he reached for her wrists, pulling her to her feet and quickly into his arms. He wrapped her in that sense of security she'd always sensed her mother felt with J.D.

God help him. Seconds before, he was shaking like a kid facing the bogeyman! Or a man facing the loss of a woman who meant far too much to him.

That couldn't be the case, Turk assured himself. It wasn't terror.

So, why was he holding her in his arms, tight to his chest, his head bent protectively over hers as he kept his own back to the door? Why was he protecting her before his own security?

"I'm okay," she whispered, her tone more hesitant than the delicate fingers gripping the sides of his back.

Forcing himself to move back, Turk stared down at her pale face, the sea-green eyes darker now with distress.

"Let's get you the hell out of here before anyone realizes anything happened." Gripping her wrist to keep her behind him Turk moved quickly for the door.

Easing it open and checking the hall quickly, Turk tucked his weapon at the small of his back before motioning Erin to stay in place, just out of sight. Crossing the short distance to his own apartment and opening the door, he gave the kitchen and living room a thorough scan before returning to Erin.

She'd managed to find her purse and the smaller-size baby Glock she now held firmly close to the side of her thigh.

Keeping her covered with his own body Turk rushed her into his own place. Closing the door, still silent, he went quickly through the rooms just to be certain, before returning to the kitchen.

"I'm going to lock your place up. . . ."

"I did that while you were in the other rooms," she cut him off mid-sentence as he strode to the door. "The security auto engages as soon as the door closes." Laying her purse on the center bar and tucking her weapon inside of it, she faced him calmly.

Calmly, as though she hadn't just been attacked inside her own home.

His jaw clenched, the terror that washed through him moments before morphing into anger.

"John D.'s trailing my attacker until backup catches up with them. They'll have him in custody soon, if he's not already."

Moving to the sink as she spoke she tore several paper towels from a roll, wet them, then applied the cool compress to her lip before turning back to him.

"I should fucking paddle your ass!" he snarled, his hands plowing through his hair as he stared back at her in bemused fury. "Do you think I dragged you over here first so you could just sash-the-fuck-shay across that damned hall without me?"

"Sash-the-fuck-shay?" A single fiery brow arched as she lifted the compress she fashioned to reveal a swelling lip and the bruising at the side of her face.

A fist slammed into his gut, pure jagged rage at the sight of her perfect creamy flesh so abused.

"God, you'll be the death of me!" Swinging away from her he stomped to the other side of the room before turning back with a glare.

"What's your problem anyway?" Frustration flashed across her face but beneath the irritation was a hesitant wariness.

"These fucking bruises on your face? The fact that some bastard just tried to kill you? For God's sake, Erin!" Pure rage ran through his senses. And there she stood, her head tipped to one side, the once-neat disarray of the tumbling curls now torn from the clasp and falling to her shoulders. The white shirt was ripped, her little vest missing a button, her hose were all but shredded, and she was barefoot. And she was staring back at him as though she really didn't know why he was so pissed off.

She propped one hand on her curvy hip and glared back at him.

"How would you feel if you had to accept Iron's help if a gang jumped you, then had to listen to him bitch because your poor little face was bruised?"

His eyes narrowed. "I'd cut the smart-assed remarks."

A mocking little roll of her eyes had him forcibly restraining the need to spank her tight little ass. The problem was, if he got her panties over that cute little ass then he'd end up doing far more.

"You know, Turk, you seriously need to do something about that double standard of yours. Now tell me what you intend to do about slipping back over there for my clothes? Since I forgot and I'm fairly certain you don't intend to let me go back."

His arms went across his chest as he simply stared at her silently, darkly.

"Didn't think you did." She sighed.

"You called J.D." Dropping his arms he moved toward her once again.

Predatory male grace and determined sexuality nearly stole not just her mind, but her breath as well.

"Yes, I called him." She stepped back warily as he stepped to the refrigerator, opened it, and pulled free a bottle of water.

"Did he tell you to get to my apartment and stay put?"

She frowned at that. "How did you know?"

"Standard procedure for female agents," he growled. "Why weren't you aware of that?"

"Maybe I'm not your standard female agent," she suggested softly as he twisted the lid from the bottle. "I could be so much more." A sexy little wink shot his blood pressure sky high and had the room feeling way too damned hot.

"He'll be here soon." Turning from her and lifting the bottle to his lips he took a deep drink.

"Yeah," she murmured. "We wouldn't want J.D. to catch you fucking his favorite agent. That would be bad."

The water shot down the wrong side of his throat as the sudden memory of the effects of fucking her shot to his brain. Hunger pulsed in his dick as he suddenly wheezed, while his balls tightened in lust.

Turning to her he glimpsed her satisfied smile a heartbeat before he took that first step to have a second taste of her. At the same second a short imperious knock sounded at the door.

"Mmm." Her satisfied little murmur came with a wicked glance in his direction. "Talk about timing."

Narrowing his eyes he let her enjoy the moment. For now.

Erin almost laughed. He'd nearly spit that nice mouthful of water clear across the room. Who knew he'd be so damned easily unsettled.

The urge to laugh died a quick death as her stepbrother entered the room behind Cooper and J.D. And John D., like his father, didn't look happy.

CHAPTER 8

H er attacker had gotten away.

Erin stood silently as she listened to her brother's report, aware of Turk close behind her. The warmth of his big body, the feeling of security he exuded kept that first, hard flare of fear from igniting inside her.

"Sorry, sis." John D sighed, his light-blue eyes concerned as he watched her carefully.

"Nothing was taken from the apartment that I could see," J.D. assured her. "Your window is being repaired as we speak. I'll have a female agent come in and pack your things. When we leave I'll make arrangements to have you transferred . . ."

"No." Surprised, the word popped from her mouth before she could hold it back.

J.D.'s eyes narrowed slowly, tension radiating through his body with such energy. Erin swore every male in the room followed suit with instinctive dominance.

Give her a break. She was going to smother from testosterone at this rate.

"What do you mean, 'no'?" her stepfather finally growled.

"I'm not leaving, J.D.," she informed him firmly.

"Then I'll fire you!" The threat was an old one. Even John D. smirked at the sound of it.

"And you're not firing me either." Erin moved carefully away from Turk, all too aware that he and Cooper were none too pleased with J.D.'s warning.

J.D. glowered back at her. "Erin, this is serious," he informed her as he leaned forward slowly and braced his hands on the counter. "You were attacked."

"I wasn't hurt."

Sometimes, it was best to simply stare him down.

"Have you looked at your face yet?" he snapped when she didn't blink. "Take a look in the mirror then tell me you weren't hurt."

She snorted at that. "It hurt more when John D. wrecked the four-wheeler last summer. And the bruises were worse."

J.D. turned to his son slowly. "You said you were alone," he reminded John D. with a hint of anger.

John D. shook his head with an air of brotherly exasperation.

"Come on, Dad, I told you she lies on me. Those innocent green eyes are hiding a heathen determined to get me disowned," he accused her

Erin rolled her eyes at his statement. Sadly, J.D. was used to them.

"I'll get to the bottom of the four-wheeler wreck later," he snapped, straightening from the counter. "Get your purse. I want to get you out of here before anything else happens. . . ."

"She said she wasn't leaving!" Turk didn't raise or lower his voice.

He stepped closer to her, tension sizzling through the atmosphere around him.

J.D. and his son turned to him, nearly identical expressions of surprise on their faces now.

"I can handle this, Turk," she breathed out wearily as she glimpsed the determination that filled his face and tightened his body.

J.D.'s smile was tight. John D. smirked back at her.

Really? she thought. Did she really have to deal with this bullshit tonight? Hadn't she put up with enough already?

"I'm not a bone," she informed them all as Turk moved in closer to her back, nearly touching her now.

John D. took a seat on the other side of the counter, propped his elbow on the counter, and rested the hard curve of his chin on his fist. The subtle wink he shot her as his black hair fell around the hard planes and angles of his face assured her he intended to be amused.

"Of course you're a bone," John D. drawled. "J.D. will never admit anyone else can take care of you."

"John." J.D. turned on him with a quiet, dark anger. "Get back to the van."

John D. grinned but didn't move.

"I'm not leaving. Leaving won't solve anything. That attack was personal. It wasn't a robbery," she protested.

"All the more reason to have you reassigned," J.D. pointed out, propping his hands on his hips like some Roman emperor surveying all he held power over.

He did not control her. She refused to allow it.

"All the more reason to stay here," she argued. "If I run I'm always looking over my shoulder until the bastard catches me unaware. If I stay, Cooper, Turk, and the others will ensure it ends here."

"Possibly ending your life as well," he snarled. "And just how do you think your mother will handle this?"

"Don't tell her," she suggested blandly. "That's where you always make your mistake. You blab, J.D."

For God's sake, why did he keep involving her mother?

"Don't tell her?" J.D. asked her as though amazed she would suggest it. "And you think she wouldn't find out?"

"What does it matter?" Crossing her arms over her breasts she found herself less than willing to continue this debate. "You can't force me to leave. I won't let you. Conserve your energy and the hair you'll end up pulling out by figuring out who it is now rather than later. Or worse yet, when he catches me unaware and kills me because none of us were expecting it."

"She's right, Dad." John D. was no longer amused.

"I didn't ask you," J.D. growled.

"If we keep her from sight," Cooper cut in then, "let no one know where she's at, someone will start asking questions. That someone would lead us to the answers we need."

"I didn't ask you either," J.D. growled, casting Cooper a silencing look.

"Then ask me." The sound of Turk's voice had her wincing. "She stays right here. No one would know. They could suspect she's here, next door at Iron's place, or downstairs at Jake's. They'll have to come looking for her and when they do, we can eliminate the threat once and for all."

Stay here? At Turk's place?

"Well, sis," John D. drawled then, obviously amused once again. "There are your options. Door number one or door number two?"

"Try door number three," she murmured.

Her brother's brow lifted as laughter gleamed in his emerald-green eyes. Behind her, Turk muttered a curse.

"And what would door number three be?" Only Cooper was brave enough to ask.

J.D. sighed. "She'll decide once she makes up her mind which of us deserves to die first." He looked at Turk. "She's staying with you. I live with her mother, I know that look."

She was quite certain he did. Since J.D. and her mother married nine years before and he'd seen their couch as a bed more times than once.

"I'll sneak over and get her clothes," John D. decided, then turned to Cooper. "Get Gabby over here to drive her car around and stay in her apartment with Jake. With a little work, she could look enough like Erin to perhaps fool whoever's looking for her."

Gabby was the bar's camera and security tech, normally hidden in the basement of the bar and buried in code and camera surveillance.

John D. was all but rubbing his hands together in glee.

"Boys and girls, let's have fun."

"Good God, I should have drowned you at birth." J.D. stared at his son as though he were demented. "Gabby will eat Jake alive, Miss Do-it-my-way-here"—he jerked a thumb at Erin—"will probably end up strangled before Turk realizes he's done it and you'll leave a hell of a mess for me and Cooper to clean up."

John D. laughed. "And just think, I'm your heir."

"It's not too late to drown you, John," J.D. assured him. "Not too late at all."

His son only laughed back at him before shooting Erin another of those cocky winks.

Damn, J.D. could practically feel life beginning to twist and turn. What was would be no longer.

So why wasn't he fighting it harder?

CHAPTER 9

Nearly a week later, Turk closed and relocked the apartment door after another visit from J.D. and his diabolical son. He was beginning to think perhaps John D. did deserve to be drowned at birth as his father had threatened.

If the little bastard kept flirting with Erin the way he was while pretending a brotherly air, then Turk would take care of that little task himself.

"I think that went rather well," Erin stated cheerfully as he stepped into the living area to glare down at where she had stretched out on his couch.

Those little tank tops were going to get her ass in trouble. They outlined her breasts perfectly.

Today, instead of jeans or oversized sweatpants, she was wearing a pair of shorts that practically made his tongue hang out of his mouth like a slavering fool.

They weren't indecent, but the material ended far too short for his peace of mind, and they fit. They fit her perfect. One slender leg was lifted and bent, her bare foot resting on the cushion of the sofa. She looked relaxed, comfortable, and just like the shorts fit her body, she seemed to just fit into his life.

"None of you threatened to kill each other, you mean?" he snorted.

She gave a small, light chuckle. "Mom says when that happens she looks for the safe room because the explosion is coming."

He almost winced. Yep, he could almost feel it coming himself.

"What usually instigates the explosion?" he asked carefully.

"J.D." She didn't even hesitate before giving that answer. "He's not allowed to screw with Mom's life or her friends' lives, but for some reason, she refuses to put her foot down on my life. And poor John D., his mother died when he was a baby, so he's had no other example to follow but J.D."

Plopping down at the bottom of the couch Turk almost felt sorry for John D. Almost. The entire time the bastard had been there he'd petted on Erin like she was a homeless pup or something.

As he sat there contemplating the other man's drowning, a delicate little foot slid to his thigh. Automatically he reached for it, gently kneading her arch as he tried to convince himself that drowning her stepbrother was a bad idea.

"John D. and I are really close though," she said.

He wondered how long he'd have to hold John D. under the water?

"How close?" He glared at the wall instead of her.

"Not that kind of close," she answered, an edge of laughter flirting with her tone. "He was always the big brother. Pulling my hair and hiding my hair bows when I first moved in. The first time I caught him unaware and planted my fist in his solar plexus he still didn't take it seriously when I told him to leave my things alone. Then I caught him coming in drunk as a skunk one night. He passed out in the garage. I spent the night chewing gum and planting it in his long, pretty black hair. The next day Mom nearly had to shave his head bald. He must have gotten the message then."

Okay, he might let the bastard draw a breath or something.

Turk narrowed his eyes on her. "Vengeful creature," he grunted.

It would be hard to get seriously aroused when a man knew a woman could do such damage, he thought.

She shrugged with a smile, lifting her breasts beneath that snug top. "He knew I'd done it, but he never told on me. Never got me back. But he did stop stealing my things."

Kneading her little foot he stared over at her, seeing the genuine affection she felt for her stepbrother, but none of the hunger for him that lit her eyes.

Okay, he might let John D. live. Maybe. If he could keep his hands off what belonged to Turk.

That almost had him stilling in shock.

His? When had he actually decided she was his?

They'd settled into a wary routine for the past week, one Turk had felt unraveling from the moment it had developed. Still, they both seemed to be adhering to some unwritten set of rules.

Erin cooked, he cleaned up and stacked the dishwasher. While he remotely helped Gabby work the surveillance cameras at the bar, she worked on reports J.D. kept her busy with.

Come midnight, normally the busiest part of the night for the bar, and for them, was when the tension developed. When the air between them became rife with arousal, with awareness.

As it was now.

"You're quiet, and you're staring at me," she said suspiciously. "What are you thinking?"

About her lips wrapped around his cock.

How sweet she tasted.

How tight she felt wrapped around his engorged flesh.

He was thinking about things he should never be thinking about and he knew it.

"I try real hard not to think too much where you're concerned," he grunted as he lifted the remote and flipped the television on. "It's too damned dangerous."

Yeah, like he might decide to actually stop pretending that he didn't want her.

Lifting her foot from his hard thigh, where he'd been absently rubbing her arch, Erin swung her legs around and rose from the couch.

"I have things to do," she stated.

She had no intentions of watching several hours of the news as they had the night before.

"Sure." He sounded distracted, he might want her to think he was distracted, but she could feel his gaze on her. Like a physical touch, stroking along her back, her thighs.

She almost rolled her eyes.

She wasn't going to beg him, if that was what he wanted. And she was damned if she would make the first move.

Her bedroom door closed quietly.

Running his hand over his face Turk clenched his teeth and told himself he was not following her.

He'd made it a week. Questions were being asked and several suspects were being investigated. Unfortunately, a lot of the bar's customers had noticed the female bartender that was suddenly absent. Just as Cooper's men had noticed those who pretended a disinterest, or too much interest.

Then there were those who had noticed his absence as well.

Blowing out a hard breath he leaned forward to the laptop opened on the wood coffee table. Waking the laptop and pulling up the surveillance cameras outside the apartment building he took note of each vehicle, comparing them mentally to those that were often seen at the bar.

Next he tapped into the bar's cameras and the program Gabby had running from Erin's apartment. Everything looked good there.

There wasn't a damned thing for him to fill the upcoming hours with. Nothing to distract himself with.

God, what was he doing to himself?

What was he doing to himself as well as Erin?

He'd spent three months keeping other men away from her, watching her like a hungry wolf, telling himself he was saving both of them by not taking her, by not giving in to whatever kept drawing them toward each other.

He wasn't saving either of them a damned thing. He was killing himself. And if he wasn't careful he'd lose any chance he may have at the heart of the woman he couldn't force himself to stay away from.

He'd lost his mind. . . .

Or had he lost something far more serious? he wondered as he rose from the couch and turned slowly to the closed bedroom door.

Had he lost something he hadn't even been aware he actually possessed?

"Erin." The bedroom door opened several hours later, Turk's tall, powerful body stepping into the dimly lit room.

She lay back on the queen-size bed, the small lamp that sat on the bedside table not nearly enough to fully illuminate the shadowed planes and angles of his face.

Erin stared at him from across the room, never shifting position. Lying back on the pillows, one arm curled beneath her head, the other rested just beneath a breast.

The thin gray cami top snuggly outlined her breasts while matching brief boy shorts made her legs look longer.

The sleepwear was comfortable, but as lust burned in his chocolate-brown eyes she realized exactly how little it was covering as well.

Turk prowled closer to the bed, his eyes darkening to nearly black as his gaze moved over her slowly.

"I'm not in the mood for one of your quickies," she informed him, though she knew better.

Her body was primed and ready for whatever the hell he wanted to give her for however long he wanted to give it to her.

Her mouth dried out as he gripped the bottom of his T-shirt, stripped it off, and dropped it negligently to the floor before his hands fell to his belt.

Sweet merciful heaven. Hard abs flexed, and the power beneath hard, sun-bronzed flesh caused her to swallow nervously.

"No quickie tonight." The dark rasp of his voice, the sensual promise gleaming in his eyes had her breathing quickening, the blood rushing furiously through her veins.

Her gaze moved to his hands, watching as he unclasped his belt before releasing the first metal button of his jeans.

"Sit up." The growl in his voice, the erotic hunger tightening his face, combined with the knowledge she may have asked for more than she could handle wasn't lost on her.

Slowly, she sat up, mesmerized, aching for him. Drawn to him in a way she promised herself she'd figure out later.

"I tried to stay away from you, Erin." Jeans loosened, he pushed them over his hips after freeing the impressive length of his cock.

"Why?" She had to fist her hands at her side to restrain the urge to touch him.

"There was a very good reason." Shedding his jeans and stepping closer to the bed, Turk wrapped his fingers around the base of his erection and stroked the iron-hard flesh slowly. "Right now, I don't even have a clue what that reason was though."

But he wasn't unaware of what he wanted.

Pushing his fingers through her hair, he gripped it, tugging at her head until the wide blunt tip moved slowly to her lips.

"Part your lips, Erin," he groaned. "Sweet baby, give me that hot little mouth."

Sweet silken lips parted, allowing the head of his cock to pierce the wet heat of her mouth.

The sight of her taking him, the feel of her mouth slowly surrounding the crest as her delicate hands gripped his thighs drew a strangled groan from Turk's lips.

Damn her! It was too fucking good.

Damn him! Because he was stepping willingly into a waiting hell and he knew it.

He knew it, yet fighting it was impossible.

"You're a fucking witch. You should be burned at the stake," he accused her as electric pleasure rippled from the engorged shaft to his tightening balls.

Innocent green eyes blinked back at him with erotic promise as she worked her lips and tongue over his hardened flesh with feminine hunger. That wicked little tongue licked and stroked, rubbed at the underside of the throbbing crest and teased that ultra-sensitive spot just below it.

Her mouth was exquisite. What she lacked in experience, she more than made up for in hunger. And the hungry demand in each suckling stroke had his body tightening as pleasure lashed at his nerve endings.

He'd never felt that curling heat in his gut that he felt now with any other woman. He'd never burned for another woman like he burned for Erin. From that first moment that their eyes met, to that first kiss, and beyond. Each day with her, each time he touched her, his need for her only grew. This hunger for her touch, the need to just hear her voice . . . God, what was she doing to him?

Staring down at her, watching her lips move over him, her expression flushed and filled with pleasure and need, he could feel himself unraveling. His release boiled in his balls, threatened to slip his control.

"Enough." Tightening his fingers in her hair and pulling her back, Turk watched as her lashes lifted languidly, her sea-green eyes darker now as arousal filled them.

"Lie back for me." The demand was a hoarse rasp as he fought the need rushing through him, demanding that he take her now.

Gracefully, temptingly, she lay back.

His lips almost quirked at the witchy, hungry look in her eyes.

"Take the clothes off," he ordered then. "Let me watch."

Let him watch she did.

The teasing, taunting movements as she lifted the little top over her head, revealing swollen breasts and tight, cherry-red nipples had his cock flexing in demand. Then those slender, graceful fingers moved to the boy shorts she wore. Slipping beneath the elastic band she pushed them down her thighs, over her knees, then discarded them with a smooth shift of her legs.

"You've tortured the hell out of me for far too long," he growled as he knelt on the bed. "Months too long."

"You tortured yourself," Erin assured him, her arms curving over her head as a sharp pulse of sensation clenched her womb before sending a heated strike of sensation to wrap around her clit.

He wasn't touching her yet. She shouldn't be feeling this.

Satisfaction curled at the corner of his lips.

"You'll regret this later," he assured her as he came over to her.

"And you know this how?" she asked, the shadows in his eyes sending a flare of uncertainty raging through her now.

He had no idea how he drew her. How the months working with him, drawn to him yet denied his touch, had created an erotic need she couldn't deny.

His head lowered, his lips brushing against hers. "Because, stubborn determination and independence are so much a part of you that it terrifies me."

A moan escaped her. Filled with need as her hands lifted to touch his shoulders, only to have him catch them and press them back to the bed.

"Keep your hands right there. Don't touch me yet, or I'll lose what little control I have left."

Releasing her wrists, he obviously thought she would obey him without question. For the moment, she let him believe. . . .

"Oh God, Turk," she moaned as excitement exploded through her at the feel of his palm curving around her breast, his thumb stroking over her nipple.

Sensation raced across her nerve endings, slamming through her senses, sending need screaming through her body. Fingers of flaming pleasure raced across her flesh, set fire to her body and her mind, and need tore through her.

She'd ached for him. Dreamed of this touch.

Lips parting beneath his kiss she lifted to him, her nipples raking across the scattering of curls over his chest and increasing the heat and the need tearing at her.

Turk's kisses were incredible.

As his head lowered and his lips covered hers, Erin realized she had forgotten just how good the feel of his lips against hers really were.

He didn't just kiss.

He sipped.

He tasted.

His lips caressed and possessed while his incredibly wicked tongue staked full possession. The hungry demand of his lips against hers filled her with a hunger that shocked her.

Oh, God, she'd waited so long. . . .

Clenching her hands in the blankets beneath her, Erin let herself sink into the morass of sensations building around her.

They sensitized her flesh, beaded her nipples tight, and caused them to ache for his touch. Between her thighs that small bundle of nerve endings swelled, pulsed, and demanded attention.

When she began lifting her arms to touch him again he pressed them back to the bed with a growling," Keep them there."

The firm dominance in his voice was previously unknown to her, but not something that surprised her.

"Turk—" She arched in an involuntary move, her breasts lifting his bare chest as his lips moved down her neck, a hand stroked to her thigh.

The stars behind her closed eyes were multiplying as their buddies began racing through her bloodstream.

Her lashes drifted up, her breath catching as she glimpsed the absorbed, erotic hunger reflected in his face as his head lowered, his lips, the moist heat of his mouth surrounding her nipple.

Sharp, furious pleasure pulsed in near violence from the hard bead of her nipple to the swollen bud of her clit. Sensation clenched her womb. Her hands fisted in the sheets beneath her, hips arching.

"Turk!" she cried his name in shocking pleasure at the erotic pulses of electric sensation.

Releasing her nipple from the moist grip of his mouth he moved lower. And he didn't waste time.

As flames began to envelop her senses, heat rushing around her, inside her, Turk wedged his broad shoulders between her thighs, his head lowered to flesh so sensitive, aching with such need she suddenly feared the intensity of it.

Erin froze.

The hungry demand of his lips and tongue instantly burrowing into the slick response of her body threw into that world of shocking chaos with no apology.

There was no slow journey into the dizzying kaleidoscope of sensation. There was no time to sense the storm gathering in her body. There was no time to fear it.

The feel of his tongue flickering at the clenched entrance, licking and probing with experienced demand had her hips arching involuntarily to the decadent caress.

Her thighs spread wide and her hands latched into his hair, sinking into the thick strands and gripping tight, Erin felt all control over her own senses disintegrate.

She would have tried to pull back, but instinct actually surged forward refusing to allow it. At the same time his lips and tongue found the curved bar as it lay along each side of her swollen clitoris.

Turk sucked the violently sensitive bud into the heat of his mouth, lips and tongue devouring it with wicked hunger, and each draw, each lick worked the piercing that curved beneath the bundle of nerves. Destructive sensation exploded through her body. It tore through her senses and convulsed her muscles as pure blistering ecstasy and rapid-fire pulses of rapture combined to destroy her with pleasure.

Turk knew the moment Erin found release, convulsing beneath him in an orgasm that drew her body taut, filling the bedroom with her cries of rapture. God, he'd die if he lost her. How would he survive it?

He should have heeded the white-hot hunger that nearly blinded him three months ago. Should have realized this delicate, fragile, young woman was becoming far too important to him.

He nearly lost all control, nearly spilled his release to the sheets in his hunger to have her as her release began ripping through her.

Thick, engorged, his cock throbbed, pulsing in painful arousal as he draped her legs over his thighs and pulled her closer, lifting her to him.

The swollen folds of her sex, bare of curls, silky and slick with dew, like the prettiest pink flower opening for him, petal by petal.

Gripping the heavy length of his cock Turk guided the wide, blunt crest to the weeping center. The feel of slick, heated flesh and his princess's pleasure swept through his mind with the force of a tidal wave.

Shudders still gripped her body, little cries falling from her lips as the pulses of release continued to clench and ripple through her snug pussy. Pressing against the entrance Turk eased the engorged, sensitized crest into the flexing entrance. His teeth clenched, pleasure searing him, electric surges of incredible sensation racing from the head of his dick, along the heavily veined shaft to tighten around the sac of his balls.

"Turk." The husky cry pulled his gaze from the slick flesh enveloping his dick to the dazed pleasure suffusing her expression.

"It's okay, baby." Reaching up he cupped her cheek, his thumb brushing over her trembling lips as he clenched his teeth against the fiery pleasure gripping the head of his dick.

"Fuck, Erin," he groaned, the feel of tight, slick silk sucking him into the gripping heat of her pussy, destroying him with pleasure.

Her head thrashed against the mattress, her fingers gripping his forearms as her thighs tightened and her pleasure began to build once again.

And he watched it.

Echoes of her pleasure milked his hard flesh as he pushed deeper inside her slick heat.

"Erin . . ." His hands slid from her thighs to her hips where he held them still, halting the instinctive little movements that had her pussy riding the hard engorged crest stretching the entrance. "Easy, baby."

Flushed, dazed, her expression was tight with the sensual hunger building again. The swollen curves of her breasts drew him as pebble-hard pink nipples topped them, a flush of arousal surrounding the delicate hue.

Feeling her hands caress his shoulders, her tight sheath gripping him as he tilted her hips to him, Turk let his lips brush hers.

A brush was all it took.

Her lips parted beneath the caress, her tongue meeting and tasting his. A pulse of white-hot lightning tore over his nerve endings, sending a surge of pleasure through his body. His hips jerked, thrust, pushing the hard flesh penetrating her deeper.

A low, keening cry filled the air around him as Turk felt the last, fingernail hold he had on his control dissolve.

The next thrust sent an overload of sensation crashing through his brain and spreading through his senses like lava pouring from a volcano. Immersed in more pleasure than he'd ever imagined finding in a woman, Turk gave himself to the overwhelming ecstasy he'd only found with this one woman.

Erin couldn't process reality. Pleasure was a brutal storm whipping through her, burning her. The pleasure-pain of the thick flesh penetrating her, driving into her, dragged her in an erotic whirlwind more devastating than the one before it.

Turk surrounded her. Filled her.

The heaving thrust of his cock burning between her thighs, stretching and caressing intimate flesh, sent waves of desperate pleasure tearing through her again.

Again, it built inside her, rushing through her body and her senses as the storm began tearing through her.

The hard length of his thick flesh impaling her in quick, hard thrusts, the engorged crest stretching her, his throbbing shaft stroking with ever increasing pleasure . . .

"Turk!" She tried to scream his name as he buried his lips at her neck. Tried to breathe through a pleasure raging through her in rapidly tightening bands of chaotic storm centers. Like dozens of tornados racing through her, threatening to converge.

A hoarse male groan was her answer, his lips moving against the sensitive curve of her breast. Then his lips lowered, covered the painfully hard tip, his tongue lashing at it as he sucked it inside.

Sensation exploded from the caress, speared to her womb, her clit, then imploded with a force that she knew she would never fully recover.

Ecstasy was a vortex of swirling, vivid sensation. It spread through her senses, wreaked havoc with her emotions then overtook her soul in a blinding burst of pure rapture.

She was only distantly aware of Turk crying her name as he stiffened above her. The pulse of his release filling her, heating her further and adding to her orgasm.

Had she sensed what was coming she would have surely tried to run in fear as it rose inside her.

Such destruction no matter its need, no matter the resulting renewal could never be eased into. The senses were far too wary of change, the soul far too insulated against such havoc. But some storms, even the soul has no protection from. A man's hunger for warmth, need for love. A woman's beckoning, wrapped in innocence, flames trapped within and a love more enduring than even the sharpest blade.

Apart, they were lost, tortured by need, tossed about by capricious winds.

Together, forged in the flames of not just pleasure, but the need for each other, the need for emotions suppressed, buried, hidden, until this moment. They came together, neither admitting to each other, but both knowing, they found much more than pleasure.

CHAPTER 10

〜

Y ou survived," Erin whispered, a grin tugging at her lips when she found the energy to tease him once again.

Lying behind her, his large, broad body sheltering her, his arms wrapped around her as his warmth surrounded her, Erin wondered at his silence.

"Did I?" There was an edge of seriousness to his tone that had the smile melting from her lips as she stared into the dimly lit bedroom, the room-darkening shades and curtains all but eradicating the light from the room.

"You're breathing," she stated.

He sighed heavily, one hand stroking over her hip to her thigh as he remained silent behind her.

She couldn't handle the silence. The least he could do was curse. Yell at her. Something.

"You'll make me crazy," he finally spoke, the dark rasp of his voice sending a tingle of response racing through her senses.

"How will I do that?" Rolling to her back to stare up at him she was faced with a man without amusement. He was serious. Watching her with the air of a man that couldn't quite figure out the puzzle presented to him.

Lifting his hand, the backs of his fingers smoothed down her cheek. "Just by being you," he said softly, his dark gaze somber.

Shrugging, she stared up at him with a little smile. "You think you know so much about me, don't you, Turk?"

"J.D.'s stepdaughter," he stated cryptically. "I've heard quite a lot about you. What I didn't know was your name."

"Oh, yeah? I wasn't aware there were that many agents who knew me." She sat up slowly, holding the sheet to her breasts as she watched him carefully.

"Everyone that's part of the agency has heard of you, Erin." He stared up at her, his expression closed now. "Wild. Determined to piss J.D. off whatever it takes. Even if it means risking your own life."

She frowned down at him. Was that what everyone thought? That her clashes with J.D., her disagreements with him were just carefully orchestrated stunts to piss him off?

"Is that what J.D. thinks?" she asked him, watching his eyes carefully, though she knew he would give very little away.

"J.D. hadn't mentioned it either way," he revealed. "Your determination to do the exact opposite of what he wants is renown though."

Erin's lips quirked mockingly as she turned from him.

"I don't try to piss J.D. off," she told him, rising from the bed as she released the sheet before moving to the leather duffel bag she'd left open in an easy chair at the corner of the room.

Pulling a black silk robe free from the bag she pushed her arms into it slowly before dragging it around her and belting it snugly.

"It's a talent then?" he suggested.

"It's a natural progression." She swallowed tightly as she turned to him. "I had a single choice at a job, working beneath his eagle eye and his protection. Anyone I've dated is so well vetted by him that by the second date I know how many cavities he has and how many his ex-lovers have. He runs over every choice I make, ensures I have no choice but to accept his dictates, and expects me to just follow along with whatever order he gives, just as anyone else would. Do you have any idea how hard it was to just have a life, Turk? To have a normal relationship?"

He just watched her as though she were one of those puzzle pieces that didn't exactly fit. She could feel him slowly putting information together. What he'd heard. What he thought himself. What he suspected. Everything he'd seen and heard as he began to dissect her like some psychological lab rat.

He reminded her far too much of her stepfather actually.

"You're just like him." She sighed then. "God." Raking her fingers through her hair she had to laugh at herself. "I'm obviously insane. Only I could fixate on a man so much like J.D. he could actually be his son."

Turk didn't flinch. He was rather proud of himself for that after the insult.

"We all know how J.D. likes to maneuver everyone." He finally shrugged as he rose from the bed. "What worries me is the fact that you seem intent on doing the exact opposite of whatever he wants you to do. I'm part of the organization he oversees, and you know what that means. Risking myself for someone simply determined to piss off the director isn't my preferred hobby."

Wow, he really had a great opinion of her, didn't he? Did he believe she'd choose him as a lover simply to piss off J.D.? Hell, she'd known when she realized how much she wanted him just how pleased her stepfather and her stepbrother would be.

"I'm more intent on doing whatever it takes to have a life of my own, a relationship he doesn't dictate," she argued, wondering why she was trying. Like J.D., he'd make up his mind and that would be it. "That's all I ever asked for, Turk."

"And what do you call your position within the CIN?" he asked, standing by the bed as he watched her, obviously more than comfortable with his nakedness.

"As an observer?" Her laughter was mocking. "A carefully designed maneuver by J.D. to ensure he can keep tabs on me while pretending to give me a life. Do you think that's all I deserve, Turk? That it's all I want in . . ."

"Fuck!" The sudden hiss of fury had cut her off in midsentence as Turk turned quickly to a monitor sitting on the dresser across from the bed.

A flip of the switch and the camera views were up. What she saw on them had her rushing to dress.

Jeans and a T-shirt, socks and boots. She dressed as quickly as possible. From an inner pocket of her suitcase she pulled her weapon free and shoved it in the small of her back as the four figures at the apartment door worked at the security.

"No time," he snarled as he armed himself as well. "We can't risk gunfire in the hall. There are kids in the other apartments."

She was pulling extra clips from her suitcase and shoving them in her jean pockets as he quickly slid the bedroom window open.

"Clear," he stated, quickly moving through the gap and turning for her.

Erin didn't wait for an invitation. Sliding through the opening she drew in a deep breath as they teetered precariously on the narrow ledge three stories up.

"What the hell is going on?" she whispered. "No one should have known where I was."

"Process of elimination," he muttered. "I'm the only security personnel not showing up at the bar. We anticipated this, just not this quickly." Reaching behind her he slid the window closed, latching it, surprisingly, from the outside.

"Oh, someone managed to surprise you?" The heavy mockery in her voice surprised even her as they began making their way along the brick ledge.

Dammit, she hadn't even been given a chance to revel in the incredible pleasure she'd found in his arms. First she'd had to deal with him and his sudden too-serious turn where making love to her was concerned. Now she had to deal with this. It was a little much.

"They'll be watching your vehicle," she guessed as they began to edge their way around the corner of the building.

"That's why Coop will have someone waiting for us," he informed her. "I received the message as the alarm went off. They were cutting through my security too fast though."

"Do you think they'll figure out the window opens? Does mine open like that?" she asked as she followed him, inch by inch, praying her feet didn't slip.

"I'll know in time if they do," he informed her. "My guess, they'll come in, see no trace of you, and assume I have you hidden somewhere else."

"How do we get out of here then?" she asked, her heart in her throat as she caught a glimpse of the parking lot, too far below.

Okay, so a fall probably wouldn't kill her, but a broken bone was still a broken bone. No doubt they'd both break something.

"Just a little farther ahead," he muttered. "The big tree that grows along the side of the apartment building is a perfect way down. I have a truck parked right beneath it."

"Good thing John D. taught me how to climb out of trees." She sighed.

Just a little farther.

She could make it just a little farther. A few more feet, she kept telling herself. She could see the tree, growing nearly to the fourth floor. It was sturdy, its limbs full and shielding.

They were going to make it.

Just a few more feet.

"Here we go," Turk muttered, reaching out and gripping a heavy limb just in front of him. "I'll go down first. The truck is right there." He nodded toward the ground below.

"Got it." She nodded quickly. "Go on. I know how to shimmy down a tree, I promise."

The look in his eyes was approving as he stepped over to the limb. "One minute, then follow. We'll be out of here quick."

"One minute," she promised.

Reaching out for the heavy limb she stepped out to it and began the countdown.

One minute.

Taking a deep breath she began moving down the tree, listening careful for Turk, for the sound of the truck door opening, the vehicle starting.

What the hell was he waiting for?

Looking down, all she saw was shadows. Nothing moved, not even Turk. The heavy foliage kept her from seeing much as she moved slowly down the tree.

Finally, she dropped to the ground on the darker side of the tree trunk, crouched, listening carefully.

She wasn't moving.

Turk should have been there. He should have been waiting for her.

The passenger side of the truck was just on the other side of the tree, the trunk was huge. It spread out on each side of her, the foliage drooping, shielding her. The heavy layer of grass beneath her feet had shielded her drop.

Something was wrong. She could feel it.

It was in the air, like an ominous presence, watching, waiting for her.

Turk's alarm system should have alerted Gabby in the other apartment. It should have alerted Jake and Cooper at the bar. Surely there was backup somewhere?

Reaching behind her back she slid her weapon free silently, thankful that she'd chambered that first round before leaving the apartment. That small, mechanical snick would have given her away the second she pulled it back.

Swallowing tightly she lowered herself to her stomach, inching forward slowly until she could see just beneath the front of the pickup Turk had parked under the tree's spreading branches.

"What the fuck do you want?"

She froze at the sound of Turk's voice.

"Hell, Turk, I thought we were friends," another voice answered, harsh, grating, and familiar. Though Erin couldn't immediately place it, she knew the voice.

"Friends don't ambush me in the dark, Gyron," Turk snapped back at him.

"Well, it's not often I watch you drop out of a tree like a cat burglar either." Gyron gave a hard imitation of a laugh. "I have to say, I was rather surprised."

"Yeah, well, it's not every day I have four bozos trying to break into my apartment either." Turk grunted. "Now, why don't you get out of here while I find me a nice little place to hide so I can figure out who they are and what they want?"

"I know what they want."

Erin felt the breath still in her chest. As she moved to launch herself to her feet she heard the sudden rustle of bodies struggling, a male grunt, and the thump of a fist.

She was moving quickly around the front of the truck, weapon held ready as she risked a fast look around the side of the vehicle to see Gyron dropping to the ground.

"Stay there," Turk suddenly ordered with a hiss. "They'll be out here any minute."

Throwing Gyron over his shoulder he was pushing her ahead of him a second later until they were once again behind the tree. There, he dropped his burden carelessly before turning to her.

"Okay?" Narrow-eyed, intent, his gaze went over her quickly.

"Ready to get out of here," she assured him, her voice barely above a whisper.

"The truck's fouled. Someone must have known it was mine." Catching her hand he was pulling her quickly around the side of the apartment building. "Come on, let's see if Jake still keeps a spare key beneath that damned sports car of his."

Still holding on to her hand he pulled her quickly across the other side of the parking lot. Moving between two pickups to keep the vehicles between them and the apartment building, he led the way along the grassy border to Jake's glistening black Corvette.

Pausing at the front of the car he pulled her down next to him, reached beneath the car, and a second later pulled free a small, magnetic box. Sliding open the panel on the front, he froze.

"Turk?" she whispered.

"I anticipated that." Erin froze, alongside Turk, at the hard voice behind them.

Turk rose slowly as Erin followed. He pulled her behind him, forcing her between him and the front of the Corvette as he faced the dark silhouette that moved from the bushes alongside the grass border.

Three other shadows moved into place behind the first, eyes gleaming in the darkness as their features slowly became recognizable.

They were regulars at the bar.

Tyler Stanley, the talent scout that often drank with Gyron and his three friends. All four of which were linked to a suspected criminal figure that operated out of Corpus Christi. Though Tyler hadn't been linked to the organization.

Until now.

"Bad move, Stanley." Turk sighed as though they were actually on the winning side here. "Did you think we weren't waiting for this?"

Waiting for them and being without backup were two different things. Right now, Erin hoped desperately, Turk had a little more up his sleeve than a bluff.

Tyler Stanley chuckled at that. "Your friends are all at the bar," he informed Turk. "Your security was incredibly easy to break. All emergency contact was blocked before it could go out. You're all alone, Rogan. Just you and Ms. Masters, and the four of us. You're a little outnumbered, don't you think?"

"What do you want, Stanley?" Turk growled as Erin slowly tucked her weapon into the band of his jeans at the small of his back.

She wasn't good enough to take down all four of those assholes before one of them shot, but maybe Turk was.

"All we want is the girl," Tyler assured him. "You're just in the way. You should have stayed out of the way, Turk. Killing you wasn't how I wanted this to go."

Turk grunted at that. "What makes her so damned important?"

"The same thing that made John Delanore and his son, John Delanore, Jr., race out here when we nearly had her last week. She's important to him."

"She's his stepdaughter." The tension building in Turk's large body had Erin nearly holding her breath. "Of course he came running. That doesn't tell me what it has to do with you or your friends."

"And he has something we want. We need her. We don't need witnesses. Tonight, you get to die. She'll die later." Tyler spoke as though killing someone were an everyday occurrence.

"What does your stepdaddy have that these assholes want, Erin?" Turk asked her then, the irritation in his tone not in the least feigned.

"Hell if I know," she whispered.

"If I'm going to die for it, I'd at least like a fucking answer," he snapped.

He was getting ready to move.

Erin could feel the energy gathering in his body.

Tyler watched Turk carefully, though the three men with him kept their gazes more on her.

"What do you think you can threaten my stepfather out of, Tyler?" Erin stepped around Turk just enough to watch the other man more closely. "He's an asshole. And trust me, he won't pay a ransom."

"He'll pay." Tyler sounded far too confident. "But he'll give me far more than money for your life, honey. He'll give me the identity of the Giovanni heir that he's hiding. And I know he's hiding him, because I traced him as far as your stepfather's home nine years ago before he disappeared."

The who?

"What the fuck is he talking about?" Turk hissed, reaching behind his hip as though to catch her arm.

Instead, his fingers curled around the butt of the weapon she'd tucked into the band of his jeans.

"The hell if I know." Erin slid back marginally, giving the appearance that Turk was indeed holding on to her.

"You don't have to know who he is," Tyler snapped, anger filling his tone now. "All you have to do is come along quietly. Do so, and I won't make your boyfriend suffer before I kill his ass."

If she was going to die either way, then she'd just die here, with Turk, rather than later. Rather than lying down and grieving for the man who had stolen her heart so effectively that she hadn't even realized how much of it he owned, she'd just die with him.

"Don't let them take me," she whispered under her breath.

Turk grunted at the almost silent plea.

"Walk away, Tyler, and this won't have to get messy." Erin knew him. He used that tone of voice only seconds before dealing with the irrational drunks at the bar.

"But I do so love leaving a mess." The cold smile that curled at the other man's lips was the first indication that he'd run out of patience.

She felt Turk shift closer to her, his arm bunching, muscles tightening to pull the weapon free when she was suddenly blinded by bright, white light.

A manacle at her waist lifted her clear off the ground as she felt herself thrown to the side. The blast of gunfire exploded around her as a heavy weight followed her to the grass, crushing her beneath it.

The scream of tires on blacktop filled the night, screeching through her senses as male screams filled the violent symphony for endless seconds.

Then, silence filled the air.

It was so deathly still now that she wondered if time had stopped.

A curse whispered at her ear then—Turk's voice—deep with irritation as his hand tightened at her hip before his weight suddenly rolled from her.

Rolling to her back Erin quickly scanned what she could see of the parking lot only to be blinded once again by the bright lights of a helicopter overhead.

The steady drone of the helicopter's motors were almost a distant sound before Turk blocked the light, reaching down for her.

"It's over," he promised her, pulling her to her feet as she placed her hand in his. "They're dead."

"What the hell happened?" She breathed out, still shocked by the suddenness of it. "God, Turk. What happened?"

She could see the bodies then. Tyler's and his two friends', sprawled out on the blacktop, their bodies twisted or lying at odd angles. There was no way they were still alive.

"The hell if I know." He breathed out roughly, pulling her to his side and surveying the scene as well. "I'll be damned if I know, Erin. But I have no doubt J.D. will figure it out. No doubt at all."

At that moment the helicopter landed in the deserted restaurant parking lot beside them as vehicles began pouring into the area. Residents of the apartment building were beginning to creep from the doors and if the black-clad figures erupting from the SUVs that braked to a quick stop were any indication, those residents would never see, nor ever know, exactly what happened.

"Turk. Erin. Let's go." One of those black-clad agents neared them, lifting the dark mask he wore to reveal his identity.

Iron's eyes were icy cold, his expression hard as he stepped to them. Dressed in dark jeans and jacket, it was obvious he hadn't had time to change into the dark military gear normally worn in such situations.

"Come on, we have to get you out of here," Turk muttered, pulling her with him to the SUV.

Of course they did. She was J.D.'s stepdaughter, and someone knew far too much if what Tyler said was true. So much, that it could change her life forever.

CHAPTER 11

⌒

Three days later

Once again Turk stood at the windows of Cooper's office staring out into the night.

He was tired.

He'd realized in the past few days, he'd been tired for a very long time until Erin had arrived at the bar. When his eyes had met hers, he'd begun looking forward to each day again rather than just existing within each night.

He'd looked forward to getting up each evening, had looked forward to leaving each morning. Because Erin had been there.

She wasn't there any longer.

Leaning his shoulder against the wall, his gaze narrowed into the darkness outside, he could feel that steel hard core of determined fury he'd once possessed, absent. The man who had joined the Covert Information Network didn't exist anymore. Not just in name, but in spirit as well.

The fury had been gone for a while, he realized. The dark, bitter anger that the evil in the world had destroyed the last innocence he'd believed in, had eased to regret, to that feeling of aching loss that came with time.

He could now remember his youth with a bittersweetness that he hadn't been able to remember it with before. The memories didn't shred his guts with helpless guilt any longer. Instead, he realized, the memories of the laughter, the good times, had returned.

He hadn't realized those memories were back until he'd lain down the night after the attack at the apartment and realized how he ached for Erin.

Her smile, filled with such innocence.

The warmth that had begun to fill her gaze, the softness of her expression that he knew, knew to the bottom of his soul, had been her love for him.

And he hurt now. His chest ached, his heart protesting the loss with such virulence that he knew, somehow, she'd made him love as well.

He had to find her.

God knew J.D. would try to hide her. That was what Turk would do under the same circumstances. Hide her someplace that no one would ever find her again. But he couldn't imagine never holding her again. Never feeling her warmth. Never seeing her smile.

Wiping a hand over his face as he breathed out wearily, he knew he'd never really rest again until he was with her.

The office door opened, causing him to turn slowly and watch as Cooper, J.D., and John D. entered the dimly lit office.

Flipping the desk lights on to fill the room with soft light, Cooper glanced at him silently, his gaze just as assessing, as considering, as it had been for the past three days that he'd helped debrief Turk.

"Turk." J.D. moved to him, his hand reaching out to shake Turk's. "Thank you for taking care of Erin. We had no idea this situation had developed as it had."

As he released the handshake, J.D. gave him a small, sharp little nod. "You're an asset to the network. I'm damned thankful you were here."

"Where's she at?" The question refused to be held back.

J.D.'s gaze sharpened for a moment.

"She's in protective custody at the moment, Turk." John D. answered as he took a seat at the far corner of the room, his expression hard as Turk's gaze lifted to his. "I'm sure you of all people realize our determination to ensure her safety."

He of all people.

Did they believe that reminding him of Cara, the sister he'd lost with such sudden violence, would cause him to back off? They were wrong if that was the case.

"The assailant you incapacitated and threw in the back of your pickup was a fount of information," J.D. spoke before Turk could protest John D.'s announcement. "The agent they were searching for was a contact for the U.S. and Italian authorities nine years before. He helped destroy a criminal organization that had held Italy in its grip for generations. His work alone identified assassins, drug lords, and individuals involved in local as well as national government that ensured the continued hold that organization retained. His identity has remained hidden, just as his location has. Unfortunately, he was tracked much further than we'd believed. The network itself is secure, but my and John D.'s association with him was revealed."

"Where's Erin?"

He really didn't give a fuck about the agent and where he was tracked. If he was part of the CIN, then no doubt once leaving J.D.'s residence he disappeared forever to those who had known him before. Turk really couldn't care less about the details at the moment.

He wanted Erin.

J.D. sighed deeply. "Turk, the risk to her . . ."

"Where is Erin?" Iron hard, the relentless need to see her, to claim her, hardened inside him until it ran soul deep.

J.D. grimaced as he turned back to meet his son's gaze.

"Erin will be relocated for a while . . ." John D. began.

"Then you'll relocate me with her." He wasn't giving up.

Cooper sat back in his chair, watching everything thoughtfully, but Turk knew the other man. His friendship with the agents that worked with him was a bond forged in the hottest fires. If push came to shove, he'd back Turk. It wasn't a position Turk wanted to put the other man in, but he would if he had to.

"The risk to her is too great. . . ." J.D. tried again.

"J.D., don't turn this into a battle," Turk warned him, his fingers clenching at his sides, fisting to hold back the rage gathering inside him. "You may keep her away from me, but I promise you, I'll cause you more trouble searching for her than it's going to be worth to you and your family."

The other man crossed his arms over his chest and glared back at him.

"You're an agent for the network, Turk. A network I run. You don't give me orders here. It's the other way around."

"Don't make me go rogue on you." There was no other option. Existing without her wasn't going to happen.

"J.D.," Cooper began as the door to the office was pushed open.

Turk didn't hear a word his friend said after that. He didn't give a damn.

Erin stepped into the office, closing the door softly. Jeans hugged her slender hips and legs, a soft cream-colored blouse whispered over her breasts before tucking into the band of her jeans. Canvas sneakers covered her feet.

She looked like a damned teenager.

The effect she had on him was anything but immature though. His entire body hardened, tensed. Every cell, every particle of being came to full, vibrant life.

Pushing past J.D., Turk moved to her slowly.

Heavy, red-gold waves fell about her shoulders and surrounded the vulnerable features of her face while mysterious sea-green eyes watched him with a hint of vulnerability, and more emotion than he'd ever seen in another woman's eyes.

He stopped in front of her, aching to touch her, his palms itching with the need, his entire body going hot with the urge to feel her against him.

"I missed you," he whispered, aching, trying to find the words, trying to find a way to tell her things that he was still fighting to understand.

She licked her lips, her gaze holding his, the promises and feminine needs reaching out to him, sinking inside him.

"I missed you," she answered, her voice soft, vibrating with so much more to say. Words she would hold locked inside her, he realized, until he gave her what she needed.

Before he realized the intent, before he was aware he was moving, he had her in his arms. Cradling her head in one hand he tipped it back, his lips touching hers. Just touching as he stared down at her, as he held her close to his body and relished the feel of her against him.

"I love you, Erin Masters," he whispered against her lips, watching her eyes dilate, the flush that suddenly mounted her pretty face. "Don't walk away from me. Give us a chance. . . ."

"I love you."

Her soft voice, the feel of her hands gripping his waist, her body bending to his, the essence of who she was, of everything they could be, sank inside him before taking root with a suddenness that stole his breath.

She loved him.

God, she loved him.

In that second Turk found what he'd been searching the night for in the long, lost years he'd watched the darkness. He'd been searching for himself. For that part of him that would complete the lonely parts of his soul.

And he'd found it the night he'd met her eyes. He'd claimed it the night he claimed her kiss.

Erin's kiss.

She completed him.

Nothing mattered.

No one mattered.

Erin felt her world suddenly come to a full stop, leveling, then filling with a bold, heated stroke of color as Turk whispered "I love you."

In the dark-chocolate gaze she suddenly saw inside him, felt herself inside him, felt him wrapping himself around her, his heat and strength holding her in one place. Right there in his arms.

"I love you." She loved him as she'd never loved anyone in her life.

J.D. didn't matter. John D.'s support had always been assured. But right here, in this moment, in this man's arms, she found the search she'd been on for so very long come to an end.

She'd been searching for herself, never realizing, never knowing, that the completion of who and what she was would end in the knowledge that she truly wasn't alone. She never had been.

Turk had been right there, waiting for her, watching the night until their eyes met across a crowded bar and fate entwined them as it had always meant to do.

They found each other in that first kiss.

And now, they would complete each other in the first of what she knew would be a lifetime of kisses.

Erin had found her way home. Years of restlessness, of searching, of never understanding why she couldn't bear the thought of putting down roots until she came here, to the place where her heart was awaiting her.

Where Turk was waiting for her.

EPILOGUE

There were others searching for the betrayer.

That changed the rules of the game.

That couldn't be allowed.

The betrayer would always be protected from outside forces, it was a vow made long ago, even before the betrayal was revealed. Even before the betrayer had been born.

The enemies from without had to be destroyed.

Could that be the key to revealing the identity of the one sought for the destruction of generations of trust? Could it be that easy to draw the betrayer from hiding?

The watcher watched, waited, and planned.

The betrayer was here, that was now a certainty.

Others sought him, other's sought vengeance that they couldn't be allowed to have. Vengeance belonged to the watcher, and no one else would be allowed to interfere.

No matter the cost. . . .

misTAKEN

by

Laurelin McGee

ACKNOWLEDGMENTS
Laurelin Paige

⌒

As it is with any book, this one was not born alone. There are too many people to name all the ones I'd like to acknowledge, but there are a few thank-yous that are essential.

First and foremost, to Kayti McGee, my work-wife—I'll say it again and again: don't cowrite, but if you do, cowrite with Kayti. You are the wine to my empty glass. The Miss to my Match. You are brilliant and shiny in all the places that I am not. I look forward to all the places this journey takes us together.

To our editor, Eileen Rothschild—I was so nervous to talk to you that first time on the phone, and then you were absolutely everything I ever wanted in an editor. Thank you for sharing our quirky enthusiasm for this series. It wouldn't have been the same experience with anybody else.

To the team at St. Martin's Press—What a great group to work with! Thank you for inviting us into and embracing us in your tight-knit family.

To Bob Diforio for making this deal happen and Rebecca Friedman for deals yet to be made. It's the best feeling to have wonderful people in your corner.

To Shanyn for keeping me together and KP for putting us together. It's an honor to be called an InkSlinging Author.

To Lisa—You gave me your idea. Ideas are gold. With this, you've given me the biggest gift anyone's ever given me. Thank you.

To Bethany—You ferry me through all the dark places. A particularly hard task when we both love the dimly lit moors so much. There's a well of gratitude in my heart for you that never runs dry.

To Gennifer—You named our book! It's perfect. Thank you for that and more.

The women who wrangle me—Wrahm, Naturals, FYW, and others (you know who you are): I make it through my days because of you. I also get distracted a lot because of you, but that's another story.

To my husband, Tom—Though I tease you for being flighty, you are my rock. Thank you for being so solid.

To my children—I'm so proud of all you are. I hope you see me as an example for making your own dreams come true. I love you, my babies.

To Mom—Finally, here's a book I'll let you read. Thanks for your never-ending support. Love you.

To my Maker—Praise is always on my heart, even when it's absent on my tongue.

ACKNOWLEDGMENTS
Kayti McGee

⌒

First and foremost—Laurelin Paige. You took me on this crazy journey, for no other reason than that you are God's angel on earth. No one can possibly convince me you aren't the best person I have ever had the honor to meet, much less call my friend. I'm inspired by you every day, to write better, be more, be better. I love you so much. You are grace and generosity and talent personified.

Eileen Rothschild took a chance on us that I could never have imagined, and then turned out to be the most badass editor ever. Bob DiForio sold her that chance, and Natalie Lakosil was so charmed by my Dream Dr Who Team (I assume) that she looked past my horribly awkward weirdness to become my agent. I am so lucky to have the best people in the business on my team.

My mom taught me that reading is more important than anything, and without that I would never have become a writer. Dad, Kerry, Laura, and Dann backed that up. McGrigsby's!

My friends: Sara, my bestie, my first reader and still the prettiest. M Pierce, you redefined what friendship is for me. I'm so proud to be pub-siblings with such an incredible author and friend. Thank you for everything. The WrAHM girls, the Order, the Dirty Laundresses, Melanie Harlow, Gennifer Albin, Tamara Mataya, my guy, Tyler, my lunch buddy Jen, my late-night buddy Leah. I couldn't live without our constant contact. I have to especially mention Bethany Hagen's perfect edits, and Lisa Otto's perfect idea. You truly made this all happen, and for that, no thanks can be enough.

CHAPTER 1

Jaylene didn't even wait for her date to get out and open her door before she stepped out of the car. He seemed to be polished enough to attempt to do so, but she wasn't that type of girl, which was probably a lot of the reason the night had gone so terribly. Even if it wasn't the reason, she wanted to be out and gone from his arrogant presence ASAFP.

Yeah, the date had definitely not been one of the best, even based on *her* track record. And she had a bone to pick about that very subject. A blind date, what had she been thinking? But having her neighbor as a matchmaker was just too strange to pass up. Seriously, who had a matchmaker for a neighbor? She hadn't even realized they still existed.

Perhaps that should have been a warning sign. The whole thing was actually . . . archaic, now that she thought about it. Especially when she'd been set up with *that* guy. Never mind what she'd been thinking. What had her matchmaker neighbor been thinking?

Instead of climbing the stairs to her own brownstone apartment, she headed straight to the one next door, intent on picking that bone right then. Jaylene Kim had never been the type to procrastinate. She eyed the group of guys drinking beers on the stoop as she approached. When she'd left to meet Blake Donovan for her disastrous dinner she'd seen the men carrying a sofa into the building. Which one—or ones—of them were moving in?

The scruffy one with the shaggy hair caught her gaze. *Oh, God, please let it be him.* He was too beautiful to not have a girlfriend—or boyfriend, they were in the hippie part of town—but who the hell cared? She didn't expect to cuddle up with him. Just having him as next-door scenery would be scrumptious.

Scrump. Tious.

But even the face of a potential hot new neighbor was not enough to distract from her mission. "Excuse me," she said, stepping between the men to get to the door of the building. A couple of them nodded a hello as she passed. The cute one, however, he remained straight-faced, uninterested. Too bad.

Though, when she threw a glance back at him over her shoulder, she found him staring after her, a shy smile curling on his lips. Damn, if that didn't send shivers down her spine. There was nothing like the sight of a beautiful man. See how her nipples perked up in this guy's presence? Take that, Blake Donovan, aka blind date from hell.

She grinned smugly to herself as she walked through the door and started up the stairs toward the Dawson unit. When she caught sight of the sisters outside their door, a basket of laundry in each one's arms, her smile vanished and her eyes blazed.

Pausing in her tracks, she pointed an accusing finger at the elder. "You!"

Lacy, the younger sister, looked up from her task of unlocking the door one-handedly. "What did I do?"

"Not you," Jaylene said. She gestured to Andy who was attempting to hide behind her mane of auburn curls. "Her."

Lacy turned to face her sister. "What did you do to piss off Jaylene?"

Andy shrugged. As if she were innocent. As if she didn't know what she'd done.

"Hey, you two know each other?" Andy asked before Jaylene could commence her attack.

Lacy scowled at the question. "We're neighbors, doof."

"But she's not in our building." Andy was clearly trying to deflect the spotlight from herself. "And you don't know any of the other neighbors by name except Mrs. Brandy and that's only because she's over here once a week to scream about the volume of your stereo."

"Jay's different." Lacy winked at her. "She's cool. She used to be running buddies with Lance. They did the marathon a couple of times."

At the mention of Lacy's late fiancé, Jaylene found her temper cooling a degree or two. But only out of respect for the dead, not because she actually felt any less pissed at Andrea Dawson. Truthfully, she hadn't known what to say to Lacy after her loss and had spent most of the last year avoiding her. Guilt kept her from mentioning Lacy when she'd met Andy. It was no wonder that Andy didn't realize the neighbors had once had a connection.

Lacy cocked her head, her eyes focused on Jaylene. "Wanna come in? We're planning a laundry-folding party, which will not be the finest of the parties I've thrown, I admit, but we do have wine."

Without hesitation, Jaylene resumed her walk up the steps. "Don't mind if I do. I've never needed a drink so badly in my life." As Lacy turned back to the doorknob, Jaylene narrowed her eyes at Andy. "Besides, your sister and I have a beef to settle. And I'm *not* folding her laundry."

She didn't think she imagined the scared squeak that escaped Andy's lips. *Good. She should be afraid. Very afraid.*

By the time Jaylene had made it up the rest of the stairs, Lacy had managed to get the door open, and both sisters were already inside the apartment.

"I'll open a bottle," Andy said, setting her basket of clothing down next to the couch. "What kind would you like?"

Though Andy was now pretending everything was copasetic between them, Jaylene recognized the offer as an attempt to escape her company. That was fine. It would only be momentary. Jay could wait to start her persecution.

"What do you have?" she asked in a pleasant tone. Two could play the nothing's-up game.

"A reddish kind and a less reddish kind."

With a sigh, Lacy interjected. "Andy's basically clueless when it comes to wine. We have a Merlot or a Zin."

"Definitely Merlot then." The deep red would be a fitting color to accompany the bloody murder about to take place. Luckily there were freshly washed towels to mop up with.

"Got it," Andy said, scurrying to the kitchen. "And good choice! It has a nice finish." Clear bullshit. All wines had a nice finish, if you said so.

"Grab some chips or something, too," Lacy called after her as she kicked off her flip-flops. She nodded to Jaylene and gestured toward the sofa. "Have a seat. I'm dying to hear what my sister possibly could have done to get you over to my apartment after nine P.M. on a school night."

Jaylene's early teaching schedule and even earlier training program put her in bed before ten on most evenings. Deciding she'd skip her morning run, she'd made an exception for tonight's date. She would have been insane not to after she'd seen the picture of Blake Donovan. He was beyond attractive, and Andy's description of the rich, self-made bachelor had him sounding like quite a catch.

Now that she'd met Blake in person, she remembered that things that seemed too good to be true usually were. Because even though the person she'd met was rich, savvy, and attractive, he was not a catch. He was a nightmare.

As Andy would well have known. "Just wait until you hear." Jay leaned back into the mismatched throw pillows Lacy had stitched out of thrift-shop dresses. Despite her irritation, Jay quickly felt comfy in Lacy's bohemian-styled apartment. She was perfectly happy with her own IKEA and fair-trade stuff, but it was fun to let her eyes roam over all the goofy little knickknacks and art pieces her neighbor matched together.

"You've got my attention," Lacy said, matching a pair of fuzzy socks from her laundry basket then pinning her eyes on Jay. "Please, tell all."

Andy reentered the living room then with a bottle, a few mason jars, and a box of crackers balanced in the crook of her arm. Jaylene had eaten a meal on that jerk's dime, but she was going to polish off the box of crackers, too, just on principle. Wine poured, Andy took a tentative seat on an armchair across from the couch.

It would almost be worth it to let the woman suffer. But Jaylene couldn't hold in her wrath any longer. She leveled her glare at Andy. "Blake. Donovan." She let the two words settle, enjoying Andy's squirm. The two didn't know each other well. They'd only met because of a piece of mail delivered to the wrong address, but Jay figured that since she was Lacy's sister, she had to be cool.

After her date with Blake Donovan, she wasn't so sure.

"Well, that name says everything," Lacy said, scowling at her sister. "What were you thinking, Andy?" Her sister's eyes darted away.

Jay continued the interrogation. "Did you actually imagine we'd hit it off, or was this your idea of a sick joke? Have I inadvertently offended you in some way?"

At least Andy had the grace to look ashamed. "No, I thought maybe you two would have a nice time."

Lacy chortled. "You obviously don't know Jay very well."

Andy sat straighter on her perch. "Admittedly, I don't know much about Jaylene. But she passed the initial screening points. They're both into exercise." She turned to Jay. "You seem to be driven. So is he. You thought his picture was attractive." Her eyes fell to her hands where she fiddled with the hem of her T-shirt. "He likes Asians. . . ."

The picture snapped into focus. "Are you suggesting that you set me up on a date with a guy who likes Asians simply because I'm the only Korean you know? That is so racist. And actually explains a lot."

"I'm not racist!" Andy's head snapped up. "I just thought this would be an easy match. He should have been quite taken with you. I don't like this job, and the quicker I can leave with a bonus, the better."

Jaylene couldn't believe what she was hearing. Could this day possibly get any weirder? "You're planning to stay at this until you marry the guy off? You can't possibly think you'll find someone for him. You must be kidding me." That called for a refill.

"I wish I was kidding." Andy grabbed for a notebook and pen off of the coffee table and slid into the corner of the sofa. "So if it went that badly, I'm afraid I'm going to need to know every last detail. Top me up, too, will you?"

Andy did look sort of pained. That was good. Because, job or not, Jay was going to describe her awful evening so Andy knew just how much she owed her. This ought to be good for a couple of more wine nights, and maybe even some cat-sitting while she was at her ex-roommate's wedding next month.

Pleased with the thought, Jaylene settled back into the cushions and began. "I got to the restaurant early. Because there was still a good half hour before our reservation, I thought I'd sit at the bar and grade some papers over a drink while I waited. It was a hot day, as you know, so I ordered a Sam Adams."

"Always a good choice." Lacy grinned. "Sorry, go on."

"I was halfway through yet another tedious and mundane essay about how *Catcher in the Rye* changed this student's life when this gorgeous man sits down next to me. I recognized him from the pictures right away. I hold out my hand for a shake—he doesn't take it."

"I'm sure he didn't notice," Andy offered.

"Oh, he noticed, all right. He stared at my hand and said 'Jamie?' in this curt tone that said he didn't approve of my name."

Andy waved her hand dismissively. "He seems to have a thing about names fitting the way a person looks or acts. He calls me Drea. Best just to ignore it."

"Well, it isn't my name, now is it? I told him he could call me Jay." Because to hell with a guy deciding what a woman should be called. Maybe she needed to invite Andy to her monthly Femme Power group meeting. Anyway. "His gaze went from my hand—still just hanging there, mind you—to the beer. And I think that must have been the moment he decided I was gay."

Her story was interrupted by a guffaw from Lacy. "You? With the trail of broken-hearted men you've left in your wake? That's rich. Andy's boss is an idiot. I suppose he thinks only lesbians drink beer?"

"Bingo." Jay touched her nose. "He actually said something similar to that later on, but we're still at the bar right now, me holding my hand out like an idiot, thinking he *has* to take it at some point because who does that? Well, *he* does that. He actually turned around and started walking to the table without ever acknowledging my unshook shake."

"Unshook Shake sounds like a song title." Lacy grabbed her acoustic guitar and started strumming softly. "I'll credit you, though."

"I wait a second before following him, because I have to grab the papers I was working on and stick them back in my briefcase. I get over to the table and he's sitting in the shady spot. I try to scoot my chair so the sun isn't shining directly in my eyes, but he says, get this, '*I prefer you sit across from me.*'" She took another swig of wine and shook her head. She still couldn't believe she'd actually followed his instructions instead of insisting on another table, or better yet, leaving. But she'd been taken completely off-guard, and just sort of went with it.

Also, the man was attractive. Beautiful men were definitely her weakness. Such a contradiction to the foundation of her being.

She shook her head—if her thoughts spiraled into all the stupid things she'd done for beautiful men and the bitterness she had at herself regarding that fault of hers, she'd never get her story finished. "So the server drops off a glass of wine and an iced tea. That's when I realize he'd ordered drinks for the both of us while I was putting papers away. And that he had taken the liberty of ordering me *tea* while he's drinking something fancy enough to require the waiter to watch him sniff, swirl, and sip."

Andy scribbled something on her notepad. "I'm sure he was probably trying to impress you. Blake's social skills aren't super developed."

"It wasn't impressive. It was a total dick move. If he was trying to impress me, he'd have ordered me a glass, too, so I could admire his taste." She took a swallow of her wine, hoping to calm her growing irritation. It didn't help. "Why are you defending him? You weren't there. And 'not super developed' is a kind way to describe his social challenges."

"I'm not defending him." Andy shifted her eyes as if just realizing that she had indeed been defending her boss. "I just think there are two sides to every story."

Not this story. Jay stared at Andy until the other girl dropped her eyes. She popped a cracker in her mouth, chewed, and swallowed the whole thing.

Lacy prodded her on. "So did you call him on it?"

Jay followed her cracker with a swallow of wine. "What do you think? I mean, I'm at a freaking loss here. Do I tell him that I feel he was being rude, or do I allow him to play the manly card and order me around a little?"

"My guess is, your feminist ass wanted to call him out, but you didn't want to reflect badly on my big, dumb sister. Am I right?"

Jay touched her nose again with the *bingo* sign. "Pretty much nailed it."

Lacy plucked a few victorious strings and laughed. "Did he order your food for you, too?"

"Um, *yes*. He very thoughtfully chose a large garden salad with grilled chicken for me. Oil and vinegar on the side. He himself enjoyed a prime rib and a lobster tail. Medium *well*. Like an asshole. You're gonna spend that much money on a piece of meat and then have them cook all the flavor out?" Jaylene's eyes flashed.

Andy looked up from her scribbling. "Some people just don't like bloody meat, Jay. And look at you. You're teeny tiny. He probably figured you lived on vegetables." She lowered her eyes. "Besides, some women would think that a man taking care of her is sweet."

Archaic was more like it. "Andy, *seriously*. What is this about? Do you have a thing for this guy?"

"No! I told you—I have a decent amount of investment in him getting future dates."

"It seems the lady doth protest too much." Jay smirked.

Lacy grinned. "I know, right?"

Andy's jaw dropped. "Lacy! You know how I feel about the asshat."

Her sister shrugged.

"So you admit he's an asshat." Jay found a certain amount of satisfaction with that, at least.

"Like I said, his social skills need finesse. But there's someone for everyone. Even the asshats. I just have to find someone to take this one." Andy ran a hand through her long auburn curls. "So, could you please just tell me what happened next?"

A part of Jay wanted to argue with Andy, not just because she doubted that there was a match for Blake Donovan, but because she also questioned whether there might really be a match for *her*.

But that was a mess of a conversation that she didn't want to start. Not when she had to work at seven in the morning. "Fine." After another sip of wine, she continued on with the telling of her horrid date. "I was beside myself trying to come up with conversation with the man. We have practically no shared interests. He works out in a gym, by the way. No rough-terrain running. Which is lame, but any-hoo." She watched as Andy noted that. "So I turned to the one and only thing any red-blooded Bostonian can discuss in the summer—I asked him what he thought about the Sox's chances for the Series this year."

"Totes what I would have done!" Lacy contributed from the corner where she did appear to be writing an actual song based on Jay's date.

"He smirked. He *smirked* at me."

"Hmm." Andy didn't seem surprised by this.

Jaylene sat forward in her seat. "And he said, 'I just bet you're a fan.' Naturally, that pissed me off. Maybe even more than him not understanding that to keep this teeny tiny bod, as you call it, I require more than rabbit food for the miles I run a day. So I was like 'What does that mean?' with my sweetest smile. And he said, 'It's pretty obvious I'm not your type.'"

"Well, he's right. You aren't. I'm sorry, Jay." Andy capped off the drinks, emptying the bottle.

"Andrea Dawson, *I* am not *his* type. And I haven't the slightest clue why you thought that I might be, but I can tell you that he was convinced from the get-go that *he* wasn't *my* type because of his false assumption that I am into women. I am loud and proud about my feelings on equal pay for equal work. I protested in the streets for marriage equality. But for some rich asshole to tell *me* what *my* sexual preferences are—that's just such a typical chauvinistic viewpoint."

"Blake, um, sort of prides himself on his intuition. No one has the heart to tell him he is wrong in everything but business. He just gets so . . . childlike and excited when he thinks he's nailed someone. It's cute," Andy said, a half smile on her face.

"Well I didn't find it cute at all. So I'm a girl who drinks beer and enjoys sports. Why can't that just be something that a blue-collar girl, born and raised in Massachusetts, might enjoy? Oh, no, this patriarchal alpha male immediately assumes that instead of being someone who could challenge and equal him, I must be someone who wishes to be him. Like a penis somehow equals success."

Jaylene was running out of breath, and could tell she was losing her audience. Perhaps she'd used variations on this speech a few too many times while convincing Lacy to sign petitions, attend sit-ins, or pledge in charity pub-crawls.

"The point being, you two"—she pinned first one then the other with her eyes—"is that I wasn't expecting Blake Donovan to be a feminist ally. But I was definitely not expecting him to be the ultimate male pig. And yet he was."

"Are you saying that just because he thought you were a dyke?" Lacy called from her armchair. She'd obviously gotten comfortable enough with the story that she was laying sideways, head across one arm of the chair, knees bent across the other, as she worked on her song.

"That and he congratulated me for having such a feminine profession. Then he told me *his* wife would not have a job but would stay home and cook and clean."

Lacy paused mid-strum. "Is this seriously what your boss plans for his marriage, Andy?"

Andy pulled a pillow down from the couch to brace behind her back. "I know it's a bit . . . old-fashioned. He's going to have to make some compromises before he settles down. Everyone does. At least he knows what he's looking for in a woman. Do you?" She fixed her eyes first on Jaylene then on her sister.

"Well," Lacy said, sitting up, "I'm not looking for anything in a woman, and as Jaylene has unequivocally stated, neither is she."

"In a man, I mean. Do either of you know what you want?" Andy paused as if letting the question settle in the air. "Does what you want actually exist?"

"It did." Lacy's words echoed across the room.

Jay exchanged a glance with Andy who was very obviously berating herself for the comment. It was the reason Jay had stayed away from Lacy. It was too easy to say something that would remind her of her dead fiancé.

"I'm sorry, Lace," Andy offered softly. "I didn't mean—I just didn't mean it like that."

Lacy shrugged. But the chords she played next were minor ones, somber in tone.

Not having any words of comfort herself, Jay swirled the wine in her jar as she contemplated Andy's question. Did the guy she wanted really exist or was he a fairy tale? She didn't want the controlling alpha male hero that all the women seemed to be into nowadays. There wasn't a submissive bone in her body, though a part of her wondered if she might like it in the bedroom.

Now that for sure was a fantasy—there's no way she could marry her feminist ideals to any type of domination, even if it was just sexually. Was it even possible to find a guy who could admire her strength but still hold her when she needed to be held? A guy who would fight for her equality yet embrace her differences? A guy who would let her be a partner as well as a lover? Perhaps the real question was, could she ever let a man do those things for her? She was stubborn and independent, both traits that made it difficult to ever let someone in. It wasn't like she didn't want a man in her life—she did. Very much so. Just after all the failed relationships she'd gone through, it was difficult not to wonder if the problem wasn't her.

Was she too hard on men?

In the midst of Jaylene's self-examination she became aware of Andy staring at her with narrowed eyes.

As if the woman could read Jay's mind, she said, "Maybe you should go out with him again, Jay. I think you could see past his weirdness if you spent some more time with the guy."

Well, maybe she was too hard on men. But not *that* man. And if she had any hope of finding out if her type of guy existed, she couldn't waste time with men who were definitely not her type. Men such as Blake Donovan.

With renewed rage, Jaylene snatched the box of crackers from Andy's hand. "You couldn't pay me enough. And I can assure you he doesn't want to date me again either. He accused me of having a men's haircut. Are you listening, Andy? He referred to me as masculine. It was in the same conversation where he congratulated me on my profession. The guy is a complete and utter jerk. Good luck matching him with anyone." She didn't add that he wasn't the first person who had referred to her as masculine. It wasn't relevant information.

"Now, I'm taking your other bottle of wine, and these crackers, and going home to lick my wounds." She ruffled her pixie cut. "Also, I'll be out of town for a week next month. You'll be cat-sitting. Pookie's diabetic, so you'll have to do her insulin. Call me sometime, Lace."

Pleased with the look of chagrin on Andy's face, Jaylene swept out of the apartment to the sound of Lacy's laughter.

With the door shut behind her, Jay paused before going down the stairs. The irritation she'd had about her bad date dissolved as she realized it wasn't really Blake Donovan she was mad at. Or even Andy.

She was mad at herself.

Because she was a strong independent woman. She didn't need a man. She didn't need anyone. So why did she feel so lonely?

CHAPTER 2

N oah was bringing the last few stragglers in from his car when the cute girl passed him again. That shaggy haircut and tight dress were downright inspirational. He dropped his eyes. He also dropped a book from the stack in his left arm.

"I got it. I'll follow you in." Her voice was deeper than he'd imagined it would be. Not that he'd planned on talking to her. If he had his way, he wouldn't talk to anybody. Easier said than done, though. Tossing a glance back over his shoulder, he confirmed his earlier suspicion that this girl was going to be trouble. At least he'd sent his brothers home.

"You can just put that . . . somewhere." He gestured around as they walked through his open door. This was the worst part about having people over, knowing they were seeing all your stuff and wondering what sort of conclusions they were drawing about you.

Everything he owned was different shades of gray. What did that say about him? That he was cold and depressed? He had been going for cool and modern, but maybe it didn't translate. She set the book and her stuff down on a silver end table (scuffed) and wandered over to the steel bookshelf (ancient) to look at his literature collection (impeccable). She skirted a few unpacked boxes (beige) on the way.

"Didn't you just move in today?" she asked. "And you already set up your bookshelf?"

"I, uh. Like things in a particular way." He scratched the back of his neck and wondered if he should be offering her something.

"I see that. Alphabetical order. You have great taste in books. . . ." She held out a hand.

"Noah." His large hand engulfed her tiny one, but her grip was surprisingly strong.

"Jaylene Kim. Jay to my friends. And neighbors."

"Well. We are neighbors. Can I get you anything, Jay? I don't have much in the house, but there's some . . . caramels, I think." Caramels. Smooth. She laughed, though, and it was musical and he thought maybe he'd say stuff like that more often if he could hear it again.

"Thanks, but I have an early day tomorrow. Work and all." Was it his imagination, or did she actually look regretful? Sometimes it was hard to tell when someone was blowing you off.

"Of course. What sort of work do you do?" He'd remain polite either way. And then stare at her ass in that dress while she was leaving.

"I'm a teacher. My days start early. What do *you* do, Noah?"

"I'd tell you, but I'd have to kill you. What grade do you teach?" He'd learned a long time ago how to deflect questions about his chosen career. Asking more questions of the other party was usually the best method. People in general loved to answer questions about themselves.

It was a bonus when he was genuinely interested in the answer.

"I'm high school English." She absentmindedly ran a hand through her hair. "Hence my uncontrollable urge to check out everyone else's bookshelves."

English. She literally couldn't be more perfect. For one, an English teacher would never abuse the word "literally."

"Did they pass muster, then?" Of course they did. Noah Harrison knew books. He'd been an English major himself, after all, though he had zero desire to teach, or go into academia. He just liked to read. Reading didn't require any social interaction. He reserved that for his professional life.

Which reminded him—there was a beautiful woman inside his brand-new apartment. And here he was pretending to be social, when he had work to do. He should walk her to the door; he should thank her for carrying the book and escort her out. But he found himself fixated on her red lips, and anticipating her approval. *Hoping* for her approval.

"You're a Plath fan. Not many men are. I'm impressed." She ran her tongue over those crimson lips, not lasciviously, but unconsciously, as if she were considering him. It was sexy as hell either way.

"She was a brilliant writer. So raw, and honest. Not many women do *that*," he said.

Her eyes narrowed. "I could name a ton! Virginia Woolf—"

"'Really I don't like human nature unless all candied over with art.' I've always loved that line. Okay, I'll give you Woolf. She laid it out pretty well. But Plath still has her beat on sheer morbidity, which I maintain you don't see much of in female writers." Was she—she was kicking off her heels. And sitting on his overstuffed sofa (gray).

"Oh, please. Emily Dickinson practically invented the morbid female poet. Plath just made it hip. Where are those caramels?"

Noah ambled toward the kitchen to scrounge some snacks. He'd wanted her to stay and chat, despite himself, but now he was second-guessing himself. Women like that, intelligent, gorgeous women, didn't just follow him into the Land of Stormclouds. And if they did, by accident, he escorted them out. And for God's sake, if they wanted to stay, he didn't offer them refreshments.

But here he was, hand out, offering not just the aforementioned caramels, but a can of Coke as well.

"So now you're candying *me* over." She popped a caramel into her sexy red mouth. Was she flirting? Because he could think of a *lot* of comebacks for that one, but they all seemed a bit too forward. He settled for just grinning at her. Let her take that as she would.

"So, Jaylene. Jay. What do you do for fun?"

"I like music. I try to go out on Saturdays when I can, see some local bands. How about you? Are you from around here?" She popped the tab of her soda and gazed at him expectantly over the top as she sipped.

"Oh, you know. I'm from around here generally. As for fun, I wouldn't say I do much. There are a few shows I follow. I like to read, as you can tell, but I have to admit I'm pretty slow. If a story is skimmable, chances are I'll regret wasting my time on it. So I pick books I have to kind of savor a few sentences at a time—are you laughing at me?" Her hand was over her mouth and it was kind of adorable. Even though he didn't really enjoy being laughed at.

"Oh, gosh, no, it's just that you're so *serious* and I asked you about *fun*." Her eyes were still gleaming though she composed the rest of her face. Noah gave her a flat look.

"Serious things can be fun." She stared back. He held the glance, lost in the depths of her eyes as long as he deemed appropriate.

"Okay, fine. I don't have a lot of fun. I don't go out much," he admitted.

"We should change that." She winked. Definitely flirting now. Sweet. He opened his mouth to hit her with a bit of the old Noah charm just as she jumped up. "Ugh, I can't believe it's so late."

Puzzled, he glanced at the clock. Ten thirty was late? Ten thirty was like his lunchtime. Which reminded him that the caramels were basically the only thing he had in the house to eat.

"You don't live in the building, do you?" He thought he'd met all the neighbors now, all but the old woman who was apparently both on vacation and an alcoholic, according to the Dawsons. Who had accosted him at about minute three of living there. "Can I drive you home? I need to go grab a couple of things anyway." He felt around his jeans to double-check on his wallet and keys.

"Oh, no. Thanks. I'm just the next building over. You can walk me if you want. I'm taking these caramels, by the way." So he was *definitely* going grocery shopping, then. He opened the door for her, ostensibly to be a gentleman, but he would be lying if he said it wasn't half to get a better look at her ass in that tight dress.

Jay hadn't been kidding. Walking her home took exactly forty-five seconds, and that was at a very slow pace. Even though in some ways he was desperate to be alone and sort this out, he was also not sure he was ready for this—whatever it was—to be over.

"Would you like me to walk you up?"

She smiled up at him, dimming the streetlight with her sparkle.

"I can handle it. I'm just there." She indicated with her hand.

Great. So now every time he walked by the first-floor apartment on the left, he'd be side-eying the window hoping for a glimpse of her even as he hoped she wouldn't see him looking. Life just got infinitely more complicated, and he'd only been here for a few hours.

"All right, then. Well. Have a good night, Jay. I'm glad I met you." Should he hug her? This was the crap he never knew if he was getting right. It was easier in books, where everyone knew just what to do and when. But before he had a chance to start overthinking it, she'd moved in and wrapped her arms around him.

Her scent was candy-sweet, sugar on honey. Forget whether it was too soon to hug, all he wanted to do now was grab her by the arms and kiss her hard. To see if it was even possible that she tasted as delicious as she smelled.

She was pulling away, thank God, before he'd acted on the urge.

"I'm glad I met you, too, Noah, I'll be seeing you." Since she didn't look back as she climbed the steps and let herself in the front door (green), he didn't have to pretend he wasn't staring at her ass again.

Groceries. Think about groceries.

Five minutes later he was in the corner gas station stocking up on chips in a can, soda, and Bit-O-Honey candies.

He didn't even like the things. Well, he didn't *know* he didn't like the things, he'd just always thrown them out of his childhood trick-or-treat bags because they looked stupid. But honey reminded him of Jaylene, and he wanted to savor that, savor her, the way he'd told her he liked his literature.

Liking his women like his literature. Wow. That was ridiculous. Or *maybe*—it was brilliant.

He stalked back down the chip aisle and grabbed a couple of strips of beef jerky. Protein was important to a man's diet. So was sex. So was intellectual stimulation.

He dumped his groceries on the counter with an exasperated sigh. Obviously it had been quite a while since he'd been with a woman. And this one was stuck in his head like a bad pop song. That would be fine, if he didn't have his work to think about.

His job was not the kind of thing one did half-assed. Your head had to be in it, one hundred percent. And right now his traitorous head wouldn't give him a break from the memory of her climbing those steps in that dress. Slowly. Climbing.

What he could do to her on that staircase.

The clerk had to repeat his total twice before he snapped out of it.

When Noah rolled out of bed, groggy and slightly nauseous from his sugar intake the night before, he was completely irritated with himself. Not for waking up at noon; that was normal. Irritated for looking at the clock and wondering what Jay was doing right then, if it was lunch in the staff room, or grading at her desk.

This had to stop. Right after he took care of the other matter at . . . hand, so to speak.

Ten minutes later, he was dressed and ready to go for a hard run. Sometimes turning the headphones up loud, matching the beat with your rhythm, and getting utterly lost was the only way to find your inner peace. And he had some good hip-hop cued up and ready to go.

Outside his new building he squinted in the bright Boston midday. Rolling his head and shaking out a little, he considered which way to go. First run from his new apartment, it was a momentous occasion in its own small way. Might as well give in—he turned toward Jay's building and set off.

The first mile was always toughest. The worst part about habitually sleeping in was that he always seemed to be running under a blazing sun. On the bright side, he always had a tan despite being the biggest homebody he knew.

As the first few blocks fell away beneath his pounding feet, Noah considered.

Jaylene Kim was his neighbor. As such, he was bound to be seeing plenty of her. Or maybe not—they did seem to be operating on opposite schedules. But even the best- or worst-case scenario meant passing occasionally on the street, both in the freezer aisle of the corner store, seeing each other across the pumps at the gas station. Probably a couple of times a month.

The one thing, the one thing Noah could say for absolute certain was that there was no room for a woman in his life. His work didn't allow for it, hell, his personality didn't allow for it. He liked to be alone. He didn't want to check in if his run took him across town and he decided to join a pickup soccer game. He didn't want to go to bed early because someone else was. And he sure as shit didn't want to be spending his run justifying this to himself.

So he gave in again, and let his mind wander. It wandered up over the curves of her dress, and around her movie-star red lips. It followed the path of that caramel along her soft pink tongue. It meandered along the words that tongue had spoken, the banter he knew they'd have if he let himself go.

He let his thoughts spin over and around her like a cotton candy cloud until he felt sugar-sick all over again and then he let it go. Enough of the beautiful intelligent neighbor. He would be inspired by her from a distance, from now on. He had his job to do, and didn't need any distractions.

It was just not going to be allowable to become so taken with the girl next door.

So why on earth did he find himself outside her window that night, throwing pebbles?

CHAPTER 3

Jaylene was feasting. It was Friday night, she had the weekend stretching out before her, all her papers had been graded, and it was time to party. She was refusing to admit how preposterous it was that she now considered it a party to let Pookie drink milk at the table while she smeared stolen caramel on stolen crackers and washed it down with stolen wine.

So what if this was the fanciest Friday night she'd had in months? She'd rather be doing this than go out on the town with Blake Donovan. She almost spit her wine out at the very thought.

That stuffy old turd, in his expensive suit, getting beer spilled on his expensive shoes at the new raw bar that was in the sketchiest up-and-coming artsy neighborhood.

Oh, God. Now she *was* depressed. All the stolen goodies in the world couldn't make it less sad that she was home alone on a Friday, dreaming up ways for a bad date to be humiliated. Maybe it was time to sign up for one of those online matching sites. After all, she sure as hell wasn't hiring Andy Dawson as matchmaker.

There were shoes in her closet she'd rather eat.

Clunk. What the hell? The fucking squirrels around here were out of control lately. The other day, she'd seen one chubby and possibly drunk fall—actually *fall*—from a telephone wire. It looked almost embarrassed when it hit the ground, miraculously alive.

Clunk. Throwing shit at her window was too much, though. She might be a feminist, but she wasn't an animal activist. Those little shits would see what it felt like to get an acorn or two to the face.

Clunk. That actually sounded like her bedroom. Oh, hell no. It wasn't enough she slept poorly already? It wasn't enough that the sun streaming in that damn window woke her not just on workdays, but ensured she hadn't had a lazy Saturday since she moved in? It wasn't enough that those little rodents owned the neighborhood trees, causing her poor elderly cat to have a conniption every time she napped in a window?

Clunk. They now wanted her. Well, Jaylene Kim would show them *exactly* what they were up against. In her bedroom, she selected her least-favorite pair of stilettos. Hefting them, she smiled to herself. The many evenings of halfhearted dart playing in bars, waiting for the band to go on, had honed her aim. In the battle of Jay versus squirrel, PETA would not be pleased.

Shoe in each hand, *clunk*, she slid the window open and leaned out. One long arm, complete with heel, snaked out as well. Her eyes darted around the oak in front of her brownstone, seeking out the culprit.

Bonk. The next missile hit her between the eyes. Blindly, she reacted and heaved the shoe as hard as possible.

"*Fuck!*" Well, that squirrel sure had a mouth on it, she thought as she rubbed her forehead.

Wait—how many squirrels actually dropped F-bombs? She cracked one eye, then the other. Shit. The squirrel she had nailed was none other than the hot neighbor. Shit, shit, shit. This was why she never dated, she couldn't even tell a squirrel from a hot guy. Shit!

"Noah?" she ventured.

"Jesus!" came the response.

"Well . . . not quite?" How exactly did one respond in a situation like that?

"Jay?"

That she could answer. "Yeah! Um, sorry about the shoe. I thought you were a squirrel." Now that her eyes were aimed at street level, it was quite obvious there was a cute guy throwing pebbles at her window. How she thought she was being attacked by wild animals was going to be unexplainable. His gorgeous, scruffy, now-bruised face grinned up at her.

"People have made a lot of assumptions about me over the years, but this is definitely a first. Wanna come down?" She yanked her head back in the window so fast she nearly decapitated herself. Did she want to come down and spend time with a beautiful and well-read man? Obviously. But he'd been so hard to read himself the other night. Did she want to spend the next hour second-guessing everything coming out of his mouth?

Hell yes, she did.

"Give me five minutes!" Pants. She needed pants. How was her face? Was any makeup still lingering from this morning's application? Did it matter?

She yanked on a pair of black skinny jeans over her lace boy shorts. The Indigo Girls tank she had been lounging in would have to suffice. As for makeup, she gave herself a stern talking to. There was zero need to "fix herself up" for a man. If he liked her, it would be about her sparkling wit and clever repartee, not her winged eyeliner. Although—red lipstick was her signature, so no problem re-upping that. How was a woman supposed to be heard in this world without bright lipstick? She again stifled the inner feminazi as she dabbed on a touch of her favorite perfume oil. Smelling good made *her* feel good, so that was all right to do.

Despite her hard words to herself, Jay paused before opening her front door and took a deep breath. *Don't think too much. Don't preach too much. Don't ruin your first Friday with a man in ages.* Blowing air and mantras through her freshly coated lips, she stepped onto the stoop, only to have all the wind knocked out of her by the man standing before her.

"Why didn't you just ring the buzzer?" she asked. After all, it wasn't like she wanted *him* to know how weak her knees had suddenly gotten. Now it was his turn to look like he'd been punched.

"I . . . I don't know. I was trying to be cute, I guess."

Damn it. It *was* cute. And romantic. Or it had been until she'd gone and threatened the man with a spiked heel to the eye. "It *was* cute. I'm sorry. No one's been cute to me in a while. And it was surprising, is all."

He smiled, and she smiled back. Oh, God, were they going to stand here staring goofily at each other all night? Jay knew she wasn't great with awkward silences. She was likely to bring up topics guaranteed to get people talking, which usually meant things that got them arguing, and before long they were back to silence again, only of a less-friendly variety.

Luckily, it was Noah who broke it, though he was staring at his feet.

"It was really nice talking to you last night. I thought, maybe since you don't work tomorrow, we could take a walk and talk some more?" He glanced up hopefully, which was adorable since *she* was the one hoping he wanted to spend time with her, and not just demand recompense for stolen caramels.

Instead of answering, she fell into step beside him.

"Indigo Girls, huh? I haven't listened to them much, but I dig their lyrics. What's that song, 'Closer to Fine?' "

Jay nodded at him. She loved that song.

"I have that on a playlist of mine for work."

"What is it that you do, again?" She still thought it was a little weird he hadn't answered that one the other night.

"Nothing exciting. Hey, I should let you know that I have no idea where we're going. I got completely lost running today and had to take the Charlie home."

"Wait—you run? I run! How did we not talk about this before?" She stopped dead for a second and assessed him again. So that lean body was due to running. Man, he could literally not be any more perfect. She was becoming quite taken with her new neighbor.

They resumed their leisurely pace, not heading anywhere in particular. His hand found hers and clasped it. Her heart started pounding furiously. He was warm, and his grip belied his strength. She hoped desperately she would not grow clammy and gross him out. In the Boston humidity, though, it seemed likely.

"I started running a few years ago. It got addictive pretty fast. How about you?" He resumed their conversation as if the entire world hadn't just shifted on its axis at their touch.

Well, she wasn't going to be weird if he wasn't.

"I ran track in high school and college and just never got out of the habit, I guess. I don't even know what I'd do without running anymore. It's more like meditation than exercise at this point."

"I know the feeling. Were you at—were you at the marathon?" He looked distant for a moment, and she wondered where his mind had taken him.

"I was home grading papers, which I can never be more grateful for. At the time, I was horridly upset about missing out. Were you there?"

"I finished twenty minutes before. I was home again. I don't really want to talk about it, though." No Bostonian really did, so she let that one go.

"Also, it keeps me on a decent schedule. I can't stay up to watch one more episode or read one more chapter if I'm going to get six miles in before work." He may have been upset about the race, as they all were deep down, but he also had impeccable manners on top of it. That was awesome. Except he didn't like mornings—they were her favorite.

"Now that feeling I don't know. I am not a morning person." *No.* She knew something was wrong.

What the hell kind of job did he have? Who got to just *not* be a morning person if they didn't want to?

She thought about pursuing the occupation mystery again, but their conversation was going so nicely, she decided to stay on course. "I'm more of a night owl on summer break. But there's just something special about getting up before the sun and seeing it join you slowly during your run. There's hardly anybody out, and the city has a whole different feel to it."

"Hardly anybody out? Now you're talking." He grinned at her and squeezed her hand a little. Her heart squeezed a little in response. "Maybe I need to run before bed instead of after I wake up."

"Not much of a people person, huh?" They took a left turn down Massachusetts Avenue.

"Nah," he replied, but didn't elaborate. It was funny, almost, how comfortable it was to talk to someone who really didn't say all that much.

"So what kind of music do you listen to while you're running?" She knew it. She was getting clammy. Shit! If she didn't wipe her palms on her jeans soon, he'd notice. But if she pulled her hand out of his, he would think she didn't want to hold hands and she *really* wanted to hold hands.

Oh, thank God. They were walking past a ramen house. She yanked her hand away and opened the door. He looked surprised, but followed her in.

"I'm starving, do you mind?" She really was. The caramel crackers hadn't been much of a dinner. They slid into a booth and checked out the laminated menus.

"When I run, I listen to hip-hop, to answer your question. What's tonkatsu broth?" Was that his foot touching hers beneath the table? Or was it the table? Should she kick it to find out?

"Pork bones. It's my favorite. I listen to punk when I run, but I've been doing audiobooks lately for just bumming around the house." She kicked it. It reacted. Not the table, then.

"Ow!" Noah yelped. She smiled apologetically. She really was sorry. Sometimes she couldn't control her impulses. But she did want to play footsie. Damn. This was why she had so few second dates, wasn't it? Self-sabotage.

"Audiobooks. I haven't really gotten into those. I'm old-fashioned about paper, I guess."

She slunk her foot back over to his beneath the table. He didn't recoil. Maybe she could salvage this after all. The charge she felt every time they touched said she sure had to try.

"It isn't about paper or no. It's about maximizing my lit time. I could happily read all day, but then I couldn't walk down to grab groceries, or clean the bathroom, or grade tests. So I do audiobooks then."

His foot slid up to her calf, and then back down. Jay tried to suppress her shiver.

Suddenly, he kicked her back. "We're even now. That makes sense about the audiobooks. I'll think on that. But I really enjoy music, so I probably won't change."

She was still blinking from the surprise. It took her a second to recover her wits, but luckily the server was there to take their orders.

"So what are you reading right now?" She mentally patted herself on the back. That was good. They'd bonded over books the first time they hung out.

"Just something for work. What are *you* reading?"

She grinned as his foot resumed twining around hers. The sensation of elation at this cute scruffy guy staring at her as if he couldn't wait to hear her answer made her drop the impulse to press him on the work thing. What if he was unemployed? It would be embarrassing for both of them. And embarrassment was a real mood killer.

"Right now I'm reading a new literary fiction novel for my book club, a critique of modern feminism for fun, and I'm listening to this series of books following women of the Tudor era. Oh, and I have a graphic novel I read at night before bed." She grinned again at the look on his face. She didn't normally smile this often. Teaching teenagers tended to wear one's sense of humor down. Her face was going to hurt tomorrow. She made a mental note to smile less.

"I thought you were going to say just a romance novel or something. Jeez." He reached across the table to grab her hand again. Luckily, it was dry and ready again. As the heat spread from their clasped fingers up her arm, she decided she didn't care anyway.

"I like a variety!" she said. "If I keep them in separate genres, I can keep multiple readings going on. But you won't catch me dead with a romance novel." She shivered again, but this time in mock-horror.

"What's wrong with romance novels?" He looked genuinely puzzled.

What the hell? It wasn't obvious?

"They're completely ridiculous. Hot alpha male with broken past and massive bank account is healed by the golden vagina of a naive girl he meets under completely contrived circumstances. No thank you. That's just a smutty fairy tale for the Basic Bitch. It's demeaning, and unrealistic. Besides, the sex in those books is always weirdly dominant and controlling."

He was staring hard at her now, those gorgeous brown eyes blazing into hers. Shit, was she going too alpha femme herself? Oh well. If he didn't like it, she didn't like him. Hmph.

Though that was a total lie—she liked him and liked him bad. But despite her attraction, she wasn't willing to sacrifice her ideals for a pretty face. This time.

Noah's pretty face blinked its eyes. Twice. "Um. Wow. So what's a Basic Bitch, for starters?"

"You know the type. Girls who are aggressively average. The kind who make duck-faces on their Instagram pics at an eighties dance party while ignoring everyone who is actually at said party. They aren't very smart, they aren't good at socializing, and they require a lot of attention."

"That sounds pretty judgey for someone who describes herself as a feminist."

That one sentence rocked Jaylene like a 9.5 Richter earthquake, knocking down her entire self-image. It was so devastatingly accurate.

If the waiter hadn't arrived with steaming bowls of ramen just then, she might have just crawled under the table.

Well, maybe that was a bit too much honesty for their first formal date. But if she wasn't ready to hear it, he wasn't sure he wanted to hear what she wanted to say. Smutty fairy tales! Okay, she might have been right. It wasn't like Noah had actually read the last few erotic chart-toppers, but from what he had gathered, her description was pretty dead on.

Just. Just. Judgment wasn't cool.

But.

Neither was alienating someone you liked.

God, this noodle stuff was awesome. Way better than the cups you microwaved that produced a soup-like product but required one to pick the peas out. Dry-frozen peas did *not* rehydrate well. They were like little pea zombies. Nasty. This, though, this was like real food.

As he gazed delightedly into his bowl, he realized Jay was half done with hers already. He picked up his chopsticks and brought a load of ramen to his lips. There was an egg in here, too! Would wonders never cease? Well, whatever her rants, the girl knew food.

And books. The girl knew books. That was hot. Almost as hot as she was. 'Cause she was definitely smoking. He dished up a piece of pork before she noticed he couldn't stop staring. Because despite that little moment of hatefulness, she was a girl with a big heart. And luscious red lips. And adorable hair that made it really, really hard to keep his hands from raking through it.

The pork went a little dry in his mouth as he contemplated. Was she too clever for him? Then he realized he wasn't actually chewing. Once that resumed, everything got better. No. She was perfect for him. He just needed to convince her of that.

"Are you almost done?" Her eyes widened over the bowl she was slurping from genteelly. Who slurped genteelly? She was awesome. He quickly slurped as well. Really, he wanted to stay in that spot with their weird kicky footsie, but they weren't going to make out in this plastic booth. And Noah definitely wanted to kiss her. Ideally, as soon as possible.

He tossed some bills on the laminate table and pulled her up by her hand. She was a little damp, which was goddamn adorable. For that whole femme front, she was totally getting nervous around him. Him, Noah Harrison. That was ridiculous. And sexy.

He wasn't going to bite. Not until he had her tied to his bed, anyway. And they weren't remotely there yet. But once they were . . . Well. He'd bet his entire next paycheck that that feisty little feminist would love the way he was going to tell her what to do.

In the meantime he had absolutely no idea how to get home.

"Should we start heading back?" he asked, grabbing her hand again, hoping she'd lead.

She did. It was pretty clear she loved to be in charge. He'd let her, for now. He didn't even say anything when she grabbed the rooster sauce and the chopsticks and stuck them in her jeans. He did slap a few more bucks on the table, though.

She steered him down a few streets quietly.

"Noah?" It surprised him, once he'd grown used to the sounds of their flats slapping the ground in rhythm.

It only took a few beats for him to answer. "Yeah?"

"This was nice."

It took a few more beats, but this time because he was wondering, was she ready for the night to be over? Was this the last time he'd see her? This was pretty early to be summing up the evening. He needed to make a grand gesture.

What sort of a grand gesture would a girl like her require?

"It *was* nice. It *is* nice. Can we spend some more time talking books? I haven't met that many well-read women." Nice one. Books were what they'd bonded over in the first place. Books might keep them going.

"Is that a female thing? Are you being chauvinistic?" No, nothing was going to be easy with this woman.

"No, Jay. I think I just don't meet many girls like you." He spun her around so she could see his eyes. They were sincere, and he wanted her to see that.

Lies. He wanted to look at *her* amazing eyes. But, he'd pretend it was the opposite.

"Huh." *What was that supposed to mean?* "What's your favorite style?"

"What?" The conversation had lost him and he was the one who had been doing the talking. He was blaming it on her eyes.

"Like, I love the South Americans. Márquez, Saramago. My best teacher friend is into the Japanese—Marakumi and such." She elbowed him.

He guessed it was meant to be a prod, but every time they touched it gave him shocks. He tried to ignore the path they traced up his arm and down his spine.

At least their dialogue was back to something he could handle. "Classic American. Salinger. Steinbeck. Fitzgerald. I like sparse prose, and definitive themes."

"Male themes." She elbowed him again. He elbowed her back. She had no idea how bad she was going to get it once he finally had her.

"American themes. Money. Power. Class. That isn't male or female." To keep her from more elbowing, he wrapped his arm around hers, their fingers interlocked. He was overpowering her, even though he bet she had no idea. Any move she made could have him on top of her in two seconds flat. The thought was arousing.

"You don't think that any of those are gender-based? Black men had the vote before women. We were the last marginalized people to become real citizens. What kind of money, or power, or class, was a woman without a voice going to command?"

"Is that why yours is so loud?" he teased her. He couldn't help it. Girls that riled easily were fun. Although he wasn't looking to end this in an argument. Squeezing her hand to let her know he wasn't serious, he turned them back onto their street. Finally. He knew where they were.

As they neared Jaylene's stoop, he could hear music wafting down from the building next door. "That's pretty," he commented.

"That's Lacy," she responded. "I didn't think she was playing these days." He tugged her up the concrete stones to the flat landing. As the notes of a lonely, heartbroken guitar (for it couldn't be anything but, in that minor key, with that slow tempo) drifted down, Noah pulled Jaylene into him.

Suddenly, he was no longer worried about the distraction she would pose. He was happy she'd come out of her apartment and met him. He *was* sorry he'd become so taken with a girl he couldn't possibly be honest with. Yet this girl made him *want* to be honest. He wanted to show her everything. As they swayed gently together to the tunes Lacy played, Noah tipped Jaylene's face up.

When their lips met, time stood still. So did his breath. And he could almost swear hers did as well. The shape, and taste, of her changed absolutely everything. The gentle humidity of the Boston evening wrapped around them as he lost himself in the gentle pressure of her lips. His tongue met hers, and he stopped thinking.

CHAPTER 4

〜

Jaylene strolled down Boylston Street, enjoying the exhilarating release that came with the last day of school. The students had finished on Wednesday, and after two days of administrative work and classroom cleanup, her summer had officially begun. It always amused her to see the students so jazzed to leave—they had no idea how even better the break was for the teachers. Now she was celebrating her blessed freedom with one of her all-time favorite pastimes—window shopping.

As she walked, lightly swinging a bag of sticky buns she'd picked up from her favorite bakery along with five of the Friday Free cookies that were supposedly one with purchase (no one would miss the extra . . . several), Jay's thoughts wandered to the scrumptious neighbor. She hadn't seen him since the kiss on the door stoop. She'd wanted to, but with her Sunday meeting with Total Equality Now and her hectic end-of-school week, she hadn't even caught him in passing. He was on her mind, though, and she knew she was on his as evidenced by the brand-new copy of the latest Man Booker Prize–winning novel she'd found in front of her door when she returned from her morning run on Tuesday. It was a simple gesture, but she clung to it.

Even having just met him, Jay was already quite taken with Noah Harrison. Any man who was willing to buy hardcover was clearly the right kind.

She was so taken with him, in fact, that he permeated into the rest of her life. While she gathered the ballots for the T.E.N. vote, she remembered that blissful kiss, the way his lips had moved with hers in perfect unison. Grading the final papers on *A Separate Peace,* she saw his face on the athletic, charismatic Finny. No, not Finny. Finny dies.

But then, as she had signed her picture in her students' yearbooks, it was his face that she saw again, his bright eyes taunting her with their come-hither sexiness. She saw him everywhere—or imagined that she did—in the line at the bank, in the crowd at graduation, at the bar with the Dawsons the night before. Even now as she approached Desires, a women's high-end lingerie boutique, she could swear he was walking out the door.

Jaylene froze mid-step and lowered her sunglasses. She wasn't imagining it—Noah actually *was* walking out of Desires. Well, wasn't that interesting. A man didn't usually visit lingerie stores unless he was shopping for a woman. Unless he was a perv. Or transvestite. And since their relationship was nowhere near the underwear-shopping phase, she knew he wasn't shopping for her. Or she guessed he could be shopping for her, but that would be weird.

Anyway, the sight was unnerving.

It was also thrilling.

She hadn't seen the man in nearly a week and just looking at him caused her heart to dance erratically. He was simply breathtaking.

Noah noticed her at about the same time that she remembered how to put one foot in front of another. They walked to each other, his smile matching the one she was sure she wore herself.

"Noah? I thought that was you." She perched her sunglasses on her head and realized she should have thoroughly checked him out before she did so. Now she'd missed her opportunity to do it incognito. Oh, well. She could wait until he wasn't looking to slide her focus down his firm body. Maybe.

"Jay." Even the way he said her name made her stomach flip. He reached to squeeze her free hand. "What are you doing here?"

"Just out for a walk." *Don't peek down, don't peek down.* "What are you doing here is the more intriguing question."

His gaze followed as her eyes darted from his stunning face to the door of Desires. He dropped her hand, his neck turning a light shade of red. "Same here. Just out for a walk."

"And your walk took you through a lingerie store?" She looked down, her attention pausing on his trim hips. What a man could do with those kind of hips . . . She might have moaned out loud at the thought.

At least her scan also told her that his hands were empty. That was good. It meant he hadn't purchased anything for anyone. But if he wasn't buying, that meant he was browsing, and that seemed awfully pervy, or, at the very least, pro-objectification of women. Not that Jaylene didn't like a nice pair of girly undies, but she wore them to make herself feel good, and certainly not for a man's benefit. As soon as she thought that, she was already picturing the look in Noah's eyes if he saw her in something as sexy as the window display. She could practically hear his intake of breath—but no, because that was a silly, girly thought. Why should she start being silly and girly with him, when he'd never once objected to her being a strong woman?

Of course she had just busted him walking out of a lingerie store. Solo. Total perv move.

But Noah didn't seem the perv type. He'd been nothing but a gentleman with her. She was sure he'd checked out her ass a few times the other night and just now he'd glanced at her legs in the short shorts she was wearing, but every time had been flirty, not disrespectful. There had to be another explanation for his visit.

She couldn't wait to hear it.

"Um." He wiped his hands on his jeans then let out an awkward laugh. "Well, yeah." His face lit up. "Hey, while we're here—" He put his arm around her waist—God, the tingles that sent down her spine—and gestured toward the bookstore a few doors down. "Join me for a little perusal?"

It was an obvious deflection, but it was also an invitation—an invitation that Jay was more than happy to accept. "I'll never turn down a little perusal." She winked. "I'm even interested in looking at some books."

Overtly flirtatious? Maybe. But it earned her a fantastic grin.

Noah escorted her to the doors of Book Nook, his hand on her lower back burning through the material of her clothing to warm her skin. Inside, he started toward the fiction section when she stopped him.

"Oh, no, you can't visit Book Nook without stopping at Literary Wine." She nodded toward the bar attached to the shop.

"There's a wine bar in a bookstore? This neighborhood just gets better and better."

Noah's hand fell from her back as they moved to stand in line. With the break in conversation and without his touch, awkwardness began to itch at her skin. It was soon replaced with clusters of goose bumps when he pulled her into his arms, the bag of sticky buns dangling at their side.

"This may not be the most appropriate place for this," he said softly, his mouth inches from hers, "but I haven't stopped thinking about that kiss since Saturday night. So forgive my forwardness—I just can't help myself."

Before she could respond or protest—yeah, like she'd object—Noah took her lips in his. It was as sweet as their first kiss, but decidedly less tentative, and also hungrier. His tongue slid easily into her mouth and stroked along her own, making her stomach clench and her thighs twitch and her mind fill with naughty fantasies.

It was brief, but by the time he pulled away she'd been thoroughly swept away. Her stomach held a swarm of butterflies that she thought was maybe more like a swarm of bees the way they made her innards buzz with lust. There was definitely sexual tension between her and Noah, and though she was not one to jump in bed without a fair amount of wooing, Jay had a feeling their physical relationship would likely escalate quickly—woo or not.

In fact, she was ready to lean in and kiss him again, but it was their turn to order.

Several minutes later, and after she'd stuffed a handful of extra napkins into her purse, Jay and Noah were walking through the aisles of Book Nook sipping Cab Sav from clear plastic cups with straws.

"This. Is. Awesome."

Jay smiled at Noah's sentiment. This shop was one of her favorite spots in town. It was another checkmark in the Noah-is-amazing column, a column which was becoming so full she was beginning to think it was the only one that existed. "I'm glad you approve. Books and wine. What else can you ask for?"

"Good company. Though calling you good company is the understatement of the century."

Her cheeks felt warm and Jay was sure it was more than the wine producing that dizzying effect. So far they'd only run into each other a few times outside and chatted casually. She wished he would ask her out for something more formal.

Then she remembered she was a woman of the modern generation—*she* could ask him out. And she would. After a few more sips of wine.

They walked down the newspaper aisles, her eyes scanning the headlines halfheartedly. *USA Today* and *New York Times* both displayed articles about the economy. The *Boston Globe*'s front page showcased a rise of drug-related crimes right in the Back Bay area, the neighborhood they lived in. Then came the magazines—stories about celebrities' weddings and divorces and babies and weight loss trends graced the covers. By the time she reached the tabloids at the end of the row, she'd finished her wine, and her courage had been bolstered.

"So," she said as they turned in unison toward the bestselling fiction section, "do you have plans for the evening?"

"Just work," Noah answered absentmindedly, picking up the latest bestselling crime thriller. He scowled at the back description. "People actually buy this shit?" he muttered under his breath.

The popular book he was holding was particularly offensive to anyone with even a minimal background in English. But Jay was more interested in the former part of Noah's statement. She realized she still did not know what her new neighbor did for a living. He'd blown her off when she'd asked before, but now he'd opened the door.

"Work?" She trailed her hand across a stack of a recent young-adult breakout novel, trying to appear casual. "What was it you do again?"

Noah threw the book down and shot her a glance, his brows furrowed as if he had no idea what she was talking about. "Oh, I meant work around the apartment." He turned his focus to the next row of books. "I'm still not all the way settled. Boxes everywhere. It's keeping me pretty busy."

Unpacking did generally take a bit of time to complete. Still. Why did Jay feel like his answer was a cover-up? Did he not want to talk about his job? Every time it had come up, he'd deflected. Which was awfully curious. Also mysterious. And Jay didn't do well with unsolved mysteries.

She put the date-asking on hold, and followed where her curiosity led her. "Moving is a bitch. Did you get to take some vacation time at least?"

"Uh-huh." He didn't even look at her.

Completely evasive.

She bit her lip and considered. Maybe he really was out of work, living on unemployment. Though the apartments they lived in were not generally affordable to those on welfare. Or maybe he did something embarrassing. She'd heard that garbage men made good money. But certainly someone who worked all day around trash wouldn't smell as yummy as Noah Harrison, would they?

She was overthinking this. If he didn't want to tell her, he didn't want to tell her. She had to respect his privacy. Even if it meant ignoring her inner Nancy Drew. Maybe just *one* little Googling later would be okay though.

They turned down another aisle and Jay spotted a trash can. Holding out her bag of baked goods toward Noah's empty plastic cup, she said, "Trade you."

"You want me to hold your buns?" he asked with a delicious smile.

She managed to hold his gaze as she played in return. "Don't you know? I've been trying to get your hands on my buns all afternoon."

He chuckled as he took her bag, placing his cup in her outstretched hand. She turned toward the trash can and he called after her. "Hey, Jay?" He waited for her to peer questioningly over her shoulder. "Nice buns."

It was her turn to laugh. God, this guy was good. Delicious and flirty and downright sexy. *And he got books!* Such a plus. He was into her; there was no arguing that. He seemed to respect her intelligence and independence yet there was no denying he had a romantic streak. Could Noah Harrison possibly be everything she'd been looking for?

Too soon to tell, she decided as she tossed the cups in the trash, but she was definitely optimistic for the first time in months.

When she turned back toward him, she found he was still watching her. He'd been staring at her behind, she realized, but again, it wasn't in an offensive way. He was appreciating her much in the same way she appreciated him. His strong runner thighs, his chest that she could tell was cut even through his clothes, the sexy bulge of his biceps . . .

"Why, Jaylene, are you objectifying me?" he teased.

She blushed. She hadn't meant to appreciate him right at that moment, and not so obviously. At least *he'd* had the decency to do it behind her back.

Trying to hide the depth of her embarrassment, she turned to the nearest bookshelf and found a random book to pretend to read while she recovered.

"Speaking of objectification . . ." Noah's voice was challenging and startlingly close, coming just over her shoulder. Damn, the man stepped quietly. "I thought you didn't read those."

"What?" She looked at the book she was holding. *A Woman's Education.* "Oh." Of all the books she could have picked up she managed to choose the most humiliating one possible—an erotic romance. Really?

Except, she didn't have to let this throw her. She was a big girl. She could pull up her big-girl panties and turn this around. "This is a romance? I hadn't realized that's what I'd picked up. The covers are so vague these days with equally vague author names to match, as if everyone who reads them is in hiding." This one, written by N. Matthew, had a dark blue background with an ornate hand mirror. It told her nothing. How was anyone supposed to know what it was about?

Noah stepped to her side where she could see him and leaned an arm on the shelf. "The vague covers make them less obvious. Some people are embarrassed to read them in public otherwise."

She shook her head and *tsk*'d. "So everyone really is in hiding. That's terrible. They *should* be embarrassing. They're a detriment to the women's movement. Its ideas perpetuated by books like this that set us back to the fifties."

He stared her down with disapproving eyes. "There you go with the judging again. Are you sure they're detrimental?"

She hated the disappointment that sat within his words. But wasn't it equally disappointing that he was challenging her on this in the first place? She shot back in kind. "Have you read them?"

"Have *you*?"

"Of course not!" The idea made her squeamish much like looking at a *Hustler* magazine. She wasn't a prude, but the current trend in romance novels and typical pornography both fell into a category of culture that showed women as subordinate and mere receptacles for a man's use.

"Then how do you know what they're like?"

"I . . ." Seriously? Everyone knew what they were like. Right? Because that's what she'd been told from her women's studies professors in college. Because that's what every article in her *Feminine Perspective* periodical said. Because there was many a discussion at Total Equality Now meetings about the very subject.

But all of those reasons were based on secondhand information, and she was smart enough to know that she shouldn't simply adopt popular opinion without a bit of research.

Well, she had an opportunity to research now. She flipped the book open to the middle and scanned a page. "Here," she said, pointing a finger at a paragraph that instantly caught her eye. "Listen to this:

I snake my arm around her waist and hug her to me, my pulsing cock pressing against her hip. "Can you feel that, chickadee? You do that to me. And because you are responsible, you're going to take care of me now. On your knees." I push her shoulder and she immediately drops to the ground. "Good girl," I praise her. She's a very good girl.

Unwittingly, Jaylene skimmed the next couple of paragraphs that proceeded to describe a very graphic, very male-dominated blow job then shut the book, replacing it on the shelf with a huff, and not entirely out of disgust. In fact, she didn't really feel any disgust at all. Which was odd. Especially because what she did feel was turned on. Which maybe wasn't quite that odd because Noah was still standing in very close proximity to her. Too close, maybe, considering how hot her blood was now running beneath her skin. She took a hopefully unnoticeable step away.

"So?" Noah asked.

"It was . . ." She swallowed, gathering her thoughts. *Concentrate on it critically. Remove emotion.* "You heard it. It was demeaning."

She turned away from the shelf, away from his penetrating eyes— no, not penetrating, she did not want to think about penetration at the moment, especially not with Noah in the equation—and started walking back down the aisle, hoping that distancing herself from the object of discussion would also distance her from the discussion itself.

Noah followed after her. "Demeaning how?"

So the conversation was to continue then. She couldn't entirely be upset about that. It was what she'd liked about Noah from the get-go. That he wasn't afraid to debate a point, and God knew she loved a great debate.

This particular debate, though, bristled her, and she didn't for the life of her know why. She felt strongly enough about her side of the argument. So what was it then?

"Demeaning how?" Noah repeated as he fell in step beside her.

Oh, yes. He'd asked her that and she'd yet to answer. She let her mind go back to the words she'd read—the hot alpha hero and his simple sexy commands . . .

No, not sexy. Sexist. "*Good girl?* Like she's a dog?" She hoped her voice sounded disgusted instead of intrigued.

Noah shook his head vehemently. "Not like she's a dog. Like what she does pleases the narrator. Isn't that what sex is about? Pleasing one another?"

"Not at the disgrace of one of the parties." They'd made their way to the shop's doors now. Jaylene pressed through, noting that though he was on the wrong side of their dispute, at least he did not try to hold the door open for her. Another point in the Noah-is-awesome column. Too bad he was also finally collecting some points in the not-so-awesome column as well. Seemed it existed after all.

He waited until they were outside and heading back toward Beacon Street before he started in again. "Why is it disgraceful to her? In that story, I mean. Because she wanted to please him? Because she willingly submitted to him in her sex life? That isn't how people have to act in the real world, Jaylene. That's the bedroom." He was worked up, obviously passionate about his viewpoint. "Not all the rules apply."

Now *that* she could argue, and with solid conviction. She didn't even need the comfort of hiding her eyes behind her dark sunglasses, though she wore them anyway. "But that's exactly where they should apply. Otherwise husbands could still rape their wives simply because they're married, and the only orgasms achieved would be by men."

Oh, God, please don't let Noah be one of those orgasm hoarders—the men who still believed that the G-spot was nothing but a rumor.

Noah waved his hand in the air dismissively. "Yes, yes, I'm not discounting any of that. There have been valid injustices done to women in and outside the bedroom, and they still occur around the world. I know. I get it. I support and admire those who fight to end that type of oppression. I even contribute to a women's rights organization that works globally."

Jay smiled at that as she mentally ticked another mark in the pro-Noah column. With as equal-rights minded that he seemed, it was interesting, actually, how convicted he was on this one topic.

He let out an audible stream of air. When he spoke again he was calmer. "But if it's consensual . . . if a man and a woman agree that they enjoy dropping their usual culturally acceptable gender roles in favor of something they both find pleasing in their sexual relationship, they shouldn't have to feel guilty about it or judged by people like you."

"Why is this so personal to you?" It wasn't like he participated in the production of erotic romance novels. And he'd said outright that he didn't read them. . . . She froze in her tracks and gasped as it hit her. "Oh, my God! You're into that stuff, aren't you?"

He stopped a step ahead of her, turning back to say, "I'm not really a reader of—"

She cut him off. "Not the reading. The sex. Dominant behavior. You like your partners submissive. I'm right, aren't I?"

He didn't respond, which was in itself an answer.

"I *am* right!" She practically clapped at her successful deduction. Okay, she did clap. But only once.

Then . . .

Oh, shit.

The thrill of victory evaporated as she realized the deeper implications of her discovery—Noah was into dominant sex. The kind of sex that undermined all the female progression that had occurred in the last half century. The kind of sex that made a woman nothing more than a man's servant. The kind of sex that she would never willingly participate in because as attractive and hot as much of it sounded, it went against her core values.

And that meant that she and Noah could never have sex. And that was really very sad.

She started walking again and he fell in with her. He was quiet and she appreciated that he was giving her time to process, but his lack of contribution only led her to think the worst.

Maybe she didn't have a precise enough picture. "So are you into all of it?" she asked. "The whips and chains and bondage and pain?"

"I'm not a sadist," he answered. "Or a masochist for that matter, though I like to deliver a nice spank now and then."

"Oh." It was so barbaric. So why did the idea of being spanked by Noah make her panties slippery?

"And I like tying up."

She shivered.

"And blindfolds."

Her mouth went moist.

"But mostly I just like to be in charge."

"Right. The boss." Just like a lot of the men in the patriarchal society she lived in. Like the men who earned higher wages than women for the same level of education and experience. Like the men who didn't take no as no. Wait—wages—what if he did porn? Shit. She'd consider that one later.

Right now, it didn't matter if bossiness was the extent of Noah's interests—it was enough to be wrong for her.

He met her gaze full on, decidedly bumping up the intimacy of the conversation. "Look, dominance doesn't have to be scary. We could . . ." He paused, likely realizing the assumption he'd made. "I mean, I could maybe try to tone it down. If it's not what my partner is into."

It was sweet what he was offering—to put his own preferences aside in order for them to be together, but what good would that do? She'd sleep with him and then probably fall for him even harder and she'd get attached and maybe he'd get attached to her, too, all the while the friction of what he'd given up would gnaw and eat at him and eventually his resentment would destroy everything good between them. It was akin to building a relationship on a lie. It didn't work to even attempt it.

"Jaylene . . ." The ache in his voice said that he not only recognized her thought process but that he shared in her disappointment.

"It's fine," she said. Though her eyes were a little watery now. Thank God for the sunglasses. Stupid, that she should feel like this over someone she hardly knew.

Noah switched the buns bag to his outside hand and laced his now free fingers through hers. She let him. It was a good-bye of sorts. There could never be anything between them. Not anything more than this. Jay was well aware that compromise had to occur within relationships, but putting her feminist beliefs to bed, so to speak, wasn't a compromise—it was a breach of integrity.

Despite the warm day and the heat that ignited from the touch of his skin against hers—and yes, her hand was clammy—Jay felt the cold front of loneliness sneaking in. Perhaps this was why so many of her friends were single. Or lesbians. Because the men willing to accept them were few and far between.

At the moment, she didn't care if the man of her dreams was impossible to find. She was too distraught that the man wouldn't be Noah. So stupid. She didn't even know what he did for a living. The suspicion of porn flitted through her mind again, but she batted it away. It didn't matter now.

They came to her steps first, both of them stopping, neither of them letting go of the other's hand. Jay wished she could stretch the moment on and on, but eventually the silence between them got awkward and something had to be said.

Coming up with nothing meaningful, she settled on her other possible epiphany.

"Noah, do you work in that lingerie store? Is that why you were there?"

"No." He laughed. "I do not."

She loved the sound of his laugh. It made her smile despite her melancholy mood. "Then why were you there? You still never told me."

He paused. Finally he said, "I'd never been in one before. I wanted to see what it was like."

There was a sense of honesty in his admission, but his pause and the fact that men just didn't go into women's underwear shops to see what it was like on a regular basis caused her to doubt. "Were you ogling the mannequins? Or hoping to get one of the salesgirls to model for you? Is that how your dominance thing works?"

"No." He laughed again. Then suddenly he grew serious. "No. Look, I know that you have these preconceived notions in your head about things like this, and there's probably nothing I can do to change your mind about them. Or me, for that matter. Which is really too bad. Because I honestly went into that store for the experience."

He took a step forward, closing the distance between them so that his natural manly scent wrapped around her like a blanket. "And the whole time I was there, the only thing I was thinking was how sexy everything there would look on you. A red see-through chemise would contrast with your dark hair so perfectly. Or maybe a black leather bustier would be nice to prop up your gorgeous breasts. And I definitely want to see you in wisps of white lace riding up your legs as they wrap around me."

Her breath caught and her pulse ticked up a notch. She should be offended, shouldn't she? She wasn't though. Not in the least. All she wanted, in fact, was for Noah to keep on talking.

Fortunately, he did. "Maybe that's a little too forward for you, and you might even call it sexist, but I call it infatuation. And since after today I'll probably never see you again in more than a neighborly sense I have to lay all my cards out. I'm into you, Jaylene. Yes, I'm into dominance in the bedroom, but I saw your eyes when you read those words. The way they dilated, the way your breathing hitched—you were turned on."

"That's not—"

He let go of her hand and placed a finger to her lips. "Don't talk."

She obeyed. Amazingly since she wasn't one to quiet easily. Maybe she did have a submissive bone in her body after all.

Wrapping his palm at the back of her neck, Noah pulled her toward him until their foreheads met. "You can admit it or not. That's totally up to you. I just need you to know that if you're interested . . .

if you're *willing* to explore another side of you, a side that's personal and private and only reserved for the bedroom, then please consider me. I'd love to be the man who shows you what's possible."

She was glad he was holding her, otherwise she feared she might have swooned. Like, actually faint from the effect of his dizzying words. They were a turn-on—such a turn-on—but more than that they were an invitation, and not just the peruse-books kind of invitation, but a deeper kind. The kind she'd been dreaming of.

So why was she turning it down?

Silly question. She knew that answer. She'd just gone over it and over it in her head as they walked. Still, she couldn't manage to actually say *no* out loud. She couldn't manage to say anything so she simply stood there, her jaw slightly dropped as she soaked in the moment. Noah didn't prod her, seeming not to need a response. He took her hand and turned it so her palm faced up. He placed the plastic twist handle of the baked goods there and closed her fingers around it. Then he bent down to kiss her—a sweet, partially open-mouth peck that he laid on the side of her lips. "I'll be seeing you, Jay."

"Yeah." She'd see him around. They'd chat and exchange pleasantries. They'd banter about books. It would be fine. She nodded once before turning and making her way up the stairs, each step taking more energy than it should. She didn't look back, but she felt his eyes on her until she'd passed through the threshold into the building and the door shut behind her. Then she felt nothing but alone.

Well, that wasn't exactly true. She still had the monologue he'd left her with. The words echoed through her brain, spinning her in circles, begging her to take notice.

She wondered about it as she wandered into her apartment, setting the sticky buns on the kitchen counter before greeting Pookie halfheartedly. Was Noah right? Could a woman actually be independent and progressive in the real world yet enjoy submitting to a man in the bedroom?

Could *she*? There was a part of her that secretly wanted that—to be taken care of and controlled. A part of her that she'd always denied.

So why couldn't she try it? If it was private and no one knew, who would it hurt? Now that she thought about it, there were a couple of women in her liberal book group that admitted to not only reading about but enjoying D/s play and it didn't seem to have any negative effect on their political beliefs. Also they did it with each other, so she'd never thought twice.

Could that be her? Could that be her with Noah?

Maybe it was something she could entertain further before making a decision. Though, as she'd already picked out a flirty dress and her prettiest pair of undies and matching bra while she'd had the internal debate, it seemed she might have already decided.

CHAPTER 5

N oah scrubbed a hand over his face and glanced around his apartment at the sea of brown. Everything finally seemed to have a place. Time to get to work. He'd delayed for longer than he should and now he was behind. At least he'd managed to completely unpack. Though he'd rather that his procrastination was due to something else, such as a date with Jaylene. Or an after-date with Jaylene. Or whatever it was called that involved nakedness and his body pressed on top of—*inside of*—Jaylene.

Was that called a booty call? Now that was too crude. An affair? Too *Night Owl*. A neighborly get-together sans clothing? Too *Wallbanger*.

Maybe he needed to write them a new book. Whatever the story turned out to be, it would star Jaylene.

Jaylene. He couldn't think about her without letting out a sigh. She was so . . . so . . . stubborn. That's what she was. Along with a host of other less frustrating adjectives such as smart, adorable, sexy, intriguing, passionate. It was the stubborn that was the issue though. He got that she was worried. She'd invested all of herself into her independence, and that was one of the things he admired most about her. She was determined. She was strong.

But underneath her strength he sensed something fragile and insecure, a part of her that yearned to let her guard down and be swept away. He could do that for her, he was sure. If only she'd let go and stop hiding.

Hell, who was he to blame someone for hiding? Wasn't that exactly what he did, not telling any of the people in his life what he really did for a living, dodging the questions, deflecting? There had been a moment outside with Jay that he'd almost told her. When she'd decided he worked in that lingerie store, he'd almost explained. But after what happened at the bookstore, after she'd correctly guessed his bedroom persona, he didn't need a reason to push her away further. So he'd remained silent.

It wasn't like he was embarrassed about his choice of occupation. Actually, that was exactly what it was. He loved his job, wouldn't give it up for the world, but there was a stigma. So many people out there were quick to point a finger, quick to judge. People like Jaylene Kim.

And here he was again, back at Jaylene. His thoughts couldn't help but circle back to her. *Might as well let it go,* he told himself. Stop fantasizing that his words sunk into her and that she'd show up on his doorstep in one of those slinky nighties he'd seen at Desires. Truthfully, that had been the reason he'd delayed working tonight—he was hoping she'd change her mind. Three hours had passed since he'd left her, though, and he was still alone. She obviously wasn't taking him up on his invitation.

Time to move on.

Blowing a tuft of hair off his face, he slumped into his desk chair and opened up his laptop. He'd just pointed his cursor over his documents file when the knock came. He paused a moment, waited until he heard it again to be sure he wasn't imagining it before closing the lid on his computer and standing.

At the entry, he calmed himself down before turning the knob. This was *not* going to be his fantasy-come-to-life, so he shouldn't get overly hopeful. He opened the door to find he was right—it wasn't his fantasy. Not exactly, anyway, because Jaylene wasn't dressed in a nightie. Also, his dream hadn't included the plate of sticky buns that was clutched in front of her like a shield.

It was better than he imagined, though, because this was real. She was here. And the sticky buns still so hot from the oven that the frosting melted down the sides like candle wax—they were a nice touch.

Without a word, he opened the door wider. Whatever was to be said, even if this was just a neighborly visit, it would be better in private. After the door was shut, he turned to her. He wanted to say the *right* thing, though he didn't have a clue what that would be. Silly since he'd been told many times that he had a way with language.

Turned out he didn't need to speak because Jaylene had her own speech to deliver. It was only two words, but they were the only two he needed to hear. "Show me."

Silently he took the plate from her hands and set it on the closest end table. Then, though he really wanted to pull her into his arms, he had to be sure she really wanted to be there. On his terms. "We don't have to, Jay. Not this time. We could—"

She didn't let him finish, pushing herself into his chest and wrapping her arms around his neck. "Show me," she said again before crushing her lips to his in a frenzied, hypnotizing kiss.

Well, lesson one would be that he directed the seduction, but this was awfully pleasant as well.

Their kiss lasted for what felt like hours. Or perhaps it was just seconds. It was consuming and passionate and time didn't exist in the space that their lips were molded to each other. Their mouths moved greedily and her hands rushed to keep up, stroking the length of his chest with urgency.

Soon she was pushing him toward his couch. It was hot how demanding she was, how out-of-control needy she felt in his arms. Only thing her direction was lacking was submission. And really, did she think he was going to give her the best night of her life on a freaking couch? He grabbed her by the ass and picked her up bodily. She made a small noise, but didn't protest as he carried her, mouths still entwined, to his room.

As they stood at the foot of his bed, his tongue tangled around Jaylene's, Noah decided to forget the whole "show me" request, and instead just let their passion play out. He'd meant it when he said he didn't have to have things happen a certain way, at least not every time. And this—Jay's aggressive fondling and scratching at his clothes—it was turning him on with a blaze he hadn't felt in quite a while.

But just as Jay had controlled all of the seduction thus far, she undid Noah's decision when she suddenly broke from his lips and fell to her knees in front of him.

"Um . . ." He had to cover his mouth so he wouldn't laugh. She did look sexy like that—her head bowed, her eyes on his feet, as if she thought that was the pose of a submissive. It wasn't so far off, but her execution was all wrong. She was missing the whole point, acting out of an assumed obligation rather than letting herself go. If she could just do that—if she could give herself over to him in earnest, then she'd see.

He'd have to teach her.

He stroked his hand down the side of her face then bent to help her stand. Her brow wrinkled in confusion, but he kissed her forehead in an attempt to ease her. "Follow my lead, Jay, okay?"

"Okay, but . . ." She swallowed. "I don't know what I'm supposed—"

He shushed her with a brush of his thumb across her bottom lip.

"I'm going to tell you. All you need to do is relax and focus on me, okay?"

She paused, taking a deep breath. "Okay."

Her mouth opened slightly and then closed again, and Noah knew she was fighting against her impulse to ask more questions. He let the silence settle between them so she could get used to it, get used to not being able to control the speed of their interaction. He knew her well enough to know this would be the hardest part for her, so he didn't try to rush it.

When he felt that she'd grown somewhat comfortable with the unknowing, he gave her the guidance she longed for. "Okay, here's the rules." He stroked his hands from the top of her spaghetti straps down her bare arms. "I'm the boss. You don't argue with me. You don't refuse my commands. If you don't like something I ask you to do, just tell me and we'll go back to something you're more comfortable with. But the pleasure in this comes from trust. If you constantly question my requests, then neither of us will be as fulfilled as we can be. I won't hurt you. Not really. Though I may bite. And spank. You are not allowed to do anything to me without permission. If you want to kiss me, you have to ask. If you want to touch me, again, you have to ask."

"Do I have to ask for permission to speak?"

He chuckled. Expecting silence from Jay was irrational. Besides he loved her voice, loved the things she had to say (most of the time), loved the sounds she made in the back of her throat as they kissed. And he certainly couldn't wait to hear what she'd cry out when he made her come.

His pants grew tighter in anticipation. "No, you can talk. But I may ask you to be quiet at times, and then you'll have to obey. Are we clear?"

"Yes, Noah." Her brows creased. "Or am I supposed to call you 'sir?'"

He barely controlled his eye roll. "Noah's fine." Yes, he liked to be the dominant in his sexual encounters, but he was by no means a true Dominant. He didn't do the leashes and the collars and the sex clubs. Not that they didn't sound fun for a night or so, but it wasn't his lifestyle. He simply liked to control the pleasure exchange between him and his lover. He was good at it.

But Jaylene couldn't know that yet. She'd find out soon enough, though. He ran his hand through her hair, careful not to let her feel like she was being petted like a dog. "Any other questions?"

"Just one." She peered up at him with lust-filled eyes that held only a hint of trepidation. "Be worthy of me, okay?"

God, that simple request tore him down, made himself question everything he'd ever thought he knew about what it meant to be a man. Made him want to be better, to be worthy of her in a way he'd never been worthy of anyone. His voice was so choked he couldn't speak. So instead, he kissed her. Kissed her in a way that told her he'd give her what she wanted. That he'd make every attempt to be the lover she didn't even know she needed.

It was then that he decided how he'd be with her that night— slow and patient. He'd boss her around, but it would be all about her. He'd teach her to relax and he'd show her how freeing it could feel to let someone else have the reins for once. He'd be worthy of her. And maybe, as she let her guard down for him, he could learn to let her in, too.

Noah's kiss was amazing. It stirred her in places she hadn't known were able to be stirred. More than anything, it made her want to move further—to rip off his clothing and force him back onto his bed.

But she controlled herself, hard as it was. When he broke from her, she couldn't help smiling. Even though it was the exact opposite direction that she wanted to be moving, she'd let him lead, and that gave her a silly kind of self-pride.

He took a step away from her and issued his first command. "Take off your dress."

It was baffling how Noah's low and gritty voice could be so spine-tinglingly erotic. The way he looked at her, the way that he appraised her as she reached behind her and unzipped, the way his eyes dilated as she moved first one strap off a shoulder then the other, letting her clothing fall to the floor in a pool at her feet—it aroused her as much as if he was already rubbing her toward an orgasm.

Usually she was the type to throw clothes off as fast as possible and get to the banging. She'd had no idea that simply stripping for a man could be so hot. She'd been braless, so when he slowly scanned up her body, he lingered at the curve of her breasts, causing her nipples to rise to attention. His gaze held so much weight, and it took everything not to cross her arms over herself and try to hide. It was as if he were touching her with his eyes, skimming across her skin like feather-light strokes of his fingers.

Imagine when he touches me there. . . .

Or wherever he touched her, because he might *not* touch her there and she had to trust that if he didn't it would be all for the best. And she did trust him, surprisingly. If she didn't, she wouldn't be there in the first place.

"Beautiful, Jay," Noah praised her, sending waves of goose bumps down her arms. "I appreciate that you're not trying to cover yourself up."

Another burst of pride shot through her. A nagging voice at the back of her brain said she was being ridiculous. She didn't need his praise to know she looked good. And she certainly didn't need his permission to decide how she was going to stand before him.

But that voice was wrong. Not because she actually did need his permission or praise, but because she wanted both and that was why she stood there for him. That didn't diminish her strength as a woman. Did it?

If it did, she wasn't thinking about that now. Now she was following as Noah led her to the chest at the foot of the bed. He sat down and turned her to kneel in front of him, her back toward him. Which was a little strange. Until he started massaging his hands through her short hair. Then it was anything but strange. It was magical.

"Oh, God," she moaned as his fingers kneaded into her scalp, sending sparks of electricity down her neck and spine. Her first instinct was to tighten up, but she breathed out slowly and leaned back into his strong hands.

Noah leaned down to brush his lips across her shoulder. "That's it. Relax. Enjoy this. Enjoy me."

His hands moved down to the muscles of her back, rubbing them with deep pressure that felt almost too hard to bear. Instead of pulling away, though, she steadied herself with deep breaths, releasing into his touch. Soon, she was loose and her tension a distant memory. Noah brought his arms around her chest then and began to knead her breasts. An entirely different kind of tension began to build up—the sexual tension that she'd somehow forgotten while he'd been attending to her. It was thrilling how he could do that—how he could dictate what she was going to feel and when—and along with the thrill was an anticipation that threaded through her with a steady pulse. She was on the edge wondering, *what next?* Already she was sure this would be the best sex she'd ever had, and Noah still had all his clothes on.

Noah broke their physical contact abruptly. "Stand up and turn toward me." Jay did as Noah asked without a second thought, immediately missing the warmth of his touch, but eager to see what he had planned.

"Undress me."

She thought he'd never ask. Wrapping her fingers around the hem of his T-shirt, she tugged it up and over his head. Her breath caught at the sight of his chest. He was thin, but well-toned. She longed to trace the dips and valleys of his sculpted muscles, and her hand reached up to do so until she remembered his rule: *No touching without permission.* She could ask though, and she did.

"Not yet." His denial caught her off guard. It also made her want to touch him even more.

But, incensed as she wanted to be, she obeyed.

"Now, my pants."

She worked at his fly and zipper and was grateful when he stood up without her asking so she could pull his jeans to the floor, leaving him in his boxer briefs. He stepped out of the pants and kicked them to the side. It was her turn to study him, her eyes settling on the thick bulge at his pelvis. Even constrained as he was, she could see his size was impressive. She licked her lips as she found herself hoping that he'd order her to her knees again, this time to take him in her mouth much like that erotic story she'd read at Book Nook. She even hoped he'd reward her with a *"Good girl."*

God, wasn't that something she never thought she'd wish for? Was she going to regret this later? She didn't want to. More to the point, she didn't regret it now. She would regret, however, not reaching out and stroking him. He wouldn't mind just a little tiny bit of a fondle, would he?

Before she could think about it, she'd cupped her hand around his shaft. He twitched once in her hand before Noah swatted her away. "Uh-uh. I said no touching. I was going to let you finish undressing me, but since you disobeyed, you'll have to wait. Touch me again and there will be further consequences."

"What consequences?" She hadn't really meant that to sound as challenging as she'd made it sound. Or maybe she had. Actually, the idea of unknown *consequences* was somewhat exhilarating.

"That's not for you to worry about." He turned her so he could nudge her back onto the bed while he talked. "But maybe there will have to be some binding after all."

If her legs hadn't already been jelly before, they were now. The thought of being tied up and overpowered by Noah . . .

Jesus Christ, what kind of a feminist was she?

"Stop thinking," he said, pushing her legs up into a bent position. "I can hear the wheels turning. And I didn't give you permission for that."

"Okay." It was easier to say than to do. But she made an effort to concentrate on nothing but Noah's hands as they stripped her of her panties. After that, she didn't have to put much effort at all into not thinking. Because Noah had settled his face between her thighs, and his mouth on her clit, and each swipe of his tongue scattered every thought before it even had a chance to form.

"Yes. Yes!" Damn, he was good, sucking and nipping at her sensitive bud, sending her up, up, up. He lapped at her mercilessly. As she neared the edge, her hands flew to his hair, needing something to grab on to.

Immediately she realized her mistake. Noah stopped his heavenly assault and eyed her.

She let go of him. "I'm sorry. Please, don't stop. I didn't mean it. I'll be better."

She was begging him. *Begging him!* But she was so close and she needed him, and the primal desire that drove her to plead would do much worse if only he'd return to his task.

He considered. "Do I need to tie you up?"

"No. I'll be good." The tying did sound hot, though. She'd admit it. But not now, she wasn't willing to lose the momentum he'd created. "Please, keep going."

"Say it." His eyes twinkled as they met hers. "Say what you want."

"I want you to make me come. Please." It was easier to say than she'd imagined it would be. And saying it was liberating, even sexy. She wanted to say it again, so she did. "Make me come, Noah."

He did then. With his mouth and his fingers, he sent her spiraling into an earth-shattering orgasm. She clutched on to the sheets underneath her as her legs shook and her hips bucked up and she lost herself in her climax.

Noah was still licking at her when she began her descent from the heights he'd sent her to. She started to sit up. "It's my turn." She thought about it a second. "Or your turn." However it was to be phrased, she meant to have her mouth on him. Now.

Noah, however, had other plans. He shot his hand up to her chest and pressed her back to the bed. "I dictate the turns. Not you." He settled a thumb on her sensitive clit, circling on it with expert pressure.

"But—" Not only did she believe in reciprocation—equal rights and all—but Jaylene was certain she couldn't take any more of the attention he was giving her. She needed—well, she thought she needed a break, but he wasn't about to give her even that small relief.

"Can you not follow the rules?" He raised a challenging brow, but didn't let up on his assault.

Jay writhed. It was too much. Sensory overload. But as tortured as she was in the moment, she didn't want her answer to be no. More, she didn't want to have to answer anything at all. She simply wanted to let go and let someone else decide for once. So she didn't say anything. And she didn't stop him. Instead, she threw her head back and let Noah decide. He chose for her to receive pleasure. The next orgasm crashed through her stronger than the first one, sending her entire body into spasms that took her prisoner and sent her soaring all at once.

She was still flying while Noah stood and scrambled out of his briefs. Then he was slipping a condom on and then he was sliding into her. They moaned together as he pulled out to the tip, then pushed in again. Out and in like that in slow, languid strokes that made her insane. She wanted him to increase his speed, to drive into her with the frenzy that she felt building up in her again. Already.

She tilted into him, urging him to go faster.

"Keep that up and I'll just go slower." His face was strained, and she realized the effort it took for him to hold back.

"Noah . . . ?" If it was what they both wanted, why was he trying so hard to bridle himself? She wanted more of him, wanted him to feel what she was feeling.

"Just . . ." He pressed his forehead against hers and squeezed his eyes shut. "Trust me. Okay?"

He'd asked again and again with his actions and his words and, though she kept saying that she did trust him, she still continued to fight. There was a lesson to be learned here. Why was it so hard for her to set her teacher mentality aside and become the student? So far, Noah's dominance had only heightened the experience. When she let go, he took her to places she hadn't known she could go. So she took another deep breath in and when she let it out, she let it all out—the doubts, the fears, the misgivings.

And she let herself really trust him.

"Okay."

He kissed her then, stroking into her mouth with his tongue in the same lazy tempo he thrust into her pliant body with his cock. They danced like that—leisurely, deliberately. Each step of their tango took her one step closer to another orgasm, the tension creeping in so quietly, the anticipation building so gradually that when she was finally at the brink, she was desperate for release.

Noah read her body well, seeming to sense when she was there. "Touch me," he demanded.

Her hands flew to him, sweeping up the planes of his taut chest with her palms, down the hard muscles of his back with her fingertips. Then, just when she thought she couldn't take the delay any longer, he told her to hold on. She wrapped her arms around his neck and he sped up, finally pounding into her with the pressure and the pace she'd longed for. It tipped her over the precipice. Starbursts shot across her vision and her entire body stiffened, her climax overtaking her while Noah drove into her. It was the most incredible orgasm she'd ever experienced, pulsing through her with incredible force, stealing her breath from her entirely.

She was so taken away, that she barely noticed when Noah grunted and reached his own climax. Next thing she knew, in fact, she was wrapped up in his arms, his hand caressing her cheek as her heartbeat returned to normal.

"You're back," he said as her eyes found his.

But he was wrong. She wasn't back. At least, she wasn't back to who she'd been before. In the course of, well, intercourse, everything in her nature had been questioned and thrown into upheaval. Now she didn't know how to reconcile this new self with her old self. More to the point, was it even possible?

CHAPTER 6

⌐

In a situation like this, there was only one thing to do. Jaylene took to the Internet. Were there other girls like her out there? Was there some kind of meeting she could attend, Girls on Top Who Accidentally Ended Up on Bottom and Liked It? Or. Something like that. Doms and the Feminists Who Shamefully Banged Them.

Nothing was coming up on those searches. At least, nothing that didn't come with an adult content warning. Damn it! Why was she still tempted to look? Noah was ruining her. Had ruined her. This was the worst. No, the worst was her complacency.

Why was she so delighted by her own downfall? She was going to have to stop wearing her "Eve Was Framed" shirt. It was becoming more and more obvious just how tempting temptation could be. And forget original sin. It was original guilt that was going to kick her out of her happy little Eden.

It had to end. It just had to. It also had to stop playing on an infinite loop inside her head. And she definitely, definitely had to stop getting hot and bothered all over again thinking about it. It was just that thinking it should end made a lot more sense before she'd gone and enjoyed the hell out of her multiple orgasms.

She finally found a sub-Reddit devoted to feminist porn and dove in. Commenters were divided as to what the definition of feminist porn actually was. Some believed it had to be by women and for women to negate all exploitation. Some merely thought that women being in charge of their own sexuality was feminist enough. In fact, a couple of those users identified themselves as being in the porn business.

Jay sat back and thought. If porn stars, women who actually performed sex acts on camera for money, could still self-identify as feminists in charge of their own sexuality, then was she really going to deny herself?

Frustrated, she slammed her computer shut again.

Why didn't anyone else seem to be having this kind of a problem? It was a significant amount of the female population that now considered themselves to be feminists, according to studies on her favorite Web sites. Judging from the success of those hideous books she had argued about with Noah, the populations had to overlap, at least marginally. So were the women buying those books just so lackadaisical about the movement? Or was there something she was missing, some secret clause in the Femme Code?

She wondered if she could discreetly suggest this as a special topic at the next T.E.N meeting. But how to go about that without identifying herself as the guilty party? Perhaps she could pretend it was a question for a friend. Perhaps she could blackmail Lacy into doing the asking.

She didn't have any dirt on Lacy, though, and she'd still have to admit what she'd done. Jay wandered over to the window and stared out at the busy street below. Life had been so much simpler last week. How did this view stay the same when everything else was now slippery and uncertain?

Well, that was dumb. She mentally chastised herself for adding to the heap of overused clichés. If she'd read that in a student's paper, she'd have marked them down for unoriginality. Heaving a sigh, she wondered idly if there was any recently poached food in the house. Then she wondered if her feminism wasn't hindering her by refusing to learn to cook. Then she decided she didn't care. As she turned away to go stare at the contents of her fridge, something caught her eye outside.

Noah.

Noah being flagged down by a well-heeled older blonde outside her brownstone. She must be lost. Oh, how nice. Probably he was going to give some messed-up directions to the poor woman and confuse her even more than she already was.

But that wasn't happening at all, because her hair was flipping and she was definitely flirting when she put that hand on his shoulder, and he was smiling back, and oh, my God, does he have a cougar girl-friend? She jumped back from the window, heart pounding.

That lasted almost two and a half full seconds before her face was mashed against the cool glass again. The blonde was slipping some-thing out of her purse and looking around. Noah was steering her toward the corner of the building. Away from prying eyes. Well, hah! Jay's bedroom window looked out upon just that corner.

She bolted for her room. Unfortunately, she had failed to account for a kitchen chair in her frantic trajectory. Precious seconds were wasted untangling herself from the floor and the chair while cursing loudly and praying nothing was broken.

By the time she got to the bedroom window, the blonde was re-treating. Damn! She'd missed the whole—whatever that was. Then the woman turned around, still tucking something into her obviously ex-pensive handbag and blew Noah a kiss. As Jay's jaw dropped, he blew one in return.

What. The. Hell. She considered the options as she watched Noah meander off toward his building through narrowed eyes. An ex-change of some kind had clearly taken place. Not just an exchange of numbers—that could have been accomplished on the street. No, this was clandestine. Something not meant for others to see.

Just like so many things had been happening in the neighborhood. Just like the stories splashed on all the papers. The thing that surely could not be true about gorgeous, intelligent, complicated Noah. He couldn't really be a drug dealer, could he? But what else? And who said drug dealers couldn't be gorgeous, intelligent, and complicated? Actually, they were probably all pretty fucking complicated.

Maybe he was just doing it to pay off his student loans. Maybe he was paying off a gambling debt. Perhaps it was blackmail. Or maybe it was the family business, something he longed to escape but didn't know how.

Or maybe . . . maybe she was losing her mind. Maybe it was completely innocent. Maybe she needed to actually go over and ask him about it, instead of jumping to crazy conclusions. She was no Blake Donovan. The more seconds that ticked away from what she had thought she had seen, the more ridiculous her assumptions seemed to her. She congratulated herself on growing as a person, instead of going off half-cocked.

Except that she had already let the idea of going over to ask him take seed. And then she had thought of going off half-cocked, which reminded her of something Noah certainly never did. And then next thing she knew, she was in her bathroom, making sure her tussle with the chair had left no visible bruises and doing a quick swish with some mouthwash before reapplying her lipstick.

And then she was at his door. And then he opened it all shirtless and sexy, and then he smiled, and then all her rational thoughts left with a whoosh and all she could think was, "And then?"

Noah was never going to get any work done ever again. He was also never going to complain, because the thought of never seeing Jaylene again after their night together was far more upsetting to him. And he *had* worried about that—that after the post-orgasmic glow wore off, she'd be a little less enamored with the idea of being dominated by a man.

But here she was. And even though it had really only been half a day since their last encounter, he was suddenly as desperate for her touch as the night they first kissed. He crooked a finger at her with a smile, so she'd understand that although it was an order, it was a sexy order. From the wicked grin he received in return as she stepped through the threshold, though, it seemed the order was well-received.

She cocked a brow as if to say, "And then?" He took a step back, and then another, beckoning her forward and into his lair. Living room. He meant living room. They stopped, staring, still silent. He moved his finger again. Closer. Closer. And then when she was close enough, he indicated she should kneel.

He was already rock hard as she dropped obediently to her knees. Her hands began to stray toward his belt before she remembered to ask his permission. He nodded his approval, eyes never straying from hers as she expertly unbuckled his belt and pulled it off slowly, loop by loop, with one hand as the other worked its way up his thigh. God, she looked good down there. Although, he'd been told he looked good like that, too. By her. The night before. The memory of giving her everything she needed until she screamed his name made his cock pulse in anticipation.

She noticed. And slowed down her undoing of his pants even further. He wanted to reprimand her, but turnabout was fair play, he thought. It was basically the same thing he'd done to her. That subversive little feminist. She was beating him at his own game, letting him "be in charge" while running the show. It made him laugh.

Well, it would have, had her fingers not freed his member and then delicately stroked the length of it, lingering and teasing around the head. Then all he could do was gasp.

"Is this okay? Is it okay if I touch you?" she murmured, so close he could feel her soft breath on the most sensitive part of him.

"I want you to touch yourself, too," he ordered. Her eyes widened. He wasn't going to let her be all the way in charge, after all. But she knew better than to argue by now, and her eyes widened again as she reached a tentative hand beneath her jean skirt. "Good girl," he breathed, so soft he didn't know if she heard. Probably for the best if she hadn't.

Then her tongue was on him, and he was past the point of caring what she heard, because he wasn't entirely sure what he was saying. She licked him up and down, alternating the pressure between the hard flat of her tongue and the light flicking tip.

When she finally took him in her mouth, it was almost a relief. For, like, three seconds, until he realized she wasn't letting up. His hands twined in her short hair, slowing her down, pulling her back.

"Why, Jaylene. Are you trying to end this before this starts?" he asked gently. She stayed wrapped around him as she replied.

"Unh-unh." The vibration sent shock waves through him and he quickly pulled away altogether. He was about to come already, and he hadn't even touched her. She was a girl to be reckoned with, that was for sure. He'd gone from taken to taken aback, and back all over again. Their eyes were still locked as she licked her lips. Good girl? No. She was very, very bad. And very bad girls needed to be put in their place.

He held out one hand to pull her up. She reached for him, but he shook his head. She drew her other hand out from under her skirt and he pulled it to his mouth. One by one, he drew her fingers between his lips. As he watched, she shivered and closed her eyes, finally breaking their contact.

That wouldn't do. He wanted to watch her, to see how she reacted to every little thing he did. He wanted to learn her backward and forward. A little pressure from his teeth at the base of her middle finger sent her eyes flying open again.

"Good girl." This time he wanted her to hear. He wanted her to hear the deepened tone he said it in; to understand, finally, that turning him on like no one ever had meant that he found her to be more of a woman and not less.

They were still separated by almost a foot. At that moment, it felt like a football field. He stepped forward, closing the gap. With one of her hands in each of his, he pulled back, allowing her to wrap her arms around him. Then finally, he leaned down and kissed her the way he'd been longing to. The passion she responded with was unbearable, her fingers clenching into his waist before moving up to his shoulders. Even though he was only pressed against her now, instead of in her, there was still a distinct danger he'd not be able to stop himself from finishing with his thoughts and her proximity alone.

So when she moved her hands around to his chest, he almost *had* to pin both of them under one of his. They were so small, and capable. He couldn't possibly give them free rein without losing total control. Instead, he pinned both of them high above her in one of his much larger hands.

Her intake of breath belied her delight in it. So. He could be what he wanted now, no second-guessing. If that ragged gasp hadn't done it, the way she arched her spine to allow him better access did.

"Good girl," he groaned again, as he propelled her toward the couch. He was done worrying about his dull apartment what with all the color she brought in. Maybe the gray backdrop just accentuated the multicolors of their fireworks. It didn't matter, because he wasn't about to stop now. He nudged Jay with his knee, spread her across his overstuffed cushions as he pinned her with his left hand.

The other ripped her camisole open. Actually ripped it, which made him smother a smile—in all his years being a dominant lover, that was a bit of a first for him. A first that made him utterly incapable of holding back any further. He reached down and found she'd wriggled the skirt off already. Uninhibited, he fisted the front of her beautiful silk panties and ripped them apart, too. Man, he was a golden god of sex! His fingers found her lacy bra next, and tugged.

Nothing. He waited a moment and pulled harder. Nothing. One more good hard pull.

"*Ow!*" she yelled. Noah immediately pretended like he'd meant to do it and shushed her. The Dawsons knew enough already, no point in alerting them to this. Knowing those girls, they'd be waiting outside the door with wine to conduct exit interviews. He smothered her protest with kisses, and removed her bra the traditional way instead.

Then she was naked, and all he could do was stare. He'd had to let go of her wrists to take her bra off, and she took advantage of that to run her hands down his arms as he hovered over her. With a swift movement, he was inside her. She sighed in frustration as he stayed put, completely engulfed, but not moving. He stared into her eyes, waiting to see how she'd react.

Her hips began to rock slowly as she tried to take control. He settled more firmly between her legs to still her. When she stopped resisting, and smiled at him, he started to slowly thrust in and out. His hands found hers, and their fingers interlocked atop the arm of the couch.

Oh, God. The couch. They were still on the couch. That would not do. He snaked one arm around behind her and slowly lifted her as he moved off the couch. This was becoming his signature move. Maybe he *was* a golden god after all. They moved slowly toward the bedroom, still connected, still kissing.

When he gently lowered her onto the bed, her body was still relaxed enough for him to wonder if he could push her a little further. From the nightstand he removed a tie, left over from his hated day job, and placed in the drawer optimistically. She stared at him wide-eyed when she realized what he was up to, but didn't protest as he tied her wrists to the headboard. It melted him a little, knowing how much faith she was putting in him. It made him want to be worthy.

Once she was secure, Noah moved down to her breasts. Drawing one taut nipple into his mouth, he rolled it with his tongue until she cried out. He moved to the other, and did the same. Slowly, he kissed his way south. Her increasingly loud moans let him know she wasn't regretting his plan. He savored that thought almost as much as her taste, because he was already where he longed to be, painting her pleasure with long strokes of his tongue.

He mimicked what she'd done to him, first covering all of her in one long lick, then narrowing his attention to her sweet spot with small, darting motions. She came for him, spectacularly, after only a moment.

As she lay gasping for air, he rose up and reentered her. Her recent orgasm had made her tighter than ever, and it was all he could do not to have one himself. Did she have any idea how she affected him? He'd have to tell her. Just after this. His body began to undulate, and he moved in and out of her. At first she just breathed, but soon he could tell she was building again from the rhythm of her hips.

The beauty of the position he had her in was that although she couldn't touch him, she was free to express herself in an almost bigger way. When she bucked, it was hotter than a mere hand on his back. When she struggled, it told him she wanted him more than she could stand.

It was so ridiculously hot.

Thank God she was clearly about to come again, because he had been holding back for too long. He increased his pace, moving deep and hard inside her, adjusting to her subtle signals. Watching her breasts bounce with their motion turned him on even more. As her vocals reached new heights, he came with a shudder, triggering her as well.

Noah's whole body collapsed upon her. How could this have happened? How could he have become so taken with a girl he hardly knew, after so long of pushing everyone away?

But he knew. There was no fighting fate. And this amazing, challenging woman was here for a reason. As his inner philosopher took over, she cleared her throat.

"Um, Noah?" He moaned into her neck and nuzzled it at the same time.

"Yeah?" She probably wanted him to untie her. As much as he hoped to keep her there from now until next Christmas, that was fair. He reached up and started untangling the soft knots even as he asked it.

"Who was that woman you were talking to an hour ago?" Well that was *not* what he was expecting. Like, at all. And it wasn't like he had a great answer, either. That woman was in love with him. Lots of people were. It wasn't real, it didn't matter. But how to express that to the girl he was in distinct danger of doing just that with?

"A chick from work. She needed my signature on something. No biggie. I work with super-cool people. You'd love them."

"I'd love to know a lot of things," Jay said pointedly. So he had no other recourse but to go back down on her until she forgot everything but his name as she screamed it.

CHAPTER 7

W ith her eyes still shut, Jaylene stretched her arms above her head, pointed her toes, and yawned. Man, there were sore muscles that she didn't recognize.

Deliciously sore muscles that reminded her of the night before with every turn of her body.

Thinking of the night before . . .

Had she really done the things she'd done? Really let Noah dominate her as she had? And had she really loved every single freaking minute of it?

Yes, yes, and emphatically yes.

While there was still much to work out in her head, her body and soul responded to her lover as if he were the only man she'd ever been meant to be with. So whether it was easy or not to fit her newly discovered interests into her rigid system of beliefs, she'd have to find a way to do it. As certain as she was of women's right to equality, she was just as certain that her own womanhood was strengthened when she was in the arms of Noah Harrison.

And thinking of Noah . . . and his arms . . .

She opened her eyes and looked at the empty bed next to her. He wasn't there, which was a bit surprising, but in the rumpled sheets where he'd slept she found a folded piece of plain white typing paper. She unfolded it and read his simple block lettering:

Jay,
Went to scavenge for breakfast. Don't move.
Noah

P.S. By don't move, I mean, please don't move. I wouldn't want to get bossy when we aren't in bed. Though you're still in bed . . . so don't move.

He'd even drawn a smiley face at the end, which made her grin from ear to ear. But, as much as she wanted to obey, she had to pee. So *don't move* was not an option.

After she'd used the tiny bathroom and cleaned up a bit from the activities of the night before, Jay looked around for something to throw on. Noah probably expected her to be waiting naked, but that expectation alone drove her to want just the opposite. She hadn't changed her personality entirely, after all. The act of defiance felt as familiar as a worn pair of running shoes.

Not feeling comfortable enough to dig through his dresser drawers, she opened Noah's bedroom closet hoping to find a robe or a shirt. She scored when she found a discarded T-shirt lying on top of a box. It even smelled like him. Perfect.

She pulled it on over her head, taking a deep inhale as the fabric passed over her nose. It fell on her nicely, hitting the tops of her thighs. She looked sexy in it, if she said so herself. If Noah wasn't happy with her in it, he'd simply have to remove it.

Before she shut the door to the closet, her eye caught on the box that had been hidden under the T-shirt. It was partially open, and inside were brown-paper-covered bricks. Several of them. *What the . . . ?*

Though it was entirely in her nature to snoop further, she didn't want to ruin her budding relationship. But brown-paper-covered bricks? That was something out of a crime novel. Like, didn't drug dealers wrap their cocaine that way? And wasn't there a rise in drug-related crime in their area? And Noah still hadn't told her what he did for a living—

Oh, God. Oh, God, oh, God.

Was Noah a . . . a . . . she couldn't even think the end of that sentence. Yes, she could. She had to. *Drug dealer.* Was Noah Harrison's occupation so secret because it was illegal?

She shuddered. There was no choice for it—she had to see. She carefully pulled back the flap of the box and reached her hand in. Taking a package in her palm she realized it felt less solid than she imagined a brick of cocaine would feel and more like . . . well, like a paperback book, maybe. Which was almost as strange. Who had a box full of brown-paper-covered paperback books in their closet?

Or maybe she simply didn't know what a brick of illegal substances felt like. Or what if she'd been right earlier, and it was porn? Oh, God, oh, God! What if he videotaped the girls he brought home, and she was about to go viral? Oh, God!

There was no time to analyze it properly because right then the front door banged open in the other room. Noah was back and Jay was at risk of being caught red-handed. Red-handed with what was still the question, a question she was unwilling to leave unanswered. So, on an impulse, she closed the closet, and quickly stowed the package in her purse, which she'd left by the nightstand. She made it into the bed just as Noah walked in the room with a handful of napkins and two foil bundles.

Were those drugs? What had she gotten herself into?

"Hope you like breakfast burritos." Noah settled in next to her with a wink.

Breakfast burritos. Of course. She almost laughed out loud at her crazy presumptions. The bundles were not drugs. The packages in the closet were not bricks of cocaine. Noah was not a dealer. Nor was he an amateur pornographer. She was being ridiculous and now that she had a minute to think about it, she felt guilty for the stolen brick in her purse. Not guilty enough to say that she wouldn't rip it open and find out what it was the minute she had a chance, but contrite nonetheless, and unfortunately for Jaylene, she'd never had a good poker face.

Noah raised a brow. "You look guilty. And I bet I know why."

No, no. There was no way he could know why. Could he? Was it the hidden cameras? Drug dealers probably invested in things like that, even if he was innocent of the porn charge.

But before she could worry further, he said, "You moved."

"What?"

"You moved. I told you not to move. Didn't you get my note?"

Relief flooded through her. "Yes, I got your note. But I had to pee."

Noah unwrapped a burrito and handed it to her. "And peeing required putting on clothing?"

She took the burrito from him, deciding it was an act of kindness rather than chivalry, and poised it before her mouth. "Maybe I was feeling a bit . . . rebellious."

"Hmm." Noah studied her with a pleased glint in his eyes. "Guess we'll have to follow up breakfast with a spanking."

The butterflies of anticipation danced in her belly. He wouldn't see any complaints from her. Whatever he was, she was going to enjoy every last moment before she knew.

Lacy bounced the brick up and down in her palm then sniffed the length of it before tossing it back to Jaylene. "It's not drugs."

Jay caught the brown-paper package she'd confiscated from Noah's closet in her lap. "How can you be so sure?"

"Because I am," Lacy said with finality, leaning back into her armchair.

"I don't think it's drugs either," Andy piped in. "It would be heavier. And shaped different. That feels like a book."

Jaylene pursed her lips. She'd spent most of the day with Noah, talking and sexing. Then, when he'd politely dismissed her so that he could get some work done, she'd once again tried to ascertain exactly what that work was. As always, he was elusive. She'd left frustrated and without answers. For some crazy reason, she felt like the brick she'd stolen held a clue to Noah's secrets. But rather than jump to conclusions—as she was often apt to do—she'd decided that she could use a little insight from some of her women friends. The Dawsons were the nearest thing to women friends she had, both in physical proximity and in the relationship sense.

Jay hadn't given them much. She'd told them she was dating the new neighbor, that she'd found this brick in his closet, that he'd acted suspiciously whenever his job was mentioned. She'd shared her concern that Noah might secretly be a drug dealer.

Lacy rolled her eyes at that before she'd even examined the brick. Now she said, "So since you know it's not drugs, you can sneak it back into the box where you found it and he'll never be the wiser."

Andy, who stood leaning behind Lacy's armchair, gasped. "Without opening it? No way."

Lacy tilted her head over her shoulder in her sister's direction. "This is exactly what gets you into so much trouble, Andy. You have no sense of ethics."

"You know what?" Andy moved to the couch as she spoke and sat next to Jay. "I'm sitting over here. Jaylene gets me. Don't you, Jaylene?" She patted Jay's knee.

"Well . . ." After the Blake Donovan debacle, Jay wasn't claiming to get Andy at all. She evaded that conversation by focusing on the package in her lap. "I do want to open it. I mean, if it's not drugs, what will it hurt? And I know there's something he's hiding from me. If he's not going to tell me, what choice do I have?"

"That's what I'm saying." Andy shifted so she was facing Jay, watching her as attentively as a child watching another open a Christmas gift.

"You are bad, bad women." Lacy shook her head disapprovingly, but she also peered over with curious eyes.

Andy winked encouragingly. "Bad is the new good. Come on; open it."

Even without the prodding of her friends, Jay knew she wouldn't simply put the package back where she'd found it without finding out what it was. She knew it was wrong and she chided herself as she slipped her finger under the clear tape and unwrapped the brown paper from around the item it contained.

As they'd guessed, the item was a book. A familiar one at that.

"*A Woman's Education*?" Andy read the title out loud.

"It's the book." Jay was more puzzled than before she'd opened the package.

"We can see that," Andy said.

"No, it's not *a* book; it's *the* book." It wasn't exactly the same as the one she'd read from. The one that had sort of inspired her antics of the previous evening, not that she was about to admit it. This one was a smaller version of the same book, like the kind bought at grocery stores. But it was the same other than that. "We kind of got in a fight over it the other day. It's an erotic story. You know, where the hero is all alpha male and the heroine's submissive and whiney and . . .

Well." Jay's usual rhetoric regarding the inferiority of women in these novels needed to be updated after her recent adventures in the bedroom. And/or the living room.

"She's not whiney," Lacy interjected. "She's not really submissive, either. That's just her role in the assignment that Mr. Holliday has given her in their sexual exploration class. Actually, she's more of . . ." Lacy trailed off as she met her sister's shocked expression. "What? I've read it. Obviously so has Mr. Sexy-No-Job. You haven't, Andy?"

As interesting as it was to discover that equal-rights-supporter Lacy had read the book, Jay was more intrigued by Noah's involvement. "But why does he have it? And why is it packaged up like this?"

"No idea. You could ask him." Lacy sat forward and glared. "Except then you'd have to admit that you stole it from his closet."

Andy shushed her sister. "You're not helping. We need a plan."

"I'm not trying to help, this is ridiculous! Your plans have a history of going awry, big sis."

"Lacy, she's struggling here. Be a little understanding."

"Fine," Lacy said with a huff. She nodded toward the book in Jay's hands. "That's the mass paperback edition. I don't think that's out yet. Let me look." She grabbed her iPad off the coffee table and began swiping at the screen.

"You said there were more of them like this?" Andy asked.

"A whole box full."

"Maybe he gives them away as gifts for some reason. And they're packaged that way so that people won't be embarrassed about getting an erotic novel."

Hadn't Noah said something about that same thing? He was a reader—he'd proven that—but it was odd that he had such a finger on the pulse of this particular genre.

"Yeah, that version doesn't come out until next month. Then the sequel is out a couple of months later." Lacy hugged the tablet to her chest. "I can't wait for that one. N. Matthew is truly an artist with his words."

"*His words*? The writer is a man?" Jay had assumed the author was a woman. She hadn't even realized that men wrote erotica for women.

Lacy nodded. "That's what it says in his bio, anyway. He lives in Boston, too."

"He lives in Boston?" Too many coincidences. Jaylene was beginning to see the bigger picture. She swallowed, not quite believing that she was thinking what she was. "Do you know what he looks like?"

"I've never seen him. He doesn't usually have a picture in his books. Maybe online . . ."

While Lacy typed away on her iPad, Jaylene flipped through the book. A scribble of black near the front of the book grabbed her attention and she turned back to find it. There, on the title page, in neat block letters were the words, *All best.* Followed by N. Matthew's signature.

Neat block letters. Just like Noah's handwriting.

"Oh, shit." Lacy's eyes were wide as she peered over her screen.

The exclamation echoed Jay's own thoughts. Because *oh, shit* was exactly how she was feeling at that moment. The pieces fit together perfectly, but she still had to have confirmation. "You found a picture, didn't you? It's Noah, isn't it?"

Lacy answered by flipping the tablet around so Andy and Jay could see it clearly. There he was—his bright smile, that floppy hair, his wicked eyes. Next to his picture, the headline of the article read: *Bestselling author N. Matthew sits down for a rare interview.*

Jay had to look away. She pinched at the bridge of her nose, her eyes closed, as she tried to fit her mind around this revelation. Noah was an erotic writer. Noah wrote books about sex. Noah wrote books about the very things that Jaylene had spent her life crusading against.

It was one thing to say that what they did in the bedroom was private. It was quite another thing to promote it.

Wasn't it?

God, she didn't even know anymore.

Andy shifted on the couch next to her. "Well, this explains . . . stuff . . ."

It did. And it didn't. It didn't explain why Noah hadn't come out and told her. He'd asked her to trust him and yet he couldn't trust her? So he probably assumed that she wouldn't take it well, and rightly so, but still. She'd deserved to know before she'd given him her faith. Before she'd given her trust. Before she'd given him her heart.

"Apparently he's sort of a recluse. He doesn't do many signings or appearances."

Jay opened her eyes to see Lacy was reading from the article. She tossed the iPad on the table in front of her. "Obviously he doesn't want a lot of people to know what he does. I guess he likes his privacy."

"Or he's ashamed," Jay said under her breath. *As he should be.*

Or maybe he shouldn't be.

Dammit, why was this so hard to get a handle on? She'd almost rather have found out he was a drug dealer.

"Are you all right, Jaylene?" Lacy seemed genuinely concerned.

And Jay genuinely felt uncertain. "I'm not sure."

"I don't understand what the big deal is? So he writes about sex. . . . That's kind of cool. Isn't it? I bet he's good in bed."

Jaylene shot a piercing glare at Andy. For someone who was supposed to be able to read people, Andy certainly had missed the read on her. More than once.

"Oh, you've already slept with him!" So maybe Andy had some ability to read people after all.

Well, no reason to deny anything now. "Yes, I've slept with him. And he's good in bed. He's great in bed, actually."

"Is he all alpha dominating like he writes about?" Lacy was practically bouncing in her chair. "He is, isn't he?"

"He is." Oh, was he. Her body still felt the after aches from their night before. "Which is part of the problem."

"How is that a problem? That shit is all-caps HOT."

"Lacy, I'm a feminist!"

"So am I! Who gives?"

Jay leaned back into the sofa at that. Though Lacy wasn't much of an activist, she'd been a big supporter of the movement, donating her time and talent to more than one of Jay's events. In fact, Jay had always thought they'd shared similar viewpoints about women and society. And now she was finding out that Lacy read the erotica books without even an ounce of shame.

So what was Jay's problem with it?

She didn't have an answer. "I don't know what my issue is, Lacy. It seems like a contradiction, I guess. I'm still grappling with the bedroom stuff. I don't know if I can accept that he writes it, too. I mean, this is what I fight against on a daily basis."

Lacy made a sound that could only be defined as scoffing. "You don't fight against this, Jay. You fight for women's rights and for equality in the world that we live in. You work to make sure that we are treated well and respected and not taken advantage of. These books have nothing to do with that. Honestly, as a feminist I think you should be giving this subject more attention. There are obviously many women who read these books, who embrace this fantasy, and just as many people who assume that makes them weak or stupid. Am I a weak woman? Am I stupid? Because I don't think so. And I love my smut books. And isn't it ridiculous that I'm not allowed to read them without receiving some sort of judgey label? Isn't that what feminism is supposed to really be about? Empowering women to be who we want to be and not what someone else thinks we should? Well, this is who I want to be."

Jaylene kept her eyes pinned on the book she still clutched in her hands. She was too embarrassed to look anywhere else. Lacy had just put her in her place and didn't she deserve it? And wasn't this happening more and more regularly over the past few days?

Andy cleared her throat.

Lacy took the cue. "Sorry if that was a bit ranty. Getting off my soapbox now."

Jaylene shook her head. "No, it was perfect. I needed to hear it. Noah said the same thing, actually. Apparently it takes repetition to get through my thick skull."

Lacy tucked her legs underneath her. "I'm impressed that Noah agrees. It's not the same since he's not a woman, but I'm still impressed."

Jay bit her lip, considering her next move. She had to talk to Noah. Had to confess that she'd snooped. Had to address his secret. "This isn't the only problem, you know. He still hasn't told me. He obviously doesn't think I can handle it."

Lacy gave a supportive smile. "But you can. Although I see why he wouldn't think so. You do, too, don't you? Are you ready to ma—woman up?"

Yes, okay. She could. She would. Because she cared about Noah, and, more important, she cared about herself. She liked the way Noah was with her in the bedroom. In all honesty, it was the type of physical relationship she'd been longing for. Why had she thought it was against the movement to deny her wants? And even if it was, why did she care?

Whatever. That thinking was over. She was turned the right way now, seeing things straight. Now she just had to convince Noah that he could trust her the way she'd learned to trust him.

CHAPTER 8

⌒

Noah stared at his screen, reviewing the last paragraph he'd written. He'd used the word *cock*, twice, it seemed. Repetitive. His editor would not be happy. But there were only so many other words to use for the male genitalia, and so few sounded sexy. *Dick* worked. But *penis*? *Shaft*? *Love-wand*? No, definitely not that.

The same was true for the female anatomy. *Clit* was about the only acceptable word. Whenever he tried using euphemisms—*bud, nub, sex*—he'd get someone bitching. Apparently using the "wrong" label substantiated the loss of a star in an online review. So he either disappointed his editor or he disappointed his fans. There was no winning.

He read his last sentences again: *My cock twitched at her entrance. I drove my cock into her, burying myself to the balls.* He'd get eye rolls at the use of *entrance* but at least he could delete the second *cock* and simply say, *I drove into her.* He called that a compromise and moved on to his next paragraph.

Except now he was distracted. Not only was writing sex *hard*—he almost laughed out loud at his own pun—but it also, on occasion, made *him* hard. Thinking so deeply about the act, who could blame him? Especially when he'd so recently had amazing sex. With an amazing girl. Scratch that, an amazing woman. He could still feel the snug fit of her around his dick (not cock, editor), could still hear the erotic sound of the bed knocking against the wall as he slammed into her.

Wait, no, that was actual knocking. On his door. He glanced at the time before shutting his laptop. It was nearly ten. Jaylene was the only woman who would think of disturbing him so late at night, not that he considered it late. At least, he hoped it was Jaylene. His deadline was fast approaching, and he should be focused on the words. But Jay was a very happy distraction.

He was grinning as he opened the door, still grinning as he took in her appearance. She wore a short denim skirt and cami—God, how his fashion vocabulary had increased since writing women's fiction—that hugged her tits and dipped at her neckline. He could probably get a sneak peek at her breasts if she weren't holding something in front of her cleavage. A book. She was holding a book.

Fuck. She was holding *his* book.

Did she know? She couldn't know. It was impossible. He'd been so careful. Maybe she'd just bought a copy because the discussion over it had led to the most incredible sex—of *his* life, anyway. Except she was holding the mass market edition, which wasn't available for purchase yet, which meant . . . well, he wasn't sure what it meant. Had she received an early autographed copy in one of his giveaways? He'd mailed some out a couple of weeks before and though he hadn't known her yet, he was certain he would have noted the address since he was about to move into the same area.

And however she'd gotten it, that didn't mean that she knew he'd written it. Or did it? Dammit, he should have come clean and told her before. Now he'd stalled long enough to make it a *thing* and in his experience, *things* were never good in the early days of a relationship.

All these thoughts raced through his mind in a matter of seconds, so he couldn't be sure that she read his panic, but if he didn't say something soon, it would be obvious. He broke in with the good old standby, "Hey!"

Should he pull her in for a kiss? He wanted to. It would be natural, but had he waited too long?

Jaylene helped by taking over the situation. "Can I come in?" Forward women were totally awesome. God bless the feminists.

"Of course. Come in." As he shut the door behind her, he took a deep breath and gathered himself. If she did know, at least she'd come by to discuss it with him. If she didn't know, then it was probably time she did. When he turned back to her, he was ready.

So was she. "It seems we need to talk," she said at the same time he said, "We should talk."

They did the obligatory awkward laugh and all he wanted to do was draw her into his arms and carry her into his bed. But there was this. Book. God.

He scratched the back of his neck and decided to let her go first. "So. What's with the book?" He nodded at *A Woman's Education* that Jay still clutched in her hands like a shield.

"I, uh . . ." She swung her hands—and the book—behind her back. "First, I need to say something. Last night, and the night before, and this morning . . . all of it has been amazing. Eye-opening and, uh, freeing, I suppose. I had no idea that it could be like that. That *I* could be like that. Thank you."

Was this the beginning of a break up speech? Because it sure sounded like a breakup speech. That's totally what it was—she was breaking up with him and bringing him his own damn novel as a consolation prize. God, did he never get away from the stigmas of his job?

Well, if it was a breakup, he might as well get his two cents in while he had the chance. "I should be thanking you. You trusted me, and that means a lot." Now he'd made their incredible sex sound like a standard transaction between a therapist and patient. So he added, "And it's been hot. Way hot."

"Way hot." She blushed and his pants tightened.

Then he was examining the meaning of those two words. Would she have said that if she were breaking up? Was there a "but" to follow? And if there was, why hadn't she said it yet?

After what seemed like an eternity, she cleared her throat. "Which brings us to this." Out came the paperback again.

He stared at the familiar cover, remembering how much pride he'd had when his publisher had first unveiled it. It had been his break into the literary world—a world he loved more than anything. He'd toyed with several different genres while pursuing his English major and in the years that had followed. He hadn't even been certain writing was his future—there was editing, and being an agent as well. The erotic romance experiment happened to be the one that struck gold. He'd gotten an agent of his own, and a major book deal. Then, the public loved it. The first novel soared to the top of the charts. He'd been blown away to see his dream come true.

He hadn't realized there'd be so much criticism. Not just bad reviews, but criticism of him as a person. How could a man write about such scandalous acts? Was he some sort of sex-obsessed weirdo? Honestly, he was just really good at telling a story. And this one happened to be dirty.

But because of the judgment he received on a daily basis, he'd learned to keep a low profile. Sometimes he wished he'd kept his pen name secret altogether. His family was mortified. He rarely did public appearances, and he even more rarely told non-industry people what he did for a living. Especially people like Jay. Based on how strongly she'd reacted to the subject of the book, he was pretty sure she wouldn't like that he wrote it. He should have told her anyway.

Something told him she already knew.

Nothing to do but find out. He nodded to the book in Jay's hand. "Do you mind telling me where you got that?"

"Um. Your closet?" She said it like a question and then corrected herself. "I mean, I got it from your closet."

Of all the answers he'd expected to hear, that wasn't one of them. "My closet?"

"I'm sorry. I snooped." Her gaze was downcast, seemingly studying his bare feet.

"You went through my closet? Through my personal things?" All the worry he had about her reaction to his occupation dissipated as something else took over—fury. Maybe it was simply a defense mechanism acting so that he didn't have to deal with the guilt of hiding the truth from her, but he was outraged. His privacy was important. It was crucial. It was all he had. "You had no right to do that."

"I know." At least she looked anguished about it. "I know! I said I was sorry. I didn't even mean to."

Sorry? He'd been betrayed and all she had was *sorry*? She didn't fucking *mean to*? It felt like a knife had been jabbed in his gut. It was cliché, but now he understood the reason the saying existed. Because that's what this pain felt like.

"You can't imagine how much this hurts, Jay."

She met his accusation with blazing eyes. "Probably as much as it hurts that you didn't think you could share this with me."

Well, she had a point there.

They stood in a silent stare-off as Jay ran a hand through her short hair. A million things came to his head to say—apologies, explanations, retractions. Nothing seemed right.

It was Jay who spoke first. "Look, I know it was wrong, Noah. I do. I didn't really mean to be snooping. I was looking for a shirt and the books were underneath and I thought they were drugs and you never told me what you do for a living, so I figured that this must be it so I sorta swiped one so I could investigate it further, and, well, yay, it's not drugs."

He remembered the shirt she'd been wearing that morning. It *had* been in the closet before that. Directly on top of the box. The box that was open for anyone looking to see into. It would have been hard for her to miss it.

Wait. Did she say . . . ? "You thought I was a drug dealer?"

She let out a strangled sort of croak. "Yeah. Funny, right?"

"Because you thought my books looked like drugs?"

"Bricks of cocaine. Yeah."

He burst into laughter. It was too ridiculous not to. "Why on earth would you assume that?"

"Because there's a rash of drug crime here. And why else would someone have packages wrapped up in brown paper?"

His anger had faded in the exchange. How could it not? He shook his head and tried to explain. "I send those for giveaways. People don't always want other people—"

"—to know what they're reading," she finished with him. "Got it. Now. This also makes more sense when I think about that cougar you were talking to. She wanted you to sign her book, not refill her coke stash."

"Yeah, I don't get recognized on the street very often, but my fans are very sweet. I always take a moment for them when they do notice me. No cocaine involved."

She bit her lip. "So I did something shitty, and you can punish me for it later if you want to, but can we talk about the more important issue here?"

There was a more important issue than a possibly trafficking charge? Good grief. But. Her suggestion of punishment had his thoughts drifting naughtily. Probably not the right time, but he was a guy, after all.

Jay held up the book, flashing it in his face as if he'd never seen it. "You wrote this, Noah. You wrote this and you didn't tell me."

She already knew, so why was it still so hard to admit?

And why was it hard to admit at all? This was his work. He wasn't ashamed. In fact, he loved his fucking book. And so did half the women in Boston. Like that blond lady, like a million more like her. He threw his shoulders back. "Yeah, I wrote it. I write sexy books. And I read them, too. And I didn't tell you because I knew you'd get all narrow-minded again, and I'm tired of it, Jaylene. Not just from you, but from everyone. It's why I don't tell people. I don't tell anyone." He exhaled heavily, as if the weight of his sigh could somehow convey all his feelings to her. She made a face.

"I wish I could say that I didn't deserve that, but I can't. I've been wrong about things. I see that now. But I've tried to change. I've trusted you, and you didn't trust me. Were you going to keep this from me forever?" Her own sigh was just as weighty as his, reminding him that he wasn't the only one feeling betrayed.

"Maybe." No, he would have told her. Eventually. Probably. But he was still feeling a tad bit contrary.

"That's no way to have a relationship. Keeping secrets from each other? I thought you wanted to have something real. Or was I mistaken about that, too?" Her arms crossed, as if to protect her heart. It broke his.

"No. No, you weren't mistaken. I *do* want to have something real with you." His hands moved futilely, wanting to hold her, to reassure her, but knowing it wasn't going to be okay.

"Good. Because I want to have something real with you, too."

"You do?" He froze, certain he'd misheard that. Judgey Jay still wanted him, even after this?

"Yes. I do. Which is why I spent all evening reading your book. It's good, Noah. It's really good." Her arms fell to her sides, the book no longer a barrier between them.

"You liked it?" He still couldn't believe what he was hearing.

"I loved it." She smiled, for the first time, and his heart started to put itself back together.

"Even though you think it's demeaning to women?" he clarified.

"It's not demeaning to women. I made some incorrect assumptions." Her grin spread, those cherry-red lips exposing her white teeth. Maybe instead of a barrier, his book could be a bridge.

"You know what they say about assumptions. . . ." He grinned back, already planning their makeup sex. Maybe it was too soon, but his relief was so palpable.

She laughed. "It's assume, you dope. It doesn't work with the word assumption. Some writer."

"You got my reference, though. And am I right that you're now thinking about my ass?"

"I'm thinking you *are* an ass." She crossed to him and threw her arms around his neck.

Without hesitation, he pulled her closer, wrapping her into his embrace. Finally, he could show her how sorry he was. Yeah, he should have done this awhile ago. Forward women were definitely awesome.

"Is this okay?" she asked, her face so near he could feel her breath on his skin.

"Well, you went through my stuff and I kept secrets from you but we've both apologized now so I'd say we're okay." More than okay, judging from the arousal he could feel moving between them in waves.

"Except, I don't think you actually apologized." She tipped her head back to fake-glare.

"Oh, right. I'm sorry I didn't tell you, Jaylene. There are a great many people who *assume*"—he stressed the word on purpose—"that if you write erotic romance that you're a pervert or less intelligent or—"

"—an oppressor of women?" It was cute how she poked at herself. Much as he was—okay, finish the conversation first, he reminded himself.

"Actually, you were the first who assumed that." He rubbed his nose along the length of hers. "I don't usually tell people because I don't care what they think of me. I like what I do. I'm good at it. But, the reason I didn't tell you was for just the opposite reason—I *do* care what you think about me. I like you."

She drew in a soft breath.

"I mean, I *really* like you, Jaylene. And I knew how you felt about erotic romance books. And I was afraid that if you knew that I wrote them, then that would be the end of us." Fuck too soon. He was going to lay all his cards on the table. It was time to be real.

"So you *assumed*? Is that okay?" She teased gently, nipping him on the neck. She was apparently going to take advantage of this brief respite in power play. He wasn't at all upset.

"You got me," he murmured. "Not okay, I know that now."

"It's understandable." She pulled back to meet his eyes. "But actually I meant, is this okay that I'm touching you? Because you didn't give me permission." As if he hadn't noticed.

"We aren't in the bedroom." As if he hadn't noticed that either.

She fluttered her lids a couple of times and peered up at him.

Oh. He was sure slow sometimes. Maybe he *hadn't* noticed. "Did you want to be in the bedroom?"

Her shrug was meant to be nonchalant, but he could read her like the blurb on the back of his bestselling novel.

"There was a mention of punishment earlier. . . ."

As he tossed her over his shoulder, he reminded himself he had meant to write a book about this. He was already plotting their happy ending as he slammed the bedroom door behind them.

BURN FOR ME

by

Shiloh Walker

Thanks to all of my readers. You all make this so worthwhile.

Thanks to my editor, Monique, for taking a chance on me.

Thanks to Aemelia for the early feedback for the series.

And thank you so much to my family, for the love and support.

You're my world. I thank God for you.

CHAPTER 1

⌒

Blackness wrapped around them, a sheltering embrace as his body moved over hers.

His hunger had an edge tonight.

He'd come to her late, appearing in the darkened doorway of her room and she'd barely had a chance to catch her breath before he was there, strong hands slowly pulling away the covers and then the mattress gave way under his weight.

Now, as his cock swelled inside her, as one palm cupped her hip and angled her up to meet each driving thrust, he buried his face against her neck as he muttered her name.

She gasped out his and had to bite back the words she knew he wouldn't want to hear.

Tangling her hands in his hair, she arched and whimpered as he shifted his angle, moving so that the head of his cock stroked the bundled bed of nerves buried deep inside her and that small adjustment had her panting. Heat blistered her and pleasure consumed her.

"Tate!"

He surged against her, harder. Faster.

She climaxed around him, muffling her sob against his shoulder.

His mouth covered hers, swallowing down that ragged, breathless sound.

Then he stiffened, coming inside her.

She wanted that purse.

Ali Holmes didn't covet a lot of things, but as she stood behind the counter of the Madison Pizza Company, she decided she was going to let herself covet that purse.

It was a safe obsession. Vivid, murder-red, butter-soft leather. It cost almost as much as she made in a week—it would have to. It was a Coach purse. She had an eye for those things, mostly because she obsessed over them. Drooled. Coveted.

Sometimes when she went shopping in Louisville or Lexington, she'd even let herself pet them.

But she wouldn't ever buy one. How in the hell could she buy a purse like that when she could barely afford to put food on the table?

It was a safe enough obsession, because she knew she wouldn't ever go and spend money she couldn't afford to waste on something like a purse, not when her two boys needed shoes, not when she needed to figure out how to fix the roof, and not when she was still scrambling to pay the bills for the appendectomy she'd had to have last winter.

The owner of that gorgeous red purse stood in the doorway, blinking as her eyes adjusted to the dim light after being out in the bright sunny afternoon.

Ali gave herself another second to lust as she gathered up a couple of menus and tried not to notice the way somebody was grinning at her.

"If you keep staring at the purse, she's going to think you plan on mugging her."

Just the sound of that voice was enough to make her heart skip, and maybe it made her knees a little weak, although she managed not to let it show as she turned her head and looked into the dark brown eyes of one Tate Bell, her other obsession.

He wasn't so safe.

Lately, she was starting to think she might have to give him up.

He was like too much chocolate, too much wine. She wanted to gorge on him, but he was oh, so very bad for her. If she could keep herself to just lusting after him, it wouldn't be an issue. Lust was nice. Lust was healthy. But she'd let herself get lost in him. Lost herself *to* him.

Maybe that wouldn't be so bad, if he could do the same.

Tate had . . . commitment issues.

Hell, screw that. Tate had emotional issues.

With a lazy shrug, she said, "Nothing wrong with looking, sugar, right?"

A smile curved his lips.

That smile . . . damn it, that smile was what started it. That was why she'd given in to him in the first place, and all he had to do was flash her that smile at any given time and it made her want to forget herself all over again.

Forget the promises she'd made herself late last night, as she lay in her bed, with the scent of him still on her skin, while her heart split just a little more.

He might share her bed, but he wanted no part of her heart and she knew that.

She knew she needed to pull away from him.

What she didn't know was if she *could*.

"You're doing a lot more than looking at that purse, Ali-girl," he drawled, lifting his sweet tea to his mouth and drinking. His throat worked and she had to look away before she started thinking about pressing her mouth to that strong, tanned line. Before she started thinking about how they'd ended up in the shower last night—he'd been all hot and sweaty from hours spent in his studio and she'd been the same from hours spent hustling pizzas back and forth here at the restaurant.

"Oh?" She cocked a brow. "Just what am I doing?"

"You're practically drooling." He dropped his gaze to her mouth.

Out of reflex, she swiped the back of her hand over her mouth. "I am . . ." Then she rolled her eyes. "You need to finish your lunch and get out of my place, Tate. I've got work to do."

"That was a subtle change of subject. Go on, go back to lusting over pretty purses. I'll pretend not to notice." He winked at her and lifted a slice of pizza to his mouth.

She sighed and turned away.

That was the damn problem. He did notice things. He noticed her lusting for purses, he noticed when she was tired at the end of the day, he noticed when something amused her or annoyed her.

If only he never noticed things, if only he wasn't so amazing with her kids.

There were a thousand *if only*s that had led to her current mess. She might not be in the shape she was in, if only he was just interested in sex; if he would just roll in her bed for a quickie, then back out, maybe life would be easier.

But he cared. He knew her. He saw when she was sad, knew when she was mad.

He saw that she was obsessed with pretty things like Coach purses that she could never afford.

It was that very kind of thing that made it hurt more when he pulled back like he did.

Pushing it out of her head, she moved away from the counter, menus in hand as she flashed a smile at the pretty blonde. "Two?"

"No." The boy at the woman's side gave her a very insulted look. "I'm four."

Ali bit the inside of her lip to keep from grinning. Solemnly, she met his gaze. "Only four? I thought you had to be six, already." He looked only slightly mollified. "I meant are there just two of you eating today?"

Then she shifted her gaze to the woman.

"Yes." The woman grinned back. "Sorry. He's very proud of the big four."

"Can't blame him." Ali winked and led them to a table. "You all in town visiting?"

The lady shot her a glance as she slid into the booth and settled her son. "No. We just moved to town."

"Oh?" The dots connected. Madison was a small town. The small-town grapevine was pretty efficient, probably even more efficient at getting the word around than any other means known to man. Pretty lady, looked like money. Young son. Just moved to town. She cocked a brow. "You bought the old Frampton place."

The woman blinked, confusion in her eyes.

"Big old place, looks out over the river. Surrounded by an old stone wall."

"Ahh." She smiled and curled an arm around her boy's shoulders. "Yes. That's our place."

I wouldn't buy that hellhole if you gave me all the Coach purses in New York City.

Ali kept the words behind her teeth and smiled. "Welcome to Madison. I'm Ali."

Tate tried to pretend he wasn't bothered as she turned away without so much as touching him. But it bothered him. A lot. She treated him like . . .

Fuck. She treated him like he was any other dumbass who came in here just to flirt with her. She gave friendly service with a friendly smile and took his order. That was it.

Okay, maybe they chatted a bit, but they were friends. They'd always chatted a bit.

Nothing had changed.

Wasn't that how he had *wanted* it? Of course it was. He'd helped set up those rules.

Friends, Ali. Just friends. Except when we want more.

But he didn't flirt with his friends when he saw them eyeing a pretty red purse. Shit, other than Ali, he didn't think he'd ever noticed what any of his friends were all that interested in, unless they shared the same interests as him. Although he'd be pretty damn amused if somebody like Guy or Adam showed any sort of interest in something like a Coach purse.

At least he *thought* it was a Coach purse. He'd spent enough time with her to see her curled up over her computer, eyeing them with something akin to longing.

Maybe he should . . .

Stop. That's a little more than friendship.

He couldn't stop eyeing the purse in the mirror attached to the wall behind the bar top. Those things were expensive. Not that he'd paid a lot of attention. He'd just happened to notice. That was all. He wasn't going to hurt over a few hundred dollars, but for Ali, a few hundred dollars meant the kids' school supplies, their shoes, maybe even some groceries.

Scowling, he made himself look away from the purse, focusing on the hunk of pizza he no longer wanted.

Behind him, he could hear Ali's voice, warm and friendly. She didn't just make small talk. That was one of the reasons why people who came here liked her. She actually liked talking to the customers, made them feel welcome.

Of course, quite a few of the guys came in here to stare at her ass.

It was one of the reasons *he* liked coming here. One of the reasons he'd started coming here to begin with, but then, he realized he missed her when she wasn't here. Without even being aware of it, he'd started coming in here on the days she worked, just so he could see her. That slow, subtle flirtation led to something more, although he'd put down the rules, because . . . well. There was only so much he had to give.

Maybe at some point it had started to bug him when he noticed other guys in there were doing the same thing he'd started doing a few years ago. Ogling just how well her ass filled out those jeans.

Guys had always checked her out. Anymore, it pissed him off.

Pretty Ali Holmes . . . his friend. Pretty Ali Holmes, mom of two, part-owner of a small, busy pizza place in small-town America. Ali Holmes, a cute brunette with silken skin and wide, green eyes and the sexiest fucking mouth. Ali Holmes . . . the girl he'd had tucked under his body last night. A little over twelve hours ago, she'd been clutching at his shoulders and gasping for air.

Now she looked at him and talked to him like . . .

He suppressed a groan as he reached up and rubbed the back of his neck. She treated him the same fucking way she treated everybody else here. Exactly the way he'd said he wanted things to be.

She'd been doing that all along, so why was it bothering him more and more?

Why did he get irritated when she eased back if he reached out to touch her hand when she brought him his food?

Why did he get pissed off if she wouldn't lean over the counter to let him kiss her? If she pulled back when he tried to lean over and do it anyway?

Why was he still feeling empty after he'd left her bed last night? It was getting harder and harder to pull away from her, but last night, it had been almost impossible. As he lay there, his face pressed to her hair, their hearts slamming together in unison, he'd thought maybe, just maybe, if he stayed there, right there, the nightmares wouldn't be so bad.

Maybe he could sleep, and not dream.

Maybe he wouldn't wake up with a scream half-choking him.

He knew better. So he'd pulled away, kissed her cheek, and without saying anything, he'd dressed, then left.

Every step of the way, he'd wanted to go back.

He wouldn't risk it, though. Wouldn't risk waking up in her bed, wide-eyed and terrified, while screams rose in his chest.

He wasn't fit company for man or beast this time of year, much less the woman he—

Stop.

He couldn't go down that road, because it was too dangerous. Those were thoughts he didn't allow himself.

Yet somehow, he realized he'd hurt her. The thought of it left him feeling empty inside and he tried to brush it off, but it wasn't as easy as he'd like it to be. Of course, *nothing* with her was as easy as he'd like it to be.

Hell, it wasn't like he hadn't left in the middle of the night. He never stayed.

But last night . . .

He closed his eyes, a fisted hand pressed to his brow as it played through his mind.

He hadn't said a word.

His heart had still been racing when he pulled out of her.

You fucking asshole.

Guilt, raw and ugly, churned inside him.

Lifting his head, he stared into the mirror over the counter, his gaze seeking Ali out. She was taking care of the young family in the booth just behind him.

The woman was probably his age. She looked like money, while the boy at her side looked like mischief squared and he chattered with Ali like he'd known her most of his life. He shifted his gaze to the purse, the one that had made Ali sigh with longing.

Then, because part of him hoped she'd turn her head and look at him, he let his gaze shift back to Ali.

She didn't look at him and that hollow ache in his chest spread. If he was smart, he'd walk away.

He didn't have the strength yet.

Maybe in a few more months.

He'd said that a year ago.

She was acutely aware when he left.

The door shut behind him and she felt it echo inside.

She'd felt the weight of his stare drilling into her.

Part of her had hoped he'd come around, maybe come up to her and try to touch her. Even though she knew if he did, she'd just pull back. He wanted to be friends, right? She wasn't going to let him keep blurring that line when there was only so much he'd give her. When he'd pull back from her in the night when *she* needed him the most.

But he hadn't come to her. He'd just stared at her, long and lingering. She'd felt the weight of that gaze and it had left her skin prickling and her heart racing. Then everything inside her turned to ashes as he left, without saying a word.

Just like last night.

She understood why. Maybe he wouldn't talk about it, but she knew. After three years of being lovers, she understood him better than he realized. Even before they'd become intimate, they'd been friends and he was an idiot if he thought she didn't know what this time of year did to him.

It was hell on him and his sisters.

He thought he kept it hidden, but nothing could hide that kind of pain.

He spent hours at the cemetery, nights awake in his studio. There would be a lot of sleepless nights ahead for him, and then in six, maybe eight weeks, he'd start to shift back to his normal mode. The pain would ease back a bit, for a while. Come Christmas, it would rear its ugly head again, then he'd be himself again come the first week of January or so.

Until summer rolled around.

Then he'd be like this again. Sad, brooding.

Lost.

Pacing the floor while he brooded and wondered. The few hours of sleep he *did* get would be haunted by nightmares.

Not that he'd ever told her about the nightmares.

Jensen had been the first one to let it slip about those, but once or twice, he'd started to drift off to sleep on the rare occasions they'd been together at his place. Although she hadn't mentioned it, she'd seen the evidence of the nightmares then.

They chased him, haunted him.

A hollow ache settled in her heart, but instead of letting herself dwell on it, she kept her mind focused on work. Noah Benningfield had just settled in at his normal spot in the back and she grabbed a Diet Coke for him.

Forcing a cheerfulness she didn't feel, she dropped into the seat across from him.

"Heya, Preach."

He slid her an amused glance and then bent back over the plans spread out in front of him. "Hey, Ali." His golden-brown hair glinted under the lights and his hands, big and strong, held the pages down as he studied . . . whatever it was. It looked like a house plan. Sort of. With little pictures on the side.

"What's that?"

He sighed and rubbed the back of his neck. "Louisa over at the coffee shop wants to make some changes on the work I'm doing over there." Although his face was solemn, his blue eyes laughed at her as he glanced up. "We've only finalized the project three times now."

"Wow. Three? That's pretty decisive . . . for Louisa."

Noah winked at her.

"She asked you if you were going to give her a discount, seeing as how you're a preacher and you're not supposed to profit from worldly things?"

Noah blinked. Then he put down the pen he was holding and leaned back in the chair. "Excuse me?"

She grinned at him. "She was in here with her book group and was telling all of them how she thought it was just *insane* that a preacher would charge so much to renovate the coffee shop. You're a *preacher.* You committed yourself to being poor and meek and mild and here you are, robbing people who only want to make an honest living."

"Robbing people. Yeah, I look like I live in the lap of luxury." He lifted a brow. "I wonder what she'd think if she saw just how much it's going to cost, material-wise, to do the work."

"I imagine she thinks you're going to spread out your hands and turn the bread into boards, Preach."

He rolled his eyes. "I stopped preaching years ago. Even when I *was* preaching, I don't recall ever having that divine power. I was just a youth minister, remember . . . maybe I got left out because of that."

"I remember." She stood up, flicking her finger on the corner of the piece of paper. "You were *my* youth minister . . . Preach. So. You want your normal or are you going to live a little?"

A grin tugged at his lips and she remembered the mad crush she'd had on this man. It had lasted a good long while, too. He'd been one of the few who hadn't tried to totally make her feel worthless when she ended up pregnant in high school. In small-town America, it was still enough to make a girl feel ostracized, but Noah had been there, held her hand, let her talk, asked what she wanted to do.

That had made her fall a little in love with him.

She'd just been a girl then. What she felt now for him was nothing more than friendship.

"Everything okay?" he asked, his blue eyes studying her, seeing clear through her.

She sighed and looked across the half-empty restaurant. Cara was taking care of her side, just a few late-lunch stragglers. Other than the new family, Noah was the only customer she had now that Tate had left.

"Okay?" She shook her head. "I don't know, Preach."

He reached out and covered her hand. "He's a good guy."

A slow, sad smile curved her lips. "Well, at least I improved over Scott, right?"

Noah ran his tongue across his teeth and gave a slow nod. He took his time before he spoke—that was Noah's way. He took his time with just about *everything*. "Scott isn't a happy man. He couldn't have made you, or the boys, happy. The best thing you ever did was leave him, you know. Even if your life is a bit harder on your own."

"Oh, I know that." She slumped back in her chair, checking on the table where the mom sat with her child. "It's just . . . hell. Tate's not really a happy guy, either, you know."

Noah was quiet for a minute. Then he squeezed her hand. "He's happier with you."

What she wouldn't give if she could actually believe that.

She wasn't making Tate happy. She was a distraction for him, a way for him to hide from the demons that chased him. That was it.

"I don't know about that. Maybe I should just simplify and fall for you." She gave him a weak smile. "You're a stand-up guy, right? You like kids. You work hard. Wanna get married?"

He didn't bat an eyelash. "Sure. I'm free tomorrow. Sound good?"

She laughed.

Falling for him wasn't going to be any better than falling for Tate.

He was just as unattainable. Noah barely seemed to realize women even existed. Maybe, though, an unattainable dream would be less painful than . . . what she had with Tate. She needed to quit brooding about this and get to work or she'd be in a funk all day. Clearing her throat, she forced a smile. "Why don't you tell me what you want to eat, then? If we're getting married, you've got to get your schedule cleared."

"I think I'll stick with my usual. Make sure you pick out something pretty for tomorrow." He winked at her. "I'll look for my cleanest pair of blue jeans, okay?"

She left the table laughing.

After she'd put in Noah's order, the pizza for the young family came up. As she made her way over to their table, she caught sight of the scowl on the woman's face. Her name was Trinity—Ali couldn't remember her last name.

"Everything okay?"

Trinity gave her a polite smile. "Yeah, I just . . ." Then her eyes popped wide as Ali deposited the pizza in front of them. "That . . . wow. Okay, that smells amazing. I had my doubts about the pizza. I'm going to be honest. We're from New York and—"

"That's where the best pizza is," the boy chirped up. "No place else can make pizza. They just pretend to."

"Micah . . ." Trinity said, her voice soft while an embarrassed smile settled on her face.

"What? That's what you said at home."

Ali laughed. "It's okay. My dad is *from* New York. Originally. Met my mom years ago, and they got married, but she wanted to come back home . . . this is home. This might be the closest you'll get to New York pizza outside of New York. Definitely the best around here."

She fished out napkins and passed them out. "Anything else?"

"Actually . . ." Trinity slid her a look and pushed the phone toward her. "I have a meeting after we leave here and I can't find the address."

Ali dipped her head to study the phone, as a grin crooked her lips. "Sure. I know where that is. I could probably save you a trip, though. The owner is right over there."

Then she glanced back and called, "Hey, Noah."

The guy glanced over his shoulder.

It was weird, standing there as the two of them locked gazes for the first time. Just a few minutes ago, Ali would have sworn that Noah was all but immune to women. He never dated. Period. The tragedies he had behind him were enough to make any man leery about romance, that much was certain.

But Ali stood there, half-caught between them, while sparks practically set the air on fire.

It was like somebody had hit the two of them with a lead pipe. That was how stunned they both looked.

Then the little boy leaned over, excitedly shoving a picture under his mother's nose.

The moment shattered.

Ali turned away, silently mouthing to herself. *Whoa* . . .

CHAPTER 2

⌒

A hot wind blew off the river.

He shouldn't be here.

If he had any kind of brains at all, he'd be back at the shop, working on the mayor's prized BMW or maybe the Indian he was restoring. If not that, there were always cars needing their damn tune-ups and oil changes and shit. The stuff he had to do to pay the bills so he could spend his nights doing what he really wanted to do—locked up in his studio with a blowtorch and bits and pieces of metal that he twisted into endless, bizarre creations. They sold at some of the small places in town and a few were even in art galleries in some of the bigger cities in the region.

Sometimes he'd get lucky and get a commissioned piece and he actually had one of those he could be working on.

His heart had led him here.

Tate knew, in his gut, he'd be spending a lot of time here over the next few weeks.

There was no other place for him.

Liar. There is one place you could be. If you'd just let it happen.
Ali.

Yeah. He could be with her and the voices that raged in the back of his mind would go silent. He could wrap his arms around her, find some small measure of peace from the demons that had chased him for the past fifteen years. The guilt that ripped at him. He could watch her boys play and maybe they could toss the ball around awhile. He could be there, be happy . . . except happy was the last thing he needed.

The last thing he deserved.

Pushing the thoughts of her aside, Tate knelt down and laid a single rose—yellow, his mother's favorite color—down.

"Happy birthday, Mom."

There was no body buried in the plot. A month after her birthday, she'd disappeared. She'd been thirty-eight years old and she'd left behind three children. Tate, Jensen, and Chrissie.

It had taken years to even get a headstone erected in the small cemetery. Their dad, the bastard, had waited years before he even *tried* to get her declared dead. Maybe he thought it made him look innocent. Maybe he thought that giving them the money from her life insurance policy would make up for taking her from them.

Tate didn't know.

The simple stone offered no closure, no comfort.

He brushed his fingers down the curve of the stone and swallowed the knot rising in his throat.

Closure.

What the fuck was that?

Anger, bitterness, grief, things that had remained rooted in his heart for fifteen years twisted inside him even as he tried to avoid letting his mind take that dark, winding road.

"*. . . trailer trash . . .*"

His mother's stricken face, even as she tried not to let it show. The way she looked at her three children and then back at her husband.

"We can't do this right now, Doug. Not in front of the kids, okay?"
The way his dad had laughed, that bitter, ugly laugh.
"We're doing it now, you. You always want to fight? Fine. Now we fight."
"I don't want to fight in front of the kids, you son of a bitch."

A sound from behind him tore him out of his reverie and Tate rose, blinking back the burn of tears that threatened. Oddly enough, the grief that had been clogging his throat eased up as he saw who was on the path behind him.

His dad.

Son of a bitch.

The monster who'd taken his mother away.

"What are you doing here?"

Douglass Bell inclined his head. "I'm here to see my wife." He tried to smile but as Tate continued to glare at him, Doug just sighed and reached up, rubbing a hand across his head. "How have you been, Tate?"

Ignoring his father's question, he focused on the first thing Doug had said.

"Here to see your *wife*?"

Disgust flooded him. Closing the distance between them, he glared down at the shorter man. He stood six foot three, a good six inches taller than his father. His height had come from his mother's side of the family and he used it to good advantage just then, but Doug didn't look away, didn't back down. "You don't get to call her your wife. You lost that right when you killed her."

"Tate . . ." Doug shook his head. "I didn't kill your mother. I loved her."

Shooting out a hand, he closed it over the front of his dad's T-shirt. The material was old and faded and it stretched under Tate's hand. Jerking his father close, he glared down at him. "You loved her. Yeah, that's why one of the last things I remember you ever saying to her was *trailer trash*. That's how you talk to the woman you love, Dad?"

"We had a fight," Doug said, his voice rough. "You are never going to understand how much I regret that night. But it doesn't change the fact that I didn't kill her. I loved your mother."

"Stop it," Tate said. "Just . . ."

Without saying anything else, he shouldered past his father, trying to ignore the ghosts and demons shouting inside his head. Too many ghosts. Too many demons.

Ali came around the corner, her feet tired, her back aching. She practically stopped in her tracks at the sight of the man across the street, striding out of the small cemetery.

Her boys, whooping and carrying on like a couple of miniature monsters, were already at the gate in front of their house and they didn't see him.

A good thing, considering the look on his face.

The crack in her heart widened.

Seeing him now, striding out of the cemetery, wasn't a surprise.

Nor was she surprised to see the older man, standing with his head bowed and shoulders slumped. Doug Bell looked like he carried the weight of the world on his shoulders.

Madison had more than its share of misery, and the Bell family was one of the sadder stories. Tate and his sisters had lost their mother, Nichole, almost fifteen years ago. Ali's heart ached as she watched him walk away from his mother's headstone, the grave empty, because her body had never been found.

Although Tate would never want to hear it, Ali's heart ached for Doug, too.

She'd seen the man grieving by the graveside too often. He hadn't killed his wife. Ali knew it, in her heart.

Tate caught sight of her and slowed. For a second, she thought he'd just change direction and she readied herself for that subtle rejection, but he didn't. He walked right up to her and she mentally feasted on the sight of him even as she tried to brace herself.

He needed a haircut. The strands, dark, dark brown, hung near to his shoulders now, held out of his face by a rubber band. She loved pulling it free, fisting her hands in his hair as he hovered over her and drove inside. She loved brushing it back from his face when he put his head in her lap. She loved watching the way he tied it back from his face when he was working on one of the bikes he liked to rebuild— a hobby more than anything else—or when he was trying to coax a few more months out of her busted-up car. She really loved the way he looked when he was in his studio creating one of those warped creations he called art. His face would be hidden by whatever he called the shield thing he wore to protect him from the sparks from his blowtorch, but she knew, under it his face would be a mask of intensity. Sweat would dampen his shirt, gleam along his muscles. Her belly tightened just thinking about it.

If she was honest, there was very little about Tate that she didn't love.

Too bad that wasn't what he wanted from her.

He came to a stop in front of her just as her boys caught sight of him.

"Tate!" They shrieked out his name and came tumbling out of the yard, barreling in his direction.

A grin split his face and she wished she could react the way they did, just run toward him and see his face light up like that.

While they waited for the kids to join them, she asked softly, "How are you doing today?"

"Fine." He shrugged restlessly.

She should have let it go. She knew that. Sliding her gaze past him, she looked at the cemetery, her gaze lingering on Doug. Then she looked back at Tate. "No, you're not."

A dark brow arched up but before he could respond, her oldest,

Joey, reached them, out of breath and panting. "I'm going to a birthday party. I'm staying up until midnight."

"Is that a fact?" Tate reached out and nudged him in the shoulder. "Just who is having a birthday?"

"Ryan Dolenz. He's nine. He lives up on the hill and we're making burgers and swimming and staying up all night."

"Sounds like a plan, Joey. Eat some cake for me." He rubbed his hand across Joey's already tousled blond hair.

"I want cake." Nolan finally reached them, his eyes big and solemn. He leaned against Ali's leg, glaring at Joey. "I want to go to the party, too."

"You can't. You're a baby."

"I am *not!*"

Before a fight could break out, Ali stepped between them. "We're staying up late on our own, Nolan, remember? Cookies? *Avengers?*"

Tate slid his palm down her spine, settled it low on her hip. That light caress sent a shiver through her. "That sounds like a fun party."

"You're welcome to join us."

She'd made the offer before. She expected the same response she always got. He'd come by and work on her car. He'd come by on the weekends and see her sometimes, play with the boys. He'd slip in once the boys went to bed . . . and they'd have their own private party.

But he never did anything that might be construed as *serious* . . . no dinner dates. No dates period. Nothing that might lead the kids to thinking there was anything going on—that was how *he* phrased it. She'd had to bite her lip to keep from telling him he was an idiot. Kids were smarter than people thought and they'd draw their own conclusions.

When he didn't answer right away, she moved in closer and reached up to brush his hair back from his brow. His eyes came to rest on hers and she asked, "Wanna come over tonight?"

A sad smile tugged at his lips and he shrugged, gazing out over the river. "I don't think I'm good company right now, Ali." He dipped his head and pressed a kiss to her lips, quick and light.

Before he could back away, she caught his shirt, fisted her hand in it. "Maybe that's why you need company. Today's not a good day for you to be alone."

"I'll be fine."

Then he pulled back and without saying anything else, he left.

Sighing, she watched him for a moment. Of course he'd be *fine* . . . or fine enough.

He'd be angry. Lonely. Hurting.

He'd get by . . . alone. Just like always.

All without letting her in.

It's not going to happen, she told herself.

It wouldn't happen . . . and as long as she kept waiting for him to give her some scrap of *something,* she'd wait around, settling for next to nothing.

Maybe it was time to let go.

It was a thought that ripped her heart almost in two.

Let go . . . she tried to imagine going through the days without having him to look forward to. Seeing him walking through town and know that he wasn't hers. Not in any way.

A knot swelled inside her chest and the pain was almost enough to have her gasping for air.

Right now, in some small way, he was hers. When he lay against her in the night, that long, hard body pressed to hers, his hand tangled in her hair while their bodies cooled and their breath calmed, he *felt* like hers.

As he continued to walk away, without even looking back, she had to wonder . . . was it enough anymore?

She just didn't know.

CHAPTER 3

"...*just get the hell out*..."

Tate stood in his studio.

His tools lay spread out in front of him.

The materials he needed to make something were right there. If he could just bring an image of something to mind, some remnant of the chaos, he could make this darkness inside him spill out. Purge himself.

He'd always been able to lose himself in his art, but right now, even that escape seemed to be closed to him.

He'd tried to sleep and the nightmares sent him gasping back into awareness before he'd managed even an hour.

It wasn't late—he hadn't slept much the night before and he'd thought he could crash for a while and then work the night through, but screw that idea.

Now, standing in the dark garage he'd converted into a work area, he tried to think past the nightmares so he could work.

But he couldn't.

"I loved your mother . . ."

"You son of a bitch," he rasped.

That bastard could talk to him about love?

How in the hell could he talk about love?

He'd taken her away—

Grief, an awful storm of it rose inside him and he was tempted to grab his blowtorch and use it, not to *create*, but to destroy. Because he didn't trust himself not to do it, he locked himself out of the studio and stormed away from his home. He had no destination in mind, not right away.

He just had to move.

Images of his mother's face flashed in front of him.

Usually, the memories were faded, softened by time, but on nights like tonight, they were keen as a blade. The screams were just as loud, her voice, angry and hurt, raged on while his father's, that big, deep voice, bellowed out, full of bile and ugliness.

"Trailer trash . . . just get on out . . . "

Minutes ticked by into hours.

He had no idea how long he walked, how far.

He found himself standing in front of Ali's.

Dully, he stared at the brightly lit windows. Inside, they'd be watching *The Avengers* and eating cookies.

The simplicity of it called to him and more than anything, he wanted to be in there, his arms wrapped around Ali. And Nolan. Nolan would probably already be asleep and that was just fine. Having that kid curled up on his lap while they finished off the movie and cookies, that sounded like . . . heaven.

"Fuck." He stared at the sky, where a thousand stars shone down on him.

He shouldn't be here.

It was the only place he wanted to be—the only place he'd ever found any peace at all.

⌣

Nolan hadn't even made it to *Puny God . . . smash, smash, smash . . .*

Ali sat in the darkened room, watching Bruce Banner as the Hulk smash Loki into the floor. Her son had his face buried against her thigh and she was probably going to have to treat the khakis she wore for stains from the icing that had been on the cookies, but that was okay.

In the hours since Tate had walked away . . . *again* . . . she realized she had to change things. Her life, as it was, sort of sucked. She had her boys, and she loved them. She had her job, which she liked and at some point, she'd take over the pizza place from her parents, but that wasn't the problem.

She was *lonely*. Deep inside, in a place that just couldn't be filled with a girls' day out, or hugs from her kids, or a talk with her mom. She was *lonely*. She loved Tate and what she wanted, more than anything, was for him to fill that void.

It would never happen. Because he wouldn't let it.

This couldn't be all she'd ever have in her life . . . a job that wore her out and a guy who'd only be there when he'd let himself.

She wanted . . . *no*, she *needed* more than that.

As long as he was around, though, she wouldn't ever let herself look for anybody else.

I can't believe I'm thinking about doing this. It was a bitter, ugly pain that had settled inside her chest and now that Nolan was asleep, she let herself really acknowledge it. Once he was in bed, she was going to lock herself in her room, run a hot bath, and . . . she swallowed and dropped her head onto the back of the couch.

Cry her damn eyes out. That was what she was going to do.

She was getting ready to boot Tate out of her life and it was going to break her heart.

Half-dead inside already, she watched as Tony Stark shot up into the sky, through a narrow little opening, and tears tried to form, but she blinked them back. No. No tears now. Not until later. Once the choice was made, she'd bawl. After she'd told him, she'd bawl.

Not while her son was sprawled asleep on her lap.

Later, though . . .

Then she heard the door open and her heart skipped a few dozen beats. Sucking in a deep breath, she turned her head just as he appeared in the doorway, his shadow falling across the floor.

Her bruised, practically bleeding heart gave a feeble, desperate jump.

The hand that lay in her lap closed into a fist.

Now. He was here *now*.

This . . .

She was right.

This was all they'd ever have. It was almost ten. He'd come here now when it was late, and Nolan was asleep. He'd hang around for a couple of hours and then he'd disappear again.

All but breathless as the pain slammed into her, she looked back at the TV. *I can't do this anymore.*

The floorboards creaked under him as he came toward her and settled down on the couch next to her. Her body shifted toward his as the cushions gave under his weight and the scent of him wrapped around her. The longing inside her spread. *You son of a bitch.* Part of her wanted to shove him away from her. The other part wanted to cling to him, wanted to beg.

Instead she just sat there as he reached out and brushed Nolan's hair back from his face.

"How long did he last?"

"Didn't manage to make it to his favorite part." *Wow. Go me.* Her voice was calm, level even. No sign of the misery she felt inside.

"'Smash, smash, smash . . . *puny god.*'" Tate's low, easy voice sent a shiver down her spine. He curled his arm around her shoulders, drawing her against him.

The words she needed to say rose in her throat. *I think you should leave, Tate . . . we need to talk. This isn't working . . .*

Already, her resolve was melting.

His strength, his warmth, seeped into her body and she closed her eyes, letting herself take all of that in, one more time. Once she said those words, though, that was *it*. She'd never have him here, in her quiet, dark house while her boys slept and they talked softly. She'd never guide him to her room, never feel his hands on her . . .

I'm not ready.

Sam, the mutt Nolan and Joey had picked out last year, came trotting in and she glanced at him. *Traitor.* Of course the dogs hadn't warned her . . . they never did. They were used to him and never barked when he came in, but tonight, she could have used the warning.

Blowing out a slow breath, she looked down at Nolan's small face and brushed his hair back from his face. The sight of him helped her to steel herself. It didn't *matter* if she wasn't ready. It was time.

She wasn't just making this decision for herself. Her kids adored Tate and they were already too attached. He wouldn't ever let anything more come of it.

It wasn't fair. Not to them.

"How did the cookies go?"

"Well. There are cookies and icing . . . they went rather well. I think we have a dozen left." Her heart banged against her ribs as he slid his hand up to her neck, a light teasing caress that sent a shiver through her. As he leaned in and nuzzled her, she had to bite back a gasp. "You can grab some if you want. You know where they are."

"I'm not hungry." His thumb stroked over her skin. His voice had that rich, almost velvety undertone that spoke of a hunger, all right, it was just a deeper, more basic hunger.

She had to close her hand into a fist to keep from reaching out and pulling the tie from his hair, feel those silken brown strands tumble around her hands.

This has to stop.

He was never going to be able to give her more than what he'd already given her and she so desperately needed more.

Blindly, she watched the rest of the movie, her son asleep in her lap while she mentally rehearsed what she had to say. Her heart felt like it had turned to stone and Tate sat there, completely, blissfully unaware.

Ending it . . . now.

How could she do this *now*?

He was raw, and she knew it, dealing with his mom's birthday, and the anniversary of his mother's disappearance hovering just a few short weeks away.

As Fury was addressing the council and assuring them that the Avengers would be around to kick righteous ass when needed, Tate shifted on the couch and slid his arms under Nolan's warm, boneless body. "I'll get him to bed."

She stayed where she was, letting him.

She wasn't going to watch. Some part of her had clung to hope, seeing how he was with her kids—she knew he loved them and maybe that was why she'd hoped all this time. He loved her kids . . . but he didn't love her. Maybe he wouldn't let himself.

Once he was out of the room, she rose and headed to the kitchen, calling the dogs. As they came running, she opened the back door, resting against the doorjamb as they disappeared out into the night.

Pain practically ripped her in two as she stood there, her heart beating in slow, dull beats and bitterness lay like ashes on her tongue. Eyes closed, she sucked in one slow breath after another.

I have to end this. I have to.

A warm hand brushed down her spine.

She just barely managed to bite back the sob as it rose inside her.

"What's wrong?"

She waited a few seconds before she responded, and still her voice was rough and husky as she murmured, "Who said something was wrong?"

"It's what you haven't said." He slid an arm around her waist.

That simple gesture twisted her heart in her chest. He pulled her back against him as the dogs came running back inside. She let the door bang shut as he pulled her closer, tucking her against his larger frame.

He slid his hand into her hair, tangling it around his fingers.

We can't do this anymore.

She opened her mouth to say it, the words hovering on the tip of her tongue, but she couldn't force them out.

Tate turned her around, his brown eyes boring into hers as he backed her up against the wall.

Stroking one hand up her side, he slid it under her shirt and the heat of his hand on her flesh was a shocking, brutal pleasure. After three years, she should be used to this. She knew she should. It shouldn't feel like she was cutting out a part of herself to think about pushing him away.

Just do it.

But then, as she tried to brace herself to do just that, he dipped his head and rubbed his cheek against hers. There was no deep, breath-stealing kiss. She might have been able to find the strength to stand against the want. She *always* wanted him and she had to find a way to live without that. The strength drained out of her legs and she had to brace her body against the wall just to stay upright.

His gentleness was even harder to handle just then. If he had just pulled her against him, shown her all the heat and hunger that raged inside, *then* she might have been able to handle it.

"What's wrong, Ali?" he whispered, his lips moving against her skin. "You look so sad. I hate it when you're sad."

She fisted her hands in his shirt and tried to force the words out.

We need to end this.

"It's because of . . ." He paused and she heard him swallow, felt the uneven ragged motion of his chest. "Hell, I've been an ass the past week. I know I have. I'm sorry."

Don't, she thought. *Please don't make this any harder.*

His arms came around her and he tucked her closer. "I'm trying not to be. It's just—"

His body spasmed.

Ali felt her heart wrench in her chest as a harsh, ragged sob ripped out of him.

You son of a bitch. Don't do this to me now. Closing her eyes, she pressed her brow to his chest and then slid a hand up to cup his cheek. Under her hand, she felt the rough stubble rasp against her palm. "Tate, don't."

"If you're nice to me after I've been an asshole . . . hell." He pressed a kiss to her palm. "I don't deserve it. I'm just ragged right now. But I shouldn't be taking it out on you. I'm sorry I've been doing it."

Taking it out on me. She wanted to laugh at the insanity of it. If only he *would* take some of his grief out on her. Maybe then she could help him with it. But all he ever did was bottle everything up. Battered, torn, she sagged against him even as she tried to find the strength to pull away.

Ali sighed against him and some of that tension faded out of her.

A fear he couldn't fully understand eased inside him and he pressed his lips to her neck. He breathed in the scent of her, almost drunk on it already. Warm and soft, she smelled like cookies and coffee and her. Soft, sweet Ali. Her body was the sweetest pleasure he'd ever known, and all he wanted to do was hold her, get lost in her.

"Don't give up on me. I'm trying."

Her hand curved around his neck.

"Don't give up on you." She was quiet for a moment, then she slowly eased back, eyeing him with a look he couldn't even begin to understand.

It left a tightness in his chest, though, and that fear came rushing back at him. He wanted to grab her back and hold her against him, but his mind was already processing what he'd just let slip out.

What in the fuck was he thinking? Why had he said that?

"Tate, giving up on you would imply we *had* something to give up on." Smiling sadly, she shook her head and moved over to the fridge. "We don't. We're friends. Sometimes, we have sex."

Sex.

No. He'd had *sex* before.

What he had when he was with Ali was a lot more than sex.

She pulled the fridge open and grabbed a bottle of wine from the shelf. He stood there in silence as she poured a glass. "You're asking me not to give up on a friends-with-benefits thing, basically." She shrugged and lifted the glass to her lips. "That's easy enough. I don't give up on my—"

He closed the distance between them and slammed his hands down on the counter on either side of her. *Friends.* Yeah, so maybe he'd been the one to suggest this thing they had between them, but she had to realize how much things had changed. He couldn't be the only one to see it. They'd slid past friends a long time ago.

"We're more than friends," he growled.

She stared at him over the rim of her glass, her soft green eyes distant as the stars.

"No. We're not. Friends is all you wanted. *Friends* is all you'll ever give me." The look in her eyes sent a spike straight through his heart.

"I . . ." He closed his mouth, tried to figure out what to say to that. Something inside him twisted. Panic fluttered inside but he shoved it down. "Ali, we . . . we're more than friends. You know you matter to me."

"I matter to you," she echoed, her voice hollow. Then she turned away, staring out the window into the night. "You know something? Scott said that very same thing to me once. But neither the kids nor I mattered enough. Not to him."

Those simple words knocked the breath right out of him. Stunned, he backed up a step, leaned against the door as he stared at her. His voice came out in a gruff rasp. "Ali, what do you want from me?"

"I guess I want to matter *more*." She lowered her head, staring at the counter where her hands rested. She clenched them into fists. Tight, bloodless fists. "I'd . . . hell. I guess I'd like a man who actually wants to *be* with me. Not just for sex, but for *real*."

"I do want that."

She turned her head, stared at him. "Do you?"

"Fuck, I just said I did," he snapped, shoving away from the wall and closing the distance between them. "What the hell is going on? What are you getting at?"

Slowly, she turned to face him, her face quiet, her eyes sad. He went to cup her cheek, but she pulled back, staring at the wall.

"Is this because of . . ." He fumbled for the words, remembering how callous he'd been, how foolish and blind. "Is it because of the other night?"

"Oh, Tate. This is about a lot more than just one night," she said, slowly turning to look at him.

It hit him, then. He got it, and it was like she'd taken a knife from the butcher block sitting a few inches from her hand. The pain was sharp, piercing, and unending. She was done. That's what this was about. She was done.

Staring into her pretty green eyes, while that pain tore into him again and again, only one thought managed to cut through it.

Like hell.

He closed his hands around her hips and boosted her up onto the kitchen counter. "No," he said, his voice gruff and ragged as he pushed her thighs apart and moved closer. He slid one hand along until he could palm her butt and then he yanked her against him and he watched the heat bloom in her eyes, felt the slow, subtle tremor that went through her.

Her skin went the color of a rose, low on her chest, bared by the skinny-strapped shirt she wore and he knew if he pulled it away, that faint rush of color would go all the way down to her breasts.

"No," he said again. "This is *more* than friendship."

The need to strip her clothes away, climb on top of her, feel her close around him was strong, grabbing him by the balls—she would feel it, he knew that. He could show her just how much *more* this was.

"More than friendship." Her lids drooped while that blush of color crept up her neck, then to her cheeks. Through her lashes, she watched him, all the while arching back so that the heat of her sex brushed against his cock. "This? This is just sex."

He opened his mouth, the word *no* trying to form.

She slid a hand down his chest, toyed with the button of his jeans. "Sex. It's good sex, it's crazy sex, and it makes me forget who I am sometimes."

His eyes all but crossed as she freed the button and then dragged the zipper down. Once she had room, she reached inside his shorts, closed her hand around his cock, and dragged it up, down. Each touch was a sweet, sweet torture and he found himself arching into her touch, even as he wanted to drag himself away.

Her eyes were distant, remote. "But this . . . this is all we really have."

He caught her wrist and pulled it back, fury and need an ugly mix inside him. Slamming her wrist to the cabinet by her head, he leaned in, his mouth just a breath away. "It's a hell of a lot more than just sex," he rasped, even as the need for her turned into a scream in his blood. "*Sex* is easy."

"Easy?" She stared at him, her eyes mocking. "Easy. Like you climbing on top of me the other night and then pulling away when I was still wet from you. Easy. Like you walking away because staying is that much harder."

He snarled. "You don't understand."

"Of course I don't." She jerked her chin up. "You won't *tell* me."

"That . . ." He shook his head, the words tripping him up. "Do you think I don't *want* to be with you? It's not that simple, Ali. But if it was just *sex,* I could get that anywhere. What I *want* is this."

He slanted his mouth over hers, desperation and desire driving him. He couldn't explain it, because she'd never understand. She hadn't been there that night, and she hadn't lived inside his skin all these years.

He could show her how he felt, though, how he wanted her.

She had to see—

She worked her hands between them and shoved him back, panting. Her hair tumbled into her face and the soft green of her eyes glinted hard as glass.

"Just sex," she said again, shaking her head. "Everybody has their preferences, you idiot. Hell, I had a favorite vibrator before you came along and I bet you had a preference for one hand over the other. That doesn't *mean* anything."

Spinning away, he stared at the floor, shame and misery gathering inside. His skin felt tight, itchy. "Fuck. I . . . I'm sorry."

Silence flooded the room and slowly, he turned, stared at her. The hollow look in her eyes cut through him like a poisoned blade. Swallowing around the knot in his throat, he shifted his gaze away. "If it was just sex, I wouldn't want to be with you all the time. I do. If it was just sex, I wouldn't hang around your restaurant four or five days a week, and I wouldn't spend half my weekend here. You've got to know it's more than that, Ali-girl."

A sigh escaped her and he turned his head to see her slip off the counter, smoothing her clothes down, pushing her hair back from her face. "I know you *feel* more. But you only give me so much. It's not enough anymore."

Frustration and fear tangled, twisted inside him. He spun back around to glare at her. "What in the fuck do you *want*?"

"I want more," she said simply. "More than this. More than you showing up at my door when I'm ready to put the kids down. More than you staying long enough to crawl on top of me, and then when you're done, you roll off and disappear until the next time. This . . . friends-with-benefits thing isn't enough anymore."

Swearing, he drove his hands through his hair. "That's not *telling* me shit. We *have* more." He went to her, and instead of *taking* this time, he tried seducing, cupping her face in his hands and pressing a soft, sweet kiss to her mouth, hoping to feel her sigh against him, hoping to feel her body yield to his.

Her breasts were a soft, sweet weight against his chest, her belly warm against his cock.

But as he stroked his tongue along the full curve of her lower lip, as he dipped his tongue into her mouth, all she did was stand there.

"Nobody else makes me feel like you do." He pressed his brow to hers. "You know I care about you. You care about me. What else do you want?"

"*More*," she said, her voice low. "Stay the night. Talk to me. Give me *something*."

He clenched his jaw. *Stay the night—*

Give her something. That was the scariest part of all. Because she wasn't talking about gifts.

"Ali." A vise closed around his throat as he stared at her.

She jerked her chin up and he knew, then and there, if he couldn't give in, if he couldn't find a way to do this, he might as well turn away and walk now. "The whole town will talk if I stay the night, Ali-girl." He floundered for a logical reason to explain why he shouldn't. An excuse. It was just an excuse and he knew it as he reached up to cup her cheek, stroke his thumb across her full lower lip.

"They've been talking about me off and on ever since I got knocked up in high school." She shrugged and reached up, curling her hand around his wrist. "I'm not worried about it. But it's not just that. Are you going to stop acting like we're *buddies*? I want . . ."

Her voice skipped and then steadied as she met his eyes. She guided his hand down and he curled it into a fist, impotent and useless.

"I need more," she said, her voice soft, her gaze steely. "I *deserve* more. I want a man in my life who doesn't mind showing up at my door on a Friday night and taking me out to dinner. Somebody who might think about being *more* in my life, later on down the road."

"I have no problem taking you out to dinner." It made him nervous as hell, if he was honest, but he'd rather do that than lose her. He'd been so careful, all his life, never to let anybody in, but he'd messed up with her. She'd gotten in past his walls and now he couldn't change that.

He had to change something, though, and fast. Or he'd lose her.

He'd lost too much and there was so little left already.

She continued to watch him, her gaze somber. "What about when it's time for the next step?" she asked softly.

Wary, he watched her.

"What next step?"

"Yeah." She nudged him back and eased away from the counter. She took her wineglass and tossed it back like it was whiskey. Over her shoulder, she looked at him, her eyes glinting in the dim light, dark brown hair framing her pretty face, her mouth unsmiling. "The next step, Tate."

Then she turned to face him and he never had a chance to brace himself as she gave him a sucker punch that sent him reeling.

"You think I *care* about you? Screw that. I'm in love with you." Her eyes flashed as she glared at him. "I have been for a long time. But . . .

that's not enough. Sooner or later, I want a man in my life who is going to want to be a *part* of my life. A part of my kids' lives. Forever. I want somebody who might want to think about marrying me. Being a father to my kids. I want more than . . . this."

I'm in love with you. The words left him reeling. His heart slammed against his ribs. In the back of his mind, voices screamed. Terror tried to choke him.

"I loved your mother."

"Trailer trash."

"We can't do this here—"

No. Not love. She couldn't . . .

But even under the terror, something sweet, something powerful shifted, tried to grow. He refused to look at it. He couldn't.

Pushing it back down, he buried it. "Ali," he said, his voice raw. "You . . . look. That's . . . it's too much. I'm a bad bet for that sort of thing, and you know it."

"Oh, Tate."

She sighed and put her wineglass down and then came up to him, cupping his face in her hands. "No. You're not. You're the absolute best bet. I adore you. My kids adore you. You can't tell me that you don't adore them. I see you with them. I know you care. But I can't make you *want* us." She pressed her lips to his.

It was a soft, sweet kiss.

Gentle.

A good-bye.

He felt like his heart was going to shatter.

Right there. Shatter into pieces and fall to the floor. Something awful and hollow settled in the spot where his heart had been.

"You think it's because I don't want you?" He fisted his hands in her hair and pressed his brow to hers, staring at her, all but falling into those pretty eyes. Most of the time, those eyes were misty and soft. He'd seen them soft with hunger, soft with humor. But now they were hard. With determination. He started to realize, then, as he stared at her. Feeling desperate, he rubbed his mouth against hers. "I want you. You know that. I want to breathe."

It was a fucked-up time to realize it, but there it was. He hadn't held himself back enough. If he had, it wouldn't hurt so much. The words ripped out of him as he lifted his head to look at her. "I love you, too, dammit. I love you, I love your kids. But . . ."

Love wasn't right for him. It never could be. He had to be careful. Had to make sure she was safe. The kids. That was why he had to keep that distance, never give in too much.

Blackness swarmed around as the voices in the back of his head screamed even louder.

Shoving away from the counter, he grabbed the gift bag from the floor. He'd spent way too much time in the mall over in Louisville that morning looking for it. Dumping it on the counter, he shot her a look and then shook his head. "Look, you . . ." He sucked in a breath, tried to get some oxygen moving inside his lungs. It might help. Had to do something to ease the ache spreading through him. But nothing helped. "Look, I do love you. I love your kids. But . . . I . . . I can't *be* what you seem to think I can be."

Desperate, he turned to look at her. "I'll give you whatever I can. But I . . ."

"I just want *you*," she said, her voice stark. "All of you."

What the fuck did that mean? It wasn't like he was seeing anybody else. He thought about her all the time. She was in his head, in his blood. He could smell the scent of her skin even when she wasn't there and he dreamt about her. Except . . . *no*. Not a good time to think about those dreams.

Shaking his head, he tried to make her understand. "I'll take you out. I'll stay the night. I . . ." Pleading, he stared at her.

"That's not enough." The pain in her eyes sliced at him, straight through the heart.

"What is?" Hands clenched into fists, he fought the urge to grab her, haul her against him. Why was she doing this? Desperation filled him, made him want to yell, but he managed to throttle everything down, kept his voice flat and empty as he watched her.

"If you have to ask, then there is no way I can explain. But it's all or nothing, Tate." She turned away.

All or nothing—The sight of her averted back was like a brutal punch, right to the solar plexus and only sheer will kept him from staggering back.

"Ali—"

"Don't." She tipped her head back and he saw her throat working as she swallowed. "I tried, you know. I tried to make myself happy on what you could give me. But it's not working anymore. This just hurts too much."

She turned away from him, resting her hands on the counter. "Please go."

Legs wooden, he took a step.

Don't do this. He didn't know if that voice in his head was a plea to himself or her.

He went to take a step toward her and then froze as she flinched.

"I'm sorry." Unable to say anything else, he turned away. He could've sworn he heard something crack as he walked away.

It could only be his heart.

CHAPTER 4

⌐

The door slammed shut and part of her wanted to tear off after him.

The wiser part remained in control. Barely.

But she almost shattered after she pulled the tissue paper from the bag and peered inside.

Tears all but blinded her as she reached inside and pulled the purse out.

"You bastard."

It wasn't red.

Trust Tate not to just grab what he'd seen her eyeing.

He went and did one better, finding a rich, vibrant shade of blue that she absolutely adored.

The buttery leather was even softer than she'd imagined it would be and she stroked a hand down it, trying not to sniffle.

A Coach purse.

The bastard.

Tate had given her presents, and more than once. Up in her room she had one of his art pieces—it was small, almost elegant, standing on the nightstand where she could see it first thing in the morning, and last thing at night.

It was also worth a good five hundred, easy.

As uncomfortable as she was accepting the presents, each time he'd given her one, there was a look in his eyes, a weird sort of light that made her accept it, something hopeful and wishful and yearning.

But this.

It wasn't even the cost.

Tate earned more in a week than she did in a month, something most people didn't realize. He was a top-notch mechanic, but he mostly did that to fill up the days and make sure he could keep buying the materials for the sculptures he created. Some part of him didn't think he'd be able to make it solely on his art, although she suspected he could make far more if he'd just focus on that.

His art, the twisted works of metal, sold for a *lot*—some of the prices had left her jaw hanging and she knew he could afford the pretty purse in front of her.

It wasn't the *money*.

It was the fact that he'd noticed.

He'd seen her staring at this purse, then he'd gone out and found it. He had the heart to notice, and he'd taken the time to find it.

He wouldn't let them have a chance at a future.

Pulling it to her chest, she sank to the floor, her back pressed to the cabinets, while she stared up at the ceiling, willing herself not to cry.

The warm, luxurious scent of leather surrounded her.

Unable to hold the tears back another moment, she started to sob.

Gritty-eyed from lack of sleep, Tate slumped in the chair and stared up at the ceiling.

It had been less than twelve hours since Ali had tossed him out of her life.

His heart felt like it had withered up and turned into nothing but a ball of dust. Dry and useless.

Sleep had evaded him and because he had been going mad inside the four walls of his empty little house, he'd escaped.

There was no place left for him to really escape to, though, so he'd found himself here, with one of the few friends he had.

Sadly, that friend was a deputy with the county sheriff's department, and he was also currently on duty. Guy watched him over the rim of his coffee cup, his gray eyes shrewd.

"You look like hell."

"Gee, thanks." He eyed the coffee Guy had gotten him with resignation. Well, if he was going to die, he might as well get it over with. Poison was relatively fast, right? He took a sip, grimaced as something akin to motor oil rolled over his tongue. "Shit. That stuff is awful."

"Well, you don't come here for my coffee." Guy shrugged. Then he leaned forward, eyeing the monitor in front of him for a moment before sighing. "Tate, I don't have anything new for you. You know that. If I did, I'd let you know . . . you wouldn't have to come to me."

Guy and Tate had either hated each other's guts or been best friends for most of their lives. For the past ten years they'd been best friends, except when Tate started thinking too much about how Guy looked at Tate's little sister, Chrissie.

Then he wanted to hate the bastard again.

He made peace with it by yanking the guy's chain whenever possible, and by using the man's law enforcement connections. Rarely more than a few months went by without Tate asking Guy to poke around in his mother's file.

Today, he wasn't here to yank Guy's chain, though. He needed to fill his mind and he needed to stop thinking about Ali. Ali. Fuck. She was done with him. Unaware he was even doing so, he reached up to rub at his chest, the ache all but ready to end him.

Yeah. She was done with him. Why wouldn't she be?

Aware of the curious look in Guy's eyes, Tate pushed all of that aside and focused on why he'd come. His mom. Almost fifteen years. To the day. *That* date was drawing down on them, closer and closer. Sometimes Tate thought it was like a dragon, breathing fire down his back, but instead of heat, this dragon's flame was made of ice. Ice and death.

"Nothing new? How do you know? Have you thought about reopening her case?" He dared another sip of the deadly coffee. It hadn't killed him yet. He knew, because the misery was still eating him alive.

Guy sighed and gave him a level stare. "Tate. It's been fifteen years. You have me doing this, all too often. I can tell you, Jensen doesn't go more than a couple of months without poking around. Anytime we hear anything that might be *remotely* connected, she's already on top of it. None of us have forgotten Nichole. There's just nothing for us to find."

Tate opened his mouth. Then, without saying a word, he shut it. Giving up on the coffee, he slumped forward and braced his elbows on his knees, staring at the dingy gray carpet and reaching for something, *anything*, to say.

It didn't even have to be related to this at all. He just needed something to occupy his mind. Anything to keep him from thinking about Ali.

It's over, he thought dully.

It was really over.

What was he going to do without her? When he needed somebody to talk to? How did he get by without spending some time with her kids? He adored Joey and Nolan.

He loved her. So much, he felt hollow inside thinking about the days and nights stretching out in front of him. Days and nights that wouldn't have *her* in them.

"Have you questioned . . ." He swallowed and forced the words out. "My father?"

"I asked him if he remembered anything new," Guy said quietly.

"Like he'll tell you." Tate closed his eyes and pinched the bridge of his nose while the memories tormented him. They were getting worse, those memories.

The anniversary of his mom's disappearance was just a few weeks away now, and he'd be alone—

"You selfish bitch."

Memories of that long-ago night rose up, grabbing him.

Him hugging the girls once he'd crowded them into his room after he'd realized the fight was just getting worse and worse. Chrissie's thin arms wrapped around his neck, Jensen shivering against his side, him a mess of frustration and fear and confusion—he should have stopped him. He'd sat in his room with his sisters, like a pussy, instead of going out there and telling the man to shut the fuck up.

Instead, he'd just sat in there with the girls and tried to figure out what in the hell was going on. His parents just didn't fight. They might argue back and forth, but they didn't fight like that.

"Doug, just stop. We're not doing this in front of them."

"The hell we're not. You started it, so let's finish it. I was never good enough for you, was I?"

"You know, living in the past is a damn sure way to drive yourself crazy," Guy said, shattering the awful spell that had held Tate captive for a few minutes.

Turning his head, he looked over at the other man. "I can't help it."

"Sure you can. You just need to decide you're going to move on." Guy shrugged. "You think I don't have bad memories of *my* folks?"

"*Your* dad didn't kill your mother and get away with it." Tate stared at the brick wall in front of him, but he wasn't seeing anything. He was seeing that night. Hiding in the room with his sisters after his mom had left. The way his dad had slammed the door, locking himself in his room.

Then a little while later, Doug had left, returning hours later.

Fourteen years old, he'd tried to convince his sisters everything would be fine.

But nothing was ever fine again. His dad woke up. They asked where Mom was. He didn't know. They waited. They all waited.

Fifteen years later, they continued to wait.

"No, he just beat her to death in front of me, and when I tried to stop him, he put me in the hospital." Guy straightened in his chair, staring out at nothing.

Tate closed his eyes, swore under his breath. "Fuck. I'm sorry. That was—."

"Don't. It's okay. Neither of us were the picture for normalcy. My dad beat my mother to death and went to prison. Your mom . . ." Guy sighed, and then shifted his attention back to Tate. "Look, there is no proof that Doug killed your mom. None."

He shot Guy a dark look. "Who else would have done it? My mom didn't get into a fight with some other husband that night. Nobody else reported seeing anything. There's shit for evidence. Besides my dad, who *else* was angry with her that night?"

"Sometimes, there isn't a point." Guy stood from behind his desk and moved around to stand in front of it. "Look, I'll poke around, see what I can find. But there's not much hope here. We don't have a body. We don't have any witnesses. There is nothing to go on. She just . . ."

"Disappeared." Tate closed his eyes. He knew all of this. It was the same shit he'd lived with all this time.

"Let it go, man." Guy rested a hand on his shoulder and squeezed. "Go chase Ali down, make her marry you. Just let all of this go. That's what your mom would have wanted, you know. All of you happy."

"Chase Ali down." He looked up at Guy. "I think Ali is tired of waiting around for me. Besides . . ."

He paused, struggling to keep the words trapped inside him. But the misery over Ali and everything suddenly came spilling out and, for the first time, he gave voice to the fear that had lived inside him all of his life. "Something in him snapped that night, Guy. Just snapped. How do I know I won't do the same thing?"

For a second, Guy just stared at him, and then he swore.

Turning away, he moved to the window and stared outside. After long, tense moments, he turned back to him, watching Tate with burning eyes. "You're a fucking moron. Do you *really* believe that? Is *that* why you keep pretending there's nothing between you two even though the whole damn town knows you're crazy about her? You think you're going to go crazy and hurt her?"

"My dad never would have thought he'd hurt my mother, but he sure as hell did it." He glared at Guy.

Guy closed his eyes, blowing out a breath. Then he opened them and pinned Tate with a direct stare. "Okay, Tate. We need to have a talk—we should have had it a long time ago."

The river unfurled under the sun, a long, glinting ribbon of blue and gold, stretching between the wooded shores of Kentucky and Indiana. It was the dead of summer and there wasn't even a breeze coming off the water. But that didn't seem to bother the boaters out there. Some sailboats, more than a few people out fishing—although it was possible they were just out there drinking and the poles were just for looks.

Tate walked alongside Guy, hands shoved deep in his pockets as he waited. It had been nearly thirty minutes since they'd left the sheriff's department but Guy hadn't said much of anything.

"You know, if I'd known you were in the mood for a nice, romantic walk along the river, we could have set up a date in the evening when it's cooler," he finally pointed out.

"Why? So you could say no?" Guy sneered. "Then again, you might say yes . . . after all, you aren't in love with *me*. You're in love with Ali, but you won't take her on a nice long walk along the river, will you?"

"Shove it, Guy." He shot Guy a dark look. Then he smirked. "Besides, you're not my type."

"Ali is. You push her away. All the damn time."

"My relationship with Ali is—" *Over*. He swallowed the bitterness that rose up inside him. Stopping along the walkway, he turned and looked out over the river. A breeze blew up and he closed his eyes, lifted his face to it. "It's none of your business, Guy."

"Maybe not. But you, being a friend, are my business. If you're avoiding trying to reach for anything real with her because you think you're going to turn into your dad . . ." Guy stopped and blew out a breath, then he crossed his arms over his chest. His eyes, gray as the storm clouds piling up overhead, met Tate's. "I don't talk about this with you. I've tried before and you never listen. You never *want* to listen, but dammit, this time you are going to, even if I have to chase you down and sit on you. Tate, your dad isn't a killer."

"Oh, don't start—"

"I fucking will start and for the first time in your life, you'll listen to me," Guy said, his voice flat. "I know bad guys. I know scum. I know guilty men and I know men who could kill and not *feel* a damn thing. I *came* from that. I saw it, every time I looked at my father. I *know* killers. I also know the weak-ass bastards who snap and do awful things and regret it. I *know* that is who you think Doug is, but you're wrong. If I had to stake my badge on this, I'd be willing to do it. I don't think your dad killed your mom—I know that man and if you'd stop being pissed off at him, for just a little while, long enough to look at him, you'd see it, too."

Tate glared at him. "*You weren't there,*" he snarled, leaning in, nose to nose. "You didn't hear them."

"No." Guy shook his head. "But I was there, day in and day out, when my dad threatened to kill *my* mom. I walked in when he was doing it . . . when he was beating the shit out of her and when I tried to stop it. . . ."

Guy looked away.

Tate jerked out of his grasp and put distance between them.

Back in high school, their senior year, there had been a morning when all the teachers had been . . . off.

Guy's seat was empty. They'd shared almost all their classes and come lunch, Tate finally heard.

Guy was in the hospital. His mom was dead.

Guy's father had been sentenced to twenty years for her murder. He'd been released on parole a few years ago, but hadn't even gone nine months before it was revoked. So he was back in jail.

Tate rather wished the fucker would rot there.

He looked down, staring at the battered leather of his boots. "Guy, our parents were different people. Your dad was always . . ."

"A monster?" He turned his head and met Tate's gaze. "Yeah. He is. He was always a monster. He beat me. He beat my mom. He beat that mean-ass pit bull of ours and threatened to kill anybody who stepped foot on our property or looked at him sideways. He's a monster. I know monsters. Your father *isn't* a monster, Tate. I've spent too many nights talking to him. I cannot believe that man is the kind of man who'd kill the woman he loved. I don't believe it." He closed the distance between them and leaned against the railing, staring out over the town while Tate continued to stare at the river. "But even if I *didn't* know your father, I know you. You would cut off your arm before you harmed a woman, man. It's just not in you. Stop thinking that you're some fucked-up kind of fruit from the poison tree. You've got a woman who'd make you happy. She's got two kids who love you and you adore them. But instead of reaching for a life where you could *finally* be happy, you run from it. Out of fear? Shit, Tate. Fuck that. Think about it. Would your mom really want this kind of life for you?"

Then Guy shoved off the railing and walked away.

Tate stood there, staring at nothing.

"Instead of reaching for a life where you could finally be happy, you run from it."

Those words haunted him. Whether or not Guy had intended that, Tate didn't know.

But as he bent over the twisting metal, watching the image in his head take form, he couldn't block them out. There was no escaping the truth of what Guy had said.

The truth of what Ali had said.

He was in love with her.

Had been for . . . hell.

Forever, maybe.

Sometimes, it seemed like he'd just been waiting for the right moment to take his spot in her life. It hadn't been a sudden thing. He could remember seeing her with that fuckwit, Scott, back in school and thinking how much better she could do. He remembered seeing her push little Joey around in his stroller, and the kick he felt in his heart, seeing the two of them.

Forever. Yeah, that seemed about right.

Once again, memories rocked him, but this time, they weren't the brutal ugly memories of his past.

He thought about nights spent in her backyard, her behind the old, brick grill he'd helped her repair, while she wielded a spatula and threatened to beat him if he came near her while she was cooking. The boys laughing as he pretended to cower away.

He thought of Nolan, the way he'd laugh when Tate threw him up in the air and vague memories of his own father doing the same tried to creep in.

Then there were bittersweet, beautiful memories of nights spent in her bed. Her arms, soft and strong, wrapped around him as he moved over her, her voice a hungry little whisper in his ear.

He'd felt so . . . right.

With her.

It was the closest to *real* he'd ever felt.

He was letting it slip away.

He did run.

"Fuck." He glared at the sculpture in front of him, the blowtorch feeling too heavy, awkward in his hands.

Swearing, he stepped back and lowered the tool.

If he kept this up, he was going to ruin the damn thing or put himself in the hospital.

He stowed his gear and moved away, staring out the grimy windows, but seeing nothing.

Except Ali. He saw her everywhere, felt her even when she wasn't there.

The need to be with her, to tell her everything he had inside him was choking him.

He wanted to be the man she deserved.

The thought of seeing her in town one day, with some other guy was enough to gut him.

It *would* happen. Madison was about the size of a postage stamp.

He couldn't stand the thought of her being with somebody else, but could he be what she wanted?

"Instead of reaching for a life where you could finally *be happy, you run from it."*

Reach for a life.

Dropping his head, he rubbed the muscles along the nape of his neck while the storm built inside him. How in the hell did he reach for a life anyway? He'd never had one. It had all stopped one hot summer night fifteen years ago.

Reach for her, he thought.

That was how he started.

If he was going to do that, though, he had to face things, figure out the mess that was his life, his past.

All of it.

There used to be a car shop there.

Tate stood at the corner, eyeing the empty building. The sign wasn't readable anymore.

For the longest time, even after his dad had stopped trying to make it work, he could make out the words Bell's Auto Care. A few others had tried to make a go with the place, set up a business, but nothing had lasted.

When Doug Bell had owned it, it had done okay. More than okay, actually, although Doug had worked long hours. For a few months, right up until Mom had disappeared, Tate had been working there, too, and that had helped some.

Tate tried not to think about that time of his life. Tried not to think about how his mom would tease his father, making the somber man laugh, even when he didn't know what to make of her sometimes.

Nichole had been silly. Strict and silly. Absolutely wonderful.

So many of those arguments had happened because their dad thought she was *too* strict.

Half the fights, though, Tate didn't even understand what they were about. The last one . . .

Something crunched behind him.

Slowly, he turned, although he already knew who he was going to find behind him.

His father stood there, wearing the overalls he had to wear at the mechanic shop where he'd worked the past ten years. The words *Assistant Manager* were embroidered under his name. He'd been an assistant for ten years. At sixty years old, he probably wasn't going to go any higher.

"The old shop looks like hell," Doug said softly, looking past him to glance at the place he'd once taken so much pride in.

There were so many things Tate could have said.

So many things he'd already said. Questions he could have asked, maybe questions he *should* have asked.

He found himself thinking of what Guy had said . . . and Ali. Maybe it was just desperate hope that forced him to look at his father. *Really* look.

Tired eyes. So much more tired than Tate had ever seen them.

Tired but kind.

He'd been angry that night and Tate wanted him to suffer for what he'd said. But people did things, said things in anger. How many ugly words had he forced back inside? How many times had he leashed his anger, afraid of letting it out?

"Did you kill my mother?" The words ripped out of him, full of desperation, and a son's need to believe.

Doug slanted a look at him. Then he sighed, his stooped shoulders rising and falling. "Tate—"

He closed the distance between them, hands clenched into fists as he glared down at his father. This man, whom he had loved so much, whom he'd looked up to, admired.

"Trailer trash."

"Go on. Get out!"

"You called her trash," he said, his voice shaking as years' worth of rage and grief came spilling out. "You made her cry and you called her trash and you told her to get out. Did you kill her?"

"No." Then Doug met his eyes. "But I might as well have. If I hadn't been so cruel to her, she wouldn't have left that night. Whatever happened . . ."

Tate barely heard the rest of it.

The word *no* echoed through him and he spun away, sucking in oxygen. He couldn't get enough. Couldn't breathe deeply enough and his heart knocked hard against his ribs.

"Tate, I'm sorry."

Blood roared in his ears and it was forever before he realized his father had moved to stand next to him.

"It was a fight," Doug said, his voice level. "I said awful, ugly things that I never should have said and I said things that I know hurt her. I'll never be able to apologize to her and I've accepted that. But I also hurt you all. Saying what I said was wrong. *I* was wrong and whatever happened to her that night wouldn't have happened if I'd just shut my fool mouth. Because I couldn't, because I let anger get the best of me, she left . . . and you kids had to grow up without your mom. You all lost her because of me."

"No. We lost her because somebody took her from us." Tate closed his eyes, struggled to keep his voice level. "That lies with that bastard, not you. It's my fault I've been blaming you all this time."

Then he took off.

He didn't look back.

There was too much crashing inside his head just then, too much noise, too much confusion.

Underneath all of it, though, he realized something painful.

He believed him.

For the first time ever, Tate really believed that his father hadn't killed their mother.

But all that did was leave him with more questions.

If Doug Bell hadn't killed Nichole . . . who had?

The storm came blowing in not long after her parents whisked the boys off.

Her dad hugged her tight, folding her in his arms and asking, "Do I need to beat somebody up?"

She tried not to sniffle against his chest. They'd had their rough spots, but there were times like this when he proved to be . . . well, just wonderful. "Won't help, but thanks for caring."

That had been nearly thirty minutes ago and not long after they'd left, the storm had started. The hard, heavy downpour hadn't let up since.

Sitting on the porch swing, staring out into the night, she watched as the lightning lit up the sky over the river and she tried not to cry. It was easy to push it all aside when the kids were here. When they were here, she had to be a mom, first and foremost. Sometimes it sucked because as a single mom, she rarely had a free moment just to herself. But in moments like this, it was a blessing in disguise because she didn't *want* moments to herself, moments to brood, moments to hurt.

Moments to think about everything that was never going to happen.

Sniffling, she focused on the raindrops, told herself they weren't blurring before her eyes.

I'm not going to cry because it's over.

I'm not going to cry because it's over.

I'm not going to cry—

She hiccupped as a sob broke free.

Bringing her knees to her chest, she buried her face against them.

Lost in the hurt, she didn't hear his footsteps. It wasn't until he closed his hands around her ankles that she even realized she wasn't alone.

Jerking her head up, she stared into Tate's gaze. His eyes, so dark they were nearly black, bore into hers.

"Tate . . ."

He tugged her legs down and she curled her hands around the

edge of the porch swing, her heart slamming against her ribs. He went to lean in and she lifted a hand, pressed it to his chest.

"Don't." Her voice cracked. "I'm not . . . we can't do this anymore. *I* can't do this anymore."

He didn't seem to realize she'd even spoken as he reached up and closed one hand around her wrist, his thumb stroking against her inner wrist as she continued to press against his chest. "Ali . . ."

His heart slammed against her palm and his shirt, soaked by the rain, was no barrier between them. She felt the scalding heat of his skin. Drops of rain clung to his hair and as she stared into his eyes, one of the drops fell, caught on his cheekbone, and rolled down. It hit her wrist and she was surprised it didn't sizzle, as hot as she suddenly felt.

It was a heat that echoed deep inside her, down low in her belly and every beat of her heart sent that heat pulsing through her until she thought she might explode.

The seconds drew out and she took a slow, deep breath. His gaze dropped to her mouth and she had to bite back a moan.

"Tate, stop," she whispered, forcing the words out. That hunger continued to pang inside her, making her skin feel tight, hot. She had to curl her fingers into a fist to keep from reaching for him. "I'm tired of only having part of you. I told you. It's all or nothing and you won't give me everything—"

He lifted her hand to his mouth, pressed a kiss to her inner wrist. That gentle caress sent shivers racing through her. Blood started to roar in her ears, so loud it took her a minute to realize he had started to speak.

"All my life, even from the time I was a kid," he murmured, his voice slow, smooth as silk. He let go of her wrist, placing both hands on her knees as he continued to speak. "Everybody told me how much I was like my father. His parents, before they died. My mom. Even my sisters saw it."

Her heart stuttered.

Tate rarely spoke of his father, but when he did, there was always a burn of rage in his voice. That wasn't there now.

There was only sadness.

"After Mom disappeared, part of me wanted to believe he hadn't done it." He flicked a glance at her. "I really did want to believe it, you know. But I understood that gut-wrenching rage. Because there were things he'd said that made me so angry that I wanted to hurt him. I wanted to go after him and beat the shit out of him. I didn't. Because of my sisters. When they were fighting, out in the living room, I was trying to keep Chrissie calm." His voice skipped, almost broke and he looked down. "She was nine, scared. Confused. Upset. Clinging to me like a monkey. She . . . hell. You remember how she was? The teachers thought she might be kind of slow, how much trouble she had with school and everything. She did just fine as long as Mom was there. Mom could always calm her down, get her focused and everything. But . . ." He blew out a breath. "But she didn't have Mom to calm her down that night. It was just me. We'd been out there, at first, when they started fighting. I don't even remember what started it, not really. We were watching a movie. Mom got on me about something . . . and then . . . *bam*. It was like a nuclear explosion. They started fighting and I ended up picking up Chrissie, dragging Jensen along with me into my room."

Memories clouded his eyes and his voice was soft, almost too soft to hear over the rain. He still had his hands on her knees and he rubbed them up and down, slowly, like he needed the touch, that light, physical contact to stay grounded.

"Chrissie was shivering, shaking so bad. Every time I went to put her down and go out there, tell them to shut up or chill out, she just squeezed me tighter. I figured I'd let them fight it out. Chrissie needed me and they wouldn't listen to me anyway. So while my dad was being ugly as hell, I just stayed in the room with the girls and listened. He said the worst things. I'd never heard him talk like that. I hated it."

She opened her mouth to say something, but she didn't know what.

Tate reached up to brush her hair back. "He didn't touch her. Dad never lifted a hand to any of us, not even to spank us. Well, except Chrissie. She got her butt swatted more than once. But she was Chrissie. Mom was more likely to do it than Dad, though. With all of us. He always said she was too strict, yelled too much, demanded too much . . ." He lowered his head, shoulders slumped.

Unable to stay still, she reached up and pushed her hand through his wet hair. Tate caught her wrist and turned his face into her hand. Her skin shivered as he pressed a soft, gentle kiss to her palm.

He never stopped speaking.

It was like the words had been trapped inside, behind a flood wall. That wall had broken and they were spilling out of him now.

"She yelled. But she loved us. A lot. Dad only yelled when things were really bad." A scowl twisted his face as he looked away. "If Dad started to yell, we were ready to run for cover. Dad was always the scariest when he was mad. That night . . ." He stopped, his throat working.

She could see him fighting with the words.

"Tate, you don't have to tell me this," she said gently.

"You wanted everything. You wanted all of me. This . . ." He paused, shifted his gaze to hers, and she saw the hell that lay within. "This is me. All of it."

He slid his hands up her thighs, absently kneading her hips. "That fight was a bad one, but I wasn't really *worried,* exactly. Not about Mom, not even when she left. She was . . . tough. If that makes sense. She could look at a person and make them back down. Even that old bastard Theo Miller wouldn't mouth off long when she told him to shove it. I wasn't worried when she left. Not at first. But I was *pissed* at Dad because he made her feel like that. Made her feel so bad she *had* to leave, even for a while. What he'd said. How he'd said it. He was so fucking ugly and every time I saw him, I wanted to punch him. Chrissie couldn't sleep, so I thought I'd get her some warm milk—it always helped when Mom gave it to her, so I figured I'd try. I saw him in the living room. He was getting his keys and I just wanted to hit him. Hurt him for saying the shit he'd said. He wouldn't even look at me. Just left. Didn't say a word. He came back a little later. Mom hadn't come home."

He closed his eyes and dropped his head to her knee. She reached up and pushed her fingers through his hair.

"Hours go by. She's not home. I realize something is wrong. I'm scared, and I'm mad, and getting madder. I could almost understand, then, the things he'd said, how ugly he'd gotten, because I wanted to do the same thing, only to him. I wanted to hurt my father, Ali."

She tangled her fingers in his hair. "You were mad, Tate. He'd been unkind to a woman you loved. That's just how you are."

"That's part of the problem. That's how I am." Slowly, he lifted his head and the look in his eyes made her heart skitter in her chest. Burning, full of an intensity that all but stole her breath. "I'm thinking, all this time, that he killed her. Not on purpose maybe. He just caught up with her, or ran into her somewhere. He lost his temper . . . he was angry, like I was. I've always believed that he killed her."

His dark eyes bored into hers and he covered her cheek with his hand. "Ali, I'm just like my father. I've always worried . . . if *he* could do that . . ."

Confusion danced across her face and then abruptly, comprehension dawned.

"Tate."

She cupped his face in her hands and leaned in, pressing her lips to his. That soft, light kiss somehow was a balm to the bleeding, gaping hole that was his heart.

"You stupid, stupid man," she murmured against his mouth. Then she sighed and pressed her brow to his, slipping from the porch swing to kneel in front of him.

He curved his arms around her waist. The feel of her was both comfort and torment. Turning his face into her hair, he breathed in the scent of her. *Let me fix this . . .*

"You honestly think that you could hurt me. Is that why you try so hard to keep a distance?"

Why did he feel so foolish about this now? Foolish, and oddly relieved, as he felt her heart beat against his own. A weight had been lifted off him some time in the past few hours. A weight he'd been carrying around for too long. Maybe even for fifteen years.

He kept his face buried against her neck. "Intentionally, no. I don't *think* I ever would . . . but a huge part of me . . ."

She eased back and covered his cheek with her hand. "Tate. Don't take this wrong. Because I love you, dearly. But you're an idiot." Temper flashed in her eyes and she surged upward so suddenly, she knocked him off balance. He ended up sitting on his ass while she started to pace.

He shifted around to keep her in his sight as she moved.

"All this time." She glared at him as she reached the end of the porch and wheeled around. "For three years, we played *friends,* all because you're afraid you're going to pull some weird *Jekyll and Hyde* bit?"

"*Jekyll and Hyde*?" He climbed to his feet, staring at her while his temper started to kick up inside. Okay, he could take feeling like an idiot, but he'd held back because he wouldn't risk hurting somebody—hurting *her.* "You know, this might sound like a fucking joke to you, and maybe I'm being stupid, but I lost my mother. She was our *world.* Our dad was our rock. And for the longest time, I looked at him and saw only the man who *I* thought killed her. I saw a man who is *just like me.*"

"Did it ever *occur* to you that you were wrong?" she shouted. "About *any* of it?"

"Yes!" He spun away and sucked in a breath, closing his eyes. He moved to the edge of the porch and leaned against it, his weight braced on his hands. Heedless of the pouring rain and the wind, he closed his eyes. "But . . . shit. I didn't let myself think about it. Until today."

He hadn't let anger get a foothold in his life, not since he'd lost his mom. He'd blamed her death on anger, after all. When he felt *too* angry, or too close to slipping there, he funneled all those frustrations into his art, into a hard, driving run . . . or sometimes, into sex.

Right then, though, he was caught, hovering between anger, self-disgust, and other emotions he couldn't name. When Ali came near, he caught her arm and she crashed into his chest, glaring up at him.

This. He closed his eyes, let himself revel in the feel of her pressed against him.

Just . . . this.

He hadn't felt whole since she'd walked away.

And even when they'd been together, he'd held back. Always.

This was probably the closest to *whole* he'd ever been. Slowly, he twined her hair around his fist, holding her gaze with his. "I know it might not make sense," he said gruffly. "I didn't let myself think it, because I couldn't. Even if I was *wrong*, at least it was an answer. Can you understand that? Do you understand what it's like . . . living with that? Not having *any* answer?"

Something flickered in her eyes and the tension that had held her rigid drained away. The hands that had been pushing him away curled into the fabric of his shirt and she sighed, gazing up at him. "Yeah. I think I do. You lost your mom—the answer, right or wrong, was something you needed. I *get* that. But you spent fifteen years blaming the wrong man. You spent fifteen years putting yourself in a box, only letting bits and pieces of yourself out because you were afraid you'd be just *like* him. You are like him, Tate. He isn't a killer. He's just a stubborn, headstrong man."

"But that's part of the problem." He pressed his brow to hers. "I don't want to be like him. I don't want to be the kind of man who'd say things that sent a woman running out in the middle of the night. I don't . . ."

"Tate." A soft sigh escaped her, ghosting over his lips. "You can have some traits without being him made over. *You* decide the kind of man you're going to be. You're more likely to hurt me by closing me out than by anything you say."

Stroking his thumb across her temple, he closed his eyes.

She smoothed her hands down his shirt and then turned her face into his neck. "You've had a rough day. Why don't you come inside for a while? You can dry off and wait until the storm passes."

He lifted his head and looked into her eyes.

"Then go home?" he murmured.

Go home . . .

Those words set her heart to racing. No. She didn't want him going home, not at all.

But she wasn't throwing herself back out there again unless she knew he was going to be with her.

"I think you need to look at all of this, and make sure you know what you want," she said haltingly, staring at the column of his throat. Much safer territory than his eyes. She felt lost every time she did that and if she looked there now and saw the heat and the hunger and the confusion and the love . . .

"I know what I want." He tugged her head back and dipped his own, pressed his brow to hers. His free hand fisted the back of her shirt and it left her feeling surrounded by him. "I want you. I'm scared to death and you'll have to kick my ass along the way, but I want you, and everything that comes with it."

Oh. Well. Hell.

Now she was *really* lost.

For a long, long moment, he stared at her and then, slowly, he slanted his mouth over hers. He pressed her back against the wall of the house, the strength of his body pinning her to it as her muscles went lax. His tongue toyed, tangled with hers. Her heart slammed against her ribs as he slid his hands up her sides, danced the tips of his fingers along her neck before plunging them into her hair to arch her face to his.

"Ali-girl." He rubbed his lips against hers before pressing a hot, burning line of kisses down her neck. "My girl."

She twisted her hands in his shirt, sucking in a desperate breath. He shifted against her and her pussy clenched when she felt the hard, heavy ridge of his cock. Hunger and need ripped through her.

Lost . . . yes. She was lost. She didn't care.

He barely had the brainpower to realize they were on the porch.

Her lit porch.

Groaning, he managed to stumble inside and kick the door shut and that was where his control ended.

Spinning around, he put her against the door and leaned back, grabbing the hem of her shirt. It was wet now, thanks to his own sodden clothes and he ran his fingers down the transparent cloth. Through it, he could see the outline of her bra, the soft swell of her breasts, the elegant line of her torso. He wanted to go to his knees before her and worship her, wanted to press his lips to every damn inch of her. Slowly, he lifted his gaze up to meet hers. "I got you all wet."

"So you did." She licked her lips.

"Should I do something about it?" He made himself hold back. He'd been so fucking unfair to her, holding back from everything they both wanted, both needed. He needed this . . . now. With her. She wanted it. But if he'd pushed her so far away that she wasn't ready for this . . .

A slow smiled curled her lips. "Well, you're a big boy, Tate. It's time you start taking more responsibility for things," she teased. "You got me all wet. Now take care of it."

As she spoke, she curled her legs around his hips and arched against him.

The contact was a jolt, straight down his spine, hitting him square in the balls. "Yes, I should absolutely take care of that."

Reaching for the hem of her shirt, he slowly peeled it up, watching as he bared each inch. Goose bumps broke out along her skin and once the shirt had cleared her head, he dropped it to the ground and leaned forward, pressed his mouth to the delicate line of her collarbone.

She shivered and he looked up, stared into her eyes. "Are you cold?"

"Umm."

"I can't tell if that's a yes or no." He nibbled his way along her shoulder, felt another shiver race through her. "I'll take it as a yes. I should warm you up. Get rid of these wet clothes."

He kissed his way up her throat and reached behind him to unhook her feet, guiding her legs down so he could deal with her jeans. "These should go, too, right?"

"Yeah." She smiled against his lips as he went to take her mouth. Her kisses—he could gorge on them. Every day for the rest of his life and never be satisfied. That was what he wanted. What he'd wanted for a long, long time; maybe he'd even let himself think about having it. "I think everything should go."

"Good idea." He undid her bra, slipped the straps slowly down, watching as her breasts swung free. The deep rose of her nipples begged for him and he paused to catch one in his mouth, plumping her breasts together as he did so. "So soft. So sweet."

She arched against him, a movement guaranteed to distract him. He wasn't about to get distracted, though, and he straightened, focusing his attention on the thin cotton yoga pants. They were gone in seconds and he boosted her back up, pressed her back to the door.

A random thought fired—*we can go to her room*—but he didn't want to be away from her, didn't want to try and navigate the house when he could be inside her.

She hissed, shivering. "You're getting me wet all over again."

"That's the idea." He slid a hand down between them, pushed a finger inside her and yes, she was very, very wet.

She gasped as he stroked her, her muscles clenching around him. Then she reached for him, yanking at his shirt. "Take this off."

He leaned back just enough, gripping the firm curve of her ass. "You take it off instead."

Their gazes locked and held as she dragged the shirt up. It caught around his shoulders and he let go just enough to finish stripping the wet mess off as she clutched at his hips with her knees.

It was absolutely insane that his hands were shaking.

He'd made love to Ali a hundred times. More.

Yet each time was a new experience.

This time, I don't have to hide—

He stilled, slowly lifting his eyes to stare at her.

"Tate?"

His heart thudded in his chest and he tried to breathe around the massive ache centered there but it was almost impossible.

An uncertain look crossed her features.

"No more holding back?"

A breath shuddered out of her. "Please don't."

Gazing at her, he eased the zipper of his jeans down, his cock pulsating, the need inside him swelling, rippling through him. His blood burned. Nerve endings seemed to sizzle and scream inside.

She reached down and stroked one finger along his length and he caught her wrist, stretched it up over her head and pressed it to the door, still watching her. He caught her other wrist as well, holding them both pinned in one hand, high over her head.

It arched her back, lifted her breasts, a position that seared itself on the back of his mind.

With his free arm, he caught one leg, drew it up. "There. Stay right there," he muttered, right there as he pressed it to his hip, opening her. Her lips parted as she stared at him, soft, broken little pants coming from her. Then he reached between them and grabbed his cock, grimacing as even that touch sent a jolt racing through him. He was ready to come, right there. The heated kiss of her wet pussy against his head was a damn near brutal sensation.

Ali gasped as he pressed against her. Slowly, oh, so slowly, she yielded. Her breasts rose and fell against his chest in a rapid rhythm, her gaze all but blind as she stared at him.

She was burning him. Burning him alive.

"Burn for me," he whispered against her mouth. "I want to feel you burn for me."

The silken, tight grasp of her pussy closed around him, the tissues clinging to him as he withdrew and then surged back in. Her head fell back, throat arched, the line, delicate, exposed. He skimmed it with his lips. "I love you."

A soft, broken cry escaped her lips.

Why did this feel different?

Bewildered, Ali stared into his eyes but even as she tried to understand everything shaking and rolling through her, he surged against her again. His swollen flesh rasped over sensitized tissues and he retreated, slowly, almost too slowly, so that she was painfully aware of the void he left behind. His gaze caught hers, held hers as he poised there, right there at her entrance.

Then he started it all over again, a slow, deep possession, until she was full with him, stretched tight around him. The pleasure battered at her and she whimpered, twisted in his arms in a desperate attempt to get closer.

"Burn for me," he whispered against her mouth again, releasing her wrists and sliding his hand down to cup her cheek.

She clutched at his shoulders, her nails biting into his flesh as she clenched down around him, already feeling the orgasm gathering deep inside her. So easily. He had her so easily.

He worked a hand between them and she keened out his name as he flicked his thumb over her clitoris. *There . . .*

She caught her breath but then he changed his rhythm, going to shallow, teasing thrusts as he toyed with the hard little nub of flesh. "Not so fast, Ali-girl."

She glared at him.

He stared back at her. The naked need, the hunger, the love she saw in his eyes left her breathless.

Desperate, she reached for him and he came to her, his mouth slanting over hers. Sinking her teeth into his lower lip, stroking her tongue against his mouth until he opened for her, she tried to gorge on him, feast. Lose herself.

His rhythm turned hard again, hard, heavy, driving. She arched to meet each thrust, gasping out his name and then he tensed against her.

"Tate!"

Abruptly, he moved—harder, faster, working one arm around her to hold her steady as he drove into her like he was trying to imprint himself on her very flesh. She loved it.

A shriek ripped from her as the climax slammed into her. Ali hadn't even caught her breath before his cock jerked and she felt him start to come. Moaning, she quivered around him, shaking at each rhythmic jerk of his heated length.

"Ali . . ."

Her name was a dazed, raspy murmur on his lips.

Because she could actually *say* it this time without him tensing up, she turned her face into his neck. "I love you."

CHAPTER 5

The sun came up over them as he made love to her again.

She'd lost track of how many times they'd turned to each other during the night. This might have been the sixth—she had fuzzy recollections of it happening sometime in the dark, but that might have been a blissed-out dream.

Now, with her face pressed against the pillow and him stretched out, half lying on top of her, half alongside, she tried to steady out her breathing.

Her heart beat like mad and she had a feeling if she looked in the mirror, she'd see a goofy grin spreading across her face.

It wasn't a bad day, she decided.

Not a bad day at all.

She didn't have to work.

The kids wouldn't be home for a while and best of all . . .

"What's the smile for?"

That was the best of all. Tate was here.

She cracked one eye open and saw him peering down at her. "I dunno. I'm suffering from oxygen deprivation so I'm probably delusional."

"Uh-huh." He dipped his head, kissing her behind the ear and then he rolled off, settling on the bed just a few inches away.

In the soft, golden glow of the early morning sun, he looked too beautiful. He was here. In bed with her.

He hadn't up and left in the middle of the night. He didn't look like he was going to take off running right now, either.

Swallowing, she laid a hand on his cheek. "I can't believe you're here."

He covered her hand with his. "Ali."

"Don't." She shook her head, wiggling closer and tucking her head against his chest. "I just. Hell. I thought about this. I wanted this. Didn't think it would happen and I was ready to just . . ."

"You got tired of waiting."

He stroked his hand up her back, his touch light and gentle, but she felt the tension mounting inside him.

"Not because I wanted to." She rubbed her thumb across his skin and felt his chest rise, expanding on a sigh. "I just realized that waiting around and hoping things would change wasn't going to make them change."

"So we talk now." He rolled her onto her back and stared down at her. "What do you need me to do? What *can* I do?"

"You already did a lot of it, Tate." Studying his face, she shrugged. "You let me in. All you ever did was keep me on the outside, sharing nothing but . . . this. It was just sex. I know that's all we talked about in the beginning, but I think we both know things changed for us along the way."

He pressed his thumb against her lips. "I always wanted more than just this. I just didn't think . . ."

His voice trailed off and the thick black fringe of his lashes drooped, shielding his eyes. She kissed his thumb and then squirmed, pushing against his shoulders until he let her up. Dragging the sheet up over her shoulders, she settled on the mattress with her legs crossed. "I know. I get it. You're *wrong*." She narrowed her eyes as he slid a look at her. "But I can understand why you never wanted to trust yourself. As long as you're willing to *stop*. Okay?"

"It's not going to be just as easy as flipping a switch." He climbed out of bed and she watched him disappear through the door. Something kept her from getting up and a minute later, he reappeared, pulling his jeans up over naked hips. She watched his hands as he zipped them up, left them unbuttoned over the lean, tanned line of his belly.

Dragging her gaze away, she looked back at his face, but he was focused on the floor. One hand closed into a fist. "I *know* I've fucked up, Ali. I *am* fucked up. I know that, I get that, and I'm going to fix this. Fix me. But I also know it's not going to be an overnight thing."

She waited a beat and then shrugged. "Well, we'll take it in bits and pieces." He flickered her a look and she smiled at him. "Besides, you might be wrong. *Overnight things* might just be the answer to getting you on track. Last night was pretty damn good, right?"

The grin he gave her was just a flash on his face and it barely showed in his eyes. Shoving away from the wall, he moved to stare out the window. "Just tell me you're not giving up on me."

"Tate." She slid out of the bed and moved to stand behind him. Wrapping her arms around his back, she pressed her lips to his spine. "Baby, I didn't give up the past three years while you had your head up your ass. You're just now starting to show some sign of intelligence. Why would I walk now?"

"You're a smart-ass." He covered her hands with his.

"Yeah. So are you. I think that makes us a matched set."

They stood there a minute and then he slowly turned around, leaning back against the wall and drawing her into the cradle of his hips, one arm wrapped around her waist. "I keep thinking about the past fifteen years. About my dad. About me." Misery was written across his face, naked and plain. "What in the hell am I supposed to say to him?"

Her heart twisted in her chest. The storm in his eyes, the pain she could see him trying to hide, was enough to break her. Reaching up, she cupped his face in her hands, pressed a soft, gentle kiss to his mouth.

Then, easing back down, she held his gaze. "Just go to him. Tate, that man loves you. All he wants is to have his son back."

"I ain't got time for you today."

"Wow. Nice to see you, too, sis." He stood in the doorway, watching Chrissie . . . no. Chris. She hated it when he called her Chrissie. Sometimes he looked at her and saw the little girl who'd clung to him that awful night. For a little while, after Mom died, he'd been her world.

Unlike him, she'd looked at their father and maybe it was the eyes of a child that had let her do it, he didn't know, but she'd looked at her father and just saw the man who'd tucked her into bed. The man who'd told their mom to ease up when he thought she pushed them too hard.

They hadn't been perfect parents, Tate thought.

But they'd balanced each other.

Tate hadn't come to grips with how he felt about that final night, but he was going to do it in bits and pieces, just like Ali had suggested.

Starting here.

Chris stood at a table and for the life of him, all he could think was that she looked like a gothic Tinker Bell. Short punkish haircut in shades of white-blond, black, and pink, incongruous as hell, but it suited her. She wore a shirt with a ragged hem that bared her belly and left the stone in her navel flashing in the light as she reached for another blossom. Tattoos twined around both of her arms, sleeves that she had started working on as soon as she turned eighteen. For her eighteenth birthday, she'd gotten her first tattoo and Dad had paid for it.

That was what she'd wanted and Dad had never been able to tell Chrissie no.

It wasn't a surprise.

She was the only one who'd believed in him, Tate realized. From the beginning.

The tattoos were a garden, blooming there on her skin, roses and daisies, climbing and vining around her arms before disappearing under the cotton of her shirt.

He thought there was a new one around her left wrist, but he wasn't sure.

She shot him a look, her green eyes unreadable.

For the most part, he was close to his sisters, but this time of year was hard . . . on all of them. He tended to withdraw. Jensen all but worked herself into the ground, picking up extra hours at the station whenever she could. Chris centered herself around Dad. The baby tiger, there to guard the old man from anybody who might hurt him.

Namely, his son.

Swallowing, he closed his eyes and lifted his head, staring up at the sky as he tried to figure out the easier way to go about this. There wasn't one, though.

What the hell.

He'd managed to bare himself to Ali. He could handle Tinker Bell over there.

"I talked to Dad."

Her hands stilled over the blossoms—badass, gothic Tink loved nothing more than working with flowers. There wasn't a week that went by that their mother's grave didn't have a beautiful display on it. By night, she tended bar over at Shakers and during the day, she had a mini florist's shop bustling in the garage tacked on to her house. Her dream was to expand it out of her house, but it hadn't happened yet.

Her lips flattened out. "Leave him alone, Tate. You've caused him enough grief, don't you think?"

"Yeah."

"I mean, *fuck*. You try the same thing, without fail, every year—"

She stopped. Without looking at him, she put down the stems she was working with and then reached for the rag in her back pocket, wiping her hands off. She gazed out the window, her hands clutching at the edge of her worktable. "What did you say?"

"I believe him."

She turned her head and stared at him.

Two seconds later, he had to dodge the roses as they came flying at him.

"Sorry."

Tate slid Chris a look as she settled down next to him. "Are you?"

A grimace twisted her face. "Well. Technically, I probably should be. In all honesty, no. I wish I had a bucket of dirty water or something to dump over your head." She sighed and leaned back, bracing her weight on her hands and stretching her legs out. "You're such a stubborn ass, you know that?"

"Yeah."

"You are so like him." Her voice was husky and when he glanced over at her, he saw the misery in her eyes. She sniffled and averted her face.

Reaching out, he slid his arm around her shoulders. For a minute, she held herself rigidly. Then she sank against him, her voice cracking as she whispered, "I miss her, Tate. Sometimes I wake up, thinking she'll come home. I can barely remember what she looked like, but I remember her voice, and how she smelled and how we danced around the kitchen some nights. I think . . . *maybe she's out there. Maybe she'll come home.*"

"I know." He rubbed his cheek against her hair. "I know, Chrissie."

A minute passed and she sucked in a breath, then pulled back, swiping the back of her hand over her eyes.

He pretended not to notice.

"She looked like you."

He watched as she turned her head and stared at him. He smiled at her and shrugged. "You want to know what she looked like. Just see yourself. Without the crazy rainbow hair and all." He smiled, pushed a hot-pink section of her bangs back. "But she looked like you. She was pretty. Funny. She yelled a lot and she drove me crazy and she made us work too hard."

"She was a good mom."

"Yeah." He caught her hand in his and squeezed. "She was a good mom."

Chris closed her eyes. "Dad . . ."

He sighed and lifted her hand, pressed a kiss to the back of it. Then, unable to sit still, he rose from the porch and started to pace. "I'm going to talk to him later. I'm trying to work things through in my head. But I needed a resolution, Chris. It's not fair—it wasn't fair to him, to you—"

"Or you."

He shot her a look.

She sat on the porch, her elbows braced on her knees. She stared at him, her green eyes vivid. "It wasn't fair to you, either. I know why you did it. Hell, *Dad* knows why. He's the one who's been telling me and Jensen all this time to leave you alone with it."

He didn't want to hear this. Turning away, he jammed his hands in his pockets, he braced himself because he also knew, as much as he didn't want to hear, Chris was going to say it anyway.

"You needed to have some kind of answer—something in your head that made sense," Chris said. "This was the only one you could come up with. So you focused on it. Because you did, you lost your father and your mother."

Tate closed his eyes.

Behind him, he could hear her coming toward him, but he didn't move. Didn't turn to face her. When she circled around to face him, he had a hard time meeting those sharp green eyes. "Are you done punishing yourself now?"

"I'm not—"

"Oh, bullshit." She shook her head. "You spent fifteen years telling yourself that you should have gone out there, said something, done something . . . stopped her from leaving. You were fourteen. You were just a kid. So was I. So was Jensen. Yeah, they had a fight. Dad shouldn't have said the shit he did. He didn't make Mom leave and no matter what . . ." Her voice tripped, then steadied. "No matter what happened to her, she didn't ask for it. The only person to blame in *any* of this is the son of a bitch who took her from us."

"We'll never know who that is."

She looked away. "No. We're never going to know. We'll never know what happened, where she is. Not after all this time. But I'm not going to let my life stop because of that. She would have wanted us to be happy—all of us."

This would be the easier one, Tate told himself. Jensen wasn't going to make it hard on him and, hey, he even got a smile out of it, just sitting there and waiting for her.

Feet propped on the edge of her desk, he had the pleasure of watching his sister threaten to throw a mouthy bitch in jail, after said mouthy bitch shoved Jensen.

Granted, Jensen had all but taunted her into it, chin up, eyes glinting with an *I dare you* smirk in them.

But Leslie Mayer had gone into the station looking for trouble, and she'd found it in the form of Detective Jensen Bell.

Jensen had grown up to be a cop. Out of all of them, she was the most solid, something that had baffled Tate for only a very short while. She'd lost her mother but that hadn't sent her down a spiral. It might have done that to Tate and Chris, but it had centered Jensen.

She'd lost her mother and she'd do everything she could to keep another child from suffering the same, another family from going through the misery the Bell family had suffered all these years.

As Leslie Mayer was led out of there by two uniformed cops, still screeching at Jensen, his sister headed over to her desk, pausing only a second when she saw him waiting there.

"You had way too much fun with that," he said.

"Hey, a girl's gotta get her kicks somehow, right?" She knocked his feet off her desk and dropped into the seat. "Why are you here? It's awful early for you. You usually skulk in your den until the day is half done."

"I don't skulk."

"Brood. Whatever." She shrugged. "You made up with Ali yet?"

He felt the hot, red crawl of blood creeping up his neck. *Half the damn town*, he mused. From the corner of his eye, he saw the grin on her face and the way trouble glinted in her gaze.

"People sure are interested in my love life." He turned back to face her. Leaning in, he studied her closely, more closely than he usually let himself.

If Chris was a gothic Tinker Bell—attitude and chaos in one tiny little package—then Jensen was her polar opposite. Every bit as slim and slight as the youngest Bell sibling, yes, and there were physical similarities, but while Chris was all clashing colors and short temperament, Jensen was order. She wore her dark hair in a neat, chin-length cut and she probably spent five minutes on it a day—including washing. Her makeup bordered on the nonexistent and her clothes were just like her, efficient and simple.

She looked like a cop.

That was all she'd wanted to be.

She cocked her head and studied him, her green eyes narrowed to slits. Lips pursed, she continued the study until Tate had to fight the urge to squirm.

"Something's different with you," she finally said.

"Yeah? I went and had my nails done. Sweet of you to notice."

She snorted. "Yeah. That's it. Let me guess, you used one of Chrissie's favorite colors she's always pushing on me . . . Razzle Dazzle Red or something?"

"Nope. I went with Fru Fru Pink." He smiled, relaxing a little as she jabbed at him. He leaned forward, bracing his elbows on his knees and rubbing his face. Man, he was tired. He felt like he'd aged a year in the span of a day. "Listen . . . I, uh, I've been thinking about things. Mom. Dad."

She was quiet for a long time. So quiet, he finally lifted his head and saw her eyeing him, a sad smile on her face. "Finally figured it out, Tate?"

He blew out a breath. "So you aren't going to throw roses or something at me?"

"Roses?" She grinned. "Let me guess. You've already told Chrissie?"

"Yeah. Know the bucket of flowers she keeps up on her table when she works?"

Jensen arched her brows.

"She pelted me with them." He rubbed a finger over the scratch on his cheek. "Fortunately, most of them didn't have thorns."

"Yeah? Then what?"

He shrugged. "We talked. Wanted to come over and see you." He blew out a breath and straightened back up in the chair, staring up at the ceiling without seeing it. "I'm going to hunt him down later and talk to him. He's probably going to tell me to get the hell out, but I'll try."

"He won't tell you to get out."

"Why not?" he bit out. Shoving upright, he moved to the minuscule window she had by her desk. Jensen didn't have an office but as one of the two lieutenants, her work area was a little bigger. By maybe two inches. She also had a window. He focused on it while temper sparked and brewed inside him. "Why not, huh? I did my damnedest to turn you all against him. I spent fifteen years hating him. I hassled every cop who'd listen to me to reopen the case and dig deeper into his story. Why shouldn't he tell me to get out?"

"Because he understands." Jensen didn't bother getting up. She stretched her legs out and rested her elbow on the desk, glancing around the room, but most of the other cops had headed out to lunch or were out on patrol. The few left were too far away to hear them, although the siblings knew they'd *try*. "Tate, you needed a target. He let himself be that target. The same way you were the target when I found out my boyfriend was cheating on me senior year. Instead of going after him, you made me mad at you instead."

Tate glared at her. "I just wanted to handle the punk myself. He shouldn't have been messing around on you anyway."

"You still let me take my mad out on you . . . it was safer."

He looked away. "Nah. That jackass wouldn't have lifted a hand to you—he couldn't handle a woman who stood up to him. Probably why he kept fucking around on you."

She sighed. "Fine. You want to play that way, go ahead. He did the same thing you do. Now *I* am going to do what Mom would have done—give more unsolicited advice. Stop standing there worrying and just talk to him."

CHAPTER 6

⌒

The old man was sitting behind the shop where he'd been working all these years.

Ever since he'd closed his place down. Hard to keep it open, when
half the people who used to bring him business started giving him
the side-eye, wondering if he had indeed killed his wife.

Gut in knots, Tate moved across the busted pavement slowly,
wondering how much of that was his fault. He'd never been quiet
about what he'd thought. Was he to blame for that, too?

A busted bit of glass crunched under his boot and his dad tensed,
slowly lifted his head.

He turned and looked and across the parking lot, their gazes locked.

Then Doug went back to eating his lunch. His actions were slow
and mechanical, like he did it only out of necessity. *I'm human. I gotta
eat. So I will.*

Tate understood that. That was how he approached almost everything in life. *I'm human. I gotta eat, gotta sleep, but I don't much care
if I do it or not. I'm only doing it because I have to.*

The only things in life that he took pleasure in were his art—and that was a release more than a pleasure—and Ali, her kids.

Fuck, he needed to get a better grip on life. Ali was everything, her kids were an added blessing he felt he had no right to.

But shouldn't there be *more*?

The wooden bench gave under his weight as he settled across from his father, but a foot or so down so he could look at the crumbling cinder block of the garage, rather than Doug. It was easier that way. Simpler.

He opened his mouth, then snapped it closed after five seconds passed with no words coming.

Clearing his throat, he tried again, but the words evaded him.

A quiet sigh drifted under the hot summer sun. Doug said softly, "Boy, whatever it is that's eating you, just let it go."

"I can't." He slanted a look at his father. They didn't look much alike—the artist in him could pick up the similarities—the shape of their hands, the set of their mouth, their eyes. But mostly, Tate took after his mom's father. Physically, at least. Everything else, though, that was his dad and that was why this was so hard. He clasped his hands together and pressed his forehead to them, staring at the table while words circled through his head.

They were *there*. If he could *think* them, he could *say* them.

Right?

His hands felt painfully empty and because he was having the hardest time concentrating, he tugged a little leather journal from his pocket and flipped it open. It was full of a thousand sketches, it seemed—he'd fill a page and then move on to the next, and the next until he had no room left. He'd then buy another one. This journal was about half full. He started to sketch and once his hands were moving, he could almost imagine the block in his head moving.

He sketched a wall. He'd add a ginormous wrecking ball smashing through it—he'd do the damn ball in the shape of his head. "I

messed up. I was wrong." He managed to get those words out as he finished the outline of the wall. He wished he could stop there.

"Tate, you had a rough life. You don't need to—"

"The hell I don't." He lifted his head slowly and met his father's eyes. His own eyes, he realized with a jolt. Not just the color, or the shape or the size. But everything about them. He realized Doug would do this, too. He'd force himself to own up to the hard shit. Maybe he wouldn't expect it of others, but he damn well expected it of himself.

The knot lodged in his throat and he threw the pencil he held down. "Fuck, Dad."

"You're too much like me, you know."

He sucked in a breath and went to say something, but before he could, Doug just continued to talk, his voice low and easy. "And . . . too much like your mom. Too much like yourself, even. If that makes sense. I don't think you could be any more contradictory if you had to." A hint of temper finally showed in the older man's voice as he tossed his sandwich down and dragged his hands over his face. "You don't want to expect anything from anybody, and at the same time, you seem to set the highest fucking expectations. How is that even possible?"

Tate ran his tongue across his teeth. Then he shrugged. "I'm an asshole?"

Doug's eyes shot to his face and then a slow, reluctant smile lit his face. "No." He shook his head. "No, you can be, and too often, you are. But that's because of the kick in the face life gave all of us. I think . . ." His voice trailed off and then he sighed. "I think if your mom hadn't gone and disappeared the way she did, you would have been a different man. You're a good man now, but you're harder. Sadder. I hate it."

Tate didn't know how to respond to that. Uncomfortable with the way the conversation was going, he sighed and shook his head. "Dad, there's no point in talking about any of that. I just . . . look. I'm sorry. I was wrong, and I'm sorry. I can't make any of it up to you."

He would have said more, but his father reached out and covered his hand with his.

It was the first time they'd touched in more than a decade. Tate recalled, vividly, the last time his father had touched him—high school graduation. He'd tried, yet again, to bridge the gap between them. Tate had told him if he laid hands on him again, he'd bury him.

Shame rose up in him, thick and dirty and black. He couldn't take this back, not any of it.

"You don't need to make a damn thing up to me," Doug said. "You're my son. The one thing I wanted to have again . . . other than to tell your mom how sorry I am . . . well, you called me Dad again. I don't need anything else."

His dad's image blurred. Looking away, he focused hard on the cinder block wall of the garage, staring at it until his vision cleared.

An awkward silence fell and he had no idea how to fill it, no idea what to say to this man who was all but a stranger to him now.

After a moment, Doug cleared his throat. "I hear you have something going with Ali."

Tate flicked him a look. Half the damn town. Probably closer to *all* the damn town. Shrugging, he reached for his pencil again and started to sketch. "Yeah. We're . . . ah. Well, we're working on it."

"She loves you."

Hands still over his sketch pad, Tate looked up.

Doug smiled. "I see how she looks at you. If you love her, boy, don't let that slip away. You have no idea how precious that is. Sometimes, you don't realize it until it's over and gone and you have no chance of ever getting it back."

I almost lost it. But he couldn't talk about it with his dad. This . . . thing was too awkward, too strange. He just met his dad's eyes and nodded. "I'm not going to let it go."

CHAPTER 7

H e'd stood here.
Just here, a hundred times.

Maybe even more.

At the foot of his mother's empty grave, waiting, wondering, hoping for answers that just weren't going to come.

For the first time, he stood there without feeling the weight of all those questions, all that anger.

"I don't think you'd want me to keep carrying all that around," he said, while a breeze kicked up, blowing his hair back from his face.

He sighed and then looked away. "Screw that. You wouldn't want it. I was wrong. You'd probably kick my ass if you could see how I've been acting all this time."

He couldn't undo it, though. All he could do was go forward.

"I'm going after Ali." He paused as the words hung there, tentative and soft. Then he nodded. "Yeah. That is something you would like. I love her."

Closing his eyes, he let himself smile. "I don't know how I'm going to handle any of that, but I love her and we're going to make it work."

He waited a few more minutes, might have said something else, but a fat, heavy drop of rain came down, fell on his nose. He shot a look up at the leaden sky and blew out a breath. "Good-bye, Mom."

He turned his back on the grave and strode out of the cemetery, but instead of heading straight to Ali's, he cut down by the river as the rain started to come down harder.

Miles down the river, far, far outside of sight, something, buried for years, shifted.

The car, pushed out of place after a year of heavy rains, started to drift.

Tate stood on Ali's porch. Although he had a key, he didn't go to the back door. He lifted a fist, knocked.

He had the words he wanted to say, and he was going to get them out. No matter what.

She opened the door, giving him a puzzled smile.

"I thought maybe I could take you out on a date," he said, while rain dripped down his face.

"Ah . . . well, the boys are here." She looked past his shoulder to stare out at the pounding rain. "It's raining kinda hard."

"I wanted to take you out. The boys. All of us." He swiped the rain from his face as Joey and Nolan appeared in the doorway, one on either side of her. They grinned up at him.

"Take us where?"

"On a date." He reached out, hoping she didn't see how his hands were shaking, just a little. "What do you think, guys? Can I take your mom out? You two?"

They didn't even blink. "Yeah! Let's go!"

They whooped and darted into the house while Ali continued to look at him, bemused. "A date," she murmured, while he moved up and caught her hips in his hands.

"A date."

He pressed a kiss to the corner of her mouth, sighed as her scent, warm and sweet, flooded him. The remnant ache in his heart faded.

"Tate, you're going to get me all wet again. You know that?"

"Yeah." He lifted his head and stared down at her. He frowned and stepped back, looked down.

She caught him, looping her fingers in his belt loops. "I don't care. So . . . tell me, what are we doing on this date of ours?"

"I have absolutely no idea."

She laughed and pressed her mouth to his. "That sounds absolutely wonderful."

TANGLED

by

Kate Douglas

To my longtime agent, Jessica Faust, BookEnds LLC,
who knows me way too well, and yet represents me anyway.
And to the amazing winemakers and grape growers of Dry Creek Valley,
who made research on "Tangled" so much fun.

ACKNOWLEDGMENTS

My sincere thanks to the folks at Bella Vineyards and Wine Caves (www.bellawinery.com/), for answering what might have sounded like really stupid questions (okay . . . they probably were really stupid questions) and who have a much nicer wine cave than the one at my mythical Tangled Vines Winery. And to the David Coffaro Estate Vineyard (www.coffaro.com/) and their wonderful Web site and online diary—a truly entertaining resource. A very special thank-you to all the winemakers and growers of Dry Creek Valley for producing such wonderfully inspirational world-class wines.

CHAPTER 1

⌒

W ell, shit." Nate Dunagan stood on the wrong side of the locked gate currently barring him from reporting to his new job at the Tangled Vines Dry Creek Valley vineyard, and honestly didn't know whether to laugh, cut loose with a primal scream, or just keep cussing. He really should have expected this, considering the day he'd had. After a ten-hour drive from Paso Robles that should have taken less than five—thanks to a grid-locked San Francisco Bay Area—a call from Marcus Reed, his new boss, telling Nate he'd be unable to meet him tonight as planned, and a dead cell phone, the locked gate was totally apropos.

Daylight was fading fast and the charger for the dead phone was stuck somewhere in one of the boxes with all his belongings in the back of the Silverado. According to his new boss, the winemaker would let him in. All he had to do was give her a call.

"Crap." Nate let out a frustrated breath, glanced at the dead phone in his hand and then stared up the driveway to a nice-looking farm-house at the end. The farmhouse was dark, but there was a light in a small cottage nearby, and a brighter light on the top floor of a fairly large barn set a couple of hundred yards north of the cottage.

That was probably his apartment. The one he couldn't get to. Marcus Reed had said it was the second floor of a remodeled dairy barn.

Nate glanced at the truck and muttered another curse. He'd stopped in the little town of Healdsburg to pick up a pizza and a couple of cold beers before heading up the valley. By now, the pizza was probably cold and the beer warm. He glanced toward the lighted cottage, back at the cab of the truck and figured, desperate times and all that. . . .

After he locked his truck and stuck the keys in his pocket, Nate climbed over the gate. Certainly not the way he'd planned on showing up for the new job. There'd damned well better be someone here who could let him in, or he'd be spending a long night in the truck with cold pizza and two warm beers for company. Still, as he trudged down the gravel drive toward the cottage, he had a feeling it was asking for a little too much, to think something might go right today.

Cassie fumbled for the cell phone that had somehow worked its way to the very bottom of her tote bag, dragged it out, and checked caller ID. Staring at the screen through two more bars of "Proud Mary," she thought seriously about sticking the phone back in her bag.

Of course, that wouldn't work. Not at all. "Hello."

"Cassie?"

"Yes."

"Marc Reed here. Has the new vineyard manager arrived? Nathan Dunagan. I was supposed to meet him at the ranch, let him into the apartment over the barn, that sort of thing, but I got tied up in a meeting. He should be there by now, but he's not answering his phone. Have you seen him?" Without giving her time to answer, he added, "Make sure he has keys, show him where everything is. Get him settled. Tell him I'll be there in the morning. Early."

"Yes, sir." She imagined a salute. Again, probably not appropriate.

"I gave Nate your cell number. He'll call when he gets to the gate so you can unlock it."

"I'll let him in."

"Good." The line went dead.

She stared at her phone. *Jackass.*

Shoving the phone in her pocket and shoving the brand-new absentee owner out of her mind, Cassie stared out the window. Damn she was going to miss this place. The cottage was okay, but nothing like this, her mom's kitchen with all the windows across the back and the breathtaking view of vineyard and redwood-covered hills.

This was her favorite time of day, when the sun slipped behind the trees.

Her favorite place in the whole world.

It should have been hers. Damn it all. It really should have been hers.

The perfect view wavered. Angry, she swept her hand across her eyes. She wasn't going to cry. It was too late for tears, for what ifs . . . for wishing she'd known before it was too late.

"Dad, I'm so glad you don't realize what you did. But damn . . ."

She took one last swipe across the spotless granite counter, folded the plain, white cotton towel over the edge of the sink, and walked out the back door of the only home she'd lived in for all her twenty-eight years.

Locking the door behind her, she walked across the yard without looking back. The guest cottage lay just beyond a tangled hedge of old roses, their stems unpruned for the past two years as her father slowly descended into the dementia that stole more of him each day.

When Marcus Reed and all his start-up billions bought Tangled Vines before the bank took it, she'd seen his purchase as both a blessing and a curse. He'd saved them from bankruptcy and paid enough that she could afford the assisted living facility her father's failing health demanded. Plus, Marcus had offered Cassie a decent job when he'd insisted that she and her wine-making skills be included in the deal.

As if she had a choice. She'd wanted to hate the man for buying the vineyard and small winery for a fraction of its worth, but he'd continued to surprise her. So far, he remained an owner in name only, and things had essentially stayed just the way they'd been when her father was still healthy and running the place with Cassie in charge.

She was still in charge to a certain extent, but she was no longer one of the owners, and no longer living in what used to be her home. Marcus Reed wanted the main house for his own occasional use and the apartment over the barn for the new vineyard manager. He'd offered Cassie the small cottage, the original house her mom and dad had lived in before Cassie was born. The catch was Cassie's promise to stay on as winemaker for at least the next five years.

Five years? Sounded like forever, but it wasn't as if she had anywhere else to go.

She'd aired the cottage out and moved some of her belongings in this past week. The rest, including most of the furniture remained in the main house. The new owner had said she could leave what she wanted and they'd deal with everything later. She appreciated that. She really couldn't deal with another thing. Not now.

Except now it appeared she had to deal with the vineyard manager. Her original plan—opening a bottle of their best Zinfandel wine and drinking it all by herself—was going to have to wait.

"Excuse me. Are . . ."

"What tha . . . ?" Cassie bit off a scream and spun around, almost tripping over her feet. A strange man stood just a dozen feet away;

she knew the gate was locked and no one should be anywhere near, so . . .

"I'm sorry." He took a quick step back, held up both hands, and smiled.

He didn't look dangerous when he smiled. Not that he'd looked dangerous before. Actually, he looked pretty impressive. Lean and rumpled in faded jeans and wrinkled camp shirt, but still dark and sexy and way too much man for her comfort level.

Especially on this side of her locked gate.

"I'm sorry I startled you," he said, answering what she was opening her mouth to ask. "I'm Nate Dunagan. Marcus Reed hired me. You are Cassie Phillips, aren't you?"

She let out a soft breath. Relieved, and more than a little interested. "I am." Smiling, she added, "I thought you were going to call." She glanced about, looking for his vehicle, except she was certain Lupe had locked the front gate. The hired hand never forgot things like that. "How'd you get here?"

He smiled again, but she thought it looked a bit strained. "I drove, but your gate's locked. I would have called, but the battery on my phone's dead, and I would have arrived a lot earlier, except I've had the trip from hell trying to get here. Would you mind unlocking the gate so I can get my truck in?"

"C'mon, Nate." She laughed, somehow feeling lighter than she had all day. "Your day doesn't sound any better than mine."

She was damned easy on the eyes. Nate glanced at her, sitting beside him in the cab of the Silverado with the box of cold pizza in her lap. He pulled in beside the barn he'd spotted from the road, and took another, more thorough look. Cassie Phillips was beautiful, in an offbeat way, with long hair that wasn't quite red curling past her shoulders; waves of curls that stopped just short of frizzy. He guessed the color was what his mom called strawberry blond, but it fit her. So did the freckles across her nose and the blue eyes, the snug purple tank top, worn jeans, and work boots.

Talk about fit—those faded jeans fit her like a second skin.

She turned and gazed steadily at him for what felt like a really long time. Long enough to be pretty unnerving. Finally she sort of nodded at the box in her hands. "This pizza smells really good, I haven't eaten since this morning, and I've had just about as crappy a day as you have. How about I help you unload your truck, show you where everything is, and then we take the pizza over to my house and reheat it." She shrugged and then smiled.

That smile changed everything.

"I'll share my salad if you'll share your pizza."

He returned her steady gaze long enough for her to look a little unnerved. It seemed only fair. "Works for me," he said. "C'mon. Show me where I'm going to be living for the foreseeable future."

She unlocked the door into what looked like a sturdy old barn on the outside. Inside, it had obviously been upgraded to serve as a tasting room. Simple and attractive, but definitely not a place he wanted to live.

"This way." She grabbed a couple of his bags, carrying them with the ease of someone used to heavy lifting. Impressed, Nate picked up a large box of miscellaneous stuff. Packing had never been his strong suit, but he followed her up a flight of stairs to a spacious second-floor studio apartment. It was comfortably furnished with a small kitchenette and a spectacular view of the vineyards and old oaks. The sun was long gone and the sky already a deep, dark blue. He imagined it would be absolutely beautiful in the morning when the sun rose over the hills to the east.

Best of all, it had a king-sized bed that was freshly made up, clean towels folded in the bathroom, and a coffeepot and fresh coffee in a canister on the counter.

All the necessities.

The two of them had all his stuff unloaded after a couple more trips.

"Is that it?" Cassie had already picked up the pizza, so Nate grabbed the two beers he'd bought. They were definitely warm, but at this point he was so tired he really didn't care.

Cassie led him to the small cottage instead of the big house. For some reason, he'd figured she lived in the house.

"No," she said when he asked. "Mr. Reed wants it for when he's here visiting, but I've got the cottage rent free. I hope that's the same deal he gave you on the apartment." She pushed the door open with her butt and he followed her into the small house.

"It is. He doesn't seem to worry much about money, does he?"

"I've noticed." She turned on the oven and stuck the pizza directly on the rack. "I've got cold beer in the refrigerator. Those are probably warm by now."

"Thanks." He opened the door on the refrigerator and sighed over an entire rack filled with bottled craft beers. Glancing over his shoulder, he shot her an appreciative grin. "This is impressive. I could fall in love right now."

She laughed, a sound so joyful Nate stopped in the process of opening his beer to look at her. She stood there in front of the stove with a huge grin on her face.

"My dad always said the way to a man's heart was through his stomach. My mom would shake her head and say no, it was through the quality of beer she kept in the refrigerator. I always keep cold beer on hand for when I bring my father home for visits."

He noticed she hadn't mentioned another man.

She rummaged through a drawer and a cabinet and pulled out

napkins and silverware, then grabbed paper plates out of another cabinet and set them on the bar separating the living area from the kitchen. Nate stayed out of her way while she mixed a big bowl of salad with what looked like homemade dressing and filled another paper plate of salad for each of them.

Last she took the hot pizza out of the oven and placed it on a wooden cutting board she'd set on the bar. Standing back, she studied the setting for a moment and sighed. "I'm beat. There are real dishes here somewhere, but I'm too tired to hunt for them."

"It's a lot fancier than I ever do. Smells wonderful."

"Sit." She reached for a bottle of wine sitting out on the counter, used a puller to get the cork out like she'd done it a million times—which, given her profession, she probably had—and poured herself a glass. Then she paused, grabbed another glass, and poured one for Nate.

"I've got my beer."

She stared at the goblet in her hand. "Yeah, but this is my wine. I want you to know what those grapes you're going to be babysitting are used for."

One sip and Nate knew for certain he'd made the right decision. He held the glass up to eye level and noted the deep red color of the wine, the way light barely made it through the heavy red. "This is amazing."

She tipped her head, accepting his compliment. "Thank you. I took over as Dad's winemaker when I graduated from Davis. I'd helped him from the time I was a kid, but he'd basically done it himself for over twenty years. He was good. I think my wines are even better."

"Did he retire?" He took a bite of pizza.

She didn't look at him. Stared, instead, toward the dark window. "Dad has Alzheimer's. It was so subtle at first that I didn't really notice, but before long it was obvious he was changing. It's horrible, really. Steady and inexorable, a truly grim march toward death."

"I'm sorry." He set his pizza back on the plate. "He can't be very old. What are you, twenty-five or so?"

She laughed. "You're on the right side of close. I'm twenty-eight, but lately I've felt years older. Dad's eighty-five. He married late, after he retired from government service, and bought the land in 1984. It was originally a dairy but the cows were long gone and there were some grapes planted. Overall, it was pretty run-down when he took over."

Shaking her head, she chuckled softly. "He said he'd always loved a challenge, that this was one of his biggest. He met my mom shortly after he moved in. He'd already fixed up this cottage, and even though there were over twenty years between them, they fell in love. They got married, and had finished building the house next door by the time I came along a couple of years later."

"Your mom?"

Cassie shrugged and glanced away for a brief moment. Then she focused on Nate. "Mom died of breast cancer when I was fourteen. That left my dad with a teenaged girl to raise on his own." She shot him a sly little smile. "That's how I learned wine making. He figured keeping me busy in the cellar was better than wondering where I was all the time. I thought it was cool because I got to taste the wine."

"It's got to be tough, watching him now." His grandfather's slow decline had been painful beyond belief.

"It is. He had a damned good life, but it's so wrong, watching time steal from him when no one else could ever get the upper hand. What makes it so hard is that he's well aware he's losing ground. He was an army colonel, a decorated veteran who spent years in the Secret Service." She took a slow sip of her wine.

Nate watched the subtle ripple along her throat as she swallowed, the way her eyes slowly closed as she savored the taste. But was she savoring, or grieving what she'd lost? Not only her parents, but the home and vineyard where she'd been raised, the winery with an amazing reputation that she'd helped build. All now belonging to someone else.

"Yeah," she said. She turned and looked at him. Her eyes glistened, but the tears didn't spill. "Time and age are proving there are some battles even the best men can't win."

"Is that why you sold to Marcus Reed? Because of your dad's failing health."

"That's the really sad part. The plan all along was for the winery to come to me, but Dad was handling the books while the dementia was beginning to take hold. He made some bad business decisions. The place was paid for, but he borrowed against the vineyard a couple of years ago to buy more land without telling me. He wanted a wine cave that's across the road. It was dug into the hillside years ago, back before prohibition. We couldn't afford the payments on the new mortgage, but I didn't find out until we were so far in arrears there was no digging our way out. This is a small winery—our biggest year we did just under two thousand cases—and he paid top dollar for the cave and surrounding vineyard. The good thing is, he got some beautiful old Zinfandel vines that still produce really well. The bad thing is, we couldn't pay the bills. We were getting ready to declare bankruptcy when Marcus Reed stepped in with enough cash to pay off the mortgage and pay for Dad's care."

She swiped at one errant tear that had obviously managed to slip free. Nate merely nodded. "But you're still here?"

"Yeah." She smiled in a sad sort of agreement. "I'm still here. I'm part of the deal. We were making award-winning wines during the whole mess, and I guess that's what Mr. Reed wanted. The awards, the accolades. In that respect, we came out okay. I still have a roof over my head, and Dad's taken care of. I have to concentrate on what's important. What really matters."

Obviously it was family that mattered. Nate's respect for Cassie continued to grow.

The conversation flowed as smoothly as the wine they drank. He told her about his childhood in upstate New York, how he'd wanted to be a farmer since he was just a kid growing up on his grandparents' farm. At first it was the idea of eating the fruits and vegetables he'd helped grow, the eggs he'd gathered, the milk he'd squeezed out of one of the two cows his grandfather kept; he liked working with his hands. When he got older, he'd discovered good wine, especially the different varietals. Curious about the process, he'd learned about wine making, which was all about the grapes, and that took him full circle, right back to the farm, to the whole concept of growing grapes to make premium wines. They talked about their classes in viticulture—his at Cornell, Cassie's at UC Davis—and Nate's decision to find work with a smaller winery, just like Tangled Vines.

He wanted to do it all: from planting the rootstock and nurturing the new vines, to pruning and trellising and every step of the process, right down to supervising the picking and the delivery of perfect fruit.

His goal from the time he'd graduated from college had been the smaller, hands-on vineyards, but all his experience to date had been with a big factory-sized operation, since they had been the only one hiring. Still he kept wanting that same intimate experience he'd gotten in college, the chance to work with the vines, with the soil. To try new things, get his hands dirty, and get to know every square inch of the vineyard.

Marcus Reed had offered him the job of a lifetime, and it was such a rush to see the same excitement in Cass, the same dedication to the process from grape to wine that Nate felt.

Cassie told him about growing up on a small vineyard, about the responsibility that almost overwhelmed her during her mother's illness, what it had been like watching her dad fail and the struggle to keep everything going entirely alone.

But she'd done it, and she'd done a good job. Her life on the vineyard, working with the wines was all she'd ever known. She loved everything about wine making, the thrill of the harvest and the rich aroma of fermenting grapes that hung over the valley during crush, the process of combining the various barrels to find the perfect blend. If not for her father's financial problems, she'd still be living in the big house, still making her own award-winning wines.

"I don't get it," Nate said. He took another swallow of Cassie's amazing wine. He'd passed on more of the craft beers for the finest old-vine Zinfandel he'd ever tasted, but one part of the equation eluded him. "Why did Marcus Reed hire me? If you're doing so well with the wines and the vineyard, where do I fit in?"

She took a sip of her wine and grinned at him. "Trust me. You'll fit. Dad was the vineyard manager for years, and the young kid who helped him, Lupe Medino, started right out of high school. We have a couple of guys who come in on a seasonal basis when they're needed. They've been thinning out suckers this past week, but the rows still need to be disked to knock down the weeds. Lupe took over managing the vineyard this past year when it was obvious Dad couldn't do it. He's really good. He's smart and he works hard, but he goes to the junior college and won't have time to do the job the way he has in the past. Plus, he's aiming for a four-year school to finish out his viticulture degree. You'll have him to help you when he's available, but he won't have time to run the vineyard."

"Makes sense. What do you know about the new owner? He told me he wants to change the name from Tangled Vines to Intimate, something about a line of some kind of jewelry he's planning to come out with next year."

Cassie merely shrugged, though it was obvious to Nate she wasn't happy about the name change. "He's the owner. He can do what he wants." She glanced away and then stared at the empty pizza box and laughed. "Wow, I sure hope you ate most of that."

She was really stunning when she laughed. Nate went to take another sip of his wine, realized the glass was empty and reached for the bottle. "I told you I was hungry." He picked up the empty bottle and held it to the light. "Must have been thirsty, too. Was this full when we started?"

This time she raised her eyes to the ceiling as if looking for strength . . . or maybe it was forgiveness. "That bottle was full, and so was this one." She leaned over and picked up an empty off the floor. "It's almost eleven. We've been eating, drinking, and chatting for almost four hours."

He'd been exhausted when he arrived this evening, but now he felt energized—he didn't want what had been an absolutely perfect evening to end. He didn't want to overstay his welcome, either, so he stood and gathered up his paper plates and the empty wineglass. "I guess that's my cue to let you get some rest. Thank you, Cassie. This was a much nicer welcome than I expected. I'm really looking forward to working with you."

He tossed the plates and set the glass in the sink. When he turned, Cassie was standing beside the counter with her plates in hand, staring at him again in that unnerving way she had. She made Nate feel as if she looked beneath his skin.

"I've enjoyed myself, too," she said. "Thanks for sharing your pizza." She tossed the paper plates in the trash and then stuck her glass and silverware next to Nate's in the sink.

When she turned, they were mere inches apart. Her lips parted in surprise and he should have stepped back, given her room. But whatever had been simmering between them all evening slowly, steadily— as if he watched one of those stupid slow-motion explosions in a movie—exploded.

He cupped the back of her head with his palm and looked into her eyes. She didn't move, but this time when she looked at him, there was nothing at all unnerving in her stare. He saw heat and desire, a need every bit as powerful as his own. As he slowly dipped his head to take her mouth, he gave her every opportunity to pull away.

She didn't. One hand rested on his shoulder, the other softly caressed the back of his neck. Just before he kissed her, she sighed. It was the smallest hint of surrender.

It was all Nate needed.

She tasted of pizza and wine. The lush flavor of grapes was heady enough on its own, but combine that with the taste of Cassie Phillips and Nate freely admitted he didn't have a prayer of stepping away.

This was probably one of the stupidest things she'd ever done. She had no time for a man in her life, not now, but damn this guy could kiss. He was tall and lean, at least six two or three, and movie-star gorgeous. When she first saw him, she'd thought of Bradley Cooper with his thick, dark hair and beautiful blue eyes, but beyond the way he looked, he was funny, smart, and compassionate. He'd kept her laughing most of the evening with his dry sense of humor, and the time had flown. She hadn't sat and just talked with a man for almost three years.

She'd never spent time talking with a man like Nate Dunagan.

The rambling conversations with her father didn't count, and she was too damned busy trying to hold things together to spend anytime in town where she might actually meet someone single and interesting. But Nate talked passionately about his work, about his hopes for the future, about what he wanted to do here at Tangled Vines.

They agreed on so much it was almost unsettling.

When he finally broke the kiss and rested his chin on top of her head, they were both breathing hard. She wanted him. The need was so primal, so visceral, it left her shaken, but that kiss hadn't been enough. Not nearly enough.

He held her face between his palms and kissed her again, lightly. "Damn. When I first saw you, I thought you were beautiful, but I never

expected to like you as much as I do. Or want you as badly as I do."
He laughed. "But I do, Cassie. Which means I'd better leave before I
use any arguments I can think of short of brute force to haul you off
to bed."

She laughed and buried her face against his chest. He felt so wonderfully solid. Strong enough to lift some of the overwhelming pressure
of trying to keep Tangled Vines alive for the past couple of years
while everything went to hell. "Nate, there hasn't been a man in my
bed for over three years. I probably wouldn't remember what to do
with you if I got you there."

He chuckled and nuzzled the sensitive skin behind her ear. But
he didn't let her go. "I imagine it's sort of like riding a bike."

"Ya think?" She gazed up at him, head tilted, and realized their
teasing had taken on a more intimate note. Was she ready for this?
She was certainly attracted. Probably too attracted.

"I'm positive."

He kissed her again, and she found herself opening to him. Holding him close enough to feel the solid proof of his erection against
her belly and the yearning, tugging pull deep in her womb. When the
kiss ended by mutual consent, both of them were breathing hard.
"Wow." She licked her lips. "Maybe you're right. It's all coming back
to me."

"Me, too." He kissed her again, quick and hard. "I don't want to
leave."

"I don't want you to go." She unbuttoned the top button on his shirt,
and then the second so she could run her fingers over the hard curves
of his chest. "We'd need protection," she said. "If I have any condoms,
they're out of date." Then she raised her head and grinned at him. "And
believe me, I am so sorry right now that I'm not prepared, because
I'd really like for you to stay." Chuckling, he reached for his hip pocket
and pulled out his wallet. "Don't give up hope. Not yet." He dug
through the notes and bills that filled the thing, and came up with

one relatively new-looking foil packet. "I've got enough for one shot, so we'll have to make it good."

She took it from him and cocked an eyebrow. "Just how good are you?"

He kissed her. "I'll let you be the judge of that."

She felt so comfortable with him, as if they'd known each other for years rather than hours, but at the same time the thrill of someone new, someone smart and funny and drop-dead gorgeous, was its own aphrodisiac.

At least that's what her body was telling her.

She ran her hand over his hair. It was thick and so dark it was almost black, surprisingly soft, like silk beneath her fingers. "I do want you to stay," she said. "It's probably the wine talking and I'll hate myself in the morning, but tonight has been the most fun I've had in so long I can't remember as good a time. I'm not ready for it to end."

He kissed her. Briefly, sweetly. "I'll do my best to keep you from hating yourself." He winked. "Or hating me, either."

A flash of caution had Cassie adding, "No commitments, no promises. Just tonight, okay? We have to work together starting tomorrow."

He ran his fingertip along the bridge of her nose and touched her lips. "No promises, no commitments. But I can tell you already, tonight is going to be amazing." Before she had time to react, he picked her up, holding her in his arms as if she were just a child. The room spun, but she held on tightly to Nate—and the condom.

And pointed him toward the bedroom.

CHAPTER 2

He loved the feel of her in his arms, but he had to admit, having that little "no promises, no commitments" clause in the conversation left him feeling enormously relieved. He had no time for commitments beyond the one that had brought him here. Not when he still had to prove himself capable of the job he'd be starting tomorrow.

He didn't have any concerns about proving himself to Cassie tonight.

It should have felt awkward, carrying a woman he barely knew into her bedroom, but nothing had ever felt quite this right before. They'd talked for hours, had listened to each other, shared some of the bad things in their lives, talked about the good things, and somewhere in there he'd felt a connection developing that had been so unexpected, so powerful, that this had become a necessary next step.

She wasn't a small woman, but she was all wiry strength and lean muscle. She felt light as a child in his arms, but there was nothing childish about her. She'd looped one arm around his neck and she studied his face with eyes as blue as a summer sky. When he laid her down on her bed, she propped herself up on her elbows and watched him as he untied her boots and tugged them off, as he pulled off her socks and then reached for her tank top.

She sat up then, grabbed the hem and pulled it over her head. She wasn't wearing a bra, and the absolute perfection of her small, firm breasts left him speechless. He'd been ready to take off his boots, but instead he bracketed her hips with both arms, leaned forward and drew one coral-colored tip into his mouth, laving the nipple into a tight peak, tasting the salty-sweetness of her skin.

She moaned and arched her back, pressing her breasts closer, but even though it killed him to pull away, he needed to take his boots off. Hell, he had to take everything off, so of course he tangled the strings into an impossible knot. "Shit." He sat there cursing at his left boot as if that would make the knots magically disappear. Then he glanced at Cassie and she was folded over, laughing so hard he figured she'd be absolutely useless, but he stuck his booted foot under her nose and she deftly unknotted the strings.

The giggles hit her hard when his boot thumped to the ground. She rolled over on her belly and buried her face in her pillow, laughing so hard her entire body shook. Nate rolled to his back on the bed, lifted his legs, and tugged off his jeans. His knit boxers stayed put, but there was no hiding the fact he was heavily aroused.

Cassie raised her head, took a long, steady look at him, and her laughter died on a tiny whimper.

That was encouraging. Too encouraging. Damn, but she looked so hot, lying there with her face flushed and her back bare to the frayed waistline of her worn jeans. Jeans covering the most beautiful ass he'd ever seen. He sucked in a breath. His body was caught on a knife's edge, so damned aroused he felt strung tight, ready to explode. He clenched his hands, took a deep breath, and prayed for some semblance of control.

Then Cassie rolled over, slipped her jeans off, and sat there in the middle of her bed, watching as he took off his shirt—the same shirt he'd been wearing since he left Paso Robles. "I should have gotten a shower first. It's been a long day."

Cassie laughed and flopped backward. "I need one, too, but ya know what? I don't care, and if you don't, we can get one after, because I really don't want to wait."

Lord, but she was beautiful, and he liked her attitude. "Me, either."

He kept his boxers on as he slowly peeled away her tiny scrap of whatever she wore that was supposed to be underwear. He tugged the narrow elastic as far as her thighs and raised his head and chuckled. "You really are a natural strawberry blonde, aren't you?"

She growled.

"Did you just growl at me?" He sat back and grinned at her. "Never mind." Laughing, he tugged her panties the rest of the way down, and once he got them off, he held the thong up and studied the purple lace. "You wear these when you're working?"

"Yeah." She flashed him a cocky grin. "What's it to ya?"

He shook his head. "I'm going to be out there in the vineyard, covered in mud, working my ass off with a hard-on, imagining you wearing these." He hung them carefully from the bedpost, and knelt between her legs. "That doesn't seem fair, ya know?"

"You gonna keep those on?" She cocked one eyebrow and pointed at his boxers, the ones that did absolutely nothing to hide the fact he was beyond aroused.

"For now. I don't want to get sidetracked."

"From what?" She raised her head as he lowered his.

"From this."

She sighed as he palmed her perfect ass, lifted her hips in both hands, and used his tongue and lips and even his teeth, nipping, licking, sucking until he lost himself in her flavors and silky textures. When he slipped his fingers inside, the rippling strength of her climax almost sent him over the top. She cried out, curled her back, and her fingers fluttered helplessly over his scalp, the tips of his ears, along his jaw.

So responsive, and so beautiful when she came. He was shaking like a leaf and Cassie was still whimpering softly as he stood, stripped off his shorts, and sheathed himself.

She was still shuddering from an unexpected, amazing climax when Nate stood beside the bed and slipped out of his dark blue knit boxers. She'd thought he was gorgeous before, but watching him as he stood naked beside the bed and carefully rolled the condom over an absolutely beautiful erection, Cassie figured she had a visual she'd be able to fantasize over for a long, long time. There wasn't an ounce of fat on him. Muscular, but the kind of muscles from hard work, not hours spent in a gym. A light dusting of dark hair covered his pecs and picked up again at his navel, and from there it led directly to evidence that Nate was ready to take this little interlude a step further.

She'd meant what she had said earlier—she refused to think of anything beyond tonight. They didn't know each other and she wasn't going to think about the fact that she never did this sort of thing. She'd had no-strings sex before in college when there was no pressure to pretend to be in love, and the joy of this night with Nate was sort of the same thing—they weren't in love. They had no baggage, hardly knew each other, but they'd talked enough that she knew she liked him.

It was all okay, as long as she didn't let herself think too much. Thinking always seemed to get her in trouble. Then Nate was back on the bed and it was once again all about sensation, the pure physical pleasure of his beautiful body close to hers. He was long and strong and his skin was hot, as if a furnace burned beneath the surface. He settled between her legs, but he didn't enter her. Not at first. He leaned close and kissed her, making love to her mouth with such finesse that she felt herself growing more aroused, knew her body was responding so powerfully to his kisses that she could come again before he even filled her.

That wasn't going to happen. She tilted her hips, reached for him and savored his hot, hard length as she positioned him against her as he thrust forward. She held her breath and Nate must have, too, because they both sighed when his balls brushed her butt and the thick length of his cock filled her.

She opened her eyes and grinned at him. "You fit. I was worried."

"No you weren't." He thrust his hips and it felt so damned good she whimpered. "You just wanted to get your hands on me." And he went deeper this time. "Didn't you?"

She laughed, a deep, throaty laugh of pure sensual pleasure. "Caught me. You're right." She'd never felt so wanton.

Grinning broadly, Nate thrust again, and again, harder and faster, then slow and deep, until she caught his rhythm, matched it, and lifted to meet him. She thought for a moment that this felt so good, they should just keep doing it all night long.

And then she remembered there was only one condom.

Nate was only going to get one orgasm, but she was pretty impressed when he dragged two more out of her before he finally buried himself deep, his face twisting in an expression of absolute pleasure.

He whispered a soft, almost reverent curse as he took her with him one last time.

Colonel Mac, as Macon Phillips preferred to be called, stared at the cards in his hand and tried to remember what game they played. It was usually seven-card stud, but he was only holding five cards, and that didn't feel right.

"C'mon, Mac. How many cards you want?"

Benny did tend to get impatient. Mac stared at his hand. Two kings, two fours, and a seven, and if Benny was asking what he wanted, this had to be five-card draw. He pulled out the seven and put it on the table. Benny gave him a card and Mac made a noncommittal grunt. That third king looked real nice though, lined up with the other two.

The game went on and he sort of drifted in and out. He was doing more of that lately, and it really pissed him off, but not as much as what he'd done to Cassie. He'd never forgive himself for getting them in such a mess. It was hard to accept, doing something so stupid. Hell, he'd made decisions that saved lives, and he'd hidden more information about people than most folks ever knew in a lifetime.

He wondered if he should tell Cassie about the briefcase? It was well hidden, and she'd be okay as long as no one went looking for it, but what if she found it? What if she let that info get into the wrong hands?

"Mac? You with us tonight?"

He jerked his head up. Hector sounded a bit testy. Mac chuckled. "Just wool gatherin', Hector."

"Leave the damned sheep alone, my dear colonel, and make a decision. You in or out?"

Mac sighed and tossed in a handful of chips. They were just chips—no money was allowed to change hands here in the Mountain Vista Assisted Living Facility social hall, otherwise known as the Old Fart's Casino by the resident old farts in question.

Just worthless chips.

Sort of how he felt, like one more worthless chip, but moving here had been his decision. Penance, he figured, except there would never be enough he could do to make it up to her. He hadn't seen Cassie for a couple of days, but he remembered her saying she was moving out of the house. That just about killed him, to think that the house he'd built for her mother, the house he wanted his daughter to have, now belonged to some rich idiot from San Francisco. It was just wrong.

And what if the new owner found that briefcase? Hell. He hadn't even thought of that.

Hal laid his cards down. Two pair, queens and jacks. He reached for the chips when Hector said, "Not so fast, Hal."

Hector laid out four tens and grinned at the other men at the table.

At least in this respect, things were looking up. Mac fanned his full house out on the table. "Three kings and two fours, gentlemen. Read 'em and weep." He reached for the pile of chips.

Benny put up a hand. "Hold up a minute, Colonel." He spread his cards on the table. A straight flush—nine, eight, seven, six, and a five of hearts.

"Not bad, old man."

Mac and the others turned toward the new voice.

"Hey, son! When did you get here?" Benny stood up and embraced the younger man walking toward the table.

"Just now. I had to come through town and thought I'd stop in and see you. Still up to your old tricks, I see."

"Always." Laughing, Benny turned toward the three men at the table. "Boys, this is my stepson, Jayson. Jay, this is Hal Munson, Hector Ruiz, and the newest member of our group, Mac Phillips."

"Nice to meet you." Jay shook hands with Hal and Hector and then smiled at Mac, almost as if he knew him.

Mac didn't think he'd ever seen this kid before, but the way his memory had been acting up lately . . .

"Colonel Macon Phillips, by any chance?" Jay's grin stretched completely across his rather nondescript face and he held out his hand.

Mac shook it. "Yes, it is. Do I know you?"

"No, sir, but I've heard of you. That book about your tour of duty in Vietnam and your years in the Secret Service was practically required reading in my political history class."

Mac chuckled. This he remembered. "That book made it look a lot

more glamorous than it was. What it was, was a long, long time ago."
Still, it was nice to know that somebody remembered. For some
reason, those days were so clear to him. Much clearer than whatever
happened a couple of days ago. Hell, even a couple of hours ago.

"When you have time, I'd love to hear some of your stories. I bet
you could put a whole new spin on current politics."

Mac merely smiled. That was the truth, though he wasn't real
comfortable talking about those days. Once sworn to secrecy, it was
hard for a man to open up about stories that should never see the light
of day.

Of course there were a few, dammit, that should have been front
and center, but they got buried when the wrong people turned up in
the mess. Wrong people being a euphemism for politicians with
more money than integrity. "I've always got time, boy." *Boy* worked
when you couldn't remember a name. Jeff? Jim? No matter. They
were all boys, now. How the hell did he get so old? "I'm just not sure
if some of those stories should ever be told."

He remembered a briefcase. He'd been thinking about it earlier, for
some reason. He'd remember later why it was so important. If it was.

The kid was here to take Benny out to dinner. Hector decided to
call it an early night, but Hal had a movie he was going to watch in
his room. *All The President's Men*. Mac had never been much of a fan
of that movie. Not at all. Sometimes the truth hit too close to home.

"Hey, Mac? You coming with me? I've got a bottle of Jim Beam."

"Sounds good, Hal. Real good." Besides, Cassie wouldn't be visiting tonight. Sure beat sitting alone in his room.

He managed to stick it out for over an hour, but it was making him
twitch, sitting here drinking with Hal and trying to pretend interest
in a movie that brought back too many things he'd rather forget. Crazy,
really, how the stuff you wished you could remember was gone like
the morning mist, and that crap from years ago filled up your brain
and kept you awake nights.

Almost like it was etched into your damned DNA. He wandered back out to the game room. There'd been a new *National Geographic* on the table earlier. If no one had snagged it, he'd take it to his room and see if he could get some sleep. It was still early—not even nine, yet. He thought about calling Cassie, but the girl worked so damned hard she might already be in bed. Ah . . . there it was. He grabbed the magazine off the table and turned to head back to his room.

"Colonel Mac? You're still up."

He spun around. Not good when a man could sneak up on you. He really needed to pay better attention. The fellow looked vaguely familiar, but . . .

"I'm Jay. Benny's son. We met earlier."

Mac nodded. He vaguely recalled meeting the kid. Here, or at the winery? "Where's Benny?"

"Dad went on to bed. Have you got some time? I'd really love to hear some of your stories. You had a truly amazing career, and I'm fascinated by that era. So much going on in this country during the late sixties, seventies, even into the eighties."

Mac nodded. "Pretty wild stuff, that's for sure." It was a nice change to talk with someone curious about those years. Everyone was so caught up in the present. Didn't they realize that those who didn't know their history were destined to repeat it? He said as much, and the kid nodded his head.

"Edmund Burke," he said. "An Irish statesman. He also said, 'The only thing necessary for the triumph of evil is for good men to do nothing.' That's what I admire about you, Colonel. You did something, something that mattered. And I'd really love to hear all about it."

He stared at the kid for a minute. He had an open face, a likable face. It couldn't hurt to tell him a few. And he was right. Mac had done a lot. More than most people would ever guess. He'd never talked about his work, never bragged about the things he'd done, but now? Now he was losing so many memories. Daily. But those old memories were clear. Too damned clear. That's why they still kept him awake nights.

He followed the kid over to a corner sitting area, sat down in one of the comfortable chairs, and tried to remember the exploits that had once kept his juices flowing. Those were good days. Mostly good days.

Except when they'd all gone terribly wrong.

Someone must have used a jackhammer on her brain. That was the only explanation. Cassie opened her eyes to bright sunlight streaming through the bedroom window. Sunlight? Oh, hell. She glanced at the clock beside the bed, threw back the covers, and raced into the bathroom.

It was after seven. Lupe probably wondered where in the hell she was. They were supposed to meet at the cave this morning and get things ready for bottling next week. Damn. She peered at herself in the mirror and cursed. Then she turned on the shower and got in before the hot water had time to reach this end of the cottage. Shivering, she soaped up, rinsed off, washed and conditioned her hair and ran one hand over her calf. Bristly but not horrible. It didn't really matter under her jeans. Didn't matter unless . . .

"Oh, shit." *Nate.* She leaned against the shower wall to keep from falling, and thunked her head so hard on the tile she saw stars. She couldn't believe she hadn't even looked to see if he was still in her bed.

Rinsing off, Cassie got out of the shower, dried herself, and wrapped the towel around her body. Slowly, she opened the bathroom door a crack and glanced at the bed. He wasn't there. She stepped partway out of the bathroom so she could get a better view of the room.

No sign of Nate. His boots and clothes were gone. She breathed a huge sigh of relief. What an idiot she'd been! The man was her new vineyard manager, not a fuck buddy. They were going to have to work together, sleeping together was out of the question . . . well it should have been.

She stalked across the room, grabbed a lacy thong out of the dresser drawer, and slipped it on. Turning, she saw the pair she'd had on last night still hanging from the bedpost, and wanted to crawl under the bed and just stay there. Crap. She couldn't believe what they'd done.

Except her body remembered. Oh, damn did it remember. Her nipples ruched into tight little buds and she felt an answering ripple of heat between her legs. She turned and saw a glimpse of herself in the mirror. She stopped, caught by the stranger staring back at her.

Her breasts were marked with streaks of red from his five o'clock shadow. So was the tender skin of her inner thighs, and it looked as if he'd left a bite mark on the side of her throat, but it wasn't the physical brands he'd left that caught and held her. It was the way she practically glowed. Hell, if she could see it, there was no way she'd be able to hide this from Lupe or anyone else she saw today.

This was not going to happen again. It couldn't happen again. She wasn't about to let it.

She finished dressing, pulling on the same jeans she'd worn yesterday, and when she couldn't find the tank top she'd had on last night, she pulled a T-shirt out of the closet.

One with a high enough neckline to cover the hickey. It was hot pink with a scrawled saying across the front: *With wine all things are better.* She slipped it on, and couldn't help but think about last night, about sharing wine with Nate. About his hands and his lips and . . . "No, dammit!"

Dressed now but still running late, she spun about and headed out to the kitchen. There was a pot of coffee already made. She poured herself a cup, and then she saw a note written on a paper napkin. Next to the note was a handful of daisies from the bush beside the front door. Sipping her coffee, she read what Nate had written.

That has to be the best welcome I've ever had on any new job. I think I'm going to love the benefits. Hope to see you later this morning. Nate

Benefits? That's what he thought of her. She stared at his bold handwriting and tried to think of something truly awful about the man.

She couldn't. But damn it all, she was going to have to try, because this was not going to work.

Still, she put the daisies in a glass of water and set them on the bar where they'd eaten last night. How the hell was she going to face him today?

And how was she going to keep him out of her bed tonight?

CHAPTER 3

‿‿

"It's almost four, Lupe. Go home. Josie's going to think I kidnapped you."

Lupe just laughed at her. "Sure thing, boss. Except she's busy checking out the new vineyard manager. Said he's hot." He winked. "You met him yet?"

She nodded but kept her eyes focused on the tablet in her hand, and the notes she'd taken during the day. "Yeah. Last night. Had to unlock the gate and let him in, show him where his apartment was."

"What'd you think? He okay? Does he know what he's doin'?"

Oh, Lordy . . . did he ever know. Her inner muscles clenched and released and clenched again from some sort of physical memory she was going to have to put a lid on. Quickly. She shrugged. "He's got a good education and all the right degrees. Has been working down in Paso Robles for the past eight years, in the Finger Lakes area in up-state New York before that."

"Cornell?"

Cassie shot him a grin. Lupe'd been studying every college in the country, trying to figure out the best viticulture program. "Yep. That on your list?"

"Too far from family. Josefina said I'd have to tie her up and ship her in a big box because she'd not go willingly." He laughed again, but his smile was so sweet it hit Cassie hard. To be loved as much as Lupe loved his smart and sassy wife? One could only hope.

"It'll probably be Davis."

"Good choice." Cassie grabbed her backpack with the remnants of her bagel, all she'd had to eat today. "I'll lock up. Say hi to Josie for me. See you in the morning."

Cassie took a last, quick glance around the cave and the barrels they'd be bottling next week to make sure everything was ready. She still had to check on the labels. All the legal stuff for the ownership and name change hadn't been completed yet, so this would be the final vintage of their award-winning old-vine Zinfandel bottled under the Tangled Vines label.

The first time she'd bottled without her dad here to help. Damn.

Intimate wasn't a bad name, it just wasn't the name her mom and dad had chosen. Tangled Vines, not just for the twisted grape vines, but for the tangled threads that had brought both of them here to Dry Creek Valley at the perfect time in their lives. Mac, leaving the Secret Service after years of work, most of it classified, and Melinda running from a long-term, abusive relationship. Him older, ready to settle, Melinda tired of trying to make a failed relationship work. They'd met and, in spite of an age difference of over two decades, had fallen deeply in love and been happy.

Was it so much to ask for? Happiness? Sometimes it sure felt like it. Cassie shook the old thoughts aside. She needed to get home and clean up, and then she really had to get into town and see Dad, maybe take him out to dinner.

One of these days, she was going to show up and he wouldn't know her. She really didn't have time to waste, and neither did he.

She'd been so late this morning, she'd brought the truck, but now Cassie was glad she had it. She stopped at the front gate and got the mail, then pulled up in front of the cottage and climbed out of the truck, not easy with her arms filled with the mail she'd grabbed out at the box on the road, and her backpack with her tablet.

"Hello, Cassie."

She spun around, grappling with mail, backpack, and keys. "Do you always have to sneak up on me like that?" Damn it all, she was so not ready to see Nate. Not now. Not tonight.

"I'm sorry." He frowned and stepped closer. "You okay? Marc Reed just left. He was here all day so we could go over plans with the vineyard. He's planning to come next week when you bottle."

"Yeah. He texted me earlier, asked if I wanted to go to lunch with you two." She paused at the front steps. "Look, Nate. I'm in a hurry. I'm going into town to see Dad, and if I want to take him to dinner, I have to get there soon. They start serving around five and I'm afraid he'll forget I called and told him I was coming."

He backed off. "Okay. That's fine. Guess I'll see you tomorrow." He turned abruptly and walked away, back toward the barn. Cassie walked up the stairs, went inside, put her mail and backpack down. She got as far as the bedroom before she burst into tears.

Obviously last night hadn't had the same impact on Cassie as it had had on him. Nate walked back to the barn with his head spinning. He wasn't angry with her, or even hurt. Mostly confused. As in, how to fix this and make it better. Last night probably shouldn't have happened, but he couldn't regret what had arguably been the best sex in his life. He really liked Cassie. She was smart and funny and drop-dead gorgeous, but she also had a hell of a lot on her plate right now.

Her world was in turmoil, and having him move in and slide

right into her bed couldn't have looked good in the cold light of day. Somehow, he had to let her know how much it had meant to him while at the same time making sure she didn't feel as if she owed him anything or had to act differently around him.

Okay. That was about as sensitive as he could manage. What he really wanted was to go back to her little cottage and screw the night away, but this job was too important to take a chance like that. Especially after what Marc Reed had said just before he left, a warning that made Nate wonder if the guy had been able to tell what he and Cass had been up to last night.

"Cassie Phillips is the heart and soul of this winery. She's smart, she's beautiful, and she's got skills I can't even imagine. I like you, Nate, and I think you'll be a great asset to this company, but if there's a problem between you and Cass, she stays." Then he'd smiled at Nate like it was no big deal when he added, *"I know it's not fair and probably not what any man wants to hear, but I can't afford to lose her, so what I'm saying is, don't fuck with the winemaker."*

Well, nothing like putting it all out there, though Nate actually had to admire the man's attitude. Cassie had proven herself—no doubt about that. He'd researched the Tangled Vines history and they consistently scored well in all the big competitions. Expenses were historically low, profits high—until her father had made some bad business decisions.

Despite those, Cassie had her record to stand on. Nate had zip. And beyond that, he really liked her. He hated that Cass might feel uncomfortable around him because of last night.

He went upstairs and looked at the pile of bags and boxes that he hadn't had time to put away. Marc Reed had shown up at seven this morning, driving in from San Francisco a lot earlier than Nate had expected. He'd barely gotten out of the shower in time to meet his boss downstairs. They'd had a full day—a good day—and Nate had been impressed with both the man and the vineyards.

They'd gotten a good look at the piece of property on the other side of West Dry Creek Road, the sloping hillsides covered with some really old vines and an absolutely magnificent wine cave. He didn't think Cassie even noticed he and Marc had been there—she'd been on the phone with a local mobile bottling company that would come in and do the bottling next week. She'd been talking inert gas and filtration, capsules, and corks—a totally different language than his part of the process.

He'd wanted to stay and listen longer, just to watch her in action. She'd been magnificent in bed last night—she was every bit as sexy in work clothes with a phone stuck to her ear.

He'd been positive she was wearing another pair of those sexy little thong underwear.

And she'd essentially just told him to get lost.

Cassie glanced at the upper story of the barn and saw movement behind one of the windows. She wondered if Nate saw her leave, wondered if he even cared. How the hell had this happened? A one nightstand. That's all it was, all it could be. She was supposed to work with him, not sleep with him. But last night . . . last night had been amazing. She'd tried not thinking about him during the day. There was so much she had to get done before next week, but she'd found herself drifting off, wishing they'd had more time to explore all the things he'd teased her about wanting to do.

Places he wanted to taste, to bite. To lick. Her insides clenched and her nipples poked against her bra. "Aaaarrrrrrgggghhhhhh!" She pounded her fist on the steering wheel and shoved Nathan Dunagan out of her mind. She was going to see her dad. Take him out to dinner, have a nice, quiet evening with him. Then she was going home and going to bed at a decent hour. Alone. She could do this.

She hoped.

Cassie parked next to the main dining room. She'd tried calling her father again to remind him, but he hadn't answered. It was early enough; she hoped to catch him before he ordered his dinner here. Or she could join him in the dining room.

"Hey, Cassie. What are you doing here this late in the day?" Annie, the assistant manager, greeted her from the entrance.

"Thought I'd come by and see if Dad wanted to go out to dinner. Have you seen him?" She glanced toward the dining room where residents were already filing in and finding tables.

Annie shook her head. "Didn't he tell you? Colonel Mac went out to dinner with his friend Benny White and Benny's son Jayson. I'm not sure which restaurant, though they were planning to stay in town to eat. I could call Benny and see where they are."

Cassie shook her head. "That's not necessary." Her dad must be having a good day if he was up to dinner out with his friend. Benny was sharp as a tack and really good about keeping an eye on her father. "Just tell him I'm sorry I missed him, that I'll come by tomorrow. It's so busy right now that I didn't get by yesterday."

"I'm sure he understands. I talked to him this afternoon and he sounded really good. Your father's got a terrific sense of humor."

"He does. Thanks, Annie. I'll see you tomorrow."

She got back in her truck and sat there a moment. "Now, what?" Her stomach rumbled, and she thought of Nate. He was probably still at the ranch, trying to figure out what to eat. She'd bought a few things for his refrigerator, but not much.

She still felt really bad about how rude she'd been this afternoon.

It wouldn't take long to stop at the market on the corner. They had a terrific deli.

Nate heard a car in the drive and glanced out the window in time to see Cassie's truck returning. She hadn't been gone long. And she was pulling in to the parking area in front of the barn. Curious, Nate shoved the last of his socks into the dresser drawer and headed down the stairs.

Cassie was just raising her hand to knock when he opened the door. She had a large tote bag full of something that smelled really good.

"I've come with a peace offering."

"I didn't know we were at war." He smiled at her and stepped back, holding the door.

She set everything on a trestle table that took up a large part of the tasting room. "We're not, but I owe you an apology. I'm sorry I was so rude today. You didn't deserve that, especially after leaving me fresh coffee." She glanced at him and then began unloading the bags.

"And flowers." He pulled a couple of containers out and set them, still closed, on the table beside the ones Cassie had unloaded.

"Well, you get half a point for the flowers. They did come out of my garden."

"Okay, but I should get three points for the coffee. I had to grind it. Don't you know about instant?"

"The devil's brew." She flashed him a quick grin. "Only fresh ground. No substitutes accepted."

"I'll make note of that."

"Silverware's in the drawer by the sink. Paper plates in the cupboard."

He grabbed a couple of knives and forks, found the plates and paper towels to use for napkins, and brought them back to the table. Cassie had laid out everything from green salad to pasta, fresh grilled salmon and what looked like enchiladas and Chinese fried rice.

"We're eating a multinational feast?"

She laughed and took a seat across from him. "I know better than to go into that place when I'm hungry. It may not go together, but I can guarantee that it's all good."

"Did you want wine?" He started to rise.

Shaking her head, she said, "You're kidding, right? Wine got me into too much trouble last night. I think I'll stick to water, thank you. Sit. I'll get it."

She filled a couple of wineglasses with water and brought them to the table. Nate held his up in a toast and she clicked the rim of her glass to his. She might be laughing, but he sensed the underlying tension. She really was upset about last night. Damn. Best night of his life and he had a feeling Cassie wasn't interested in a repeat. "I'm sorry you feel that way. I shouldn't have pressured you."

"You didn't. I wanted you. If things were different, I'd be doing a lot more than going home to sleep alone after we're finished with dinner." She reached across the table and wrapped her fingers around his wrist. "Last night was really wonderful."

He liked the fact her hands were callused, her nails short and square. He turned his wrist and grabbed her hand. "But?" He tilted his head and stared into those beautiful blue eyes.

"But this isn't the right time, Nate. I've got to concentrate on my job, on making this last bottling of Tangled Vines absolutely perfect. In a way, it's my dad's legacy. He built this winery. Did you know this was a dairy barn at one time? Years ago there were cows out here, not grapes. He left a couple of acres of the old vines the family had planted for their own use, but everything else, he planted. He loved the place, but it's going to have a new name and, at some point, a new winemaker. I want everything to be perfect for this last wine that's all his."

"Will he know?" Nate squeezed her hand, ran his thumb over the backs of her fingers.

She sat there for a long moment, staring beyond Nate, lost in whatever memories his question had pulled free. Finally, she shook her head and sniffed.

"For a while, probably. I'll take him a case. I haven't brought him out here and he doesn't want to come. The fact I'm not in the main house, that I'm living in the cottage . . ." She shrugged. "That would hurt him too much. Even seeing you living here, running the vineyard instead of Lupe. I think it would be too confusing. And it would be so damned hard, to see him hurting. No matter how confused he's gotten at times, he still has such horrible guilt over losing this place. There's nothing I can do to fix that."

They finished eating, and Cassie stood and started gathering the leftovers. Nate grabbed the dirty silverware and glasses, and they had it all cleaned up within a couple of minutes. Cassie packed everything up in the tote and handed it to Nate. "Stick this in your refrigerator upstairs. I didn't leave much food here for you, and I know you haven't had time to get to town."

"Thank you." He took the bag and set it on the table. Took a risk and asked her, "Will you let me kiss you good night? Friends?"

She tilted her head and stared at him in that unnerving way she had. "This is probably a huge mistake." But she stepped into his embrace and wrapped her arms around his waist.

She fit absolutely perfectly. He cupped the back of her head in his palm, wrapped his free arm around her, and pulled her close with firm pressure against her back.

And he kissed her.

She sighed and kissed him back. And then, as much as he wanted to take this so much further, he ended the kiss and stepped back.

She stared at him a moment, blinking owlishly, and then she smiled. "G'night, Nate. I'll see you tomorrow."

"If you've got some time tomorrow, I'd like to walk the vineyard with you, find out the history of the various sections, what you've got planted where."

"Give me a call. Once I get going, I'll have a better idea of my schedule. Good night."

"Thanks for dinner, Cassie."

She turned and waved as she headed out the door. "And the kiss," he added, but he didn't think she heard.

Benny and his kid walked Mac back to his room. They'd had an excellent dinner in town, lots of good conversation. The best part was, Benny's kid picked up the tab. Mac waved them off and thanked both men for an enjoyable evening, and then he went into his room.

That was the most fun he'd had in a long time. Benny had worked for a Washington security firm back in the seventies, and his stories from inside the beltway were every bit as good as Mac's. In fact, their work had overlapped at times, though they'd never met before both of them had settled here in Healdsburg.

Mac had talked tonight about things he'd not spoken of for over forty years, and he had to admit, it felt good to get some of that off his chest. He had to be careful, though. Some of those bastards he'd collected information on were still in politics, and they'd continued to move up the ladder, taking all those steps on the backs of innocent people.

One in particular, and because of him, Mac's career had gone down in flames. It still made him angry, but what was a man to do? All that information, years of intelligence gathering, and he'd been forbidden to use it. Early retirement hadn't been bad, though. He'd met Melinda, they'd had Cassie, built Tangled Vines.

The hell of it was, though, he'd lost the vineyard. The winery. His daughter's house.

But he still had the briefcase.

He crawled into bed, thinking about the secrets he'd held on to. Cassette tapes and photos, hard evidence that could end careers, and he'd saved all of it. So many years, so much left in the dark corners of his mind.

A mind growing darker by the day.

Cassie parked in front of the cottage and carried her purse and keys inside. It was still warm out, the evening was calm and it wasn't completely dark. She wasn't ready to go to bed, didn't want to work on anything that required using her brain, and she really didn't want to think about Nate.

Not easy, especially after that kiss. So sweet and totally nonthreatening. But she knew what he could do with those lips, that tongue. Those teeth.

Her breasts actually felt heavy. All she'd done was think about him. "Girl, you are so screwed." She put on a sweatshirt to keep the mosquitoes away, grabbed a flashlight, and went outside. At the back edge of the property that ran along the west side of Dry Creek was a favorite spot of her mother's, a two-acre parcel of very old, gnarled and twisted vines. They'd been part of the original homestead and had withstood flood years and dry years, and her father's original intention to pull them out and plant new stock.

But her mom had stood firm. She'd said they were survivors, and so was she. She'd loved the vines. Loved their age and their shapes, the way the grapes hung in heavy, dark purple clumps, year after year. They didn't produce much, but Mac had given in—as he always did with the wife he adored—and the vines stayed.

Her mom hadn't, but Cassie and her dad had agreed that Melinda Phillips's spirit was still here, in this little bit of vineyard that she'd loved. So were her ashes. They'd scattered them, just she and her dad, after Mom died. Even if it was only in their imaginations, Cassie and her father had agreed that, ever since that solemn day, the grapes from this two-acre plot had given something to the wines he and Cassie made that no one else could match.

Probably why Cassie always felt closest to her mom out here. The juice from these grapes had something special. Year after year, she'd blended them with the other lots of Zinfandel in measured quantities, and they'd always produced award-winning wines.

It made her feel as if she had her mom's blessing.

"Cassie? Is that you?"

At least he didn't startle her this time. She'd thought that was him walking down the road. "Hi, Nate. What're you doing out here?"

He stood in front of her, forcing her to look up. "I saw someone hanging around the door to the cave a few minutes ago, so I walked over to check. Everything's locked up tight. Couldn't find anybody, but I know there was someone there."

"How could you see anyone?" She stood up and gazed through the darkness at the single light still visible over the heavy door to the cave. The cave and the few acres of old vine grapes were on the other side of the narrow road, across from the main vineyard and houses, and the door itself was hidden behind trees between here and the hillside.

"From my bedroom window. I noticed the car, first. He'd parked it on the road and must have hopped the fence. I used my binoculars. Average-size guy, dark hair, but too far away to make out features. He tried the lock on the door, looked around, and then walked back to the car. A minute later, I saw lights on the road. Had to be him driving away. I went over to check, and everything is okay."

She frowned. "Thank you. I appreciate your checking, but what could he have wanted? I mean, we have our wine archived—bottles of our wines from over the years are stored in the cave. And the barrels of wine, of course, but nothing worth stealing."

"I don't know. That's a good lock on the door, and the electronic keypad is top quality, so it should be secure. It just seemed odd that someone was trying to get in." He glanced at the old vines and nonchalantly said, "These really need to come out. Marc and I were talking about trying some Chardonnay down here by the creek. It's cooler and . . ."

"You pull these vines out, I can guarantee my wines won't win another award."

He laughed and walked over to one gnarled old vine that looked more dead than alive. "I find that hard to believe. How old are these?"

"From records Dad got when he bought the property, this section was planted around 1906, same year as the San Francisco earthquake. They're Zinfandel, just like the others, but the flavor is richer, more robust."

"There's no irrigation."

"They've managed for over a hundred years."

"I still think they need to come out."

She stood there with her hands on her hips and studied him for a moment. "I think you're wrong."

"There's what, an acre? Acre and a half?"

"Two acres." She pointed north along the creek, but the vineyard was lost in shadow. "It's a narrow parcel but it stretches to the north end of the property."

"They can't be producing enough to make any real difference in your wine, and you could use this land to put in more Chardonnay."

"Why would we want more Chardonnay?"

"Because you had to buy grapes last year. You don't have enough acreage if you're planning to market it. What did you get last year? Two hundred cases?"

"We don't buy grapes, we grow more Zinfandel than we can use, so we trade with a couple of our neighbors. The fruit is all from Dry Creek Valley."

"At least think about it?"

"No, Nathan. You think about it." She folded her arms across her chest to keep from making fists. Damn him! "I'm the one making the wine, not you. You grow the grapes. I need these grapes to make the kinds of wines that win awards, that people want to buy. That our boss

likes to serve at his fancy parties and dinners. Before you start tearing out my vines, you'd better clear it with him."

Nate matched her stance and gazed at her for what felt like a very
long time. She noticed a tic in his jaw, so he was obviously pissed.
Finally he let out a long, slow breath and shoved his hands in his hip
pockets.

"Actually, Cassie, they're Marc Reed's vines, and it was his idea to
tear out this section and replant with Chardonnay. You'll have to take
it up with him."

He didn't give her time to answer. Probably a good thing. Cassie
wasn't sure she could say anything without either cursing or burst-
ing into tears. Instead, she stood there, angry and so frustrated her
entire body shook while Nate merely turned and walked away, back
up the road to his apartment.

CHAPTER 4

⸎

Three days with the mobile bottlers going full tilt, a couple of mechanical issues, nine hundred and eighty-four cases of Zin and two hundred and sixteen cases of Chardonnay later, Cassie needed food, a shower, and sleep. Not necessarily in that order.

"Lupe. Go home to your wife before you drop."

Lupe wiped his hand across his sweaty forehead and laughed. "Yeah, or she finds another man. One who keeps better hours."

"There is that." Too tired to laugh, Cass shot him a grin.

"Don't worry. I'm almost done. And Josefina loves me best because I'm hot." Then he laughed and said, "Also dirty and reeking of wine. Where would she ever find a catch like me?" He'd been rinsing out the used barrels and stacking them outside to dry. Now he paused and shook his head. "I'm outta here. Be sure and call, let me know when these are dry so I can get them sulfured and stored. I've got a crazy week at school."

"What am I going to do when you leave for college?" She was teasing, but the concern was real. He wasn't much more than a kid, but

Lupe knew this winery almost as well as Cassie did. And he was so easy to work with. No games, no power plays. Happily married.

It would be so much easier if Nate were married. Then he wouldn't be out there, a constant thorn in her side. A damned magnet to her libido.

For whatever reason, she'd been perfectly happy without sex for the last few years. One night with Nathan Dunagan and she'd been unable to sleep, unable to avoid looking toward his apartment at night to see if the lights were on. They'd hardly exchanged two words over the past nine days, and as much as he drove her nuts, she missed him.

And she was counting the days, dammit!

Lupe grinned at her. "You will do fine when I'm gone. Josefina's baby brother will be in high school next year. He's going to want a job."

"Is he as smart as you? Does he work as hard as you?"

Laughing, Lupe gave her a kiss on the cheek. "Yes, and yes, but he's not nearly as good looking as me." He bowed deeply with a dramatic sweep of his arm. "Nor as charming. G'night, Cass."

She was still laughing when she heard his old truck start up out in front. But as soon as Lupe was gone, Cass's mind spun right back to Nate. He hadn't said anything more about tearing out her mom's vineyard, and she'd been too busy to bring it up when Marcus Reed and Nate came down to watch the bottling.

The minute she saw tractors moving in to take out the vines, she planned to raise hell.

A vehicle pulled into the lot outside. Cass checked her watch. Almost five, and Nate was the only one who might still be working. She wiped her hands on a damp towel and walked to the front of the cave. A dark car sat in the lot, a man about her age standing in front of it, making notes on a digital tablet.

"Can I help you?"

He glanced up, shading his eyes against the sun streaming over the hilltop. "Are you Cassandra Phillips?"

"I am. What can I do for you?" She stayed in the doorway and folded her hands over her chest. For whatever reason, something about this guy didn't feel right.

"Name's Andrews. I'm with the FDA. You're scheduled for a food and beverage safety inspection, and since I was in the area, I figured I'd get it done today."

"I don't think so." She'd had a long day. This joker had to be kidding.

"You don't think so?" Andrews actually smirked, the jackass. "I have complete authority to inspect the premises. I insist that . . ."

"No, Mr. Andrews. You don't." She paused, and stared at him long enough that the smirk disappeared. "I don't know who you are, but we had a full inspection done less than a month ago and passed with flying colors. I've been bottling all week, I'm tired, and I am shutting this place down, locking the doors, and going home to bed."

She stepped back inside, shut the door, and locked it behind her. Then she went back to her office nook, grabbed her backpack and cell phone and headed to the front of the cave. When she walked outside, the inspector—or whoever he was—was sitting in his car, talking on his phone.

Cassie carefully locked the door, got into her truck, backed out and left him sitting there, but as soon as she got across the road and on the drive to her cottage, she pulled over behind a row of olive trees where she could still see the man, and called Nate.

"Cassie? What's up?"

"There's a guy in front of the cellar, says he's with the FDA, here to do an inspection. Thing is, we had an inspection about a month ago and passed just fine."

"Did you ask for his credentials?"

"No. He gave me the creeps. I'll check with the local office tomorrow after they open, but do you mind taking a look? He's average size, dark hair. Made me think of our nighttime visitor last week."

"I'm almost there."

She glanced up and saw his truck flying up the driveway. She'd left the front gate open on this side as well as in front of the cellar. It wasn't like she could lock the guy in there, but as Nate paused at the gate on this side of the road to check for oncoming traffic, the man pulled out of her lot and headed south, toward town. Nate got out of his truck, walked across the road, and locked the gate.

Then he walked over to where Cassie was parked and planted his hands on the bottom frame of the open window. "Damn. I didn't get a good enough look, but he could have been the same guy from the other night."

"That was my first thought. Thanks for checking, Nate."

"Anytime." He paused a moment, gazed toward the cave, and then turned to her again. "You okay? You've had a pretty rough week. Bottling done?"

She nodded. "All done. We still have to sulfur and store the barrels, but Lupe will do that in a few days, once they're dry enough." She yawned, and then started laughing. "I'm exhausted. Thanks for checking on that guy, and for locking up." He stepped back, she put her truck into gear. "I'll see you tomorrow."

He waved as she drove the short distance to her cottage, but she noticed that he got out of his truck and locked her gate behind him before he left. She wondered where he was going.

"None of your business, Phillips." She went into the cottage and dumped her things on the couch in the front room. Nate had looked tired, too. She wondered what was keeping him awake nights.

Heading into the bathroom for a shower, shedding clothes along the way, she hoped it wasn't the same thing keeping her awake. If it was, they were both in big trouble.

Nate watched for the dark gray sedan, but the guy must have been in a hurry. There was no sign of him anywhere along the road. He'd either been in a hell of a rush, or he might have taken the second bridge rather than the one closest to the wine cave. In that case, because West Dry Creek Road was narrower and slower than the main route, he could be behind Nate. There were only a couple of places where you could cross over the creek between the vineyard and town.

Nate pulled into the shopping center and headed straight for the deli. He found himself buying twice as much as he usually got for dinner, but Cassie had looked exhausted, and since she hadn't mentioned the old vines, he was hoping she'd forget about them, at least long enough to share a meal with him.

He hadn't been able to get her out of his mind, and that was an absolutely unique experience. Sort of humbling, too. Women liked him. He'd never had to chase one before, but he'd never met a woman like Cassie, and he honestly didn't know where to begin. In a way, he was sorry they'd ended up having sex so quickly. They hadn't had time to build anything beyond the first, fragile bits of friendship, but he'd never, ever regret the sex. His body tightened with the mere thought of what it had felt like, sinking into her, feeling the heat and strength when her body clasped his.

Okay . . . He shot a quick glance around the crowded deli buffet. This was not the time and definitely not the place to be thinking about his one night with Cassie Phillips.

Or how very much he wanted to do it again. And again.

Just not at this moment.

He was still grinning at the direction his errant thoughts had taken him when he carried his selection to the register, paid, and then put everything in the big tote bag he'd brought with him. Dinner taken care of, he headed back up the valley. If there were lights on at her place, he'd at least offer to feed her. Nothing more. Not until they got things between them settled—that argument over the old vines had him bothered.

The more he thought about it, the fact she'd gotten so angry and emotional made him wonder if there wasn't something else going on. There had to be, and the only way to find out was to be straightforward and ask her.

Cassie grabbed a huge football jersey, all that was left of a long ago romance with an old college boyfriend, and pulled that on with nothing more than a tiny pair of panties underneath. Now, every time she slipped into one of her lacy thongs, she thought of Nate and what he'd said. Did he really do that, look at her, picture her wearing slinky panties under her jeans, and get aroused?

In some perverted corner of her mind, she really hoped he did, because she was spending way too much time thinking about him, about how much fun she'd had that first night. She wished he was with her now so they could talk about the vines, about the winery. Anything to help her relax. After the week she'd had, every muscle ached and yet she was too keyed up to go to bed. The shower had felt wonderful—she'd stayed in until the hot water ran out, which was just plain extravagant considering the fact she was on a well, but after a week of not shaving her legs or conditioning her hair, it had been long past time for a bit of maintenance, not to mention a little self-indulgence.

Her stomach growled, a not-so-subtle reminder she'd forgotten to eat. She was standing in front of the refrigerator, staring at the empty shelves with a glass of wine in her hand, when a truck pulled up in front.

Nate? The gate was locked, so it had to be him—now that he had his own keys. She glanced down at her faded and stained gold-and-blue Aggies football jersey that hit halfway down her thighs and sighed. With her damp hair caught up in a frizzy knot on top of her head and the tattered jersey, she wasn't ready to see anyone, much less a man who managed to irritate, confuse, and fascinate her in equal measure.

He knocked on the door. She started to yell at him to come on in, then remembered she'd locked it. That guy at the cellar still had her feeling uneasy. "That you, Nate?"

"It is," he said. "Bearing food for the starving. Hope you haven't eaten yet."

She opened the door. "Eat what? The cupboards are bare. I haven't had time to get to the store all week. Lupe's wife, Josie, has been sending me sandwiches or I'd have keeled over days ago."

He walked past her with a glance at her jersey and a big grin. "Nice outfit. Grab some plates and silverware. I'm starving."

She had real plates this time, and set napkins, knives, and forks with each on either side of the bar. She grabbed a bottle of beer for Nate and set it in front of him. He popped the top with the opener bolted to the bar and then started opening up containers.

"I love this. Not only international but multicultural cuisine." She scooped up spicy chicken curry and poured it over Chinese fried rice. Nate cut a square of veggie lasagna and set it on her plate.

"I had this for lunch a couple of days ago. You really need some."

"Thanks." This was nice. Better than nice. He was sweet and thoughtful and while the sexual vibe was simmering just below the surface, it wasn't a bad feeling. Far from it. She really liked him when he was like this.

Well, of course she did. He was feeding her. Hard not to appreciate a guy who came rushing to the rescue when you had a problem, or showed up with a delicious dinner all ready to eat. They ate and talked. She told him about her week and Nate talked about his. He brought up the possibility of hiring Josefina's little brother before Lupe took off for UC Davis in a few months so Lupe would be able to train him, and Cassie agreed.

He asked about her dad.

She sighed. "I've only seen him a couple of days this week, just short visits in the evenings, which aren't his best times. He's doing okay,

I guess, though he seems bothered about something. It's hard to say." She shrugged. "I think if I were losing all my memories, I'd be bothered, too."

"Does he have things to keep him busy, to help keep his mind active?"

She liked the fact Nate honestly seemed concerned, even though he'd never met her father. "He's got three good friends there. That's why he picked this place. Dad wasn't committed or anything like that. He picked the place where he lives and moved by his own choice, long before the deal closed on the vineyard, but he was well aware that bad business decisions were not normal for him. Buying that cave was a bad idea, financially. Great for the wine, but disastrous for our finances. That's when he finally saw a doctor and got the diagnosis. After that, I don't think he felt he had any other choice. We both know he's not getting any better."

"Wait a minute. You're saying he knew you couldn't afford it when he bought it? He didn't discuss it with you?" Nate set his fork down. His intense gaze made Cassie feel light-headed.

She knew what it was like to have that focus on her for a totally different reason, and no matter how wrong it was, she wanted it again. No. That wasn't going to happen. She sucked in a sharp breath and nodded. "I knew he was buying it, but he told me he had money in another bank. Turns out he'd forgotten he'd spent it years ago when we replanted some of the older vines.

"Anyway, Benny White, Hal Munson, and Hector Ruiz are old friends of Dad's. Benny worked in Washington, D.C., when Dad was back there, though they didn't meet until Benny retired and moved out here. Hal owned a tractor repair service in town and Hector was our vineyard manager when Dad first bought this place. They've been friends for a long time, and they're all widowers with family around, so they've got company in and out and enough guys to make up a nightly card game."

"Doesn't he miss the vineyard? You said before he doesn't come out here."

Cassie shook her head. She'd asked him so many times to come out and see the place, see how beautiful the vines looked. She couldn't even get him here during bud break in March when the new green leaves looked almost fluorescent against the dark trunks. "He said he doesn't want to be reminded of what he's lost. That it makes him sad to think of what he did to my legacy."

She glanced away. Being the center of Nate's focus left her raw, even more uncomfortable when she was talking about her dad's mistakes. He'd been a wonderful man and the best father ever. She wanted to remember that, not the fact he'd gotten old and his razor-sharp mind had failed him so badly. "I think the hardest thing for him would be the reminders of Mom, the fact that he can't go out in that old section of the vineyard and talk to her every day, the way he used to."

"Why that section, Cass? Why is he closest to her there? You are, too, aren't you?"

She frowned. "I thought I told you. That's the reason the grapes from those old vines are so special. We scattered Mom's ashes out there when she died in March of 2000. I still go out there and talk to her, and the wines we make from that little plot of grapes are some of the best you'll ever taste."

"Why didn't you say something?"

"Would it have mattered?" Her eyes swam with tears. She really didn't want to cry. Not now, not when Nate was being so nice, but damn it all, it was so hard sometimes. So blasted hard to keep moving forward when everything felt like it was turning to crap around her.

"It matters." Nate reached across the countertop and took her hands in his. "It matters a lot, Cassie. I imagine your father always figured his ashes would be scattered beside your mom's, didn't he?"

She nodded.

"I'll talk to Marc. He's not an unfeeling jerk." He laughed. "I was really surprised to find out he's a year younger than me. The guy's a gazillionaire and he's only thirty-four. Honestly? He's really a very nice and thoughtful guy. The more I get to know him, the better I like him. I think you will, too. I can't imagine he'd want to pull those vines, knowing the emotional attachment. Where, exactly? If we can't save all of it, at least the area that's important."

"I'll show you tomorrow."

"Good." Nate stood, gathered up the empty containers, and stuck the leftovers in the refrigerator. Cassie felt absolutely wasted. Her anger at Nate and even Marcus Reed had kept her going all week. His offer to intercede, to try to save the old section of vineyard wasn't at all what she'd expected. She stood and gathered up their dishes and silverware.

Nate took everything out of her hands. "Go to bed, Cassie. You look exhausted. I'll finish putting this stuff away and lock up when I go."

"You don't have to . . ."

"Yes. I do." He leaned over and kissed her and it was so sweet, so perfect, she leaned into him, silently begging for more. Breaking the kiss, he swatted her lightly on the butt. "Now go."

She went.

She was almost asleep when she heard the front door open and then close, and then the sound of Nate's truck as he drove the short distance to his own place.

Mac closed the door behind him and gazed about the small apartment. It wasn't a bad place. He'd certainly lived in worse. He'd met some good people here. A lot of them were older than he was, but all of them were pretty sharp. That came from using your mind, staying active. He was doing that. Melinda would be proud of him. She'd loved his sense of humor, the little word games they'd played.

He missed that. Missed the challenge of a smart, young wife. Missed holding her, snuggled in close against him. Damn, he missed everything about her. She'd left him much too soon, but at least tonight had been good. Dinner with Benny and his son, only this time Hector went along, too. Hector hadn't heard any of Mac's stories from when he was in the service. That was all so long ago, and it was fun telling those tales of famous people he'd known, of some of the clandestine things he'd been involved in.

Old news, and that kid of Benny's ate it up. Mac had kept quiet for so long, but what was the point? All of those rich and powerful people were probably gone. They should have died in jail, and a few of them had. Just not the important one.

Not the one that mattered, and didn't that still stick in his craw!

He got ready for bed, but something kept nagging him. Something they'd been talking about tonight. There were some things he'd be better to keep quiet. Some things that were better off never mentioned again. At all.

Damned if he could remember what they were.

Cassie lay in bed for a moment, enjoying the fact that she'd slept until six, and the only pressing thing she had to deal with today was paperwork for the accountant. If she could get everything together early enough, maybe she could stop by, pick up her dad, and take him to lunch. They'd hardly seen each other for the past couple of weeks.

As quickly as his cognitive abilities seemed to be failing him, she was afraid there wouldn't be all that many more good visits. She'd stopped by briefly last week and mentioned they were ready to start bottling. He'd asked her why she was bottling now, when they should be gearing up for harvest.

Harvest was almost six months away.

Cassie put the coffee on and headed down the driveway to pick up her paper. Nate was walking back after unlocking the gate. He had her newspaper and his in his hands.

"Delivery?" He held it out for her.

"Thank you. Such service." She took the paper from him, and smiled. "Thanks for last night. I was so tired I probably would have gone to bed without eating. You saved me from being horribly grumpy this morning."

"My good deed, eh?"

"Definitely." They stood there, smiling at each other. She loved his smile, and it was so much easier to give in than fight the fact that she really just flat out liked the guy. "I've got coffee on, if you'd like a cup."

"Not instant?"

"Sacrilege. Fresh-ground Colombian this morning. But I want to read my paper."

"Works for me." He took her arm and quickly guided her toward the house.

After he got his cup of coffee, Nate grabbed a stool at the bar and spread his paper out across the granite counter. Cassie curled up in a comfortable overstuffed chair by a window that caught the morning sunlight, sipping her coffee and catching up on news.

The house was quiet, the birds outside the only sound beyond the crinkle of newspaper and the sound of the refrigerator compressor occasionally going on. But Cassie was so keyed up, she couldn't concentrate on the page under her nose.

She was so terribly aware of Nate, of the fact he was here in her little cottage in a setting that was wonderfully mundane. The paper spread out in front of him, the cup of coffee sending spirals of steam into the air. His hair stuck up in back, as if he'd just crawled out of bed.

She wondered if his heart raced, if he thought of their night together. If he imagined her naked and sprawled beneath him, entirely sated after he'd taken her over the top so many times she'd lost count.

Because that's how she saw him now. His beautiful shoulders and chest filling her vision, his strong body rhythmically thrusting against her, the solid length of him filling her deep inside. Reaching climax, taking her with him one last time, his lips twisting in a grimace of what could have been pain; what she knew was pleasure. Her heart thudded in her chest and the edges of the newspaper crinkled loudly, startling her as she tightened her grasp. She raised her head and caught him looking at her. Their gazes locked—blue on blue—for a brief instant.

He didn't say a word. Merely smiled, sipped his coffee, and went back to his paper.

Cassie shifted in her chair in the tiny nook she called her office. She'd lost track of how long she'd been here in the wine cave, but she hadn't even had a chance to call her dad. The idea of lunch with him had faded within the first hour when she realized how much she had left to do. She'd spent all morning and well into the afternoon gathering information for the accountant. Then, when she was putting things away, she'd come across an old ledger of her dad's.

Since then she'd traveled through his memories.

He'd kept precise notes—temperature, rainfall, dates that deer, pigs, or turkeys had gotten into the grapes. Pickers he'd hired during harvest, how much each one had been paid, the kinds of notes most business people kept.

Except her mom had added notes. That she'd seen a coyote at dawn, or the day two bald eagles perched on top of the barn. That she thought her beloved Mac really needed to get his nose out of the ledger and meet her in the bedroom. Cassie couldn't believe she'd never read through this before, but the teasing comments between husband and wife had her laughing and sighing, and a couple of times wiping away tears.

And then her stomach growled and she glanced at her watch. It was almost six. She stuck the ledger in her backpack along with her tablet and cell phone, pushed the chair back and stood. As she turned toward the door, she sensed more than saw movement. Grabbing her phone, she punched in a quick text to Nate: *Cave. Hurry!*

She didn't want to panic over nothing, but a shiver ran along her spine, an almost visceral sense that she wasn't alone. She stepped back inside the office area, turned the phone on vibrate, and pushed Send. She stuck it in the back pocket of her jeans and stepped toward the door again.

The cellar was bathed in shadows. The brightest light was here, in her office. Small, low-wattage LED lights kept the cave from total darkness, but the glow of daylight coming through the barred window on the door only lit a very small area.

She turned off the light in her office and stood in the darkness for a moment to allow her eyes to adjust. Then she walked purposefully toward the door.

He rushed her from behind a rack loaded with wine barrels, hooked his arm around her neck and brought Cassie to her knees. She couldn't scream, couldn't breathe, but she kicked back and up with her right foot and caught him between the legs.

He cursed and squeezed tighter. Her vision went from sparks of light to darkness. Twisting her body, she fought his hold, but he was bigger, stronger than she was. She turned her head just enough to take some pressure off her throat and gasped for air.

He shifted for a better hold, and she sunk her teeth into his forearm.

"Damn! Son of a bitch!"

He hauled off and hit her, catching her jaw with the side of his hand, breaking her hold on his arm. She tasted blood and gagged. He hit her again and again, harder this time, with a weapon of some kind. She screamed, not in fear but in absolute rage.

Slipping one hand free, she grabbed his throat beneath the dark ski mask covering his face. Digging in with her fingers, for the first time in her life Cassie wished she had fingernails. Long, sharp fingernails so she could rip into the bastard.

Suddenly she was free and her assailant was scrambling out of her grasp, standing over her holding an ugly black handgun with both hands. Pointing it at her.

"Cassie? Are you okay?"

She raised her head, but she couldn't see very well. There was something in her eyes, but she knew Nate's voice. "I've been better." Her voice sounded raspy and her throat hurt. A lot. "He's got a gun, Nate. Be careful."

"I see that. He's got a problem, though. The sheriff's coming. There's only one way out of this wine cave, and a real narrow road if he wants to escape."

Nate sounded so calm, so matter-of-fact.

"Stop talking. Keep your hands up." The guy waved the gun at Nate. "Over there. Move it! By the racks. Down on your knees, hands behind your head."

"Whatever you say." Cassie heard Nate walk across the floor, but once he was in the shadows, she couldn't see well enough to find him.

"Don't move. Understand?"

"I'm not going anywhere." Nate still sounded amazingly calm, as if he were the one in control.

There was a quick scramble of footsteps and the door to the cellar opened and then slammed shut. Before Cassie even tried to get up, Nate was pulling her into his arms.

It was a good five minutes before the first sheriff's deputy arrived. Nate was still holding her, pressing a clean handkerchief against her forehead, whispering meaningless words to her, just being strong and exactly what she needed.

Two hours later Cassie had answered all the deputy's questions, and it was obvious her assailant had gotten away. She'd turned down the offer of an ambulance, but Nate insisted she go to the ER for a quick checkup. She went, too sore and tired to argue, too angry and frightened to feel confident of her own decisions. And so full of questions.

Who was he? She was certain it was the same guy who'd pretended to be with the FDA. She'd called. There was no inspection scheduled.

Whoever it was, he wanted inside that wine cave badly enough to commit a serious crime. But why? None of this made sense. But tonight?

Tonight she was just too damned tired to care.

CHAPTER 5

⌒

D on't even think of trying to get out of the truck by yourself. Let me help you." Nate pocketed his keys and went around to the passenger side. The fact she hadn't argued concerned him, but he opened the door and caught hold of Cassie just above her waist, lifted her out, and then carefully helped her stand. When she had her balance, he looped her tote bag over his shoulder, lifted Cass in his arms, and carried her to the cottage.

"Are you okay?"

She sighed. "Other than pissed off, sore, confused, and totally frustrated? Sure. I'm great. Good to go."

He chuckled. "That's what I thought." He set her carefully on her feet, steadied her, and then held the tote bag so she could find her keys. When she merely handed them to him, he knew she must be feeling like hell.

Nate opened the door and went to pick her up again. She shook her head and groaned.

"I should have just answered. Shaking head? Not good." She touched his hand and gazed at him. At least her eyes were clear. "Let me walk. I need to make sure I can."

She held his hand like a lifeline and walked slowly into the cottage. Nate flipped on lights and led her to the overstuffed chair by the window.

"Can I get something for you to drink?"

"Ice water, please?" She eased herself into the chair and closed her eyes.

A minute later, Nate was back with her glass of water. Sitting forward, she held it in both hands and stared at the surface as if it held answers to some of the questions they'd been trying to answer. A moment later, she raised her head, and it broke his heart to see tears so close to falling.

Squatting in front of her, he used both thumbs to wipe the moisture from just beneath her lids. She sniffed, raised her head. Closed her eyes. Nate took the glass from her, set it on the table beside the chair, carefully wrapped his arms around her, and held her close. It was no surprise when her shoulders shook and he heard a catch in her breath.

"Let it go, sweetheart. Just let it go and get it out."

She slipped her arms around his waist, pressed her face to his shoulder, and cried. Her body trembled as if she still fought it, but it was a losing battle. She'd had too many unwanted, unexpected changes, and the attack tonight would have put anyone—man or woman—over the edge. He held her without speaking. Gently rubbed his hand along her spine, so aware of each knobby bump, the lean strength of her muscles, the warmth and the life of her.

She was so damned strong. She'd been assaulted and was bleeding, had a gun pointed in her face and she hadn't panicked. Hadn't done anything stupid. She'd scared the hell out of him tonight. She'd been fighting for her life when he'd raced into the wine cave. He'd heard her scream, her cursing, but at first he couldn't see her in the darkness.

The second his eyes adjusted, he knew what he saw would be forever burned in his mind—that son of a bitch had her down, had been hitting her with the barrel of his handgun and there was blood everywhere. Cassie was fighting back for all she was worth. When the guy spotted him, at least he'd turned her loose. But when he'd scrambled away from her, that gun had been pointed straight at Cassie.

Bleeding, bruised, and obviously injured, she'd raised her head when her attacker scrambled away, and her first thought had been to warn Nate.

He'd never been so fucking terrified in his life. Gently he pushed her hair back from her face and kissed her temple. Between the bruises. "I have never been so afraid for or as proud of anyone as I was tonight. Cassie, you were absolutely amazing."

She sucked in a harsh breath. "If you hadn't come, he would have killed me. I'm positive of that, but why, Nate? What's he want? Why is he after me?" She sat back and wiped her eyes with the back of her hand. Nate grabbed a tissue out of a box beside the chair and handed it to her. He'd tossed his bloodstained handkerchief in the trash at the hospital.

"Whatever it is that guy wants, it's got to be in the wine cave. I'm almost positive he's the fake FDA guy, and probably the same one who tried to break in a few nights ago. But what? Could it be something from before you guys bought it?"

She shook her head. "I don't think so. The cave was empty. The place had been totally cleaned out before it went up for sale. No hidden doors, nothing but stone floor and walls covered with that sprayed-on concrete. That was all done long before we bought it. The original cave was earth and stone when it was built back before Prohibition."

His legs were cramping, so he picked her up and sat in her chair with Cassie in his lap. It was late and he was glad they'd had a sandwich while waiting in the ER. Once they knew she didn't have a concussion, it had been a matter of waiting to get her stitched up, but that had taken awhile. She had stitches on the back of her head and one bad cut—also stitched—over her eyebrow, not to mention the bruises on her face and throat. It made him sick, seeing the individual marks of that bastard's fingers on her throat.

"Do you think your father might be able to help? Would he remember anything?"

Slowly she shook her head. "I don't know. He's good some days, bad on others. It's impossible to say."

"We'll go see him in the morning. Mornings are best, you said. Maybe we should just bring him out here, see if he remembers anything at all. We have to figure this out and put a stop to it."

"I'm a mess, Nate. I don't want him to see me like this. It'll just upset him."

"Upsetting your dad is the least of our worries right now. This guy's too dangerous. He could have killed you." He sighed, holding back the frustration that was tying him in knots. Couldn't she see the danger? Instead of cursing, he kissed her. "I know you don't want to, but we have to find out what's going on."

She blinked back tears. "I look awful."

"No." He cupped her face in his hands. "You couldn't look awful if you tried. You're beautiful, Cass. Absolutely beautiful."

They didn't discuss whether or not Nate would spend the night. It felt perfectly natural for him to undress her and help her wash up. He stripped off his clothes and stood with her in the shower, helping her keep her hair and stitches dry. He washed her as if she were a little kid, gently cleaning away the blood and dirt and then hosing the soap off with the handheld shower.

She hurt all over, and she shouldn't have been aroused. Shouldn't have leaned into his caring touch, needing more from him, wanting him even as she had to admit there was no way she could handle making love tonight. But she'd never felt as cared for—almost as if Nate loved her. But he couldn't, could he? It was too soon. Her life was such a mess right now, but somehow, Nate made it better. He gave her hope that everything would turn out okay.

It was after ten when he tucked her into bed and turned off the light, but he didn't crawl in beside her until about half an hour later, after he'd locked up.

She was only half awake when the bed dipped and she felt him beside her. He gave her a chaste kiss on the cheek and then curled his strong body around hers. Safe in his arms, she slept through the night.

This time, Nate was still there when she awoke at dawn the next morning. She heard him moving around in the kitchen, smelled coffee brewing, and the sound of the door opening and closing. By the time she was ready to face him, he was sitting at the bar with his newspaper spread out on the counter. Hers was on the table beside the overstuffed chair.

"Good morning."

He raised his head and smiled at her. "How are you feeling?"

"Better than I expected." The bruises were still visible, dark purple to almost black around her throat, but a lightweight turtleneck would hide the worst of them. The cut over her eye was swollen and the stitches on the back of her head itched, but considering what might have happened . . .

"Good. Sit. I'll bring you coffee."

Normally, she would have argued with him. Not this morning. She went to her big overstuffed chair and sat.

It wasn't until almost ten that they finally went into town to see her father, after Nate had checked to see if the deputies had found out who had assaulted her. They'd searched the area, but found no sign of the man.

Nate and Cassie found Mac out on the tiny patio near the dining room, sipping a cup of coffee, staring at his newspaper. When he looked up, it was obvious from the shock on his face that he noticed her injuries.

Or maybe it was seeing her with a strange man. "Good morning, Dad." She leaned over to give him a hug.

"What happened to you?" He frowned, staring at the cut on her eyebrow, the bruises makeup couldn't hide. Then he glared at Nate. "Who are you?"

Cassie reached back and grabbed Nate's left hand. "Dad, this is Nate Dunagan. He's the new vineyard manager."

Her dad stared at Nate's outstretched hand. After a brief pause, he shook hands, but he immediately turned to Cassie again. She was thankful she'd worn the turtleneck sweater, because he studied her with a clarity she'd not seen in him for a long time.

"Did he hit you?"

"No, Dad. He saved me. A man attacked me in the wine cave last night when I was doing books. Nate came and scared him off, and then took me to the ER. See?" She grinned and pointed to the stitches. "All those years growing up in the country and these are my first stitches, ever."

"That's because your mother watched you like a hawk. But why would someone attack you? What happened?"

He gestured toward the empty chairs and she and Nate each took a seat. For the time being, he was so normal, so sharp, it hurt.

"We don't know, Dad. He's tried to break in before. I was wondering if there might be something of importance in the cave other than the wine. There's not a safe in there somewhere, is there? Or any hidden door or anything that might hold valuables we don't know about? Maybe something from the previous owner?"

He stared at her for the longest time, and she noted the moment his mind slipped. His gaze flicked over to Nate, then back to Cassie. "Who's this young fella, Cassie?" He held out his hand to Nate. "I'm Mac Phillips, Cassie's father. I don't think we've met."

Nate stood, smiled, and shook his hand. "I'm Nate, Mr. Phillips. I'm a friend of your daughter's."

"It's Colonel," he said. "Colonel Macon Phillips, but you can just call me Colonel Mac. That's what my men call me. Colonel Mac." He frowned and a look of confusion clouded his still-handsome features. Then he turned away, and stared at the roses growing along the edge of the small patio area, smiling at whatever memories held his attention.

Cassie sighed and shared a sad smile with Nate. Then she stood and walked around to her father, leaned over and gave him a hug and a kiss. He didn't respond.

They left him staring at the roses, and headed back to the vineyard.

Nate really wanted to take Cassie back to the cottage, but she insisted on checking the wine cave. She led him through the front part of the cave, into the office nook toward the back.

"There's got to be something here, somewhere. I'm thinking there might be a hidden safe or some kind of storage built in to the wall. The cave's a perfect place to hide things—safe from fire and moisture, good locks on the door—though I haven't got any idea what we're looking for."

She pulled a couple of flashlights out of an unlocked metal cabinet in the small office, handed one to Nate, and shut the door. It wouldn't close. She opened it wide and stared at the mess. "I really need to clean this out one of these days. Dad was such a pack rat." She shoved a tattered briefcase farther back on the bottom shelf. This time the door snapped shut.

Two hours later, Cassie seemed to run out of energy, though Nate knew her mind must still be spinning. Still, it wasn't until much later, after dinner, that she finally sat down with a glass of wine and talked about her dad.

"Today was the worst I've seen him. The way he lost it in mid-conversation. I had a feeling he didn't even recognize me for a moment, but it's hard to say."

"I'm sorry. I know it's tough." He sighed and shook his head. "One thing for sure, I don't think we can count on him for answers at this point." Nate spun his wineglass between his fingers and stared at the light reflecting off the deep red contents. He wasn't sure how she'd react when he said, "Someone is still out there. I don't want you to be alone tonight."

She shook her head. "I don't want to be alone, either." Then she raised her head and gazed at him with an intensity that hit like a punch to the solar plexus.

"Not because I'm afraid, but because I want to be with you. I've been such a bitch." She chewed on her lower lip a moment, and then faced him straight on. "I've always prided myself on being honest and straightforward, but I've been blowing hot and cold with you, and I'm sorry. I'd like to blame the circumstances, but that's not it at all. I felt such a strong attraction to you so quickly that it scared me. And we had sex when we hardly knew each other. That's just not me."

She shot him a quick grin. "Though I have to admit, it was the best sexual experience of my life, and I really, really want to do it again."

That made him laugh, but he couldn't look at her when he answered, so he went back to staring at the glass of wine in his hands. "Truth? It's not me, either. I'm not a 'one-night stand' kind of guy. Never have been, and what happened between us threw me. I've never been with anyone like you, Cass." He raised his head and smiled at her. "I'm still not a 'one-night' kind of guy. I want more nights with you. A lot more nights."

"Me, too."

"Will you come to my apartment? Stay with me tonight?" He glanced at his dirty jeans and the bloodstains on his dark shirt. The same shirt he'd worn last night. "I need to get a shower and a change of fresh clothes for tomorrow."

"On one condition."

He was almost afraid to ask. "Which is?"

She stood and grabbed his hand. "We come back here for real coffee."

She'd thrown clean clothes, her phone, and a toothbrush into her backpack. It was a beautiful, dark, moonless night, and the stars overhead were magnificent. Cassie held tightly to Nate's hand as they walked the short distance to his apartment over the tasting room. The new owner planned to use the lower floor for private parties and such, but for now it was merely a nicely remodeled former dairy barn that had once housed their barrel racks and wine-making operation.

But did it really matter? Cassie realized she was thinking of anything and everything but the man holding her hand. The man she was almost positive she'd been slowly but surely falling in love with.

How was she supposed to know? It had to be love. Either that or she really did have a concussion, because he made her feel things she'd never felt. Made her want things she'd never dreamed of. It was simple, really. Mostly, she just wanted Nate.

The shower was huge—bigger than the one she had in her cottage, and there was no question at all about sharing. At least tonight she could wash her hair, but it was absolutely hedonistic to have Nate do it for her.

He turned her so that her back was to him. His hands were so gentle, his touch like magic over her bruised skull.

"I could definitely get used to this." She leaned forward and balanced herself with both hands pressed against the tile.

"Go right ahead." He kissed her shoulder, then carefully rinsed out the shampoo and added conditioner. His hands were big, his palms and fingers callused. Strong.

He was so wonderfully strong. As he gently massaged conditioner into her hair, she felt his erection swell against her, riding the crease between her buttocks. She tightened against him, felt him grow larger, but Nate merely rinsed the conditioner out of her hair and stepped back to wash his own.

Cassie grabbed the washcloth, soaped it, and ran it across his broad shoulders and back, and under his raised arms. His body was ribbed with muscles, yet his skin felt like silk. Even the hair on his chest was sleek and silky. Pressing herself against his back, she soaped his chest, scraping his nipples lightly with her blunt fingernails. She felt his groan, felt his back vibrating against her breasts.

She stepped away when he grabbed the handheld shower and rinsed off. When he put it back in the holder, she slipped around in front of him and went to her knees on the slick tile. He brushed her damp hair back from her face and watched as she cupped his sac in her palm and then wrapped her lips around the broad crown of his erection. This time she heard him groan as she licked and teased his thick length and then slowly, rhythmically sucked him deep, then pulled almost free.

After a minute, he clasped her head gently in his palms. "Enough, Cass." His voice was strained, rough. "Damn. I want us to do this together."

He helped her to her feet and finished rinsing the two of them. Then he wrapped her in a big, fluffy towel, dried himself and followed her into the bedroom. She stopped beside the bed, clasping the towel between her breasts. "I brought clothes for tomorrow, but I forgot a nightgown."

He leaned close and kissed her. "I don't think you're going to need one."

"I hope not." She dropped the towel on the floor and crawled across the bed.

Nate reached into the top drawer of the bedside table and pulled out an entire box of condoms. Unopened. "This time, I'm better prepared."

She took the box out of his hand, studied it, and then gave it back. "Three dozen? Think that'll be enough?"

Standing beside his bed with a damp towel around his hips and a full box of condoms in his hand wasn't exactly the way he'd figured tonight would end, but after coming so close to losing Cass—losing her before he'd ever had a chance to really get to know her—made tonight beyond special.

She challenged him, she made him laugh, she turned him on. Damn how she turned him on, and when he'd raced into the cave and saw her fighting with that guy, he knew then that, impossible as it might be, he loved her.

But he really hadn't thought he had a chance with her. Not beyond friendship, and that wasn't enough. Not nearly enough. He ripped the box open and set it on the bedside table, dropped his towel and crawled across the bed until he hovered over her. Her blue eyes sparkled and she stared at him with a look of pure joy.

He kissed her, and when that wasn't enough, he kissed her again. She wrapped her arms around his neck and pulled him close. "So, big guy. What's on the agenda?"

"Sex. Kissing. Maybe a bite or two." He nipped the juncture where her neck met her shoulder. She scrunched her shoulder up and her head down and snorted. He sat back on his heels and just looked at her. She sprawled against the stack of pillows he'd shoved to one side, still damp from her shower, her normally fair skin flushed with arousal. Her hair hung in wet corkscrew curls past her shoulders. Her dark, coppery nipples were almost the same color as her hair.

"Make love to me, Nate." Leaning forward, she brushed his hair back from his forehead and then pulled him close for a kiss. "I want to feel your weight on me, feel your heart beating against mine. I want you hot and hard inside me. You make me feel safe, Nate. As if none of the ugly stuff can touch me when you're here. I don't want to waste another minute."

Her eyes were swimming with tears and he thought of brushing them away, but he kissed her instead. Kissed her lips, her throat, the soft curves of each breast. Then he sheathed himself and parted her feminine folds with his fingers. She was so lush, so wet and hot and ready for him, and when he entered her, when he filled her completely and their bodies connected as deeply as their hearts, he knew this was right.

She arched into him and he filled her, over and over again. So quickly it seemed they balanced on the edge, hovering for such a brief time before tumbling together, all harsh breaths and thundering hearts, soft cries, and sweet kisses. Pressing deep, holding still as his climax ebbed, as her feminine muscles slowly rippled around him with her orgasm, he felt her slowly relax. He rested his weight on his elbows and cupped her face in his palms. "I will keep you safe, Cass. You can trust me to watch over you. I won't ever let anyone hurt you." He kissed her.

She smiled. Her eyes drifted shut. It was obvious the last couple of days had finally caught up with her. Once again he brushed his lips across hers, but this time he whispered what was in his heart. "I love you, Cass. I never expected this, but I love you."

Her eyes remained closed. She didn't say a word. He wasn't even certain she'd heard him. That was okay. He was a patient man.

She was drifting . . . drifting in the vineyard, floating between the rows, and Nate was there beside her. She saw her mom sitting by one of the old vines near the creek and tugged on Nate, dragging him over to meet her. "He's mine, Mom. And I love him." Her dad was there, holding Mom's hand, smiling, and Cass was holding on to Nate, and all of them were laughing, the sun was shining, and grapes hung heavy on the old vines.

"Cassie? Cass, wake up."

"What?" It was still dark in the room, but she reached out and felt denim. Nate was dressed. "What's wrong?"

"I hear voices. Sounds like they're over at the wine cave. At least two men. I've called the sheriff, but I want to go over and see what's going on."

"I'm coming, too." She was out of bed, pulling on her jeans and slipping her feet into her boots. No idea where her socks or underpants were, but that was okay, and damn it all but where was her shirt? She found her tee on the chair and slipped it over her head.

"Here, put this on. It'll keep you warm. It's chilly out."

She took the heavy dark blue fleece coat Nate handed to her. It was big, but blissfully warm. "Flashlights are downstairs. I'm ready."

She followed him quietly down the stairs and took the small but powerful flashlight he handed to her, but she didn't turn it on. Instead, it went into her pocket along with her cell phone. She checked to make sure the sound was muted.

Outside, even without a moon she could make out the lighter crushed gravel of the driveway. The night was absolutely still. A coyote howled, and then others picked up the sound. The soft rush of the creek grew even quieter as they moved farther away, closer to the road.

She heard voices and tugged on Nate's sleeve. He covered her hand with his and put a finger to her lips. They reached the gate and she could see them—two men in the beam of the overhead light that illuminated the front of the cave.

It was him. The one who'd attacked her. But the other? It couldn't be!

She grabbed Nate's arm and tugged him close, whispering. "The one trying to do the code? That's my father."

"Damn. I thought it looked like him. But why?"

"Listen."

Their voices were faint, but still audible.

"C'mon, Colonel. You know you can do this. The country depends on you."

"I know. I understand, but it's been a long time. Maybe Cass changed the code."

"I hope not. I'd hate to have to bring her out here."

Her father raised his head. "You will leave my daughter alone."

"Then open the fucking door, old man."

Her father stopped and stared at the man.

"Nate." Cassie whispered against his ear. "He's got a gun."

"Where the hell's the sheriff?" Nate leaned down and kissed her. "I need to get closer."

"Follow me." She led him through the darkness to a section of downed fence. They stepped over the loose wire and ran quietly across the road, then moved closer to the cave using a row of grapevines as cover. At this distance, the voices were much clearer.

Her father had sounded like himself a moment ago. Now his voice had that quavery, confused tone she'd heard more and more lately.

"Tell me again why you want me to open this?"

"To protect your daughter. Bad people want those papers, remember? You asked me to take them somewhere safe."

"That's right. The briefcase. I knew it was important." He tried another combination on the door. This time it swung open, and the younger man rushed inside. Cass's father just stood there, looking more confused than ever.

Nate grabbed her hand. "The briefcase in that cabinet. That's what the bastard wants."

"I have no idea what's in it, but Dad did some really sensitive stuff during those years. It could be anything."

"Crap. I was afraid of that. Stay here." He leaned over and kissed her.

"Nate!"

But he was off, running across the parking lot toward the open door to the cave. Cassie took off after him just as the dark-haired man raced out the open door with the heavy briefcase under one arm. Nate was almost on him when he raised his right arm, aimed that same gun he'd once pointed at Cass, and fired.

Nate went down. Cassie screamed and her father, moving like a man half his age, launched himself after the one with the gun. Another shot echoed against the hillside. Cassie reached Nate as the sheriff's car pulled into the driveway in front of the locked gate.

Sobbing, she dropped to her knees beside Nate. He'd gone down hard without a sound, but she had no idea where he'd been hit. She touched his neck and found the strong, steady pulse right where it belonged. Relief had her sobbing as she tried to turn him over. She knew she had to apply pressure to the wound, but he was such a big man, and so damned heavy.

She was only vaguely aware of two men racing across the gravel lot with guns drawn. One of them pulled her father away from the dark-haired man. The guy was moaning, but he stayed down.

One of the deputies reached Cassie.

"Help me turn him over, please." Damn, she had to stop crying! "I can't tell where he got shot."

"Nate's been shot?" The deputy was a big man and he carefully rolled Nate to his side. Cassie grabbed her flashlight and raced the beam over his torso, but there was no sign of blood. He gasped for air and groaned as she ran her hands over his body, but it wasn't until she found the bullet hole in his shirt pocket and the shattered cell phone in its metal case behind it, that she finally took a deep, calming breath.

She pulled the phone out of his pocket and showed it to the deputy. "Look. It saved his life." She tugged his shirt away, and the dark contusion covered an area too damned close to his heart. "Oh, Nate."

He blinked and gazed at her. "What happened?"

"You got shot."

CHAPTER 6

I did? I feel like I got kicked by a mule." Nate managed to sit up
with the deputy's help. He patted his hands over his chest. Found
the hole in his shirt. Cassie showed him the phone, and he sat
there, still slightly out of it, staring at the shattered plastic in the badly
dented case.

The first deputy was giving first aid to the injured man. The one
who'd helped Nate sit up walked over to check on Cassie's father.
The old man had found a quiet place out of the way—a bench in
front of the cave entrance—and he sat there clutching the briefcase.

Cassie gazed down at Nate with eyes so filled with love, he fully
expected her to say the words. Instead, she said, "Can you walk?"

"I think so." Nate grabbed the hand she held out to him and she
tugged him to his feet. There was a lot to be said for a strong woman.
They both walked over to check on Colonel Mac. Cassie squatted
in front of him with her hands on her dad's knees. "Dad, you've gotten
so thin and bony. Look. You've got a big tear in your pants." She pointed
to a rip in the right pants leg.

"Actually," Nate said, "I think it's a bullet hole." He sat on the bench beside Mac. "What happened, Colonel? And thank you. You saved our lives."

"That son of a bitch told me he'd kidnapped Cassie, that I had to let him inside the cave or he'd kill her." He hugged the briefcase tighter. "Turns out he works for the senator I once investigated. That's why they made me retire, you know. Because I discovered things I shouldn't have. I made some very powerful men very uncomfortable, and it's all in here."

He patted the briefcase and stared at the wounded man lying on the gravel drive. "Damned fool. Benny's going to hate this but his son was willing to kill for this info. Looks like when I tackled him, he fell on his own gun." He chuckled. "I hope it hurts like hell, after what he's put the two of you through."

He glanced at the hole in his pants. "That bullet that went through Jay is the same one that went through my pants. All because of this." Mac stared at the briefcase and then shoved it at Nate. "You take it. Take it to the newspapers. What's in there should have been made public over thirty years ago. It's time."

Cassie sat on the other side of her dad and took his hand. "You were so brave, Daddy. I am so glad you're okay." She sniffed and wiped away tears with the back of her hand. "You saved us."

Her father turned and looked at Nate, and there was no sense of confusion, no lack of comprehension when he slowly nodded and then patted him on the shoulder. "You take good care of her, you hear? She's very special, my girl is. Very special." He gazed into the darkness and softly said, "I'm so tired. Will you take me home, now?"

"Sure thing, Dad." She glanced at Nate and sighed. "I'm going to take him over to the house. Marcus won't mind for one night, will he?"

"Not at all. Just a minute. I'll come with you." An ambulance was pulling in as Nate walked over and spoke briefly with the deputy. He walked back to Cassie and her dad. "We can go now. They'll want to talk to us tomorrow." He helped her dad to his feet and glanced once again at Cass. "Can he walk that far?"

"He just took out an armed assailant. A little walk shouldn't be a problem." Then the three of them headed back to the house Colonel Mac had built for his wife so many years ago.

Cassie helped her dad while Nate held on to the briefcase filled with the sort of stuff that just flat scared the crap out of him.

Cassie led her father into the master bedroom. He'd been the last person to sleep here—she'd kept her own room after he moved into the home, but it was fitting he should sleep here tonight. A pair of his pajamas still hung in the closet. "Here, Dad. Do you need any help?" She set his pajamas on the bed.

He kissed her forehead. "Send your young man in. I dressed you when you were little, but you don't need to dress me."

She laughed and hugged him. "I love you, Daddy."

"I love you, too, sweetie. But do you love that young man of yours?"

She nodded. "Yeah, Dad. I do. I love him so much it hurts."

"Shouldn't hurt, sweetie. Maybe you need to let him know. Take the poor boy out of his misery. Now go get him. I'm tired."

"Yes, sir." She kissed her dad's leathery cheek and left the room.

Nate was waiting when Cassie stepped out of her dad's room. "He wants you to help him get ready for bed." She stood on her toes and kissed him. "My room's the first door on the left. Will you stay with me?"

"Are you sure?"

She nodded. "I love you, Nate. I wanted to say that to you before, but I didn't have the nerve. Then tonight . . ." Her voice caught and she sniffed, wiped her eyes with the back of her hand. "Tonight when I saw you go down, all I could think was how stupid I was, what a horrible coward that I hadn't told you how I felt."

Cupping her face in his palms, he said, "I love you, too, Cass. Let me help your dad, and I'll come in as soon as I can." He kissed her, tasting salty tears and the sweetness that was Cassie. "Now go."

She nodded, turned toward her bedroom, and shot Nate a heated glance over her shoulder that had him hurrying to her father's room.

Colonel Mac was wearing his pajamas and a flannel bathrobe, but his shoes and socks were still on. Nate went down on one knee to help him take them off.

"Not yet." The old man stood and headed toward the door with a flashlight in his hand. "This will only take a minute, but I want you to come with me."

Nate grabbed an extra flashlight off the counter and followed him out the door. They didn't go far—Mac stopped at the edge of the old vineyard. Turning around, he glared at Nate. "Do you love my daughter?"

Nate grinned. "I do. I love her very much."

Mac nodded. "Good. I'll just be a minute."

He took a few steps into the vineyard and paused by a particularly large and gnarled old vine. Nate quietly waited. Barely a minute later, Mac turned and headed back to the house. As he passed Nate, he said, "Come on. What are you waiting for?"

Grinning, Nate followed him back to the house and down the hall to the master bedroom. The colonel glanced over his shoulder and said, "Close the door."

Nate shut it.

Mac walked across the room to a picture on the wall, moved it aside and uncovered a small safe. A few twists of the combination and the door swung open.

He reached inside, pulled out a small, black velvet box, and held it out to Nate. "I had to ask Cassie's mother for permission. It was hers, you know." He smiled as he flipped open the lid to expose a beautiful emerald-cut ruby in a gold setting. "Mel didn't wear it much. Only when we went out." He chuckled, obviously remembering those nights. "She loved this ring, though. Said it was the color of good Zin. She wants it to go to Cassie and so do I. And I have a feeling you're going to be needing a ring before too long."

He shoved it into Nate's hand. "Take it."

Nate stared at the box in his hand. This wasn't at all what he expected. "I don't know what to say, except that I love Cassie and I just hope she'll say yes."

"You're a good man, Nate. You were willing to take a bullet to protect my daughter. That says a lot about a man. I want you to make her happy."

He raised his head, made eye contact, and said, "I promise, Colonel. I will do my best."

"Good. Now get out of here. I need my sleep."

"Yes, sir. Good night." Tucking the box in his pocket, he added, "And thank you, sir. For your blessing as much as the ring." The colonel was already in bed. He merely grunted and rolled over as Nate quietly shut the door behind him and headed down the hall to Cassie's room. Nate tucked the small box with the ring in his pocket and stepped into Cassie's bedroom. She was already in bed, but still awake.

"Did I hear you go out?"

Nodding, Nate began stripping out of his clothes. "Your dad wanted to talk to your mom. I took him out to the old vineyard. He only stayed there a minute, but he seemed happy about it."

"Thank you. I'm so glad." She swiped her hand across her eyes and sniffed. "That's the first time since he moved into town. He said he was too embarrassed to talk to her."

Sitting on the edge of the bed, Nate pulled Cassie across his lap. "What a night." He kissed her.

"I know. I keep thinking how badly I feel for Benny. I had no idea Andrews was his son. Benny's last name is White."

"Stepson. He was a teen when Benny married his mother, according to the deputy. Still, something like this isn't easy." Nate yawned. "Let's get some sleep."

Cassie scooted across the bed and slipped between the sheets. "It's only a queen. I hope you'll fit. And, Nate, I want you to know, there's never been another man in this bed." Blinking back tears, she raised her head. "And there will never be another man but you in my bed."

He pulled her close. "Your father asked me tonight if I loved you, but I think he'd already figured it out. I told him yes."

She was smiling when he turned off the light, and they met each other in the middle of the bed. "Let me hold you, sweetheart. That's all I need tonight. I want you in my arms, knowing you're safe, knowing that you love me."

He pulled her close, tucked her head beneath his chin, and she snuggled against him as if they'd slept this way forever. It felt like a beginning. A beginning of forever. As Nate drifted off to sleep, he decided he liked the sound of that. Liked it a lot.

Bright sunlight flooded the room, but it was Nate walking in and sitting on the edge of the bed with a cup of hot coffee that woke her out of a sound sleep. So many dreams last night, memories of her mom and dad, of the three of them here in this house, of picnics out in the vineyard. It was so restful, sleeping here again, in her old room.

So filled with good memories, though waking up to Nate and a cup of fresh coffee made a whole new memory. "Good morning." She sat up and took the cup he offered. "Did you go back to my cottage to make this?"

"I did." He smiled and brushed her tangled hair back from her face. "Did you sleep well?"

"Mmmmm. This is good. There's hope for you, yet. And yes. I slept really well. I dreamed a lot. Good dreams. Must have been from sleeping in my old bed." She set her cup on the bedside table. "I hope Dad slept okay." She spun her legs around to get out of bed, but Nate caught her up in the bedspread and held her on his lap.

He kissed her. "Sweetheart? There's no easy way to say this, but I am so sorry. Your father's gone. He passed away sometime during the night."

"Oh." She blinked, but she couldn't stop the tears. Nate held her while she cried, but it wasn't very long. It was fitting for a man who was ready to go, to die in his own bed in the house he'd built with his own hands so many years ago. "He seemed so good last night. So sharp when he had to be. I thought . . ." She shook her head. "I don't know what I thought."

"You should go see him, sweetheart. I checked in on him a couple of minutes ago. He was smiling. At first I thought he was still asleep, but then I realized he was gone. I have no doubt your mom was waiting for him."

"He was ready." She got up and went to the closet door, found an old bathrobe and put it on. She really needed to empty this place out for the new owner. "I'm going to miss him, though the father I knew was fading so quickly. Last night, as traumatic as it was, was one of the best nights he's had in so many months. He was a hero."

"That he was. And when we turn that briefcase over to the newspaper, he's going to be an even greater hero. I've been reading some of the stuff in there. It's explosive, but it's not something I would have felt safe sharing while he was alive. I think there's a good chance that Jayson's actions relate directly to the senator your father investigated so long ago. It could get ugly."

She stood on her toes and kissed him. "Then it should. Come with me? I want to say good-bye to Dad, and I want you with me. He was able to let go because of you, Nate. He's been so worried about me. He met you, and he wasn't worried anymore. He knows I love you."

Nate hugged her close. "That's good, because I love you."

"It is good, isn't it?" She took his hand, and together they went in to tell the colonel good-bye.

Three weeks later . . .

Nate walked Marcus Reed across the rough ground to his car. The memorial service for Cassie's father had ended a few minutes ago, and Marc was needed back in San Francisco. His response to Cassie's request had been all anyone could have hoped for, and he'd promised this piece of ground would never be replanted, as long as he owned it.

But there was one more thing. They paused beside Marc's new Tesla. Nate gave his boss one final pitch, and hoped like hell he'd agree. "Will you think about it, Marc? If there's any way you can bring yourself to sell this small piece, just the three acres we discussed, I'll do whatever I can to come up with the money for it."

Marc nodded. "We'll work something out, Nate."

He gazed across the acres of neatly trellised vines and then stared at the older, head-pruned vines where Cassie stood talking with some of their neighbors. It was hard to tell what he might be thinking.

"I hope we can. This piece of ground is special to Cassie. I already owe you so much, Marc. If you hadn't hired me, I would never have met her. Never have found . . ." Laughing, he shook his head.

Marc winked at him. "I recall advising you not to fuck with the winemaker. Shows me how well you pay attention."

Nate laughed. "I didn't. I fell in love with the winemaker. That's totally different."

"It is, Nate, and I envy you that." He opened the car door and grabbed a manila folder. "I forgot to give this to Cassie. Would you mind?"

"Not a problem." Nate took the folder from him. "We'll see you in a couple of weeks."

Cassie stood among the gnarled and twisted old vines near the creek while Nate walked Marcus Reed to his car. They'd scattered her father's ashes here today, in the same rich soil where her mother's ashes had been spread so many years ago. A few of the neighbors had come for the short service, and her dad's poker buddies from the home had been here as well. Even Benny, more quiet and reserved than usual. He'd been badly shaken by his stepson's horrible betrayal.

"Take care, Cassie."

"You, too, Myrna." Cassie hugged the last of the neighbors to leave and waved good-bye to them. She saw Marc Reed's Tesla slowly pulling out of the parking area. He'd become more than her boss over the past couple of weeks. Now she counted him as a friend. He'd stepped in with Nate and the two men had taken care of all the details associated with death. They'd left her to handle the work at the winery, which was the best therapy she could have asked for.

"You okay?"

She glanced up as Nate—looking so dark and sexy in navy slacks and a sky blue shirt the color of his eyes—crossed the driveway and then wrapped her in a tight hug. She sniffed. "Everyone has been so terrific. Even Marc." She sighed. "Dad would have been so happy, the way everything worked out."

He set aside a big envelope he'd been holding and kissed her. "Cassie?"

He had such a mysterious smile. "What?"

Holding both her hands, he went down on one knee in the dirt. "I love you, Cassandra Parsons Phillips. I fell for you, oh, about five seconds after the first time I saw you. I'm sorry your dad isn't here so I can ask him for your hand in marriage, but he already guessed my intentions. Besides, I figured that if I asked you here, where both your dad and your mom are resting in peace, that he couldn't refuse. I hope you won't, either. I want to marry you. Will you do me the honor of accepting my proposal? Will you be my wife?"

Nate freed her right hand to pull a small black velvet box out of his pocket. She covered her mouth. This wasn't happening. Nate? After less than two months he was asking her . . . but if he loved her even a fraction as much as she loved him, it made perfect sense.

He held the box for a moment without opening it. "Your father gave this to me the night before he died. He said it was your mother's. We walked out here that night so he could ask her for permission to give it to me to give to you." He chuckled softly and added, "So even if you turn me down, you still get the ring." He opened the box, and if she hadn't been crying again and laughing at the same time, she might have been able to see it better when he slipped the ring on her finger. She could tell it wasn't a diamond. Blinking away the tears, Cass held up her left hand. It was her mother's ring, a deep, wine-red ruby set in a wide gold band.

It was absolutely perfect.

"Yes," she said. "Nathan James Dunagan, yes. I will marry you."

He stood and drew her into his arms, rocking her slowly as she laughed and cried and tried to see her ring through the tears.

"Good. And soon, I hope. Before harvest. I'm going to be really busy during harvest."

He hugged her and she hugged him just as tight. "I'm free whenever you are." And she kissed him there in the vineyard. She was positive her parents approved.

A few hours later, Nate remembered the envelope Marc had given to him for Cassie. They were in Cassie's small cottage, Cassie in his lap in the big overstuffed chair in the front room, each of them having a glass of wine when she opened it, read the official-looking documents inside, and burst into tears.

Nate took the papers out of her hand as she clung to him, shaking. He had to read it twice before he raised his head in disbelief.

"It's a deed, Cassie. I asked Marc last week if there was any chance of him selling the house and the old vines, about three acres total, to us. I can't believe this—he's given you five acres of property—the cottage, the original family home, an acre and a half of five-year-old trellised Zinfandel and the two acres of old vines." He raised his head and laughed. "Your dad would love this—the old vineyard is listed on the deed as the 'Mac and Melinda block.'"

"You told me he was a good guy." She kissed him. "But he's still not as good as you."

He held her close, kissed her, and thought of how both their lives had changed in such a short time. How much the two of them had to look forward to. "That works for me."

He stood with her in his arms, and headed down the hallway to the bedroom. "Where do you think you're going?"

He kissed her again. "Why, to celebrate, what else?"

"The deed?"

"No, silly. The fact that Cassie Phillips said yes."

ABOUT THE AUTHORS

#1 *New York Times* bestseller LORA LEIGH is the author of the Navy SEALS, the Breeds, the Elite Ops, the Callahans, the Bound Hearts, and the Nauti series.

LAURELIN McGEE is the pseudonym of Laurelin Paige and Kayti McGee. Laurelin Paige is the *New York Times* bestselling author of the Fixed trilogy. Kayti McGee, when she isn't writing, loves to make up recipes.

SHILOH WALKER is an award-winning writer and avid reader.

KATE DOUGLAS lives in California and loves happily-ever-after endings.

Don't miss Lora Leigh's
SCORCHING
Bound Hearts novel

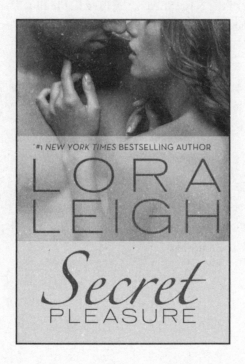

Available **8.4.2015** wherever books are sold.

St. Martin's Griffin   St. Martin's Paperbacks